For my mother,
who never thought
I'd show an interest in art

THE LOST PROVINCES

THE LOST PROVINCES

A Novel

by Stephen Glazier

AVON
PUBLISHERS OF BARD, CAMELOT AND DISCUS BOOKS

THE LOST PROVINCES is an original publication of Avon Books.
This work has never before appeared in book form.

AVON BOOKS
A division of
The Hearst Corporation
959 Eighth Avenue
New York, New York 10019

Published by arrangement with the author
Library of Congress Catalog Card Number: 80-69635
ISBN: 0-380-77255-8

First Avon Printing, March, 1981

Printed in the U.S.A.

Book One

I

I first visited Paris in the spring of 1907. The English King Edward VII had just taken leave of that city, though I saw little connection between his departure and my arrival. I saw so little then.

I let a room in the Rue du Sommerard, a quiet street of a few blocks' length near the Sorbonne. Proximity to that august center of learning comforted my father back in Washington and secured continuation of the monthly stipend on which I had been dependent during my unhappy sojourn at Harvard and without which I could not have survived long on the continent. I was fortunate enough to gain admission to the Académie Julien and there pursued my ill-defined artistic inclinations.

Paris lay all around me, unattained, shrouded in fog as gray as the stones of its ancient buildings. My concierge, an irksomely accommodating Madame Adelaide, took me rapidly in hand. The expression in her gray eyes seemed to say: "I am a woman who has seen and experienced everything, and my judgments are swift and unerring, Monsieur Peavey." Her assessment of me as a dabbler and dilettante hopelessly out of his depths colored every relation between us.

My room with Madame Adelaide was a small fourth-floor garret beneath a sloping mansard roof. It faced across the Rue du Sommerard, and on a clear day I could barely see the spires and buttresses of Notre Dame. During my first days in Paris I spent many hours at this window, one hand upon the cold brass *espagnolette,* the other twisting the frayed lace curtains, watching bundled students trundling their books to and from class, street cleaners and delivery boys on bicycles, children of the left bank playing a sidewalk game whose object and rules I could never decipher. I moved a tiny writing desk—the room's only furniture save a chair and bed and chamber pot—to a position by the window where the light was angular and intense. There I sketched rooftops.

While it was merely exhaustion and the residual nausea of my long ocean crossing which kept me thus cloistered for several days, I think my withdrawn manner did much to stigmatize me as a lost soul in the wet gray eyes of Madame Adelaide. She must have imagined me terrified in my room, peering out, for she always glanced up and waved as she came and went on her daily errands or left pastries for me with a swift knock at the door. I could hear her retreating footsteps on the stairs when I opened the door to retrieve my treat. Toward the end of my first week, as my stomach finally righted itself and my head cleared, I emerged from this self-imposed isolation into the glorious, teeming vitality of the city of which I had so long dreamed but whose power and mystery I found I had underestimated.

One crisp morning in late March, having taken my customary coffee and croissant *chez Mathieu,* I strolled into the Luxembourg Gardens beneath a shimmering spring sun. A thin fog hung in patches round the bare budding trees of the park, and an intimation of blustery spring storms blew across the pond, capsizing two toy boats. I sat in a green metal chair with the day's *Paris Herald* until the boy came asking for a few sous. Then I rose, crossed behind the palace, and emerged before the Odéon Theatre.

A modest crowd had gathered in the treeless cobbled square. Above the sea of bowlers and bonnets and brimmed caps which bob on every Parisian head, I could see festooned between two massive pillars of the Odéon a crudely painted sign: "*La Famille Jollicorps.*"

Several costumed acrobats were performing on faded rugs spread before the theatre steps. A lean, muscular young man juggled three orange balls while balanced on a barrel. Kneeling beside him, his little brother watched intently, one hand resting on the head of a scruffy dog. Before the barrel a girl of twelve or thirteen performed gymnastics and twisted herself into an impossible posture: her head between her legs, which bent back so that she touched her shoulders with her feet. She held this contortion with a smile of serene indifference on her thin face.

A battered cart, canopied across flimsy supports and tethered to an equally battered horse, stood to one side of these performing children. A woman, gaunt and wispy like a single silhouetted reed at sunset, with mantic eyes and a flowered hat, sat on the cart steps. She wore a long dress of thin plain cotton and hunched in her shawl over a small table on which lay a deck of cards, a globe, a drawstring reticule, and other small props. A monkey watched from atop the canopy.

Out of the cart stepped a man, the father perhaps, a lank harlequin who seemed to glide dreamlike across the steps of the theatre while his children mimed before him. As he began to speak, his delicate hands plucking flower petals and sparrows from the air, the strumming of a stringed instrument issued from behind the canopy. The frail woman rocked over her table and sang in a delicate, remote voice and an unfamiliar dialect.

Something in the slimness of this Jollicorps family, the haunted resignation in their eyes and contrasting boldness of their movements, the certainty in the presence of bewilderment, was at once beguiling and pathetic. Many in the silent crowd were as deeply struck as I by their performance. Even a squadron of schoolboys in knee pants and brimmed caps, mincing through the crowd and mimicking the performers, could not break the spell. The motley father cast evanescent figures in the air and droned in his throaty dialect. The vanishing illusions of his hands were complemented by the sweet diminuendo of the woman's voice in exquisite harmony.

The tale and tune concluded, the hidden guitar fell silent, coins were tossed upon the rugs, and the small boy put his dog through its paces. "Come, Cuntz," he shouted in a high-pitched voice as the dog leapt through gilded hoops and then it too balanced on the barrel while its bantam master shouted encouragement and danced about in comic pants with garters and pointed slippers.

Behind this pair another Jollicorps appeared: a massive, flushed and bejowled clown, the eldest of the troupe. He seemed to diminish the others by his presence, formidable and stern in his ruffled collar and floppy hat. He carried oversized black dumbbells, apparently hollow, which he tossed in the air. When they came down they crushed his great bulk to the earth. Soon the girl contortionist cried out, "*Mon oncle, mon oncle,* can you toss me through the air like that?" And he obliged her.

My gaze was repeatedly drawn to a young man in the crowd. It may have been his girth and the bowler hat several sizes too small for his head, or perhaps the rapt expression in his large brown eyes, but I felt him to be an element of the performance, or at least of its pervasive mood.

I was startled when he returned my gaze and came lumbering toward me from his station by the steps. Fearing I had disturbed his reverie, I glanced away, but he brought his stout frame to rest beside me, laid a soft hand on my arm, and fixed me with his dark eyes. No threat inhabited his stare; only a keen, wistful penetration.

"You like the *saltimbanques*, eh, my friend?"

I nodded. "The *saltimbanques*?"

"That is what they are called. You will find them in all the great cities of Europe, performing in the streets and traveling about in their wagons." He paused. "They are true sons of the people: versatile, cunning, dextrous, intrepid, poverty-stricken—and liars all."

"I see," I said, somewhat taken aback.

"Of course you do not see," he corrected me affably. "But you shall." He turned to watch the girl contortionist achieve another exceptional posture.

"She is remarkable," I offered, and he replied: "Yes. Today Claudie is the most remarkable creature in all of Paris."

"Ah, then you know these . . . these *saltimbanques*?"

"Merely as an observer. They do not know me."

Together we watched the remainder of the performance. My attention focused on the girl Claudie and on my companion watching her. She was indeed a remarkable creature: so frail, so fraught, with just the faintest flaxen thatching of hair deep in the hollows beneath her slim shoulders and the tiniest crescents of breast beneath her leotard. Her hair was wound into a pale plait and wrapped about her head. Something in her manner and her eyes suggested that this chit of a girl had already experienced a full life, both difficult and rewarding. Yet her precocious knowledge of life, rather than deadening her or rendering her prematurely resigned, had miraculously generated a rebirth of innocence which beamed through a face as ingenuous as could be imagined.

"She's quite a little pretzel," I joked, and the spell was broken.

"Please?" replied my companion, and I explained to him in French what a pretzel was.

"You seem to be a clever American." He abandoned his pout. "I myself am a reckless Parisian. I know an excellent little bistro not far from here in the Rue St. André des Arts. I should be pleased to offer you lunch there in exchange for the stimulating conversation I suspect you are capable of."

"Oh boy. I dare not refuse such an offer," I exclaimed. We added our coins to the pile of bronze growing, sou by sou, on the rug and set out together.

"I am Guillaume Malaimé."

"Clayton Peavey." I extended my hand.

We were seated in a cramped dining room on one of the narrow winding streets of the quarter. The room smelled of basil and roast duck, fresh bread and full-bodied red wine. Guillaume whispered in the proprietor's ear, shrugged, and put his hands in his pockets, but the proprietor shook his head vigorously, clapped him on the back, and strode into the kitchen barking orders as he went. We were soon drinking our soup.

"We always eat best when we are broke," Guillaume said and he winked.

Outside it had begun to rain. Schoolgirls in bright pinafores with parasols scurried beneath arabesqued parapets. A fat woman in frieze leggings drew a canvas awning over her fruit and flower stand while her daughter built a charcoal fire in their tiny ceramic brazier. A motor-driven omnibus—recently introduced in Paris—wheezed to a halt in the middle of the street. Its operator cranked and fumed over the engine while passersby laughed at him. Soon a Moto Naphtha petrol cart arrived and he began to refill his tank. In midstreet a dray drawn by a single white horse passed slowly and bicyclists negotiated the puddles.

The electrical workers of Paris were on strike at this time, and despite the darkening skies the streetlamps remained black. Our jovial proprietor brought two plain tapers with the wine, and I watched the candle shadows dancing across Guillaume's face as he spoke.

"I am a poet and a critic," he told me. "I consider myself a scholar and I have been called a pornographer. I know all the great young minds of the city—Paul Fort, Jarry, Max Jacob, all of them." The names meant nothing to me. I smiled. "We still meet weekly at the Closerie. Did you say you wrote?"

"No, I am a painter. I have been taking classes at the Académie Julien and—"

"Why, that's wonderful. Painters and poets are together the standardbearers of the new spirit."

"I hardly consider myself a standardbearer for anything," I replied with well-warranted modesty.

My artistic inclinations—pretensions, Father always called them, while Mother smiled demurely and elder brother Eugene tried very hard to look superior—had gradually submerged during my school years, surfacing only occasionally in the idlest doodlings and sketches, stick figures and cartoon characterizations of my parents' friends in Washington which clung barely within the bounds of good humor, all of this lacking the consistency, conviction, or inspiration necessary to a true artist.

"But why are you called a pornographer?" I asked.

"So that strikes your fancy, does it? Truly it is a work of scholarship—editing, translating, annotating. I have been engaged by a small publisher to organize the, shall we say, restricted works in the national library.

Have you read any of the Marquis de Sade?" I told him I had not and feared I should find the works dull and offensive, but he flared up at this: "Perhaps you might, though I hope not, for this fellow de Sade who appeared to be of no importance throughout the past century may well come to dominate the new one."

He was in the habit of making such extreme, challenging statements, as much I suspected for effect as out of genuine belief. I felt I must sift his words for truth, sort the constantly molting self-fabrications from the real substance of self.

"And what do you paint, Clayton Peavey?" He liked the sound of my name and missed no opportunity to employ it.

"I have worked in oil, landscapes and that sort of thing," I hedged, then plunged. "Are you familiar with Little Nemo in Slumberland?" He shook his head. "I suppose not. It is one of the color cartoons in the American press, a wonderful work with its flights of fantasy and palaces of ice by a man named Winsor McCay. It appears in the *Paris Herald*. I think that is the sort of thing I most admired until this winter when a small sampling of Cézanne appeared in Cambridge." His interest perked at my mention of Cézanne and he urged me on. "The dealer who accompanied that exhibit described the retrospective at the Salon d'Automne, which I have since seen myself, and spoke fervently of the new spirit in France, the posters of Toulouse-Lautrec and the work of the Fauves. I became greatly excited, dropped out of the university, and here I am."

Guillaume grinned. "But the Fauves were merely a harbinger of things to come, monsieur," he said. "The Fauvist cage is no longer an outrage. The beast is in hibernation." He snorted. "You understand their significance, of course?"

"Well . . . I . . . it has to do with the abandonment of traditional perspective and the use of fantastic colors to serve expression and—"

"Bah. It is nothing less than the death of imitation in art. Paint landscapes, paint still lifes. Paint anything you like. It is not what you paint nor what you see that counts, it is *how* you see it. And that is all."

Someone had begun playing popular tunes on an Aeolian pianola in the next room. Our conversation lapsed while Guillaume tapped out the rhythm with his pudgy fingers and I swished my cognac around the snifter, "meditating with The Autocrat" as the *Times* advertisement for Old Hennessy described it.

"So you see, I am a foreigner like yourself," Guillaume told me in his apparently perfect French. "I learned early of life, Clayton Peavy. An illegitimate alien —or so my bourgeois friends would have it—fathered by a reprobate Roman and bundled about Europe by my poor mama." He paused over this reference to his mother. "But I have not deserted her."

"Nor she you," I ventured, and he nodded.

"I wish I could find such loyalty and such love among the gay young women one meets in Paris. They are so lovely, but so vain and fickle. And I . . . I am *malaimé*." He stifled a laugh behind his hand.

I noted his infatuation with the young contortionist in the Jollicorps family and he grew animated at once.

"Ah yes. She is pure movement. Did you notice her hands, my friend?" I admitted I had not. "They are a woman's hands. So wonderfully expressive, full of age and wisdom, strong yet delicate. She holds them as a ballerina, with the most subtle arc, yet I know she is untrained." His own fleshy hands fluttered preposterously over the table. "It is pure intuition and her movements are pure motion, the motion of the new dance."

"Do you think so? She seemed a trifle awkward to me."

"Exactly. Her imperfection achieves purity. Hers is the purity of the new art, which is pure painting, just as music is pure literature."

"I'm afraid you've lost me there. Music is pure literature?"

"You will meet the gang, Clayton Peavey. Then you'll understand."

At this moment an uproar commenced in the street outside our café. The evening crowds parted for a short young man with black shoulder-length hair. Swathed in a hooded cape and carrying a crook-handled umbrella, he staggered with abrupt, puppetlike movements, intentionally butting people and loosing a torrrential and incoherent stream of language. I took him for the inveterate drunkard he obviously was, but Guillaume rose from his seat.

"It is Père Ubu himself," he exclaimed. "He has returned to Paris." Repeating the name "Père Ubu," he dashed out the door. But before he could reach him the unruly drunkard had boarded a bus and was disappearing in the direction of the Place St. Michel.

Guillaume returned, hastily motioned to the proprietor, then addressed me.

"You must excuse my rudeness, but that fellow is a dear friend of mine and one of the great spirits of this city. He has been recuperating from a lengthy illness in the country. You shall meet, I guarantee that, my friend, and you shall not forget Père Ubu. But I must be off now . . . a meeting at the *Mercure*—a trifling article, a pittance in return, such is the lot of writers, eh? Meet me tomorrow where the *saltimbanques* dance and we shall continue our talk. Until then, Clayton Peavey." With a tight wave he tossed his tiny bowler onto his head and departed, leaving me to confer with The Autocrat by candlelight. . . .

This was not my first venture outside the United States. I was born in 1886 in Berlin, where my father was attached to the American embassy. In the maneuverings which followed the death of William I and led to the resignation of Bismarck two years later, Adam Peavey was transferred back to the State Department in Washington, and there he remained, mired in the foreign service bureaucracy through several administrations, finally rising to a Republican undersecretaryship, a red-brick Georgetown residence, an engaging social manner and the paunch and punctilio to go with it.

Father always claimed I was a born diplomat. I think he mistook my prudent orchestrating of family affairs, particularly where they concerned Eugene, for social grace rather than simple pragmatism. From an early age I had a quick wit and a droop of dark hair which hung charmingly close to one eyebrow and which my mother's friends found irresistible. They never tired of toying with it, though I refused to take them seriously. I took very little seriously and forever hid my native intelligence and ironic perceptions behind an ingenuous facade, my droop of lank hair, my spindly fidgeting body, and my unstinting playfulness—what Father regretfully called my archness, though it was merely peevishness.

A lack of ambition combined with Father's coercion and the offer of a bountiful support to determine my course of study. By the fall of 1906 I was preparing my undergraduate thesis in international affairs under the much-maligned Professor Stallwarts at Harvard. Like Washington, Harvard seemed to exist largely on its reputation and inflated self-image; it was of interest to me solely because it *was* Harvard. By the time the Cézanne exhibition arrived, and with it talk of Fauvist beasts intent upon devouring the traditions of the old century and exploring the potential of the new one, I was bored. Suddenly my imagination soared. This excited state happened to coincide with the unhappy termination of a romantic relationship and renewed pressures from Father regarding graduate school and my future. I was impelled to action. I could no longer keep plugging away at the League of the Three Emperors and the nationalist movements in Serbia and Bosnia. Nor did the Harry Thaw murder trial in New York captivate me as it did so many of my countrymen. As the press yellowed and my academic outlook blackened, I realized with a sudden numbing sensation that this might be my last chance to escape the path which had led poor Father to Georgetown and his diplomatic paunch. I took a leave of absence from Harvard (once admitted one cannot entirely remove oneself from that fabled institution, barring certain sins against the university itself, for which one is expunged) and came to Paris.

Father grimly accepted it as a final fling—nay, a first fling would have been more like it—and exhibited a benign acceptance of my frivolous behavior. Mother was always quietly amused by my irreverence, which she shared, and seemed genuinely pleased by my precipitate action. I think she had an artistic soul, despite herself, and she sent me wildly optimistic letters. Perhaps she was only humoring me. One cannot tell with mothers.

The day following my meeting with Guillaume I arrived shortly before noon at the Odéon Theatre, but the *saltimbanques* failed to appear and so did my friend. For an hour I sipped wine and nibbled crudités in a nearby café and then, bitterly disappointed, I began to wander. To my delight, in the Place St. Sulpice I espied the banner of *La Famille Jollicorps* draped from their wagon to one of the stone lions guarding the octagonal fountain at the square's center. A chill spring breeze ruffled the banner and rattled its wobbly stake.

The young acrobats were amusing a small crowd. I stood beside the church, looking down a long row of elms. The performers were dwarfed by the vastness of the *place,* the towering church with its stacked Doric and Ionic colonnades, the spray of water in the tiered fountain, the indifference of the passing crowds.

I crossed the square as the sonorous bells of St. Sulpice tolled twice. Stationing myself near the wagon, I could observe the performance before the fountain and also watch the *saltimbanques* crouched in the wings, out of view of the audience, arranging costumes and props and speaking quietly together.

Claudie knelt by her father, pensively tracing designs on the stones. Her hands were large for her tiny frame, as Guillaume had observed, and combined the delicacy of her father's hands with the toiling strength of her mother's. When she became aware of my presence she laughed and in a single agile leap disappeared inside the wagon.

An old woman had taken the opportunity afforded by the crowd to display her shabby textiles in a leather portmanteau. Out in the broad square several boys kicked a ball back and forth while couples strolled hand in hand beneath the shadows of the buttressed church. In the crowd before the fountain a *flic* in his police cape and square hat stood near a pale Moor with a lopsided mustache and green knit skullcap who coughed violently into a curled fist and moved away. Two bicyclists wove unevenly along the outskirts of the crowd.

Claudie emerged from the wagon as a song began.

Guillaume Malaimé, my curious friend, stood at the forefront of the crowd caressing her with his eyes.

"What is that song?" I startled him. He spun away, then slung his arm across my shoulders.

"It is the legend of Our Lady of Tusenbach, patron saint of the league of performers from Ribeauville."

The woman's hollow voice wavered above us, and young Claudie danced the sinuous dance of a lively little girl growing old before our eyes. The fat clown turned a Barbary hand organ distractedly, and the elder brother perched idly upon his barrel, one hand on his hip, oblivious of his balance.

At the song's end Claudie did a sort of pirouette from the lip of the fountain but caught her heel and tumbled directly in front of us. Guillaume lunged forward, caught her fall, and set her down. His hands rested on her slender shoulders, his eyes on her face.

"Oh, thank you, sir. I am so sorry," she began. "I did not mean . . . Thank you for your help. I'm so clumsy, so sorry."

"You could not possibly distress me," exclaimed Guillaume. "Fall upon me as often as you wish, my angel. Beat me with your wings and I shall rise to heaven with you."

"What's that?" snapped the elder brother, descending from his barrel. He wore a wispy pale mustache on his upper lip and a steely expression in his green eyes.

"This gentleman caught me when I fell," explained the little girl. "Now he tells me I am an angel."

"An angel?"

"Just so, young man. Your sister has graced me with her fall. How was she drawn to me? I think I know. It is because I alone in this crowd recognize her purity. I alone appreciate what she is and envision what she will become."

"What's all this? What do you want from us? Please

take your hands off my sister, sir, and quit your fancy talk."

"I want nothing from you. I have already received much more than I deserve."

"Is it Claudie you want, then? But she is a child and she is not for sale, whatever you may think."

"No, Sébastien, I believe the gentleman is sincere," the girl said confidently, shooting a quick glance at Guillaume to reassure him. I saw his knees sag and moved close behind him, fearing in the brother's recognition of this growing rapport between them a rising anger.

"You know nothing of these things, Claudie," said the brother. He knocked Guillaume's hand from her shoulder and dragged her back toward the wagon. Guillaume pursued them and I him. Behind us the fellow in the green knit cap coughed into his fist. Others in the crowd pushed forward to watch.

"Oh honestly, Sébastien, you are too hasty. Please let me be, I am quite all right. This is all so stupid," protested Claudie. She sounded half annoyed, half amused, but her brother's grip was firm. Guillaume caught them directly before the fountain. Their altercation now occupied center stage. Four stone clerics sat at the center of the fountain. As Sébastien and Guillaume struggled over the girl, the Evêque de Clermont smiled benignly out at them, a pen in his hand and a pigeon on his shoulder.

Guillaume said, "You have insulted me, you young fool, and dishonored your sister." The color rose to his cheeks as he took the girl's hand. She was stretched between them now in an absurd and unlikely posture. Her brother's patience was exhausted.

"Let her go," he shouted, as he himself let go and charged Guillaume. In an effort to protect himself Guillaume raised his free arm across his chest, catching the smaller lad across the side of the face and sending him reeling backwards.

Guillaume glanced at me, his eyes raging and confused, and I stepped behind the barrels, wondering whether my time to arbitrate had arrived.

Before I could move forward, young Sébastien leapt upon his barrel and stood towering over Guillaume, preparing to pounce upon him. On the steps of the wagon the fat uncle appeared in an old Zouave jacket bursting its buttons, his funny hat tilted askew.

As Sébastien balanced on his barrel and dipped once, Guillaume dropped the girl's hand and, again acting on instinct and in self-defense, stumbled forward with his arms raised. I heard his foot scrape the pavement and thud against the oaken barrel, the uncle's voice bellowing, "Sébastien, get down," a series of violent hacking coughs in the crowd, a rising murmur of excitement, Claudie's high-pitched shriek, and the clanging of a trolley bell like the signal for the next round at a boxing match. Sébastien twisted awkwardly, put one hand to his side, and fell backward off the barrel. He landed heavily at my feet and lay prone before the fountain.

For a moment no one approached him. The crowd was silent; the fountain splashed. We waited for Sébastien to rise, but he did not move. Claudie came to him, knelt, and touched his face.

"Mama," she cried. "Mama, Mama."

The woman limped across to them, clutching her elbows with her hands, shivering within her shawl. She lifted her son's face, touched his eyes, and began a dreadful keening like a sick cat.

I stood over them, puzzling how the acrobat could have lost his balance and how he could have injured himself so seriously in his fall. Remaining before the barrel, Guillaume looked from the fallen *saltimbanque* to his sister and back again. In the corner of my eye I saw a caped *flic* brandishing his baton as he approached.

"Stand back from the boy, Kasia," commanded the uncle clown. He knelt by the body, placed a massive hand on the woman's shoulder, and pronounced the words: "He is dead." At once the sharp keening recommenced. Claudie clung to her dead brother for a moment and then composed herself. With a grim expression she walked slowly to her father, who stood by the wagon. The uncle spoke with the policeman.

Realizing the suspicion which might fall upon me as accomplice to Guillaume in this incident, and the complications which could ensue from my position as a visitor in France, I felt the urge to slip quietly away. Already the accusations of the spectators were in the air: "It was an argument . . . yes, I think he pushed him . . . over the girl, of course . . . and she no more than a child . . . the other stood behind the barrel and he seemed to shove into it . . . that one over there . . . it was only an accident . . . accident indeed, they teamed on him like a pair of professionals . . . the poor people . . . just look at them . . ."

As these words flitted about I became aware of the teary eyes of the woman fastened on me. Her face was stark and tense, and she seemed to sense my desire to escape and see in that an admission of guilt. Guillaume stood rigidly by the barrel.

"Come over here then," the policeman addressed me, and I obeyed in a trance. "May I see your papers, please?" I showed him my American passport and my visa; he shook his head. "You'll have to wait here for the van. There will be questions, sir." He turned to Guillaume. "And your papers, sir." Guillaume shook his head. "No papers then, sir? Well, I'm sure the inspector will have something to say about that."

A second officer appeared and was sent to call for the prison van while the policeman questioned the fat clown.

"Arbogast Zorn," he repeated his name. "Originally from Mulhouse, though that was many years ago. We are, as you can see, traveling performers. Our home is the streets of Europe."

"Then you are German," stated the policeman.

"No, French," growled the clown. "From the village Thann between Mulhouse and Belfort. We are French and shall remain so," he added.

As his interrogation continued I noticed that Arbogast Zorn, this large flushed clown with weary eyes and soft jowls, regarded Guillaume and myself without accusation or anger. Rather he seemed concerned for us. He scanned the crowd, as though searching for clues or other suspects. When I suggested that it had been an accident, the policeman admonished me to keep my stories for the inspector, but Arbogast Zorn nodded and told them that "yes, indeed, it could well have been no more than a freakish accident, occurring in the heat of a stupid dispute."

"That's not for me to decide, sir, nor for you," the policeman said.

He had begun to examine the body. Opening the boy's purple blouse he found a hollow cylindrical object, about six inches long, on a leather strap around his neck. A long-nosed face with almond eyes was carved in ebony on the cylinder.

"What's this, some sort of whistle?" he asked.

"Yes, that's it, a whistle," replied Arbogast Zorn. "Do you think we might keep that? It is a family heirloom and quite valuable to us." He reached to take the strap from the body.

"No, sir, nothing can be removed from the body until it has been examined at the Préfecture. Odd thing, isn't it? You'll have it back after the investigation." He withdrew the amulet from the clown's fist.

As we awaited the van, the policeman casually rolled a cigarette of black tobacco and lighted it. The bitter smoke drifted over to me, and I shuddered as I considered my position. Guillaume was silently rubbing his broad chin. He searched vaguely in the faces and objects surrounding him until he found Claudie.

"You will forgive me, won't you? I shall find you and comfort you, my angel. I promise you that. Remember." But she shook her head, her whole body trembling with the sobs which finally burst forth as she buried her face in her father's side and revealed herself to be just a little girl after all. The dog nuzzled against them where they stood by the wagon.

At last the prison van—what is vulgarly called a salad basket in Paris—drew up to the fountain. Behind it came the morgue carriage in which the body would be removed. Guillaume and I were searched and shoved into the van, which was divided lengthwise by a central corridor with several compartments on either side. We were placed on opposite sides of the corridor. Within my compartment I had to remain squatting, my head resting on my knees.

Before the municipal guard slammed the door, I looked once more at the tableau by the fountain: the family huddled around the father, the uncle conferring with the police, the gaunt mother with her haunted eyes staring at me, the crude banner toppling to the stones as its support shook loose, and the wisps of bitter smoke hanging over the body and drifting into the van. The smoke nauseated me. As the horse-drawn van rocked along the cobbled streets I crouched in my compartment and retched between my legs.

I had been in Paris one month and was on my way to prison, accused of complicity in a street murder, and with no apparent defense.

II

The prison van jolted down the Boulevard Raspail and across Montparnasse. I clutched my head in my hands, the stuffy little compartment filled by the acrid smell of half-digested wine. At last we turned into the Rue de la Santée. Through the tiny grated window I saw the tall black walls of the prison, a forbidding windowless facade beneath overhanging eaves.

The driver exchanged words with sentries at the gates and we passed into a rectangular courtyard whose walls were lush with climbing vines. The outer walls of the Santée Prison were not of brick nor masonry but an unfamiliar, coarse, blackened conglomerate stone which I had observed nowhere else in Paris, as though it had been reserved exclusively for this building. Within those walls a sense of desperation overcame me. I had entered a place utterly outside my world, from which chance of return was purely arbitrary. The fact of my innocence, the absurdity of the entire episode, and the likelihood of consular intervention on my behalf provided little solace.

When we were removed from the van I had a brief opportunity to converse with my fellow accused. He gazed about in blank bewilderment.

"Well, we've certainly landed ourselves in a mess," I said with as much levity as I could muster, but he seemed not to comprehend my words. The guard warned us not to speak. At the last moment Guillaume called out in a frightened voice.

"I am ruined, ruined," he said. "Mama"—he accented

the second syllable and his voice rose—"will never recover from this. It is the end." And he was led away.

I was taken into a small room, stripped, searched and prodded roughly. All of my orifices were examined for tiny weapons or other contraband which might be concealed there. I was given faded, loose-fitting, unpleasant-smelling prison garb and placed overnight in a holding cell on the lower level of the prison.

From the sounds and smells I experienced that first night I deduced that I had been tossed in among the lowest class of criminals inhabiting the Santée, presumably due to the nature and victim of my alleged crime and to my own circumstances. The following morning I was released into the company of these street rogues—dissolute vagabonds and apaches of the sort who survived on stolen milk and rolls from other people's doorsteps; in short, hardened criminals, many of them Mohammedans and other illiterate foreigners with little regard for themselves or each other.

Breakfast was served at a long table, rather like a pig's trough. The most feral of the inmates swarmed over this slop. A feast of swilling, slurping, and clawing commenced. I thought I'd starve in such conditions and abstained as much out of distaste for the fare as the apparent danger to myself should I attempt to partake.

One pock-faced creature with a twisted arm demanded the nature of my crime. I told him it was murder. This seemed to elevate me in the estimation of the inmates but did little to gain me a breakfast, and I was returned hungry to my cell.

So often when one least requires time for introspection it is accorded bountifully, and thus it was that day. My head throbbed from hunger and doubt. At last a scowling turnkey arrived with a great jangling outside my cell. I was jostled along a maze of corridors, up and down narrow twisting stairwells, and into a small, brightly lit room. There I was left for some time with only my isolation and my fear.

The heavy metal door swung to and a man entered. He wore pince-nez, an imperial beard, and a perfectly tailored gray suit. He was in his mid-fifties, small and trim, with a small mouth tightened by years of prying into others' lives. His thick twirled mustaches were rimed in gray, but the hairs which bristled from his nose and ears were jet black. He scrutinized me and crossed with carefully measured gait to the table where I sat.

"Inspector Guy Pernicieux," he introduced himself. "And you are Monsieur Peavey, yes?"

"That's right, Inspector. I wonder if you could tell me whether the American embassy has been notified yet of—"

"I shall ask the questions here, please," he admonished me. With nervous fingers he drew a pen from his pocket and began tapping it lightly on the table.

"I only wanted to be certain—" I began, but he motioned me to silence.

"Of just one thing can you be certain, Monsieur Peavey." He smiled. "That in your present circumstances you may be certain of nothing." He derived obvious pleasure from his wit and paused. "I do hope you shan't prove as uncooperative as your colleague," he said, and added, "I suppose you shall begin by denying any involvement in this unhappy business?"

"Begin and end," I snapped and lapsed into dour silence.

He sighed. "But yes, it has become a great deal more complicated than we at first suspected. Tell me, Monsieur Peavey, why did you come to Paris?"

I recounted my tale of academic apathy, hope for inspiration, the Académie Julien, and my desire to redirect my life. "But my father is with the State Department, and if you will merely contact the embassy, as you are required to do, there will be no problem resolving all this."

"Do not instruct me on my duties, please," he snarled, but his snarl lacked fang. "I am well aware of what I must do. As for that, the embassy has already been advised of your situation, your visa has been revoked, and following the completion of our investigation you shall be deported. At the very least you may expect that. And then—" He drew a folded report from his pocket, adjusted his pince-nez, and perused this paper while I squirmed. "Yes, it is all quite odd. Not a Frenchman in the lot. Your victim was of Alsatian ancestry, born in Algeria. You are an American, your fellow intrigant is Polish-Italian by ancestry, raised in Monaco, born we cannot be certain where. My colleagues at the Sûreté have already expressed an interest in the case. One cannot be too careful with undesirable aliens in our midst. Especially in these times."

"I protest, Inspector. You have assumed our guilt and act as though the burden of proof lay upon us. Where is the justice in that?"

"Ah, but it does. You are obviously unfamiliar with the justice of the Napoleonic Code, Monsieur Peavey. And what justice did you show that poor lad in the street?"

"I know nothing about that. I was merely a spectator at his death."

"And your comrade in this work? Was he also a mere spectator?"

"I don't really know. I only met him the previous day. He bought me lunch and asked me to return to watch the *saltimbanques* and—"

"So you were enticed to consort with foreign rascals

and street performers by this Guillaume Malaimé. Do you know who this fellow is?"

"I thought he was a poet."

"Exactly," he sneered and fell silent.

The Inspector pursued an obscure and patently captious line of questioning designed to intimidate and eventually to break me. The enormity of my predicament gradually came clear: I was accused not merely of an incidental street murder, but of collusion with Guillaume and unknown others in some sort of plot. Pernicieux spoke to me as in a dream, and glumly I answered his questions about all manner of irrelevancies. At last I shook off my daze.

"Imagine what you will," I beseeched him, "but I know nothing of all this. I came here to paint. I met Guillaume and witnessed this acrobat's death with as much surprise as anyone. Those are the facts and all the rest is immaterial."

"We shall see. The Deuxième Bureau will wish to interrogate you. Your countrymen are aware of your plight and will take appropriate action when we have done with you." He gave a stifled little laugh and rose. "But do not think I shall prosecute this case lightly. The reputation of Inspector Guy Pernicieux has not been made easily, and I have no sympathy for foreigners come to ruin Paris and create international incidents. We shall meet again. A pretty prospect, eh, my fine young fellow? And so, good day."

I was led back to my cell. Dinner was served as breakfast had been. Again I did not eat. I lay awake late into the night, listening to the clanking of those enchained down the hall and the heavy boots of the warders as they passed. I breathed the prison stench as shallowly as my aching chest permitted.

At midmorning I still lay upon my rack, feverish

and nauseated, hands chapped raw by the stone chill of the Santée. Throughout that second day of incarceration I waited: for another interrogation; for the inevitable communication from the embassy; for sleep to come. But nothing happened, no one came. A grotesque singsong lyric infected my brain: down the oubliette, down the oubliette. . . .

When the light of midday sat upon the window ledge I hung by the small grilled opening and breathed the city air as I gazed at the courtyard below. This little vined garth had an almost charming quality, as though it had been plucked from someone else's story and deposited in mine. Bright green strands of ivy dangled from the walls and swayed slightly in the breeze.

A number of prisoners were taking their exercise in the bull ring. Among them I noticed Guillaume; it was the first time I had seen him since our arrival at prison. He paced the yard with his hands plunged deep into the pockets of his undersized prison trousers, his shoulders hunched and large head dipped, eyes cast upon the cobbles, like a great sea lion circling minnows in a tank. He appeared quite ridiculous in his ill-fitting garments with his raging self-pity, but I could not bring myself to laugh.

Shortly thereafter the yard was cleared and I was called from my cell to exercise. The warders were obviously being careful to keep us two desperate criminals apart, lest we plot further atrocities or engineer an escape.

Several Moors clustered along one wall of the courtyard. As always they appeared to be conspiring. I tried to flex my muscles and unlimber, but felt only a deepening chill which no amount of exercise could thaw. Discovering the narrowed eyes of one grizzled Moor fastened on me, I tried to involve myself in the exercise, but finally was forced to acknowledge his half-concealed motion to approach.

The fellow had an ashen pate and wore a knit cap pushed far back on his head. His bloodshot eyes glowered at me suspiciously. The smell of him made me stand at arm's length. How long had he inhabited these cells, taken his meals at the communal trough, conferred with his fellows in corners of this high-walled court, waited, waited for release which would not come?

"You do not exercise?" he asked. I shook my head. "You do not eat?" I shrugged and leaned casually against the wall. "Not good. Tonight you eat." He grinned.

"I think not," I said. "Thank you anyway."

"Ahmed," he introduced himself, the sound caught in his throat, and extended a dark, rough hewn paw. Though loath to touch it, I shook his hand. "Do not be afraid. Ha ha. I am Glaoui," he said proudly, as though this should mean something to me.

"What do you want of me?" I asked.

"Boy was traitor. Abd el-Aziz must fall. The land of Moulay Idris shall be pure once more." I looked thoroughly puzzled, and he leaned against me with a crusty brown smile. "Tonight you eat."

I was amazed to find him true to his word when I arrived in the dining area that evening. He forced his way through the crowd and secured for me a plate of turnips and potatoes and even a gristly beef knuckle.

"Must be strong in Santée," he explained and urged me to eat. When I broached the subject of the dead acrobat he shook his head and began a disjointed, garbled lecture on life in the Santée. I explained that I did not intend to spend so long a time there that the mechanics of prison survival should become important to me, but he only laughed and shook his head. When again I asked what he wanted and why he had singled me out, he moved unpleasantly close.

"You protect Hafiziya. No matter why. We never forget. We protect you." He laughed his glottal laugh, and that was all I could extract from him. I must admit that his friendship, and even the miserable meal, buoyed my spirits. That night I slept deeply, with genuine anticipation of the next day's exercise period and another chance to converse with the Moor Ahmed.

The following day I was taken from my cell and conducted with exceptional courtesy into a small chamber where I found Guillaume. We were left alone by the guards.

I went to grip his hand in greeting, but he shrank from my touch.

"And what cause have you for that apish grin, Clayton Peavey?" he inquired testily. His cheeks were pale and his hands clung together.

"Well . . . here we are alone together. Perhaps they have discovered their mistake and will release us."

"I see no reason for such optimism. We are rushing headlong toward destruction and you appear not the least troubled." He pouted and I nearly laughed. "Laugh at me if you wish. Join the others in my ridicule. I expected no less." He paused and looked at me severely. "I have examined my cell very thoroughly. History is etched into its cracks and scars. I am the last in a long chain of . . . criminals." He hesitated over the word. "Our lives are connected by the occupation of that cell, and each of us has left a mark there. Have you noticed the names scratched in the walls, the carving in the woodwork?" I shrugged. "They are all there. And their crimes. Shall I carve my name in those walls as well? Will that be my heritage, the extent of my infamy, or must my name be dragged through the public journals, my shame paraded before my friends, my poor mother driven from her home?"

"My dear Guillaume, I think you exaggerate. After all, we are innocent."

"And what does that matter? We are held for murder, the most heinous of crimes, cast in among the lowest form of life. I cannot breathe here. I am suffocating."

I rose and approached, hoping somehow to console him, but he leapt from his seat.

"Last night I lay awake far into the night. When I finally slept I dreamed. Terrible dreams, filled with silent anguished cries which I could not wring from my chest. I awoke from one such dream but could not recall it. My head had slipped to one side and the moonlight illuminated the bed frame inches from my face. Carved in the wood was the name 'Dédé of Menilmontant' and beneath it his crime: 'Murder.' It is an endless continuity of crimes and criminals. Who was this Dédé of Menilmontant? Whom did he kill? Did his sweetheart mourn for him or was he forgotten in prison? What color were his eyes, this Dédé? How much have we in common, he and I? I have no further use of this world and I relinquish forever my place in the society of good men."

The door opened and two guards entered. Guillaume had been pacing the tiny cubicle while I sat marveling at his capacity to dramatize his own life even as he lived it, to conceive an entire world peopled by the convicts who had dwelt before him in that cell.

"Well," I suggested, "it will make marvelous material for a story. Or at least a touching poem." But he stared at me in horror, raised his hands in a gesture of despair, and staggered before me out of the room.

We stood waiting in the sunlit courtyard. At a small grilled window on the upper level of the prison a face appeared, a cigarette dangling from thin lips. For an instant I thought I had made eye contact with this anonymous man, but I resisted an urge to smile or wave. We were placed by silent guards in a prison van, and as the van drew out through the gates I glanced back at the window: the man smiled and raised a hand toward me, then turned his stare back out across the tiled roofs and treetops of Paris.

We traveled through the streets of the Latin Quarter to the Seine and downriver along the quai to the Pont St. Michel. Across the bridge the van drew up to a barred underground passage beneath the Palais de Justice and we were conducted inside through marble halls into a courtroom presided over by a judge in brilliant red robes.

From a side door Inspector Pernicieux appeared, accompanied by a diminutive gentleman dressed all in black and a jovial, balding man who I could tell instantly was an American. He gazed about delightedly while observing the prim Pernicieux so as not to misbehave.

"The court wishes to apologize for the inconvenience shown you gentlemen over the past three days," said the judge in clipped, flat tones, his French so starchily formalized it seemed to have been spoken by a machine. "All charges against you have been dropped and you are herewith released from custody." He addressed the American. "Monsieur Darlington will please advise his countryman on the procedures for securing a new visa. You both have our deepest sympathy for this unfortunate incident." He swept aside our file, the court attendant called the next case, and we were escorted out.

"But I don't understand. What's happened? Why were we held and why have we been released?" I asked angrily of the American Darlington.

"You have been released, my dear boy, because you are innocent. *Res ipsa loquitur.* What could be simpler than that?"

"Then what *did* happen at St. Sulpice? How did that boy die?"

"It was an accident," explained Inspector Pernicieux with a smug smile. "Nothing more than a compromising set of circumstances and a tragic accident."

"I don't believe it. He was an acrobat, he couldn't just fall and—"

Darlington interrupted me. "Are you protesting your release? Do you wish to confess?" He giggled. "I think it best you say nothing at all," and his thin eyebrows jiggled up and down.

The little Frenchman in black surveyed me closely. He gently touched his pursed lips with an extended forefinger and his eyes flickered across Guillaume. Then he conferred with Pernicieux.

"Who is that man?" I asked Darlington.

"Don't ask me that, dear boy. Don't ask."

We stood with Guillaume in a gallery by a little garden outside the courtroom. His mood was dramatically altered from a few hours earlier in that little chamber at the Santée.

"So French justice has demonstrated its humility, eh, Inspector?" he said. "And that is all?"

"Quite," replied the Inspector.

"New evidence has shown—" began Darlington, but the fellow in black coughed him to silence. "I think you should both be quite thankful this is all over," he concluded. He laughed and took my arm. "Now come along with me to the embassy. Ambassador White tells me he knows your father. He was quite alarmed to hear of your predicament and is looking forward to greeting you personally and seeing your affairs set straight."

I looked from the vapid Darlington to the little man in black and then to Guillaume.

"This is far from over," said Guillaume, and I felt certain he was right.

"Nonsense," interrupted Inspector Pernicieux. "It was all a mistake. Just an accident." He edged closer, his indulgent smile tinged with solicitude. "Let us try to forget." He turned warmly to me. "But you are a painter, Monsieur Peavey. As a matter of fact I myself have dabbled in art for many years. A Sunday artist, by the quai with my palette, you know. It is a stimulating recreation."

As though intentionally rising to this bait, Guillaume spoke. "Oh, do you paint?" His mockery was barely concealed. "Then you must visit us in Montmartre. Perhaps we can infect you with the new spirit."

"No, no, I am a common man with common tastes," proclaimed Inspector Pernicieux. "I have no need of infection."

"Well, I hope you will consider my invitation." Guillaume sounded sincere. "No recriminations on my part." He smiled charmingly. "A man must do his work, eh?" and he winked at the Inspector.

"Precisely, monsieur. A man must do his work."

Before I departed with Darlington, Guillaume handed me a slip of paper with an address on it. Though I was perplexed by the day's events, Darlington's doting banter drew me across the river to the Avenue Kléber and I nearly forgot my suspicions as we entered past the marine at the door and I was succored once more into the bosom of America.

III

"Everything seems to be in order, but you'd best avoid any more trouble or we'll have to send you packing, my boy." Gilbert Darlington returned my freshly restamped passport. "And do steer clear of that Guillaume . . . Malaimé, or whatever he calls himself."

"But he's my only friend in Paris. And he's a poet."

"He's not what he seems, of that much I *am* sure. It would behoove you to forget you met him. You'll find new friends."

"I don't understand," I said as we stepped into the embassy foyer.

"You needn't understand," Darlington assured me, then spoke under his breath. "Your release this morning was not due to the confidence of the French courts in your innocence."

"It wasn't?" I feigned a naive and casual interest in the hope his indiscretions would continue. They did.

"Well, *your* innocence, of course, dear boy, of that we feel confident. But as for that other fellow, the French police are not through with him. I believe he has been released for surveillance."

"What makes you think that?" I asked. He brought his small head near mine, glanced furtively about the long empty foyer, and continued.

"I shouldn't tell you this, but some rather curious evidence has come to light regarding the dead lad." He paused, I waited. "It seems none of his visible injuries could have been fatal. He simply collapsed and the coroner has yet to determine the precise cause of death. The only unusual marks on the body were a pair of small welts on his side—perhaps insect bites or some sort of sting, though we cannot be certain." He coughed. "Then there is the matter of the hollow mask he wore around his neck. Traces of gunpowder were found in it. All very mysterious indeed." He seemed pleased by the mystery of it, then straightened and reverted to the patronizing tone of his official role. "Now, forget what I've told you and forget what's happened. Start afresh and you'll be just fine, my boy."

"I'll certainly do that," I replied. Shaking his moist hand, I turned to go.

"Oh, I almost forgot." He handed me a stiff engraved card. "The new Ambassador wanted you to have this. It will admit you to the reception in his honor next week at the Ritz. He said any son of Adam Peavey's should be our guest."

"Tell the Ambassador I appreciate his graciousness and I hope my little problem has not caused him any embarrassment."

"Not at all," replied Darlington, and with a half-salute he disappeared into the recesses of the embassy while I pocketed my invitation and stepped into the Avenue Kléber.

Despite my intense curiosity about Guillaume and the death I had witnessed, I walked back to the Rue du Sommerard half convinced that I would abandon him, act prudently, and begin anew.

Madame Adelaide met me in a fury on the first landing.

"So you have returned for your things, have you, you scoundrel? And I thought you were such a shy, sweet boy."

"What seems to be the trouble, Madame Adelaide?" I inquired blithely.

"What seems to be the trouble? Three days in the

Santée and he asks me what seems to be the trouble. We'll have no murderers in this house."

"But, madame, I am not a murderer. I have been cleared of all charges and released with the apologies of the court."

"I don't care about that." The gray eyes glistened furiously but she saw nothing. "I don't know what you've done nor what you will do, but I don't like police inspectors nosing around my house asking questions, and I don't need troublemakers as boarders."

"So the Inspector was bothering you?"

"And with good reason. This is a respectable house. The other boarders won't stand for it and neither shall I. Now, collect your belongings and be gone."

"But, madame, surely you won't throw me out in the street. I am no longer even accused, much less convicted—"

"That's enough now. I won't hear any more of your lies. Be gone, be gone." She finished in high agitation, waving her plump arms in the air as though swatting flies, and dithered off shaking her head and muttering to herself.

Unable to allay her suspicions, I had no choice but to pack my bags, organize my sketches and notepads, and don my favorite checkered tweed suit and derby. Within hours of my release I found myself struggling with my belongings through the gray afternoon, feeling misunderstood, lost, and bitter.

I sat for an hour in a café on the Boul' Mich', reading *Le Matin* and consoling myself with The Autocrat. Beneath lurid descriptions of the fatal explosion of the French battleship *Iena* at Toulon and the continuing sensationalism of the Thaw trial in New York was a brief notice on the death of a street performer in the Place St. Sulpice. It was reported that two suspects—one of them "the foreign-born poet, pornographic writer, and spokesman for the so-called New Spirit, Guillaume Malaimé"—were being held at the Santée.

Madame Adelaide's hasty, though I suppose justifiable, reaction in no way precluded making the fresh start recommended by Darlington. I might still find new rooms in the quarter, resume my classes at the Académie Julien, tour the galleries, and carry on. But this now seemed a rather mundane course to pursue. Moreover, I owed it to Guillaume to warn him what Darlington had said. Finally—and this may have been the most compelling argument—in Guillaume I recognized a kindred spirit and through him entrée into the artistic avant-garde of Paris. Such an opportunity might not present itself again. He was not what he seemed, said Darlington, and I could not doubt that. His fabrications had been transparent to me from the first, though I took them to be the product of a too fertile imagination rather than the necessary subterfuge of a rogue. My abstemious nature struggled with my curiosity. Part of me had even begun to consider abandoning the entire venture and returning to Professor Stallwarts with my tail between my legs.

I left the café with my mind in a muddle. The day was icily overcast and the raw wind seared my cheeks and chafed my hands and lips. My arms ached from lugging about the valise and portfolio, but I was drawn ineluctably to the Place St. Sulpice. It was vacant but for a few pigeons and an old man talking to one of the lions, which spouted water at him. Growing rapidly as overcast as the day, I sought out the little bistro in the Rue St. André des Arts where we had lunched that first day. Either my memory failed or it had disappeared. In total gloom, my shoulders throbbing and eyes watering, I walked to the river, reaching it at the Pont Neuf, and descended the slanting, cobbled walkway to the quai. There I sat with my back against the wall and glared across the river at the Palais de Justice.

The wind off the river drove me deep into my overcoat, but still I stared angrily at the Dépôt and Palais, blaming these visible manifestations of French injustice for my dilemma and my discomfort. A few fishermen in low rowboats poled past, headed upriver. From beneath a pair of plane trees dusty workers in denim overalls approached along the wide quai and gazed curiously at the American crumpled there. This was no spring day for walks by the Seine, no matter how romantic one's disposition or how hardy one's constitution. Bearded stone faces beneath the parapets of the Pont Neuf—stained and streaked with water—seemed to be laughing along with the Parisian workers and several scruffy boys who stood down the quai tossing stones into the river. Even the waters lapped back at me. I had suddenly come to dislike Paris itself and regretted ever having come. I sensed a growing suspicion of everyone except Guillaume—an apparent inversion of logic—and began to "recognize" people. Who was that fellow in the green knit cap watching from the bridge? The little man in black who had accompanied Inspector Pernicieux at court: was that he down the quai by a stone post? Would I be seeing these same faces everywhere from now on, chasing me through my days and filling my dreams at night? Why had all this happened? What about Ahmed at the Santée? What were his motivations? Must I suspect everyone henceforth? If I did not reach some understanding of the mystery which had befallen me I *would* suspect everyone, see faces I recognized reflected in every window or watching as I sketched or sat in a café. There was no starting anew. Darlington did not understand. Guillaume needed me as much as I needed him.

I reached into my pocket and drew out the slip of paper on which Guillaume had written an address. It read 13 Rue Ravignan.

"This is as far as I go," the taxi driver informed me, stopping in Pigalle. It was dusk. Street globes flickered along the boulevard. "It's near the Place Jean Baptiste Clément. Up the Butte that way," he waved. I handed him a five-franc silver piece and alighted on the curb.

A ripe streetwalker, her sallow complexion eerily illuminated, leered at me from beneath a streetlamp. In the shadows behind her an apache of the district lurked, his cap pulled down over his eyes. The woman moved her shoulder suggestively as I passed, but I shook my head and began to climb.

As soon as I left the boulevard I entered a district of dark, narrow streets, barely wide enough for a small carriage to pass. I set down my burden and inquired of several passersby who gave me conflicting directions to the Rue Ravignan.

As I resumed my climb the street grew narrower and turned to steep steps beside an irregular picket fence. Stunted plane trees hunched in a park, long deprived of unobstructed sunlight. This tiny park was itself at an angle on the hill and the few benches tipped precariously beneath the trees.

Along one side of this humped triangular *place* stood a decrepit, long, flat building resembling a barge on the Seine. The windows were shuttered, the walls wood slats, the roof strewn with odd-shaped extensions, gables and skylights and chimneys, the whole thing patched together by woods of various shades and textures. By the door numbered 13 a water faucet dripped into a clotted culvert.

I entered a labyrinth of intersecting corridors and

halls with stairwells leading in all directions. Everywhere the walls were splattered and scrawled with crude designs and slogans, and water seeped out of cracks beneath exposed, rotting joists. Hearing music and voices down one hall, I ascended rickety wood stairs. Out of the dark loomed a pale, balding, skeletal man with wispy side-whiskers and eyes set deep in dark sockets. He was wrapped in a heavy anorak.

"I am looking for Guillaume Malaimé," I told him.

"Ahhh, so this is the reknowned American villain," he enunciated his odd welcome, a smile barely tracing his thin lips, his voice quavering out of the corner of some dream. "This way, please," he whispered and led me down the hallway toward the sound of songs and laughter in many voices and tongues.

When the door opened on that atelier in Montmartre a drunken celebration of Guillaume's escapade was well under way. The revelers were young and gay and unrelentingly bohemian, and they had assumed every conceivable posture in every corner of the long, littered room. As party to the great deeds I was accepted into their midst with some fanfare and given a place of honor near Guillaume.

He was boisterous, flushed, and red-eyed, engaged simultaneously in several conversations. A young woman with small, gentle eyes, as slim and youthful in appearance as the girl Claudie though clearly much older, returned frequently to refill his wineglass. It took me some moments to penetrate the persiflage.

"How wonderful that you've come. We were about to go to Frédé's for more drink and then to the cinema. You'll join us, of course."

I nodded. "I was booted out by my concierge. Said she would not have murderers for lodgers."

"Hah. But, of course. Typically bourgeois sentiment. Frightened out of her wits at the disgrace. So you've come to stay with us." He seemed almost delirious with joy, the exaggeration in his festivity evoking the distress I suspected lay beneath it. But all of this was drowned in the red sea.

"I hoped to find a room in this quarter, as you said it was more vital than the left bank. But seriously, Guillaume, might we have a word in private? I—"

"All that can wait. Have you been to the cinema before?"

"Yes, once in New York. It gave me a headache."

"Hah. A good one. A headache." He laughed uproariously and nearly tipped from his seat. The slim woman rushed to assist him.

"This is Marie," he introduced us. "My comrade Clayton Peavey. Marie is my beloved muse. She illuminates my life like a little sun and paints exquisitely in just her own style. And that is all," he proclaimed. Several heads turned. Marie wrinkled her flat little nose and eyed me with a warming mixture of sweetness and candor. For a moment I thought I recognized her as a classmate at the Académie Julien. "Isn't it marvelous?" Guillaume railed on. "Everyone thinks the arrest is a tremendous opportunity. I've contacted the *Paris Journal* and shall publish on it immediately. But is it a hoax, a stunt, a mistake, a tragedy, or a joke? Hah, that is the question they'll all ask. For us infamy is preferable to anonymity."

"And so easily come by," observed the skeletal mystic who had discovered me in the hall. He remained firmly wrapped in his anorak and teetered in place as he spoke.

"But go on, Clayton Peavey. Forget your hardships, forget the foolish concierge and the officious Inspector who claims to be an artist. Forget your sorrows, my friend." He resumed his quaffing while I wandered off into the celebration.

The room was an artist's studio, though none of its occupants was taking a proprietary attitude toward its contents. It appeared a place where people camped out but did not live. Unfinished canvases were propped along the walls, and a clutter of brushes, tubes of paint, Chinese chalks, charcoal, crumpled papers, and bottles of paraffin covered the tables and much of the floor. An odd assortment of cylinders, pistons, springs, and other mechanical devices was arranged like a still life. The floor was strewn with empty wine bottles, fowl bones, broken pieces of porcelain, dead flowers, and crushed cigarette butts. At the far end of the room a man with huge mustaches and a worker's cap played an accordion beneath a Victrola horn and people danced, though not with one another, but in total abandon of partners or prescribed steps, like whirling tops or wind-up toys gone haywire.

Without warning I was swept from behind into this fray. Twisting, I discovered a radiant young woman with marvelously puckered lips and large eyes whose slant was accented by dark flaring brows drawn down to her cheeks. She led me out among the dancers and spun in her long, tube-shaped dress, her feet cracking out a rhythm on the floor and her dark curls bouncing. I imitated with modest facility until the wine and the girl's frankly lascivious manner made me forget my inhibitions. Soon I was whirling and clapping my hands in time to the click of castanets and bootheels.

As I watched my partner's firm derrière rippling her tube dress I began to imagine the pleasure of rippling that flesh myself. The promise of such satisfaction glowed in her open arms, but then she abruptly turned from me and danced with another.

A number of Spaniards huddled together around the smallest of their group, whose eyes glowed darkest and voice rang loudest and whose studio I guessed this to be. One of the Spaniards produced an old guitar and began plucking out an accompaniment to the mustachioed accordionist. I observed Guillaume motioning to me across the throng and, without ever capturing my erstwhile partner's attention, I slipped out of the dance.

"Now, what is wearing so heavily upon your mind?" he asked.

"Well . . . I don't want to upset you." I panted and bent forward to draw a deep breath. "But that American consular officer who led me away this morning told me about odd evidence in the case and how the Inspector is still suspicious and might be—" I stopped short, my attention caught by a row of wooden masks on a table behind Guillaume. At one end stood a long-nosed face of dark wood in profile, a nearly exact replica of the hollow vessel found on the dead *saltimbanque*. Guillaume noticed my apprehension and followed my eyes to the mask and back again.

"You are impressed by Negro art?" he asked and I shook my head. "We are all quite excited by the faces arriving from the Ivory Coast and from the Pacific Islands as well." His soft hands wove tapestries in the air as he embarked on a discourse. "The opposite ends of the spectrum of civilization appear to coincide. These primitive peoples have the same eye for geometry, for the discordant angularities of light and displaced anatomies, as our most farsighted European artists. One wonders—"

"But that face. It is identical to the one the dead boy wore."

"Why yes, I believe it is," he said in an enigmatic tone.

"Where did it come from?"

"From Africa, I suppose. Now what was it you were about to tell me? That I must beware the meddling Inspector?"

Suddenly I felt wary of Guillaume's glib unconcern, recalled Darlington's admonition to avoid him, and determined to withhold my information. I was startled into silence by the possibility of threatening collusions I had not previously even imagined. Guillaume sensed my misgivings and draped an arm around my shoulders.

"This has been an ordeal for you, my American friend. I am not ignorant of the dangers of officialdom, though I may appear indifferent to them. I too wish to find the *saltimbanques* and understand what has happened. We shall seek them together and learn the answers to your questions. But now—" He raised his voice and empty glass. "To Frédé's. To Frédé's," he repeated and the call echoed in response around the room.

"Freddie's?" I grumbled, still befogged by my suspicious concatenation.

"Not Freddie's, Frédé's," corrected Guillaume's Marie with an encouraging grin. Within moments the party had disbanded and my portfolio and valise were stashed behind a small black trunk. With the tube-dress vamp clinging to my arm, I sauntered out into the night on my way to Frédé's.

"Do you know what day this is?" someone asked as we trooped into a small cottage whose tilting sign bore the words "Lapin Agile." We had descended sharply on the quiet side of the Butte past Sacre Coeur. The Lapin Agile was half hidden beneath a stand of trees; ivy surrounded the windows and a flower pot sat outside the door. "It is March 23—the fête day of St. Guillaume," the questioner answered himself and aroused a flurry of excitement.

"Did you hear that, Père Frédé?" said Marie. "Guillaume has returned to us from the Santée on his fête day. What can you do worthy of such an occasion?"

This question she addressed to an older man with the playful glaze of a longtime toper. He wore a black fur cap and long white beard and reminded me of a Russian count. When he spoke his voice boomed and he welcomed these cavorting, poverty-stricken young artists as old, dear friends.

A small zinc bar stood before us; above it, arranged in a chromatic scheme, a row of bottles. To the right a door opened onto the cabaret proper, whence voices and music could be heard. Our party was conducted into a private room where unsteady wood benches lined long wine-splotched tables.

"Sing me a song, St. Guillaume," bellowed Frédé, "and all shall drink free."

This offer met with a chorus of cheers. Guillaume rose and with upraised hands and mock solemnity silenced the congregation.

"I have returned to you as from the dead," he intoned, "and I cannot sing tonight. But I have a verse for you, if you will hear it." He paused, shut his eyes, clasped his large hands, and spoke so softly it was necessary to strain over the sounds from the next room to hear him. As he recited, his priestly hands rose and drew calligrammes through the air in counterpoint to his words:

"Avant d'entrer dans ma cellule
Il a fallu me mettre nu
Et quelle voix sinistre ulule
Guillaume qu'es-tu devenu?"

Several of the Spaniards, who had not understood the verse but were well aware of the promise its execution entailed, cried, "Bravo." Frédé cut them off.

"Ah, you will make me cry, St. Guillaume." He addressed us: "He is a genius, this man." He embraced Guillaume, with real tears on his cheeks. We took this as a sign to cheer and resumed the festivities, which increased as the free bottles appeared.

Guillaume uttered that terrible last line—"What sinister voice wails; Guillaume, what has become of you?" —and with those words all my suspicions, my animosity and fear, dissolved and I recognized the deep hurt his blustering flamboyance sought to deny before the group. Ashamed of myself for having doubted him, I felt doubly certain that I must help and even protect him.

"Frédé is a wonderful man," he lectured me later. "He sells fish from a cart during the day so that he may extend us credit at night. I love him."

I wanted to express the same sentiment toward Guillaume, but could only nod thoughtfully.

Soon it was time for the cinema, and all of us, now so drunk we had to support one another, paraded back into the bar with shouts of "Rigolo, rigolo"—the local wag word for a joyful amusement. We took leave of Père Frédé, who insisted that I sign a log book which stood open by the private chamber. All the signatures were coupled with sketches, lines of verse, aphorisms, calligrammes, or other artistic tidbits, and I thought blankly for some minutes over what I should add by my name, doodling without watching my hand. Most of the gang were in the street when Guillaume's Marie returned arm in arm with the girl in the tube dress to draw me away from my shapeless doodlings. At a glance the girl recognized them.

"Why, it is Père Frédé himself," she said. "How

charming," and she eased against me, flicked the hair from my eyes, and kissed my neck.

The cinema was not far away, in a dilapidated building near the Gare du Nord. As we strolled I told Guillaume of my conversation with Darlington and my meetings with the Moor Ahmed at the Santée. Above us the Moulin de la Gallette was silhouetted by a misty moon, its arms turning slowly in the breeze.

The benches were hard and backless and the flickering gray images on the suspended screen barely held my attention. The projectionist cranked frantically and a magnified, slow-motion film of tiny insects commenced. The extreme close-ups in space and time transformed these little creatures into prehistoric monsters inhabiting an alien world. This was followed by "A Visit to Peek Frean and Company's Biscuit Works," which filled two reels and was interminable. By this time I had settled comfortably against Catherine, the girl in the tube dress who had apparently claimed me for the evening. My eyes fluttered open and shut rather like a pair of little cameras. When the third feature began, Catherine poked me and spoke.

"This is the new Film d'Art," she whispered, her wine breath rustling warm and sweet across my face and her hand resting lightly in my lap. "Mmmm," I responded. "You must watch, Clayton," she said. And I tried.

This self-styled Film d'Art featured prominent actors from the Comédie Française, among them Sarah Bernhardt herself, mouthing mute performances before a stationary camera. The film sped up, slowed down, and a variety of mackled and multiple images asserted the artiness of the production. It was pointless and thoroughly tedious and when my snores became obvious

Catherine nudged me. She had to awaken me several times during the show.

I was thankful, however, to be awake for the evening's final feature, a glorious piece of sensationalism entitled "Electrocuting the Elephant." The effect when the large floppy ears suddenly stood straight out from the head was quite astonishing.

"It is a miracle," exclaimed mystic Max as our party emerged into the dark night. "And a poetic experience of the most intense kind," added someone else to general accord. I was anxious to grope onward toward whatever consummation awaited me with Catherine, and anything which delayed that was a bore. But this was not to be just yet.

"Come, Clayton Peavey, now we must seek our *saltimbanques*." Guillaume spoke softly, his voice a disembodied spirit encircling me like the cool air against my flushed cheeks. I clung to Catherine's hand, but Guillaume was insistent.

"You can't be serious. It's nearly midnight." I glanced longingly at the vamping Catherine. "And besides, Guillaume, tomorrow will be much better. I'm so stewed and—"

"She will wait for you, my friend." He smiled. "This is important."

"But where are we going?" I admit I was beginning to whine.

"To the circus," he replied with a laugh and led me off into the night.

IV

The Cirque Mediano in Montmartre was a favorite haunt of Guillaume's gang. It was located at the junction of the Boulevard de Rouchechouart and the Boulevard de Clichy.

We bridged a switchery of railroad tracks and walked silently beneath tall elms and silver maples down the center of the boulevard. An old bum slept on a green bench curled around a sack—did one eye peek open as we passed? Along the boulevard busy shops with cheap clothing in open stalls were barred and the crowded sidewalks deserted but for a few disreputables like ourselves: apaches leaning against a kiosk in the woods of the Place d'Anvers, bad boys in black strutting their apprentice vulgarity, and the inevitable brace of *flics* swinging their batons as they marched along the curb.

A few departing spectators still milled outside the structure which housed the circus—wood-slat walls roofed in canvas, a semipermanent tent. The wind was blowing and the first drops of rain had begun to fall as we entered.

The evening's performance was long over. Crumpled broadsides advertising the show swirled overhead in the drafty tent and whistles of derision seemed to linger, resonating on high. Perhaps it was only the wind.

A group of clowns and acrobats waited impatiently beneath gas lanterns by the bar for payment from the circus master. We crossed the dirt ring toward them. Costumes were half shed and makeup smeared so that these performers appeared suspended between their mundane humanity and the painted festivity of their roles, no longer onstage yet not fully returned to the wings. An old clown stepped away from the bar.

"The time has come for the clowns to be masters." He bowed over his ceremonial greeting, to which Guillaume replied: "And that is all."

The clown's name was Darius Boppe. He had rich chocolate eyes and an aspect of enduring lassitude.

"Guillaume," he said. "This is a coincidence. A friend of yours was here this evening inquiring about you."

"A friend?"

"So he said. He left no name nor message. Looked to be a very pale Moor." I nudged Guillaume, and Boppe nodded. "Do you believe in coincidence, Guillaume?" he asked. "I do not."

Guillaume shook his head. He drew a piece of paper from his pocket. Glancing at a creature with a dwarf's body but enlarged arms and head who had sidled away from the bar toward us, he changed the subject and said, "So how goes the life of a clown, Coco?"

"Nothing changes. The paymaster is late and it is beginning to rain." He shrugged. "Giving so much laughter to others we have little left for ourselves. But we survive."

The half-dwarf shifted his drooping eyes onto a doll-like midget in ruffled skirts and followed her back to the bar.

"My friend Clayton and I have had a rather unpleasant experience and I hoped we might get some information from you. Are you familiar with a troupe of *saltimbanques* who go by the name *La Famille Jollicorps?*"

Bobbe rubbed his white forehead. "Yes, the Zorn brothers. Gaspard and Arbo Zorn. I have worked with them at the Mediano . . . but that was many years ago." He paused, lost in remembrance. "Why do you ask this?"

"Three days ago one of them—a boy—was killed in the Place St. Sulpice." Boppe frowned at this news but betrayed neither surprise nor sorrow. His eyes retained their impassive glaze. One felt nothing could upset this man, not because his passions were absent but because they lay dormant, numbed by denial or submerged beneath a higher calling. "Monsieur Peavey and I were mistakenly arrested for this crime. Since our release this morning we have been unable to locate the family. It appears they have left Paris. I wondered whether you might have seen them or heard from them recently."

"No," he said abruptly. "The Zorns no longer visit the Cirque Mediano." He paused. "As for myself, I remain here. I do not go out seeking more misery."

"What misery?" I interjected. "Are the Jollicorps miserable?"

"They have been. Many Alsatians are miserable today. It is our fate until the day of revenge." He stared at me quite icily.

"Can you suggest how I might find them?"

With his chocolate eyes Darius Boppe studied Guillaume. His silence was filled by the rain on the tent and the clanking tools of workmen dismantling a suspended grid for trapeze artists. All around them this latticework spread, and Darius Boppe seemed to hang at its center like a spider in its web. He lighted an aromatic cigarette and spoke, more slowly and with even less animation than before.

"They never rest long. Perhaps they've gone to Brussels or Luxembourg." He offered the cigarette to Guillaume, who drew a long, pensive puff and exhaled slowly. "But they are more likely to have traveled south for the carnivals in Bordeaux and Bayonne. They often remain there in early spring or across the border at Bilbão." He seemed to measure his words, calculating just how much of the veil to shred. "But it is many years since I have seen them and they may have found fresher fields to reap," he backtracked. "Why do you seek these *saltimbanques?*"

"To protect them. For explanations. Out of regret and mercy—and love."

"You have many reasons. Perhaps you will find them with so many reasons." The paymaster had arrived at the bar, and a fracas was developing among the tired, half-drunk performers waiting there. In a dialect I could not understand, Boppe called out to a young gymnast bulging in his leotard.

"One more thing, Darius. I know it is late and you are tired." The clown returned his gaze to Guillaume and slowly nodded as the sweet smoke ran across his lips and up his cheeks. Guillaume unfolded the paper he had been holding, on which had been sketched the African mask with its long nose and almond eyes. "Where would you seek such a mask?" he asked.

"Now that is an easy question." Boppe smiled. "You know Clovis Vogel, don't you, Guillaume? He was a great clown, one of the founders of the Mediano along with Boum-Boum, Arbo Zorn, and myself. Now he is an art dealer. I think your little Spaniard has sold through his gallery. Vogel bought a pharmacy in the Rue des Martyrs which he is converting into a gallery and curio shop, selling whatever oddities he comes across and distributing the medicines as well." His painted eyebrows rose. "We go there often. I have seen such faces in his shop."

"Of course. I know Vogel's shop. We shall visit him tomorrow."

"I'm sure Clovis Vogel can help you. But you must

approach him cautiously. He must see an immediate profit or he will protect himself and his sources."

"Thank you, Darius." He slipped a small, twine-tied packet into the clown's hand. "And if you hear of the Zorns or *La Famille Jollicorps* you will let me know, won't you?"

"I shall remember," replied Boppe. "But Guillaume, listen to me. I have been honest with you, perhaps more revealing than I should, and so I must take a certain responsibility. This is no game you are playing. If you take this path it will lead you far from Paris. Consider carefully why you are following it; and do not go dauntless or on a whim where you do not belong. There has already been one death—at least one death."

He bowed and wearily meandered across the rutted ring to rejoin the clowns by the bar. As we walked wordlessly away angry voices rose behind us and a single glass shattered.

"We live at the fore edge of society," Guillaume mused as we trudged up the narrow streets of the Butte toward the Rue Ravignan. The rain had eased; a light mist brushed our faces. "Clowns, artists, madmen, poets, cripples, and criminals—all lead marginal lives. I believe it is in the margins of life we find truth."

"You knew that old clown would be familiar with our *saltimbanques*, didn't you? But how? How can he know where our path leads? And all that ominous talk of death. He knows more than he said."

"And admits it," countered Guillaume.

"I must admit *I'm* confused." I sniffed the moist air. "One moment I suspect you of complicity in all this and the next I feel certain you are as innocent as I."

"Not that innocent, Clayton Peavey." He grinned.

"In truth I hardly know myself where I stand. We must wait to see what Clovis Vogel tells us."

We walked on in silence, our hoary pantings drifting behind us as we climbed. My weariness had exceeded fatigue and I felt numb; frozen into place on an unfamiliar grid.

"I love words," Guillaume embarked, his priestly hands reaching for wafer-thin layers of meaning in the night. "You wonder about the truth, the meaning of events. I marvel at the magical power of words, beyond their literal meanings. The hidden essence of a word. Mallarmé's spark." Yes, one could take communion from those hands. "We must always look behind the meaning of a word, or an event, to understand it. This is the secret property of words, which is the special concern of poets just as the secret properties of light are the special concern of artists."

"But words mean specific things. Light is open to infinite interpretations, all equally valid."

"No, Clayton. Just as each man sees a different light, so it is with words. We dissect them, dislocate their sense, then reassemble them to discover a new reality. It is happening all around us today. The cinema, painting, the flight of aeroplanes, the acts of clowns, the ways of men."

"But it is like an illusion," I complained.

"Not at all. Precisely the opposite. Everything is possible, suddenly, everywhere and with everything, all is possible if only we have faith in our intuitive understanding of what lies around us. Believe only what you see, but believe that totally. That is the path to enlightenment, and all the old techniques of pleasing, they are the illusion."

We had reached the tilting triangular *place* outside the studio. A cat howled on the roof as we entered by the dripping drain.

Everyone had passed out or gone home. Marie and Catherine lay side by side on a couch, their faces nearly touching. Catherine's arm was lifted and her slender wrist draped across the other girl's shoulder. We were both touched by the tender poignancy of this scene and stood a moment in mute admiration, without any desire to disturb them.

"Come, let us say goodnight to Max," Guillaume whispered. We crept down the halls to a door on the back side of the building at ground level. The smell of rotting things permeated and a dim light shone beneath the doorframe.

Max was sitting in the dank room, wrapped in his heavy anorak, reading *Le Temps* by oil lamp. The low flame cast a dull light across his pale forehead. The room was bleak, frigid and bare and coated with filth, and smelled of petroleum, frankincense, tobacco, and ether.

"Success?" he muttered without taking his eyes from the newspaper in his hands.

"Marginal," I said. Guillaume smiled. "At best," he added.

"Ah. I am so sorry," replied Max, but it sounded less an expression of sympathy than the wan warning of one who had discontinued use of direct forms of communication. "Perhaps I can help."

He turned, seeming to creak on rusted sockets as his chair scraped across the floor. He unfolded the mirror of a small poudreuse and tilted it forward into the horizontal position. From beneath the mirror he removed a small, round pastille tin. In the tin was a tiny curve-handled knife and a hornpiece of white powder. Max began to chop this powder on the mirror with the knife.

When a spoon and flame and silver syringe appeared, Guillaume motioned me to the mirror and scooped a bit of the powder onto the long nail of his right little finger. He sniffed it into each nostril, refilled his tiny tray, and held it up to me.

"It is cocaine. From your side of the world," he explained. "It will make you feel much happier. And far more secure."

I could hardly deny that I was not feeling particularly happy, much less secure, at that moment. So I sniffed.

"Well, well . . ." I grinned the sheepish provincial grin which no French person could resist.

Max's eyelids drooped. The oil lamp flickered low.

"We must leave him to his meditations. Thank you, my friend." The hint of a tremor ran along Max's eyebrows in response to Guillaume's gratitude, and my own which I was quick to voice. The eyebrow appeared to move but not the skin around it. There was no visible eye: only two pale blades of white slashed across dark withered prunes of eye sockets.

Our host did not escort us to the door.

"All form is an accident." His stark laughter billowed from the corner of the room like the mist of his atomizer, breathing in, breathing out. I felt a new numbness all over; a delightful, warming anesthetic. I could taste the cocaine at the back of my throat and creeping across my palate to the tip of my tongue. "Madness subverts form," he called after us.

"This is wonderful stuff," I told Guillaume. "I feel such a sense of clarity and perception."

"Hah," he scoffed. "You're probably a good deal less perceptive than you think. But it has many uses."

The girls lay intertwined upon their couch, two goddesses torn from a Toulouse-Lautrec poster, all arabesques and curlicues, with Catherine's hair washed in bountiful waves across her shoulders and Marie's arms.

Guillaume shook Marie gently by the shoulder

while I knelt timidly at the foot of the couch, wondering if perhaps I had returned too late for pleasure. As the girls rose from their sleep I was swept down by arms and legs and laughter and we began to tussle on the couch. Soft hands pawed at me, ruffled my hair, tickled and massaged and punched. It was so playful that I totally forgot my natural inhibitions and enjoyed the two girls. "Rigolo, rigolo," cried Marie, but Guillaume was distracted and remained seated rigidly outside the fray. At last I centered on Catherine and she on me. Her soft lips found mine, and she drew me to her. I was barely aware of Guillaume and Marie slipping quietly away.

I have never been boastful of my prowess as a lover, but on that night it seemed I would remain erect forever. No amount of coaxing, squirming, caressing, and lapping by the delightful Catherine could prevail upon my recalcitrant penis to complete its task. Twice she was reduced to a quivering mass, nails clawing my back, head thrashing and hair flailing, while I remained half-detachedly riding the waves of this glorious sea. Above us the rain hammered on the roof. "Oh, Clayton, Clayton," she cried as I arched in response to the delicious taste of her gossamer skin across my body. Suddenly, without warning, in a flash my numbness passed, I was unleashed from its hold and Catherine with me, and soon we had drifted together into an exhausted sleep.

I had barely fallen asleep, or so it seemed, when Guillaume stood over me, the half-light of dawn in the window behind him. I awoke instantly, sat up with a start, and my head throbbed violently. Soon the pain subsided and was replaced by that sensation of clarity.

"Come, my friend. We must flee Montmartre," he said.

"What?" I drawled over the word and fell back on

the couch. Guillame shook my shoulder. Catherine stretched a long graceful arm and smiled without opening her eyes as I rose and tottered across the cold floor.

"I have been thinking. I was a fool to return here last night. If they have been to the circus they will soon visit the studio. It is no longer safe here."

"Who?" I asked a moment later, struggling with my valise and portfolio into the little *place* in the morning.

"I don't know." He shook his head.

It was a bright primaries morning, the perfect blue of the sky and green budding trees, the parks and buildings and air itself washed clean by the night's rain. A matutinal chill still hung in the air as the big yellow sun slanted across the green and red mansards of Montmartre. It was warm against my face and neck.

"What a beautiful day," I said and began to whistle.

"It is indeed. Too lovely for fear and suspicion."

"Where are we going now?" I asked, but I felt so exhilarated by the morning—my fatigue drained by the lovemaking, my strength miraculously renewed by a few hours' sleep—that I hardly cared what he might answer.

"To my mother's house in Auteuil. It is not too far from here, in the outer districts of the city. We will be safe there while we think."

We dropped off the Butte through the Cimetière du Montmartre, an elegant park, thickly wooded, with marble slabs and stone tombs set amidst flower beds, intersecting paths, and tall ivied walls. Beyond this we passed along a wide boulevard bereft of traffic and through nearly pastoral scenes: a young shepherd boy with his small flock on a gaudy green and yellow meadow, cap atilt and sheep baaing in the dawn.

I had ceased whistling and commenced grumping, for we must have walked nearly ten kilometers when we finally entered the suburban district of Auteuil: neat rows of nondescript little bourgeois houses, all adjoining and all very much the same. The Rue Molitor was shaded by maples and plane trees. Guillaume turned in at a small brick house with ornamental stonework and two slim gables on the second floor. We passed through an unattended garden and into a carpeted vestibule.

From behind a door came the sound of a man's and a woman's voice in heated dialogue. Guillaume hesitated, put his hand to the door, raised it to knock, then opened the door and entered.

A woman rushed to meet us. She was tall and robust, with elaborately coiffed hair piled atop her head and ringlets tickling her powdered brow. She had a broad chin and forehead like Guillaume's and wore a collar of Breton lace across her shoulders. It pinched her neck, and a fold of skin overhung this collar like a popover in its baking shell. Her eyes were unnaturally red.

"Mama!" Guillaume opened his arms to her, but she braced herself at the sight of him and began screaming.

"So it's you. What have you done now? What have you been up to this time, you rascal, you worthless ingrate? Why are you trying to destroy me after all I have suffered?"

"Mama, please. This is my friend Clayton Peavey, an American whom I—"

"Ooh la la, and you bring your accomplice with you. Villain! What will you do next?"

"But Mama," he pleaded. He was cut short when his mother stepped back into the room.

On the edge of a stiff-backed chair, his pince-nez raised in one hand of protest, his entire body nipped into place by a gray three-piece suit, with the little black hairs bristling from his nose and ears, sat Inspector Guy Pernicieux. He rose and dipped his head in greeting as we entered the room.

V

"The arrant American as well. We are twice blessed," said the Inspector. "Darlington warned me of this."

"Darlington?" I stammered and he fixed me in his vigilant gaze.

"But of course," he replied. "*Some* people are trying to look after you."

"I can look after myself," I said, but it felt a childish retort lacking conviction.

"Can you indeed?" said the Inspector, and he smiled at Guillaume's mother as though an understanding already existed between them.

"So you have met the Countess," said Guillaume.

"Pardon me?" asked the Inspector while Mama reproached him: "Guillaume."

"Mother, I would like to present Clayton Peavey." He turned to me. "Clayton, the Countess Angelica."

I must have looked confused as I took her hand, for she blushed and explained haltingly: "Well, by birth only, you understand . . . we lost everything . . . long ago." She lowered her eyes and I assured her of the honor I derived from our meeting.

"And now, Inspector," Guillaume turned to attack. "Perhaps you can tell us why you've come here to disturb Mama and continue harassing us over this unhappy incident."

Inspector Pernicieux opened a copy of the morning's *Paris Journal* on the table before us. He indicated an article beneath Guillaume's byline describing his recent "exploits." "This was very foolish," he said. "You needn't attract more attention than you are already receiving."

"I think the manner in which I conduct my life is my business."

"Guillaume, you understand nothing," interjected his mother. "As usual." In other circumstances she might have appeared quite a glamorous woman, but that morning she was flustered and trying to maintain a dignity she inherently lacked. In this she fit the room. It too presented a facade—Art Nouveau chic with potted ferns and an uncomfortable ottoman, etched-glass lamps, and a curlicued Louis Quinze chair—but the whole assemblage a bit shoddy and out of place in the sitting room of this respectable little house in Auteuil. A small *ecce homo* of Flemish character, with a particularly doleful expression, hung directly behind the Countess.

"Don't you see, monsieur?" the Inspector appealed. "I have not come here to harass you but to inform you of your somewhat delicate position, which you have so obviously misconstrued, and perhaps even to provide you with protection."

"Protection from what?" Guillaume eyed him suspiciously.

"From yourself," said the Countess, but the Inspector raised a hand of forbearance.

"Please, madame," he cautioned her. "I know how upsetting this has been for you. If the young gentlemen would sit down we might be able to reach an understanding."

We sat side by side on the backless ottoman while the Countess sniffled beneath her *ecce homo* and rustled her ruches in organdy and tulle.

"First, let me assure you that in no way does any suspicion fall upon either of you relating to the death of the lad. We have that business half solved already."

"Half solved?" I asked.

"That is, we know the circumstances and general identity of the murderer—and it was murder, my friends —but we have not apprehended the individual. And that is where you may be of some assistance to us, inasmuch as you insist upon injecting yourself so publicly into this affair."

"What do you have in mind, Inspector?" demanded Guillaume, lighting a cigarette.

"The murderers, I fear, will be looking for you. I gather you hold the same view and have come here this morning thinking this a safe place to elude their pursuit." He paused to adjust his pince-nez and I thought he was far less a bumbler than he appeared. This revelation did not comfort me. "In that you may be momentarily correct. What I propose is that you return to Montmartre and continue your life there, under my protection and the protection of the Sûreté, until your enemies reveal themselves. Then I think we shall have our murderer, and perhaps a great deal more as well."

"And you've come to us this morning with this preposterous scheme?" Guillaume goaded him.

"I came merely to ask if your mother had seen you and to extend the offer of protection. It is an offer you would do well to accept."

"But who are these *enemies?*"

"Of that," replied Inspector Pernicieux, "I am not totally certain. My colleagues at the Deuxième Bureau have taken an interest in this case, but I am not privy to all their information."

"What is this Deuxième Bureau?" I asked. "You mentioned it at the Santée too."

"It is the intelligence branch of the armed forces," said Guillaume disgustedly.

"Exactly right," added the Inspector, and we all sat silently a moment mulling over the implications of that.

"Would anyone care for a coffee?" asked our hostess. "Or . . . or . . ." She glanced at the Inspector. "Or perhaps an aperitif?"

"It is barely ten o'clock," Guillaume scolded her.

"It is too early for me, madame," replied the Inspector. "But please, if you need a little something to calm your nerves, do not be ashamed. This has been a most unsettling morning for you."

Her grateful smile betrayed more profligacy than anxiety, and Guillaume, to my surprise, joined her in a *porto* while the Inspector and I drank our coffee black. She set a tray of Roman sweetmeats before us: rose-petal fondants, dried figs with aniseed, quince flavored cotanniata—all of it throughly nauseating.

"Are we feeling better?" asked the Inspector. I wondered whether he was employing the collective referrent or merely being condescending. "Now—"

In the momentary lull Guillaume had picked up the *Paris Journal*. He was reading his own piece. A sly, whimsical smile twisted the corner of his mouth.

"Oh la la, he is so proud of himself," said his mother. "Aren't you, Guillaume? What could be better for your campaign than an arrest? And the acrobats. Doesn't your friend paint acrobats? Isn't that part of the grand scheme?"

"He did paint them, yes, Mama." Guillaume smiled indulgently. Despite the jousting and superficial hostility it was instantly apparent to this observer that they were, and had been for some time, utterly interdependent, ballasts in each other's stormy lives.

"What campaign is that?" asked the Inspector idly.

"I think Mama is referring to my efforts to prepare and educate the public regarding the coming changes in art."

"Really? You will have to advise me of your secrets. I am a painter myself, you know."

"But of course, Inspector. Only it is not a matter of secrets. It is all based on the new relationships of time and space, a recognition of the intuitive understanding of these scientific phenomena among the most primitive peoples, and then simply putting two and two together."

"To get five," added the Countess. "It don't sound like science to me."

"Oh, doesn't it, Mama?" Guillaume corrected her.

"No, it doesn't. More superstitious nonsense, like that Madame Blavatsky you were so excited about last year."

"For an advocate of miracle workers and fortune tellers in some of the seamier arrondissements of this city you are certainly quick to judge."

"And that terrible man Père Ubu," she chattered along, oblivious of his remark. "My goodness but it is hard to see the art in it."

"I quite sympathize," said the Inspector, and he smiled at Guillaume's mother. Did she blush or was that merely the flush of that first glass of *porto* after her early morning traumas? One could not tell. "But I agree with what you said regarding intuitive understanding," he addressed Guillaume. "I have always felt that art flows from some source other than the intellect. One does not go about painting a picture as one goes about solving a murder."

I was about to extol the virtues of intuition in crime solving, but Guillaume, much pleased by the direction of the conversation, exclaimed: "There, you see, an artist. Behold your own divinity, Inspector, you *are* an artist. I can see it."

"No, no, I am merely an inspector with the Paris Préfecture and have been for some time." He paused soberly and fingered his waistcoat. "And it is in that capacity I have come here this morning. Vaunt your adventures at will, monsieur, but remember this is a serious business for some of its other participants."

Guillaume ignored his warning. "I refuse to believe it," he said excitedly. "You must let me see your work and judge for myself."

He had instinctively located the Inspector's weakness, and the old boy eagerly capitulated. "Well, I don't know," he excused himself. "Of course, I should like you to see my little paintings. Perhaps we can combine business with pleasure and make my surveillance an artistic exchange between this old generation and your new one."

"Wonderful. And you *must* show your work, Inspector; you cannot hide it. Perhaps your hour has come. I am a critic, you know, and might help to establish your reputation." The Inspector looked shyly at his feet, and I coughed.

"Ah yes, Monsieur Peavey, what are we to do with you?"

"If it's all the same to you, sir, I would like to remain with Guillaume in Montmartre. It's what I've come for. Unless—"

"I believe Monsieur Darlington and your friends at the American embassy can be assuaged, though there has already been some trouble regarding our handling of this case. You did not tell me your father was a personal friend of the new Ambassador."

"I most certainly did, Inspector. That first day in prison I told you that and you—"

"Of course, of course. Nonetheless—"

"But who did kill the boy?" I asked abruptly.

"I am not at liberty to say while the case is still pending." The Inspector fidgeted. "But do believe that these people's interest in you is not benevolent."

"While yours is, eh, Inspector?" parried Guillaume over his second *porto*.

"I suppose I cannot convince you of it, but yes, my interest in both of you has been, from the first, benevolent. You are not murderous fellows, that is quite clear. There now, that is my profession of faith."

As ours were not forthcoming, the interview ended.

It was agreed that we return to the Rue Ravignan that day. Despite honeyed entreaties, the Countess could not prevail upon the Inspector to remain for lunch, and he soon departed, advising us to watch for a workman come to install a new pump in the square outside the studio. This workman would be our guardian. Pernicieux promised to visit us himself as soon as possible.

At the door he said something which I found troubling and which, in his benevolent style, he refused to explain. "You were unwise to mention the mask to that Moor in prison," he told me. "They think you have it and they want it." I was left with another enigma: I had no idea who was telling what to whom but all sorts of people seemed to know things they ought not to know. How they learned them was a mystery to me.

Through a porthole window near the door I watched him go. Then I joined Guillaume and his mother in an aperitif. The room was stuffy with cigarette smoke.

"That Inspector is a sweet old angel." The Countess Angelica glowed over her *porto,* and her left eye watered slightly as though moved by this expression of sentiment.

"Goodness, Mama, you do go to excess."

"And you, my son?" She did not challenge him with this but stated the truth, flatly, and brushed at her cheek. "He means well toward you, Guillaume. You must believe that."

"Well, I don't," he replied churlishly and changed the subject. "I see the Kaiser's dear Professor Schiemann is still in Paris, trying to make mischief for the Entente Cordiale."

"I didn't know you were concerned with the Entente Cordiale," I chided him. Memories of Professor Stallwarts and my immediate past reared unpleasantly in my mind.

"Oh, I don't give a damn for the English," he said. "But I hate the Germans. Did I not tell you of my *Wanderjahr* with the rose of Hildesheim?"

"No. Another of your—"

"Yes, another unrequited love. The first. She was the English governess for a German viscountess; I was the son's tutor. Naturally, we became friends. For her it was never more than that. I loved her, she pitied me." He paused over the memory. "There is but one woman I have loved whom I will never lose," he added and his eye caught his mother's for a tender moment.

"What is this *really* all about, Guillaume?" she asked as we basked in the wine's warmth over our cheese. Guillaume neatly skived off a piece of goat's cheese, added a pinch of salt, and raised his eyes to hers. He recounted the events leading to Inspector Pernicieux's and our own arrival there that morning, abetted by my details of the days at the Santée.

"Truly, I am still unconvinced the Inspector wants to do more than spy on us," he concluded. "But if he wishes to call it a guardianship, so be it. You understand that I must stay away from Auteuil until this is over."

"Of course. I always have Jules." Jules, I would learn, was a moderately prosperous Jewish financier and the Countess' longtime companion and benefactor. "It is best you not involve me in this sordid business. Why, if Madame Dubord or Madame Michel learned what mischief you are still up to . . . oh . . ." She put her plump hands to her cheeks and primped the curls on her powdered brow.

While we completed our lunch the Countess and I

exchanged family lore. I told her of America and she spoke of her noble father and her early life in the Vatican. Guillaume interjected ironic comments as he puttered about the little house selecting a few items he would bring back with him to Montmartre. They were a sharp contrast, and an image came to me of the mother as a thick impasto of pigment smeared roughly on a canvas, while Guillaume was hundreds of tiny, multicolored dots, none of them quite the color of his whole but complementing each other and cohering miraculously into a solid form: a Pissarro personality, different from whatever angle one viewed it.

We left her beginning to doze beneath her *ecce homo* in her comfortable little bourgeois house full of oriental bric-a-brac and swirling arabesques.

Outside the lovely spring morning had turned cloudy, and as we rode back to the Rue Ravignan I detected the first ticklings of a cold at the back of my throat. I curled in my overcoat, not listening as Guillaume rambled on, but teased by the rapid, rolling surf of his voice into a snug euphoria which lasted the length of our trip.

VI

The man sent to watch over us seemed neither inspired nor amused by his task. He had served two decades in the Sûreté and was well acquainted with the older habitués of Pigalle, including the more infamous madames of the red-light district. By his account the Sûreté was the lowest form of service in the Paris police, an urban foreign legion to which hopeless or incorrigible officers were consigned. Most of its members, particularly the vice squad and undercover corps, were, like Charles, illiterate drunkards.

Charles had a thin hooked nose at the center of a drooping face. An intermittent facial tic stretched the sagging flesh upward from his neck to his right temple and twisted his mouth. He applied himself listlessly to repairing the little green fountain with its four allegorical figures which stood near the top of the humped Place Ravignan, but this cover was so transparent he quickly abandoned it and spent his days happily sitting at Frédé's or another of the cafés we frequented, drinking the cheapest red wine and enjoying the company.

It became a favorite game for Guillaume and myself not simply to distract and escape Charles' haphazard vigilance, but to devise the most obvious stratagems and still have them succeed, as they invariably did.

"The Inspector must hold us in rather low regard if he thinks Charles can protect or watch over us," I speculated to Guillaume. "Either that or he doesn't care."

"But who is watching him who watches us?" Guillaume demanded with widened eyes and a single raised eyebrow. Who indeed?

For several days life in Montmartre settled into a pleasant routine. We talked and drank, ate when we could, and walked everywhere, walked till my legs ached and talked till my head spun. I had developed a raging cold—forever a bit of wetness at the tip of my poor, raw nose—and all of Guillaume's friends suggested ways to alleviate my suffering.

I swallowed nearly every form of liqueur and brandy to no avail.

"Try Eno's Fruit Salt," suggested Marie. "It rectifies the stomach and makes the liver laugh with joy," she mocked the advertisement. But it was not my inner organs which troubled me. I believe it was the bock beer from Hannover which we drank that spring, darker and richer than any beer I had known, which finally clarified my system.

So we passed a blissful interlude in heady conversation and did not pursue, nor were we pursued by, manifestations of our little adventure in the Place St. Sulpice. Neither did the Inspector make an appearance, and I began to think he had forgotten us. I had little trouble forgetting him.

Any excuse for a feast or fête, the most minimal sale of a poem or painting, was enthusiastically embraced. Despite the apparent disorder and spontaneity to life I learned rapidly that there were patterns, and to these we adhered strictly. Mondays we met at Max's for a soothsaying session amidst astrological scrawlings on the wall and the smell of cats and mildew. Tuesdays were reserved for literary forays across the river to the Closerie des Lilas. Wednesdays Marie entertained at her mother's house, and the following day we all went to the circus. Afternoons were spent at Frédé's playing chess or tossing darts or just being witty.

I had begun developing a theory on the shape of French mouths. "You French all have such prominent mouths and lips, but I think I have discovered what makes them unusual," I told Guillaume and several of the others over bocks at Frédé's. "You start with a thin, bony face, which immediately exaggerates the lips. Then, for some unfathomable reason, many French, men in particular, have buck teeth." Guillaume had begun laughing. "Finally, anatomical considerations aside, we have the language itself, with all those long vowels and rolling r's so that you are always pouting and pursing and puckering. A very peculiar effect."

"A very peculiar theory as well," said Guillaume with obvious delight.

The subject of mouths reminded me of Catherine, whom I had not seen since my return from Guillaume's mother's, and I asked after her.

"She has gone back to her boyfriend," he told me.

"She has a boyfriend?" I was startled. "Yet she gave herself to me that night."

"Yes, she did. That was that night and that night only," explained one of the gang, a sturdy young painter from Brittany with sandy hair and laborer's hands. "Did you expect something more?" Everyone was surprised that I had.

But there were Sylvie and Laurence and Marie-Jésus and the models from the *ginguette* shows with whom to console myself, and I quickly ceased wondering about Catherine.

I *had* begun wondering when any creative activity occurred. Although there seemed to be unlimited time for speculation and theorizing, for the concoction of rites, code words, symbols, and propaganda, there was little evidence of artistic output. Occasionally I saw Guillaume scribble a few lines on a napkin or the corner of *La Phalange* or *La Revue Blanche*, but no one had the time nor inclination to sit quietly alone and work.

"I am *always* working," Max contended in his wavering voice. He sat in the sunshine dandling the little daughter of one of the gang on his knee and reading her tiny palm. I asked how this could be construed as working. "Observing life is the first duty of the artist," he explained. "Then allowing one's observations to take root in the soul, so that they become insights and grow within you like a flower. When it is time for the bloom to appear it will be there. One needn't worry." And he returned to telling the fortune of his four-year-old playmate.

I felt content to let my cold and the distress of those days in prison and immediately afterward pass slowly out of my system. My sole artistic endeavor was a painting executed on the outer wall of the Lapin Agile using the tail of Frédé's donkey, Lolo, as a brush.

Père Frédé fancied me from our first meeting. "You are so American," he told me. "In your checkered tweed suits and derby hat and wide colored ties. No one else could dress like that and not look silly, yet for you it is perfectly natural." He led Lolo over to me and, amidst great hilarity from a rapidly growing congregation, insisted that I permanently adorn his pocked walls.

It was a Saturday afternoon and we had drawn tables into the shade of the sycamores along the Rue St. Vincent. Montmartre at this time was still half city, half village, and one felt that the real urban dwellers, down the hill on the other side of Pigalle, were a race apart. They came huffing past on their way to the hills beneath the Moulin de la Gallette carrying little girls in bright gingham dresses and picnic baskets overflowing with cheese and fruit, long thin loaves sticking up at the corner like antennae. Many of them dawdled by our village inn, forming a second gallery for my painting and whispering curiously among themselves. It was a bright, warm day, and all the men were in shirt sleeves and straw hats. The bock beer chilled in Frédé's basement tasted particularly sweet. I whistled as I worked. When it was completed I proudly examined my mural, which drew critical acclaim and a great variety of insightful interpretations from the gang. Lolo kept her rear to the work throughout, held in place by Frédé and the Breton artist with broad shoulders, but with a quick swish of her tail she managed to scumble nearly half the design.

"But it is for the best," Guillaume consoled me. "It was merely the instrument of your art taking part in the creation. Now the paintbrush itself has a mind and will of its own. And that is all." He drew near me with a glance at Charles, who sat half-dozing in the sun, unaware of the creativity so close at hand. I had virtually forgotten the reason for Charles' presence, but Guillaume spoke softly to me. "Today we must visit Clovis Vogel," he said, as matter-of-factly as though saying that today we would all go to the cinema or dine at Marie's. I shrugged. The shop was near and I had no idea why we had not visited it long ago. With a wave to Père Frédé and a pat on the rump for my faithful accomplice in art, I gathered up my derby and followed Guillaume down the hill toward Clovis Vogel's pawnshop, pharmacy, and art gallery.

The Rue des Martyrs ascends steeply from the beginning of the Boulevard de Rouchechouart, not far from Pigalle. It is broad by Montmartre standards, a tall building with chipped walls along one side and a few small shops down the other. Clovis Vogel's shop was near the bottom.

I stepped down and ducked through the low doorway into a dark cave. Behind me Guillaume was distracted by an acquaintance passing in the street. For a moment I stood alone in the darkness.

When my eyes became accustomed to the dark I beheld an apparition: a scowling, aged dwarf in a serge suit with arms so long for his body that his knuckles scraped the floor as he moved toward me, followed by a miniature dog.

"Monsieur Vogel," I began, glancing back to the doorway for Guillaume but disbelieving that this could possibly be Monsieur Vogel. A high-pitched snort from the dwarf confirmed my doubts.

"What do you want?" he demanded, his hand on the hilt of a sheathed knife which hung like a sword in its scabbard by his little legs.

Terrified by the sight of this creature with his huge head and arms dangling like a tiny baboon, I could not attempt an explanation before Guillaume descended the stairs. His undersized bowler toppled from his head in the low doorway.

"Ah, Monsieur Guillaume." The receptionist's tone whined when he attempted a smile. "And what have we here?" He eyed a small wrapped parcel beneath Guillaume's arm.

"This is my American friend Clayton Peavey." He ignored the dwarf's question and retrieved his hat. "You would do well to treat him as you treat me, Otto."

"Of course, Monsieur Guillaume, of course." He scowled at me nonetheless. "I tell monsieur that you have come." He turned and began receding into the depths of the cave.

"I thought that little dwarf was going to attack me when I first came in here," I told Guillaume. From behind me the nasty voice crackled once more.

"I am not a dwarf," said Otto proudly. "I am a

noué." He shuffled off, his forepaws stuttering along the floor boards as he went.

I scratched my head, but Guillaume smiled. "A *noué* has the body of a dwarf with a man's arms and head. Another circus performer," he explained. "Vogel is an old fox," he added. "You must not take him or his servant too seriously. They prefer to start out negatively and let you earn their friendship."

"Not many bother, I suspect."

He nodded.

We browsed the bins and shelves, the maze of corridors and discarded objects which constituted the outer room of Vogel's shop. A set of mottled porcelain and a Satsuma vase stood near an oriental screen with but a single rice-paper pane intact. Centered before the screen was a puma rug, the cat's beady eyes blazing with the ferocity of the *noué*'s. Stepping gingerly around the rug I nearly tripped on a grapnel hook with barbed flukes flanked by a brass cuspidor, a bass drum missing one head, a parasol, theatrical gels stacked against a black wood stove, and a collection of files, adzes, scrapers, and rasps. I stood gaping at this horrific display when Guillaume came upon me.

He pointed to the wall above me. Glass-faced vats were arranged at eye level. Each brimmed with colored tablets: square, round, and triangular in a great variety of sizes. Gelatin capsules filled dusty jeroboams and five-liter glass jars.

"Clovis' pharmacy." He smiled. "I met Marie here."

"Here?"

"At this very spot." His eyes glowed and his thick lips curled at the happy memory.

I was about to ask some ill-advised question concerning Marie's habits and vices when the clunking knuckles of the *noué* and the sound of voices bespoke our patron's arrival.

Clovis Vogel was prepossessing only by comparison to his manservant: chalky and hunched, flaccid of flesh, blanched all but a crimson wen festering in the middle of his tall forehead and bloodshot eyes which squinted in the darkness as though he had just come into bright sunlight. A tall, Germanic woman with a long nose and intimidatingly intelligent eyes glided before him through the clutter of the shop.

"I think you will be most gratified by your choice, madame," he said flatly.

"If not, I should have chosen otherwise," snapped the woman in what sounded like an American accent. I looked up in astonishment but her uncomfortable wool suit was already disappearing up the stairs into the street.

"And now . . ." Vogel turned on us with a lewd smile. "What have we here?" he repeated the *noué*'s words.

Guillaume made a gesture of withholding the parcel and introduced me. I shook Vogel's hand and set it back in place at the end of his arm. He had an inert, empty demeanor which suggested too much indulgence in the bounty of his converted pharmacy. "I'm afraid Otto was a bit grumpy with Monsieur Peavey," Guillaume forced the conversation, preventing Vogel from taking the offensive.

"So you have met my little sparrow, Otto le Moineaux?" he inquired. "And these are his wings." He laughed a baneful, barren laugh while Otto snorted through his bulbous nose as though restraining laughter and petted his little dog. Vogel lightly touched the purulent wen on his scalp, with just the fingertips, and grinned, but it seemed to take seconds for the grin to spread across his face. His skin was like a puddle of watery farina. He waved vaguely for us to follow him into the recesses of his cave.

Vogel's back room was a small art gallery, better lit and less fusty than the pawnshop in front. Paintings familiar to me as those of members of the Place Ravignan crowd hung on the walls: several Fauvist fantasies in shocking colors, a selection of harlequins and nudes, framed posters, one of Marie's works, and a number of imitative pieces. Stacks of art books and periodicals covered the floor and tables.

"Clovis was a clown at the Mediano," Guillaume informed me.

"But now," he said with derision, "I am just a *forain,* a merchant with my stall. I am no longer a *banquiste.*"

Looking at this erstwhile clown in his lumpy suit I wondered what made old clowns so tired. He possessed the atrophied emotions and languor I had detected in Boppe, only he had gone far beyond Boppe, withdrawing into his shell like an ancient turtle, too long out of water, the neck and limbs dried and cracking, the shell itself turned brittle.

"You have visited the Mediano?" he asked me, emerging from his haze. I nodded. "It is not a grand circus but a popular circus in the grand tradition." He paused. "So much has changed; even Boum-Boum is gone now. And people forget quickly."

"We are interested today in Negro masks," said Guillaume abruptly. Vogel eyed him curiously, assessing the prospects, and conducted us to a panel where hung several masks similar to the one we sought.

"I have a Wobe mask from the Ivory Coast," he began, indicating the first. "And here is a true Mpongwe from Gabon. What is it you seek, Guillaume?"

"Something like this." Guillaume showed him the sketch.

"Ah," he coughed. "One moment." He maundered off scratching himself. I heard him pottering about in a corner of his gallery, hunched over a pile of artifacts.

"He will find something for us. He never misses a deal. Marie began to sell her paintings through Vogel, but he suggested she sleep with prospective buyers as added incentive for the purchase. She did not take kindly to that suggestion."

"But why do you do business with such a man?" I protested. "Surely—"

"And with whom are we to do business, the Académie Française? He sells the paintings. You saw the American lady leaving as we arrived. She will pay for our work. No one else can or will sell the works of the new school. Those who could, won't."

"So you tell your friends I am a pimp," Vogel grumbled. "Perhaps you do not wish to know about the mask?"

"I have something that will loosen your tongue, Clovis my old friend." Guillaume smiled. "Something new and entirely different."

"Let me see it then," the voice rattled in his sunken chest.

"But first—" cautioned Guillaume.

"Your mask. There is much interest in masks recently." He lapsed again, or was he merely tantalizing us? "Only last week Madame O- came here inquiring about such a mask."

"Madame O-," exclaimed Guillaume. "The medium?"

"Is there another?"

"Who is Madame O-?" I asked.

"Madame Orgueil is one of the most respected, and

respectable, mediums in Paris. She has a salon near the Faubourg St. Honoré visited by many distinguished Parisians."

"And some not so distinguished," Vogel muttered. "Madame O- is a disciple of Stanislas de Guaita, disciple of Levi, magus, alchemist, Rosicrucian. She knows many secrets." He paused. "Perhaps she knows yours as well." He glowered at me with his bloodshot eyes.

"Do you think," I ventured, "this mask could be Moorish?"

Again the wintry glare focused on me, and he touched the sore spot on his head. It was the color of a clown's nose, bright red, but dislocated on his chalky countenance, as though he were a living specimen of the distortions being attempted in the canvases of the artists of the Place Ravignan. Yes, this man was a clown, but a terrifying clown for any child to behold.

"If by that you mean the indigenous handicraft of one of the Arabic or Berber tribes living within the sultanate of Morocco," he spoke rapidly, "I would have to say no. Their source is farther south, along the Ivory Coast or Dahomey."

When he ceased talking, the scrannel voice damped by the atmosphere of the shop, I reflected on the way this last speech poured from him, as though the words had been wound on a spool in his head and all at once unraveled through his throat; as though it were a prepared statement. But prepared for whom?

"I see," I said. "Then—" I was about to mention the Zorns, but Guillaume, sensing my intent, silenced me with an upraised hand.

"Did Madame Orgueil purchase such a mask?" he asked.

"She wished to. You may know she is a collector of magical and occult symbols. She asked if anyone had come seeking such a mask." He grinned. "But no one had. And I had already sold mine. I suggested she visit the Musée du Trocadéro and filch one of theirs."

"Then you did have one. To whom did you sell it?"

"Ah, I have forgotten." He laughed and coughed, his body wracked by the cough. When it subsided he lighted a thick, yellow cigarette and his eyes slid half shut.

Guillaume unwrapped his offering, a painting of houses on a hillside. Vogel examined it and shrugged. "The usual terms," he said and Guillaume nodded.

An unsteady desk stood along one wall, cluttered with papers and torn journals, books open to marked pages, yellow cigarette butts, bits of wire, and pencil stubs. Vogel went to this desk and made notations in a faded, leather-bound notebook which he replaced in a drawer. Above the desk, neatly framed and carefully hung, was a small plaque bearing the words: "*N'en parlez jamais; pensez-y toujours.* —Gambetta." I puzzled over this a moment.

"I don't get it," I told Guillaume.

"Never speak of it, but think of it always," he translated for me but did not reveal what "it" was.

"An appropriate motto for many things in life," Vogel said with a bright glint in his eyes.

He conducted us back into the dim front room of his bizarre pantechnicon. Otto clambered down from a pile of folded rugs. We thanked Vogel for his help and were about to depart when he motioned us to a table. Piled on it were journals in several languages: *The Era, Der Artist, Le Voyageur Forain.* He picked one up.

"If you wish to get a message to Arbogast Zorn," Vogel said quite distinctly, "post it in these journals. Their home lies here, in these pages." He nodded. "They will see it here."

I picked up *Der Artist*. Its cover was filled by an elaborate woodcut print depicting trapeze artists, clowns, leaping horses, trained lions, and other circus scenes. Inside were employment schedules, performance reviews, addresses, traveling arrangements, advertisements, and agency listings for all manner of performers. Vogel obviously knew of our interest in the Zorns, must already have spoken to Darius Boppe, and had been awaiting our visit. Given the self-serving turpitude of the man, I wondered why he had offered this last information gratis, without even being asked, and conjectured that it might have to do with the motto on the wall. His mood had visibly altered when I called attention to the quotation. Life suddenly stirred behind his lethargy, disinterest dissolving to reveal an instant of conviction, something yet alive within that grotesque form, or something capable of being stirred to life. The key lay with the Zorns and with Boppe and somehow, I felt certain, with that ambiguous quotation which might be applied to so many facets of life.

We arrived back at the Rue Ravignan to find our watchdog waiting for us in the *place*.

"Where have you been?" he spluttered as his face twisted in a series of violent tics. "Now we are all in for it."

Charles did not normally react with such anger to our ruses or brief disappearances.

"What is the problem, Charles?" Guillaume laughed. "We've just been down the Butte to a gallery while you slept in the sun."

"What wonderful timing you have," he said. "The Inspector was here this past hour looking for you. Found me asleep and with no idea where you'd gone. He'll be back, but I don't know what will become of me." He bit his twitching lip and cursed our timing again. "I'll be back on night duty in Pigalle again with the apaches and ruffians."

"And no more contented naps in the sun, eh, Charles?" I baited him. "Well, perhaps the Inspector will be merciful." But poor Charles was irreconcilable and told us we would not sneak off again without his knowing it.

"Perhaps not," said Guillaume, but I sensed his mind already turning to plans for a visit to Madame O-, while I grew apprehensive over what had finally brought Inspector Pernicieux to Montmartre. I was beginning to agree with Darius Boppe that there was no such thing as coincidence.

VII

While Guillaume made discreet inquiries as to how we might be invited to a seance at the salon of Madame Orgueil, life continued along its prescribed path in Montmartre.

The day following our visit to Clovis Vogel's shop, Inspector Pernicieux reappeared, innocently bearing a small canvas. He scolded us indulgently and scolded Charles, but reassured him that he would not be relegated to night duty in Pigalle for this single negligence, provided it was not repeated. And indeed Charles' watchfulness did assume a semblance of efficacy for a period of perhaps thirty-six hours following the Inspector's visit.

The canvas depicted an underwater world of fish and giant tortoises, mermaids and tufts of seaweed swaying in the currents of the Inspector's imagination. It was executed in a primitive pre-Impressionist style, the pigments smoothly applied and the colors and proportions all painstakingly correct, but it had a lively, fanciful quality one could not ignore. Guillaume was entranced.

"You see," he proclaimed. "A genuine artist, without pretensions and without intellect." The Inspector took some umbrage at this remark, but was quickly appeased by the extravagance of Guillaume's praise and his desire to see more of these "delightful fantasies."

Two days later, a Saturday, we lunched at Inspector Pernicieux's modest flat on the top floor of a battered old building not far from the Place de la Bastille, chosen apparently for the abundance of light in a large second room which he used as a bedchamber and studio.

The Inspector ate with frantic enthusiasm, sopping up the sauce on crusts of bread and washing it down with glass after glass of wine. He admitted the murder case was bogged down and that he could not account for the failure of our "enemies" to show themselves. Both he and Guillaume were far more stimulated by talk of art than crime.

"And you have been painting for how long, hidden away here in your private world of dreams?" Guillaume asked.

The Inspector looked curiously at Guillaume, whose flamboyant language always seemed to amuse and befuddle him. "Twenty years now I have dabbled in these dreams, as you call them," he said. "Since my wife died and my career at the Préfecture slowed to its present pace I have had little else to occupy my time."

"You have done well," Guillaume told him. Most of his pieces were quite large and rendered in the same precise style as the charming little sample we had seen in Montmartre. He preferred underwater motifs and explained that he had spent a great deal of time at the aquarium and loved the movement of underwater life. All the works had a deep, aquamarine background with beams of sunlight filtering down through the rocks and growths. Monsters of the deep, giant squid, and bearded Neptunes peered from behind rocks or the hulks of sunken galleons.

Guillaume insisted that Pernicieux show his paintings in certain galleries to which he had access and return to Montmartre to meet the rest of the gang. He proposed a banquet in his honor for the following weekend, which Guy Pernicieux was at length prevailed upon to accept. When we left him his eyes were twinkling with boyish glee, and I could see his hands eagerly preparing to take up a brush.

"You can't be serious about his showing those works?" I asked Guillaume as we ambled homeward along the Boulevard Beaumarchais.

"But I am quite serious," he retorted. "I know, I know, the man lacks any sensibility of what we are doing today with color and form. He paints in a style long dead, but he paints with authenticity and his paintings brim with life. He is limited, of course, but within those limitations his talent is unbounded. So many of our friends strut about proclaiming themselves geniuses and protesting the failure of the philistines of bourgeois French society to recognize them. This man lives in that society, is part of it, accepts it, yet goes far beyond it. I think he is truly a genius and, given time to devote himself to his painting and proper publicity, in a few years he could become a significant force in the art world."

I could only shake my head in amazement and reiterate my skepticism. I was still not certain whether Guillaume was mocking the poor Inspector, and myself, or whether he was sincere. Guy Pernicieux appeared no genius to me.

It was the same day, on our return to the Rue Ravignan, that I met Apolline.

Apolline was an actress and poetess, a friend of the sandy-haired Breton who frequented Père Frédé's. She was unlike any girl I had encountered before, living totally in a spirit world of phantoms, visions, sound poems, and dreams. At first nothing she said made any sense to me; later it all made perfect sense.

She was a petite girl, very frail, a slender boyish figure with virtually no breasts or hips to mar its delicate symmetry. She wore her dark hair clipped very short, also boyish, and had enormous liquid eyes on a sharply sculpted face. These dark eyes instantly fascinated me, or I suppose anyone who met her, for they were penetrating, riveting and a bit frightening, awe-inspiring, yet perfectly tranquil and without intimidation, as though they perceived and saw through everything yet betrayed no reaction. No pretense was possible before such eyes. She stared unblinking at persons and things or into space for so long one feared she had gone into a trance, then emerged from this state quite suddenly, with a terse remark related to whatever had been passing in the conversation around her. She never drank alcohol, and she rarely smiled.

She was curled in a corner on the floor like a lost child. In the half-light of a foggy late afternoon I hardly noticed her. Guillaume was telling Didier, a dramatist, and Max about the Inspector's paintings. Paul, our sturdy Breton painter, was setting out a collection of pistons and gears and other mechanical devices as a still-life arrangement for his next canvas. Apolline sat beyond him in her twilight world.

"He has a very gentle strength." A deep voice billowed from her corner. She rose and crossed to us with wide, unblinking eyes, her feet barely seeming to touch the floor.

"Who, the Inspector?" the dramatist asked her, and she nodded, though she was looking at me. Introductions were made, but when I went to kiss her cheeks in the informal and universal French greeting, she shrank from my touch and her eyes widened.

"Apolline does not like to be touched," Paul explained. "No harm done. Don't worry, it is only one of her little quirks."

I shrugged. When her eyes returned to my face she

repeated the phrase "He has a very gentle strength," but this time I knew she meant me and not the Inspector. She did not bother to elaborate.

I quickly discerned that her physical reserve and her abstinence from alcohol were part of her spirituality. Unlike Max and many of the others who relied upon varying combinations of wine, absinthe, ether, hashish, opium, and cocaine to achieve their insights and revelations, Apolline dwelt constantly in that heightened state. It was natural for her. I was drawn to this innocence, this transparent purity of spirit, for I too found the gang's indulgence wearing.

We began to converse with our eyes while the others rattled on in their usual fashion. Whenever I glanced at her she was watching me.

When Guillaume and Didier went out for food, pleading exhaustion I remained in the studio. Paul was absorbed in his mechanical construction. I puttered about abstractedly, peering into things, staring out the paint-splattered window at the irregular buildings across the courtyard, then returning to study Paul at work. His thick hands turned the metallic objects this way and that with patience and total concentration. In the next room a piano played gentle, lyrical melodies, soothing like twilight calm after a blustery afternoon. At last I went to Apolline in her corner, shrugged, tipped my head to one side, and looked down at the floor beside her. She nodded and I sat down.

Thus began a wondrous night. She finally spoke in her rich, hollow voice—so deep to come from such a thin chest—but only in phrases at first. She asked me to tell her why I had come to Paris, how I had met Guillaume, my life's story.

"Of course, I already know all of this," she noted. "But I would like to hear it in your voice. And . . . when you cannot explain in French, speak in English. It is of no concern to me what language you use."

So I told her and she questioned me, drawing out details of my two months in Paris that I thought I had already forgotten, and explaining to me the meaning of certain serendipitous events. "It was meant to be" she repeated each time I came to an inexplicable circumstance or prescience on the part of someone related to the affair of the *saltimbanques* and the African mask. She was another nonbeliever in coincidence, I could see that, but of a quite different strain from the clowns.

The others returned. I ate, returned to her, they disappeared, and Paul continued working. She and I continued our conversation.

Later we were alone in the night chill of the studio.

"Are you not cold?" I asked her. She had so little flesh and wore a thin smock and no socks.

"Yes, the air is moist tonight." She gripped her arms with her thin fingers and I felt myself leaning toward her, wanting to warm her in the most obvious way I knew. But before I could initiate this movement she rose, frightened eyes batting.

"No, Clayton," she said. "You must never touch me. Never. We cannot be friends if you wish to touch me. Banish all thoughts of that from your mind, for I will know when they are there. I can see your thoughts as clearly as I can see your face or your hands. Do you understand?"

"I . . . I only meant to comfort you. You said you were cold. I . . . you . . . you are a very fine person, Apolline."

"But not so cold as to need your warmth," she said and sat down beside me. Her numinous presence was pacifying and I soon found that my desires, and my baser feelings for her as a woman, had vanished, as she had willed them to. It was hard to imagine her as an actress, hard to conceive of her being anything other than herself. We talked late into the night, in the darkness, the chill. She recited her poetry: vaguely symbolist, full of the sound of words but conveying little sense to me. She suggested I translate her poems into English, but I said this was impossible. She said it was not impossible for me as I understood them and understanding was all that was required.

"We will work together," she told me with conviction, and I did not argue.

Near dawn, during one of the lengthy silences which broke our conversation, her eyes shut and she slept. I crept back to my cot in Guillaume's studio and slept as well, a sleep filled with dreams of mermaids and fish swimming in an underwater world, thin vaporous mermaids with large dark eyes who floated about me in a diaphanous mist, so close I felt the tingle of their silken presence though I never touched them.

In the early afternoon I awoke, but she had gone and my cold had returned. Guillaume seemed pleased by my new friendship. "She is special," he said, and I agreed. "She is not dangerous," he added, but I was not entirely sure about that, nor about why I was drawn to her.

When the midafternoon sun broke through I went to Père Frédé's for coffee. *Le Temps* had arrived, and I idly perused its pages. An English actor and amateur boxer, living on a houseboat moored at St. Denis, had been murdered and his body found in the Seine. Another in the rash of murders in Paris this spring, said *Le Temps*; probably the work of apaches. I imagined red Indians raiding the quais and chuckled. I read on. President Fallières had received the new American Ambassador, Henry White, at the Elysée Palace. A reception would be held at the Ritz Hotel on the morrow. I recalled the engraved invitation I had received from Darlington and returned to the studio to find it. It was indeed for the next day, and I determined that I would attend—as a change of pace, a chance to speak a little English, and a possible source of information. It would surely be amusing. Guillaume and I toyed with the idea of attempting to have him admitted in some disguise, but abandoned it.

Guillaume disappeared for several hours. Charles became uneasy, and I too wondered, for he invariably took me along on his escapades, no matter how trivial. He returned at sunset, his broad face beaming with accomplishment.

"Good news," he told me when we had slipped away from Charles. "Your new friend has arranged for us to visit Madame O- this evening."

"Apolline? Really?" I was about to say I was surprised but realized I was not.

"She has taken part in several of Madame O-'s seances. She is something of a medium herself. You suspected?" I nodded.

"Will Apolline be there?" I asked, my stomach contracting apprehensively.

"I think not," he said. "Best not to mix too many spirits and too many influences. It will be clearer without her." Guillaume was proud of me, a recognition of new powers on my part dawning in him. "It was meant to be, eh?" he said.

The seance would begin at midnight, and we were to arrive one hour earlier, so that "the conditions could be adjusted to our presence."

"As for Charles," Guillaume added, "we shall retire early tonight and so will he. By dawn when he awakens we will have returned and he will never even suspect our absence."

VIII

Madame Orgueil's *salon des séances et sciences psychiques* was located in a little impasse in the shadow of the Church of the Madeleine.

We marched through the arched arcade along the Rue Rivoli. Across the street the Louvre loomed, endlessly housing the creative output of centuries. It was a forbidding presence, ominous. "Dead," muttered Guillaume, reading my thoughts.

We turned away from the river, caught a brief glimpse of the column at the center of the Place Vendôme, and proceeded up the Rue Duphot to the Place de la Madeleine. The massive church was a square, squat fortress of God, built in the style of a Roman temple and utterly lacking the Gothic grandeur of Notre Dame. Sculpted saints peeked between paired Corinthian columns surrounding it on all sides. We found the doorway to Madame Orgueil's salon in a narrow passage adjoining the square.

The normally dilatory Guillaume had taken elaborate precautions to ensure our timely arrival at Madame O-'s. We were, in fact, among the first guests. My companion was resplendent: his maroon evening jacket lapelled in façonné velvet, a flowered foulard ascot worthy of Oscar Wilde, his waistcoat bursting between those velvet lapels. I was in my checkered tweeds and baggy trousers, and I felt a fidgety querulousness returning even before we were shown into the receiving sala at Madame Orgueil's.

The only other person in the sala was a pale gentleman with a thin mustache and heavy-lidded eyes. He responded in monosyllables to our attempts at conversation and seemed to have something else on his mind.

Shortly other guests began arriving. First came a society matron who knew the doorman and was apparently a regular participant in these affairs. She was swathed in powder and pearls, rear bustled and well trussed.

Following her an airy dilettante alit, twirling a harewood cane in long beige gloves. He wore a coat cut to midthigh, curled mustaches, and a little tuft of beard on his lower lip. He was accompanied by a voluptuous young woman whom I took to be on hire for the evening. Both appeared flushed and tipsy. I later learned they had just come from a lengthy dinner party and a performance by Madame Bernhardt in *Bouffons*.

This company eyed one another, made idle conversation, and tried to assess the aspirations and psychic aptitude of the others. Shortly before midnight we were conducted by an extremely dignified butler into the *salon des séances*, where Madame Orgueil sat on a small stiff-backed settee, her hands clasped in her lap and eyes shut as if in meditation.

The room was abundantly foliated in Art Nouveau excess, an Alexandre Charpentier nightmare of carved mahogany paneling with long-stemmed bas relief flowers and brass inlays, pastoral murals of pastel nudes overhung by twisted torsade draperies, embroidered tapestries, oriental fans and ferns. A stained-glass lamp with tasseled cover cast no light, the only illumination being provided by a pair of gas-jet fixtures flickering in amber globes and a set of purple tapers in a candelabra behind Madame O-. Sweeping, rhapsodic curves overlapped in every corner of the room. Nowhere could the eye turn without being caught, distracted, held, and mystified by some curio or curlicue. At the center of this room stood a heavy circular table topped in black velvet with eight armless chairs set around it.

When we had been shown to our seats and waited a respectful moment in silence, Madame Orgueil opened her eyes and emerged from her trance.

She was a woman of fifty or more, well proportioned and fair, with a very stiff posture and self-possessed bearing. Her face was creased by age and her eyes were pale green, nearly translucent. She welcomed us in a quiet voice, modulated yet proud.

The seat directly to her right remained vacant, and we awaited the arrival of the tardy guest. As midnight approached the matron in pearls became uneasy and complained over this irresponsibility, but Madame reassured her. The late guest strutted in at three minutes before the hour.

He was not what I expected. Although dressed stylishly, his face and manner betrayed a hardy existence. Nor was he embarrassed by arriving late. Without excusing himself, he took his place at Madame's right.

"Good evening, Aristo." She nodded to him, and he returned the greeting mutely.

This fellow Aristo, though he hardly seemed a gentleman, much less an aristocrat, was short and slim with a taut face and spiky black hair standing out all over his head. He had a small, pointed chin and small, black, expressionless eyes: no, not expressionless, villainous. His presence made me instantly uneasy. The rest of the guests seemed harmless enough, and Madame O-, though no doubt a calculating charlatan, possessed an enchanting radiance that suggested contact with a higher plane.

"We must concentrate together to ensure that there are no interfering energies present," she explained. "Once the conditions are satisfactory we may proceed." She gazed at Guillaume and me as she continued. "For our new visitors, it is all quite simple. Place your hands palm down on the table in front of you, thumbs touching, the little fingers in contact with those of the persons to your right and left."

We did this, my right hand touching Guillaume's and my left the pinkie of the buxom young woman with the dandy. Aristo's hands were further evidence of his ill-breeding: small and chafed, the nails torn and an unsuccessful effort made to clean them. Madame Orgueil had soft, large hands and wore a ruby-eyed asp bracelet, her wrist wrapped in the silver tail which extended onto the back of her hand where the serpent's head reared, ready to strike.

After clearing the room of interfering energies the candles were extinguished. A mild incense was lit, and by the amber glow of the gas jets we were treated to a brief demonstration of Madame O-'s skills.

These included the obligatory table tilting and slate writing common to mediums and other practitioners of the occult sciences. Madame O- spoke in a soft steady stream of phrases, a serenely discerning voice broken only by her breathing.

The pale gentleman who seemed to have something else on his mind was asked to write upon a slip of paper where his heart lay that evening and to entrust the paper to the aging matron. This done, we heard a distinct scratching, like a thumbnail across hard wood or chalk across a slate, and the blank slate, which had disappeared beneath its flap, reappeared with the words "*In the mountains*" written on it. This was the phrase written by the pale gentleman. I was impressed by the skill of the performance and sniffled.

"Now, Monsieur Malaimé." The translucent eyes swept across the table to Guillaume and fastened on him with haughty recognition. I smiled self-consciously but suddenly felt a severity which intimidated me while arousing my suspicion. Where should I be looking, what repeated movement or unimportant detail was obscuring my sight? "You are interested in a mask?"

"Yes."

"And you wish to contact someone regarding this matter?"

"He who possessed it."

She placed her hands on the black velvet. The asp reared and its tiny eyes faceted the reflected light of the lamps—ivory tusks on ruby. "Let us place our hands on the table as before," she instructed us.

Hands around the table: the asp, Aristo's scuffed claws, the white manicured hands of the dilettante and somewhat puffier powdered little mitts of his paramour, my own mediocrities neither one way nor the other, Guillaume's large soft hands with the palms pressing the velvet and his fingers raised and bent, then the hands of the pale gentleman, less pale than his face and lined as from the sun or a dry wind, but not from violence or abuse like Aristo's. He held them with the palms arched and just the fingertips touching the table, as though resting lightly on the keys of a piano. After him the wrinkled forepaws of the matron who frequented Madame O-'s, well suited for dealing whist, hands raised and fingers spread, eager to pounce on some unsuspecting spirit. These were hands that would guide us tonight. A calm receptivity settled over us as the little fingers made contact around the circle. I noticed that Guillaume's finger quivered slightly as it touched mine.

"I see a girl," said Madame O-.

"There is always a girl," I whispered to Guillaume, who inhaled through his nose and tipped back slightly in his seat, his eyes rolling as though suspended in a doll's head when his center of gravity shifted. "Shhh," shushed the matron.

"She is very young," Madame O- continued. Fifty percent chance on that, I thought; either she's young or she's not. Madame O- glared at me as though sensing my thoughts.

"She is like a pretzel," she intoned caustically and I gulped on my silence.

Madame Orgueil removed her eyes from me, though there was little left from which to remove them. Several of the others looked puzzled.

"But it is not she?" Guillaume shook his head and his hand twitched. "Please, monsieur, do not disturb the balance. I feel that the conditions are nearly perfect. I feel that we shall make a very strong contact this evening. I feel—"

A distinct rapping reverberated along the carved mahogany walls behind us. "A noisy guest," chirped the matron.

"Yes," replied Madame Orgueil. "A noisy guest."

A second rapping was accompanied by the toppling of the candelabra and a rippling through one of the tapestries. The buxom one nearly burst. Even I was impressed. I had not mentioned the pretzel even to Apolline, though the idea of a collusion between her and Madame O- had occurred to me and been dismissed.

"He died quite recently," continued Madame O-. "And he was also young," she added.

For a moment neither she nor our noisy guest addressed us. Then a faint cloud began to form over the velvet tabletop and the table itself began to rock and shift beneath our hands like a boat. Fingers bent and curved. Palms shifted to accommodate the movement. And within that lactescent cloud the face of Sébastien Zorn took shape.

I wanted to glance at Guillaume, to check his expression for confirmation of what I was seeing, but I dared not for fear the vision would be gone when I looked back. As the cloud dissipated, Sébastien's thin naked torso and arms became visible. They were pierced by arrows, but no blood ran down his skin from the feathered shafts imbedded in his flesh. He shrank in size and walked slowly across the black velvet toward Guillaume and me.

A shiver frisked my spine.

"He comes as a saint," whispered Guillaume. I looked at him and hurriedly checked to see that Sébastien was still approaching, then glanced back at Guillaume. His wide eyes stared straight ahead as unblinking as Apolline's.

"If you wish to ask the spirit something, you may do so now," Madame O- suggested.

"Were you murdered?" he said.

Sébastien laughed, gripped two of the arrows in his chest, and scrutinized them as if to say, "What do you think?"

"But why the arrows?" Guillaume asked.

"Do not question the appearance of the wraith," Madame O- cautioned him. "The reality of sight is not so clear as the reality of insight. Look through the wraith."

I stared and in the distance heard a wind howling, high and shrill, no Paris wind, no city street howl, but a fearful keening over a vast landscape.

"Then . . . who killed you?" Guillaume asked.

Sébastien ceased his slow approach and looked abruptly over his left shoulder, as though his attention had been caught by something. He seemed to consider for an instant the matron seated at Madame O-'s left. As he turned he grew larger, filling the table. Billows of the creamy mist swept up around him. He broke off the shafts in his hands and dropped them with a clanking at our feet. Again the table shook violently.

With his left hand, an enormously long forefinger extended, he pointed at the pale gentleman with something on his mind.

"This man?" Guillaume's voice rose. "This man killed you?"

The pale man looked extremely startled and peered in the direction of that accusing finger, trying to make it out more clearly. From our perspective there could be no mistake.

"Do you mean to say that this man is your murderer?" Guillaume insisted in disbelief. His voice rang out.

"You will disturb the conditions," Madame O- warned him. "Do not repeat questions."

It was already too late. The fog thickened. As the vision of Sébastien turned toward Guillaume with a puzzled expression and then the beginnings of laughter, he remembered: "What about the mask?" The vision shrank and faded. "What about the mask?" And one final desperate "Where have they gone . . . your family" as with a splintering crash the wraith was consumed in its vapors and disappeared with a whoosh. "But the mask," he spluttered like a dying ember doused with sand.

"Gone," said the matron. And he was.

But the pale man remained.

"There must be some mistake," he said a bit stuffily, as though the butler had given him the wrong hat.

"Only *we* can make mistakes in our interpretation of what we have seen," said Madame O-. "The wraith does not make mistakes."

"But in this instance . . ." Guillaume hesitated. We both stared at the pale man. The heavy-lidded eyes betrayed no anxiety, merely perplexity. "I assure you, madame, that this man had nothing to do with the death of the lad. I witnessed the death and this gentleman was not there."

The pale man nodded.

"Then we must seek other explanations," Madame O- said as she removed her hands from the table. An assistant turned up the gas jets, set right and lit the candelabra which had fallen. For a moment we eased back into a nontranscendent reality. Madame O- addressed the pale man.

"When I asked you earlier to write upon a slip of paper where your heart lay this evening you wrote: 'In the mountains.' What did you mean by that?"

"Each spring after the thaw for many years I have gone to the mountains with my family. I have watched my children growing into men and women there. It is very lovely when the wild flowers make their brief appearance." He spoke with great dignity and self-assurance in the formal French of someone who has learned the language as an adult. "But this spring I shall not see the tiny yellow flowers."

"Why is that?"

"I am in Paris. My wife is dead; my children grown. I have . . . other business."

I was puzzled. Guillaume asked the man, "What mountains, monsieur? The Pyrenees? The Alps? The Vosges?"

The pale man regarded Guillaume thoughtfully and then in his precise cadence he said: "The Atlas mountains."

"The Atlas mountains," I gasped. "In Morocco?"

"Yes," he said. "My family has lived for some time on the plains beneath the Atlas mountains." He did not indicate whether he meant many years or many generations, and the ambiguity of his statement unnerved me. He was not a Moor, but the weathered hands, the whistling wind, the sound and sense of the desert were undeniable.

"I must say I am at a loss, Madame Orgueil," admitted Guillaume. His keen audacity had deserted him and he slumped with his broad chin cupped in his hands, staring across the table. "We keep coming back to Morocco."

"Then perhaps that is what the wraith intended. Perhaps that is why he pointed at this gentleman when asked about his murder. Your answer may lie in Morocco."

"It seems rather farfetched to me," I said and blinked at Madame O-. "But what will happen?" I asked her. "What should we do?"

"I cannot read your mind nor tell the future," she replied. "Nor am I here to give advice. I can only help you contact the spirits and give you my interpretation of their visits."

"And what is that interpretation?" inquired Guillaume.

"I have told you." She was growing impatient. "You must go south. To the mountains. That seems quite clear."

"And the mask?" I asked.

"Yes, the mask." She smiled indulgently at my persistence. "As you may know, I have a large collection of masks and dolls and icons from around the globe—the work of many years studying primitive magic and the Gnostic and occult sciences. Perhaps in my collection you will find a mask similar to the one you seek and I can suggest its possible significance. I hope we can arrange for you to return and examine my collection."

"But tonight—"

"It is not possible." She motioned around the table. "We have other guests."

"Quite right," said Aristo gruffly. It was the first thing he had said all evening. "I came here tonight seeking information about a friend, and all I've heard is talk of masks and Morocco and this American casting suspicions on all of us. I've had enough. Let's get on with it." He snarled and glared at Madame O-, but she was not a woman to respond to coercion.

"I'm afraid you will upset the conditions by your vehemence," she said calmly. "I think it unlikely you will make contact with your departed friend."

"Well, I'd better for what this has cost me," he rasped. His little claws clenched nervously.

"You must not threaten Madame," admonished the matron as the dandy nodded accord. "That won't accomplish anything."

Nonetheless Aristo insisted, and for some time we attempted to contact his friend without avail. The pale gentleman, too, had lost his concentration, and lengthy litanies from Madame O- failed to unearth his dead wife. Ours was the only success of the seance, and the matron congratulated us on it enthusiastically.

The pale man maintained his restraint and dignity throughout the evening, despite his inexplicable, disturbing involvement in our affairs. When we adjourned, he departed before we could question his reasons for coming that evening. Madame O- refused to reveal his name to us, saying it would be unprofessional to do so.

"But I do hope you will return to examine my collection of artifacts," she said as we prepared to depart. "Even if you learn nothing I think you will find it a most stimulating diversion." She smiled blandly, without apparent pretense, her smile full of the obfuscation and deft manipulation I read into every one of her movements and into every word she spoke.

"I hope we can do that. And perhaps we can attempt to contact Sébastien again," Guillaume added as he dropped a sealed envelope of franc notes onto a silver tray.

"I believe this wraith is reluctant, though he came quickly tonight. But you have frightened him. It may be necessary to have some physical object, such as the mask, in order to attract him again. We can attempt it, of course."

"One thing still puzzles me," Guillaume said. "The arrows. The wraith was pierced by arrows."

"And he did not die from an arrow?"

"No."

"Are you quite sure?" Guillaume nodded and I supported him. "Then they must mean something else. Perhaps he is a saint or a martyr." But to what cause could this young street acrobat have martyred himself, I wondered. "Let me ponder the possibilities and perhaps I shall have an answer for you when next we meet."

But I didn't believe her.

We could find no taxis at that hour and so we walked in silence. Near Les Halles I heard sounds and saw light. A new day was beginning. Litter covered the ground and big-bellied men bibbed in blood-splattered white aprons hooked legs of lamb on spikes. Pallets, crates, and stacked baskets stood all about them in the covered streets between pavilions. The smell of fresh meat filled the air. I wiped my nose with the back of my hand.

"We have received our dispensation," said Guillaume at last.

"What's that?" I muttered.

"We must go to Morocco. It was ordained from the start that we should go."

"Well, I don't know. It's a terribly long journey . . . and you're not likely to find the *saltimbanques* there."

"Certainly not, but what else might we find?"

"I shudder to think," I said. "They're not a very civilized people, you know, and from what I hear things are a bit topsy-turvy down there these days."

"But Madame Orgueil knows far more than she admits."

"Or far less than she pretends."

"No, no, Clayton. Did she not impress you? The pretzel?" I shrugged. "And she quoted from one of my critical essays."

"So she has done her research well," I said.

"One of my unpublished essays."

I stopped short and hesitated before asking, "Could Apolline have seen it?"

"No one has seen it. It was what she said about the reality of insight transcending the reality of sight. We must use our minds, our hearts, and our intuition to see things as they really are. She tossed my own words back at me. I believe in this woman, Clayton Peavey. There can be no doubt of her powers."

"And what about that man? The one Sébastien accused."

"That is baffling. I suspect he was merely a medium by which the message to go to the Atlas mountains was passed to us. Nothing more."

An image from the Greek myths lodged in my head: Atlas supporting the earth on his shoulders. My own burden at that moment felt equally heavy. "And the girl, Guillaume? I thought you wanted to find her and *La Famille Jollicorps*."

"I do," he nodded slowly. "And we shall. But we must take each step as it comes. There can be no short-cuts."

"And no coincidences either," I said as we turned from the Rue des Abbesses onto the steps leading to the Place Ravignan.

Two police vans were parked in front of the studio. Lights gleamed in several windows, and *flics* bustled busily back and forth with torches. We rushed across the square and were immediately accosted by two officers. Behind them a groggy Guy Pernicieux appeared, wrapped in an ulster. Without a word, his eyes burning with that fastidious impatience which for him passed as anger, he led us to the room where Charles had been sleeping.

Poor Charles had paid for our sins, whatever they might be. He lay with arms outspread on the floor in a pool of blood. His face was eaten away, as raw as the racks of lamb at Les Halles. Bits of bone jutted out with the eyesockets hollowed and the eyes gone. The blood was smeared or tracked over half the tiny studio as though his murderer had wallowed in it.

"My God, what happened to him?" I stammered through my nausea.

"Someone washed his face in vitriol," Inspector Pernicieux snapped. "And then cut his throat for good measure." I groaned. "Yes." The Inspector was roused by my horror, almost pleased by it. "Death is horrible."

"But why would anyone do this to poor Charles?"

"Perhaps because he would not tell them where you were."

"But he did not know," said Guillaume.

"And that bit of cunning on your part cost him his life."

"It's not our fault," I complained.

"Of course it is." He grabbed my arm. "Look at him. It is not pretty what vitriol does to a human face. Perhaps now you will believe me when I tell you this is a serious business." I nodded. "And, by the way, where were you this evening?" Guillaume told him. "I see. Playing at children's games with ghosts and quacks, looking for answers to questions you ought not to be asking."

"But it could have been a personal quarrel or an old grudge," Guillaume countered Pernicieux's accusations. "Charles made many enemies in this area over the years. Could it have been apaches? They use vitriol, don't they?"

"Yes, it could have been many things," Inspector Pernicieux said. "But it was not. Apaches do not kill like this, they come for robbery. These people came simply to kill whomever they found here, as viciously as possible."

"How can you be so sure?" I asked him.

"Because of this," he said, barely able to control himself. I sensed in him a deep distress, that he truly cared for Charles and for us.

He led us closer to Charles' body. Someone, presumably the murderer, had taken a paintbrush and written in Charles' blood on the floor. It was a symbol I did not recognize:

"What is it?" I asked.

"I do not know what it means," replied the Inspector. "But I do know what it is."

"Yes?" I waited. He frowned at Guillaume, who twisted his mouth and looked away.

"It is Arabic," he said. "An Arabic word."

IX

This second death—the gruesome murder of Charles—dissolved the last of my playfulness toward our adventure. The death of Sébastien, despite its attendant circumstances, had been neither our responsibility nor, but for the mistake of the Paris police, our affair. Such was not the case now. Leaving aside the remote possibility of other motivations (and the Arabic symbol seemed to rule this out), Charles' death was directly related to his work as our guardian and it could very well have been Guillaume or myself lying in a pool of blood with his face half eaten away by vitriol. I recalled Boppe's words that night at the circus: "There has already been one death—at least one death."

Charles was replaced by more efficient watchdogs, one by day and another at night. Experts appeared from the Sûreté to inspect the scene of the crime. A dark powder was dusted about: "It is Dr. Bertillon's new technique for identifying criminals—we call it fingerprinting," explained one officer. A silent, dour-faced linguist from the Quai d'Orsay arrived to examine the Arabic symbol. The little man in black whom we had seen at court came twice and asked us a few odd questions about guns and Madame Orgueil.

With strong misgivings I agreed to Guillaume's stipulation that we not tell them of the pale man at Madame Orgueil's or of our visits to Clovis Vogel and Darius Boppe. "We must not endanger them," Guillaume rationalized. Once again I wondered how deep was his involvement in all of this. Given my renewed suspicions and sense of foreboding I was happy for a chance to get away from Guillaume and attend Ambassador White's reception. This also provided a convenient opportunity to learn something of affairs in Morocco.

"It is the first sensible thing you've done since I met you," commended Inspector Pernicieux when apprised of my plans. "At least for one evening we shall know where you are and feel certain of your safety."

Constantly conversing in French had become a strain, so I looked forward to speaking with my own countrymen, notwithstanding that they would be of an age and orientation I would have shunned at home. Abroad, though, one's perspective is quite altered, and with mounting anticipation I donned a rented swallowtail coat, fastened my cummerbund, and shortly before eight set out by two-wheel fiacre.

We rolled up the Rue de Castiglione into the ancient, gabled Place Vendôme, the stone obelisk at its center illuminated by the bright lights of the Ritz. A brilliant collection of vehicles stood before the hotel: a luxurious barouche with satiny white horses, a Daimler Landaulette and a silver-gray Rolls-Royce with capped driver buffing its bonnet, Vauxhalls and Benzes, victorias and landaus. The best of the opposing centuries arrayed in uneasy coexistence.

Beneath the discreet gilt letters proclaiming the entrance to the Hôtel Ritz I passed into a long, carpeted hallway of cabriole chairs in gold brocade and dark marble-topped tables. The carpet hush seemed to infect voices: one naturally spoke more softly within the Ritz; to do otherwise would affront the walls themselves.

The reception was in a long courtyard with ivied laths, Greek statuary, and white garden furniture. Bewigged footmen in scarlet livery bore trays of champagne and hors d'oeuvre. Little Mr. Darlington took me quickly in hand, conveyed me about, and made the necessary introductions.

"You have certainly seen your share of excitement since last we spoke," Darlington sniped at me. "A most foolish fellow." He smiled fondly.

I heartily agreed that I was "most foolish" but declared I had determined to mend my ways.

"After last night's horrors I should hope so," he replied, shaking his head and tut-tutting as he presented me to several members of the diplomatic corps.

They were all there, faces I knew or, lacking that, names I had heard over the dinner table in Georgetown: Forrest Cobb and Earnest Drivel from the State Department, the Englishmen Empson and Dudley, Bruno Billy, Thierry Le Barrois, some Rothschild or other, and all De Rigueur and Pro Forma.

"So this is Adam Peavey's wayward son?" one of them greeted me. "I remember you when you were this high." All the stock lines were being trotted out for the occasion. "So glad you could join us."

"You must tell us all about it," the man's wife gushed. "Consorting with those self-styled beasts on the Butte . . . those scamps."

I opened my mouth to reply.

"International ententes are all the fashion nowadays," came a clipped urbanity from behind me. "So vague and ornamental, you know, and without meaning."

"True, but I think the French public has grown bored by the Entente Cordiale. King Edward's visit this spring was counterproductive."

"Oh, I think not," said an Englishman. "But isn't it dreadful about that poor chap Dr. Mauchamp. I say, Darlington, what is the latest news?"

Darlington shrugged and brought me around to meet the Englishman.

"It seems religious fervor and ignorance have combined in the most elemental fashion to create an uncontrollable mob," said a Frenchman who looked only slightly less out of place in his formal attire than I. He returned my smile, nodded, and continued. "No one is safe. Mr. Harris of the *Times* reports that Europeans have taken refuge in the walled Jewish quarter of the city, if one can call that refuge." He shook his head and lighted a long Turkish Matinée cigarette.

I introduced myself and his eyebrows shot up.

"Ah yes, the young American. You are quite the *cause célèbre* tonight." I looked startled. "Were it not for these terrible reports from Morocco we should all be at your feet begging for accounts of your adventures. But pardon, I am so rude. Gilles Blin of *Le Temps*."

I shook hands with the young journaalist and was about to ask him about "these terrible reports from Morocco" when a countess in a fluff of tulle and feathers descended upon us. "What *can* be done to stop these outrages?" she squawked. "There was that Charbonnier fellow, and the other, what was his name, an American I believe, and now poor Dr. Mauchamp."

"The problem," said the *Le Temps* reporter, "is the indecision and weakness of the French government. If we wish to secure our position and maintain our dignity we must inspire respect in the native population and not tolerate such monstrous behavior."

"And those Germans encourage it," declared the Countess.

"You exaggerate, madame," said an American at my elbow. "The Germans are merely concerned by French imperialism."

"French imperialism, is it?" The Countess examined him through a lorgnette with a tortoise shell handle. "And what would you prefer, monsieur? Syndicalism? Anarchism?" She was quite ruffled but suddenly espied a

Belgian gentleman across the room. "Why, there is Monsieur Leghait with Prince Radolin. I wonder what they could be conferring over?"

"It appears they are conferring over Dom Pérignon," replied the *Le Temps* man with a snicker, but the Countess had already taken flight, her feathers all aflutter.

"What is all this about?" I asked.

"Hadn't you heard? A French missionary in Marrakesh, a small city in the south of Morocco, has been killed and hacked to pieces by the rabble there. The latest in a long series of attacks. Clemenceau has called a special Cabinet Council for tomorrow to determine reparations. There is talk," he lowered his voice, "of the Army of Africa crossing from Oran and occupying Oujda, but one cannot be sure."

"I see," I said, feigning as nonchalant and half-hearted an interest in affairs Moroccan as I could. "But why should this doctor be killed? What's the problem?"

"Puh," he laughed at my ignorance. "What isn't the problem? The Sultan is weak and frivolous. The country is in a state of chaos. Conspiracies on all sides, foreign intrigues. Several British cannon have disappeared. Religious zealots in the countryside, arousing the tribes. Brigands and bandits receiving weapons and ammunition from European agents in Tangiers. A highly volatile state of affairs, I assure you."

"But Monsieur Pichon"—this was the French Foreign Minister—"has said the Sultan is a puppet. Is that true?" I fumbled beneath my mask of naiveté.

"Oh, did he?" cracked a voice behind me, and turning I found the new Ambassador himself, Henry White. "And how did you know that, Clayton?"

"I read the papers."

"Do you, indeed?" Ambassador White smiled. "I

have been kept informed of other of your activities and I think you would do well to spend more time reading and less adventuring."

"Yes, sir," I said and gazed at my shoelaces.

"Be that as it may, I am glad to see you've come tonight. I was hoping we might have a chance to—"

The arrival of President Fallières took the Ambassador from me, and I was left wondering what he hoped we might do.

"Do you know the Ambassador?" my journalist friend asked, obviously impressed.

"Well, my father knows him, and I have met him once or twice in Washington . . . not really," I hedged, but my innocence was lost.

"Listen," he said. "If you really want to hear the inside story about this business in Morocco—"

"Oh, I do. It's quite fascinating, international intrigue and all that." I grinned.

"Well, an American missionary has just returned from North Africa. I'll introduce you when I can."

I thanked the man from *Le Temps* and drifted off, champagne in hand.

I overheard snatches of conversation on the nature of the Moor, the responsibility of local officials and the honor of France, superstition and ignorance, life in the Bois, German interests in North Africa, and even a remark or two relative to the murder of a Paris police officer the previous night in Montmartre. On and on they went, pribbling and prattling their way through another of those endless receptions and dinners which made up the diplomatic life I despised. I had begun to tire and to despair of hearing anything but foolish gossip when my friend Blin of *Le Temps* approached with a bespectacled, timorous gentleman in a priest's collar.

"This is Father Quirk. Clayton Peavey, a friend of the new Ambassador's."

"Well, not exactly a friend, my father—"

"So pleased to meet you." Father Quirk beheld me admiringly. Without prompting he launched into what must have been his standard spiel for the evening. "I cannot say why these things happen, only that there are misunderstandings on all sides. All sides. Poor Dr. Mauchamp was such a fine man, but he did not understand the confusion of these benighted people. You see—" He checked to see that he was not boring me. My eyes widened in appreciation of his tale. "You see, the French government has been trying to set up a wireless telegraphy station, over the protests of the Sultan, I might add. But an innocent enough business. For some reason the rabble fear the antennas. What I believe happened is that Dr. Mauchamp received some geological survey equipment he had ordered, wrapped in rugs in long packages, and the people mistook it for hidden antenna poles. As small a thing as that can set them off, particularly where it concerns a European. They say his companion's fate is unknown, but that his family have been murdered also. A terrible, terrible business."

I commiserated with Father Quirk, who had no further insights to impart. "They are a poor, benighted people who must be civilized. God save them," he repeated, growing more morose while I grew impatient to escape his clutches. Even the treacly grasp of Darlington seemed preferable to this interminable moralizing. I was relieved to feel a tap on my shoulder.

A liveried footman informed me that my presence was required outside the courtyard. I followed him beneath gleaming chandeliers, and we wended our way through the crowd into a darkened hallway, where a small door led into a room fitted with several Louis

Quatorze armchairs and a mahogany writing desk. In the room were Darlington, Ambassador White, and a rigid American with ruddy cheeks and vacant eyes set in a tiny head on a massive body.

"Clayton, this is Colonel Struck." The Colonel clasped my hand far too long and far too firmly.

"Howdy," he said. "Judd Struck's the name." I replied in kind. "I guess it's a relief for you to be among your own again," he said.

"It certainly is." I smiled at him.

"I cannot remain long away from the reception," the Ambassador said in a voice cultured and cultivated by years of dealing with similar matters. "But before I leave you with these gentlemen there is someone I want you to meet." He opened another door leading off this room. A thin, balding Frenchman entered. He was clothed in a suit of fine cut and a discreet but emphatic air.

"This is Monsieur Sirot." The Ambassador's introduction rendered the name "Zero." The man's handshake was confident, but far less abrasive than the Colonel's. "Monsieur Sirot has been doing special work for the French government recently, and your affairs have come to his attention."

"The Troisième Bureau," chirped Darlington. The Ambassador coughed.

"The Troisième Bureau?" I exclaimed.

"That's right, boy, the Troisième Bureau," repeated the Colonel, except that on his lips it sounded like the home of an Homeric rabbit: the Trojan burrow.

"You are grotesque, Colonel," taunted Darlington, and Colonel Struck glowered at him.

"My dear Clayton." The Ambassador was at his ingratiating best. "We feel you can, by way of your inadvertent position in a set of circumstances of which none of us is too certain, be of great service to your country."

"I'm not sure I am fit to be of service to my country," I blurted. Darlington shook his head as though he had misheard me. The colonel gaped, obviously unable to comprehend such a sentiment. Ambassador White smiled.

"Perhaps not," he said. "Based upon your misconduct over the two months you have been in Paris, and the fact that you are here at all and not back in Cambridge completing your studies, I suppose that may be so, but I did not call you here to chastise you. You see, you really have little choice in the matter. I do not intend that as a threat. You are in grave danger and the only sensible thing for me to do—and this is what your father has requested—is to revoke your visa and send you home. Directly from this reception."

"And to avoid this banishment?" I inquired. "What service am I to render?"

"Given your penchant for doing whatever you take it into your head to do, we cannot allow you to carry on without some sort of protection. The French police have attempted to protect you, but you saw last night how effective their security is." I nodded, and the Colonel snorted over the weakness of the effete French. "Monsieur Sirot's organization is in a position to provide you discreet and thorough safekeeping. In return they want information from you."

"What kind of information?"

"Regarding your friend Guillaume . . . Malaimé, I think he calls himself. That is not his correct surname, of course."

"Well, I suppose not. But what is his correct name?"

"There are two theories regarding that. But in order not to prejudice you or make your work more difficult, it is best you not know. They are only theories, and either, or both, may prove false."

"And you suspect Guillaume of—"

"Certain involvements. We do not know. But *you* are in a position to find out. You have been placed there by chance more adroitly than we could have maneuvered one of our agents into this position. Will you help us?"

I thought for a moment. The cipher from the Troisième Bureau had proved just that: he remained silent, his expression stoic, noncommittal.

"I haven't much choice," I said.

"That's the damn truth," said the Colonel.

"But—" I eyed the Colonel.

"Colonel Struck is in charge of security for the Paris area. That is why he is here tonight. Darlington will be your contact for the passing of information, inasmuch as you are already acquainted and this relationship is known to Guillaume."

"But what should I do if Guillaume wants to"—I hesitated—"leave Paris?"

"Does he?"

"He has a hundred different plans." I shrugged. "You never know what he'll do."

"Then by all means go with him."

"Only do let us know where you're going this time," entreated Darlington. "You've been such a bad boy in the past."

"I have, haven't I?

"Of course, we must trust you not to play a double game," said the Ambassador with a shrewd smile. "If you wish to cast your fate to the winds in that manner I cannot stop you. You can do little damage other than to yourself in that way, Clayton." The Ambassador's honeyed kindness poured from his cool gray eyes. "Your father strenuously objects to this whole business, of course, and I am loath to let you remain in Paris. You are in danger from more than one source. But since you wish to remain, why not work with us, receive our support and protection, and serve your country and the cause of justice at the same time? If you prefer to go home, I'm sure our nation can survive the loss of your fledging services."

"No," I said quickly. "I don't want to go home. I want to stay."

"As I thought," the Ambassador said, and he shook my hand. "The Colonel and Monsieur Sirot will provide any information you may require. And I beseech you, Clayton. Do not play a double game. It's not worth it and you'll find yourself like that Paris policeman last night. Or worse. You must believe me." He shook my hand again, excused himself, and left the room.

From the laconic Monsieur Sirot and the idiotic Colonel Struck I gathered that Guillaume was suspected of involvement in revolutionary activities tied to the communist internationale and irredentist movements in Italy. This seemed likely enough, given the cast of characters in Montmartre. How it posed a threat to the French or American governments I could not see. When I asked about a possible connection to Morocco, Monsieur Sirot admitted they were considering this. He told me that the Arabic symbol scrawled in blood on the floor by Charles meant "revenge" and referred specifically to traitors.

"But revenge for what?" I asked. "And who is the traitor?"

He shrugged and said that remained to be determined. Then he asked me a single question: "Did your Madame Orgueil know how the young *saltimbanque* came by the mask?"

"If she did, she did not share that information with us," I replied.

Darlington promised to make daily visits to a certain café near Pigalle where I was to leave messages with a waiter named Pierre. I told him this was a risky arrangement, and he agreed to devise a better one. When I questioned Monsieur Sirot about the work of the Troisième Bureau he became more reticent and our conference ended.

Darlington ushered me back into the courtyard, where I remained for some time in a puzzled and increasingly piffled state. When I departed, shortly past midnight, none of my confidants approached me, though the Colonel winked as I passed him on my way out. At the door the Ambassador told me how glad he was I had come and how much he hoped to see me again.

Alone in my carriage on the way back to Montmartre I tried to take stock of my position. Something ludicrous in the intelligence operation to which I had been enlisted made me giggle; but perhaps I was only lightheaded from the champagne, my persistent cold, and the exhaustion of the past three days—the night with Apolline, the visit to Madame Orgueil's and the death of Charles, and the reception. Finally it was my fatigue which rescued me from the impossibility of sorting things out, and as the fiacre bounced along the empty boulevards I was swept into the comforting arms of that kindest panacea for man's worries, sleep.

X

I awoke late the following day. It was raining and I never really awoke at all but lay abed through the dreary afternoon, somewhere between dream-filled sleep and an illusion of consciousness. Congested and hungover, I listened to the rain running off the roof tiles and watched two flies buzzing listlessly above my bed.

The previous night's giddiness was replaced by more somber reflections on my situation. Caught in a welter of interests seemingly at cross purposes, I felt myself buffeted about helplessly in all directions. There was my friend Guillaume, an enigma, accused on the one hand and mysteriously pursuing the *saltimbanques* on the other, and now quite intent on going to Morocco, which, from the sound of it, was no place to visit. There were several opposing groups of Moroccans from what I could gather—the man Ahmed in the Santée swore to protect me, the murderers of Charles obviously had other ideas, and the pale man at Madame Orgueil's, although perhaps not a Moor himself, had some connection with the Atlas mountains. Then there was the French police and Inspector Pernicieux, noticeably absent from last night's meeting; the U.S. government and this Troisième Bureau, whatever it might be, with their interest in Guillaume; and finally there were the clowns Boppe, Vogel, and Arbogast Zorn. What they had to do with any of this I was hard put to figure.

As for Clayton Peavey, what choice did he have? Betray Guillaume and cooperate with the friendly Ambassador who reminded me of all the congenial diplomats I had met over the years and whose generosity of spirit I knew could be turned off and on at will? Or allow them to send me home to Professor Stallwarts and what now seemed so far away and so utterly boring? Or play my own little game and, very likely, end up dead? It was not a happy set of alternatives from which to choose.

I debated whether to tell Guillaume of the meeting at the Hôtel Ritz and the suspicions leveled against him, or whether to tell Darlington and Colonel Struck of the clowns and the pale man at Madame Orgueil's. I thrashed at the bedclothes, felt more alone than I ever remembered, and drifted fitfully to sleep.

Wednesday it was still raining and I had resolved nothing. Guillaume had gone off to make arrangements for Inspector Pernicieux's banquet, scheduled for that Saturday. As for Morocco, he had either forgotten or put aside for a time his intention to go there. I asked after Apolline and was told by Paul that she had been cast in a play and was rehearsing daily somewhere on the left bank. Thoughts of her aroused a fierce dichotomy of longing and dread in me: I desired her obsessively though she was totally inaccessible to me, I wanted her to be my confidante yet knew she was uniquely unsuited to that task. I really had no one I could trust or with whom I could even discuss what to do.

The days passed. I made my way down the Butte to the café in Pigalle designated by Darlington, found Pierre, and left the message that plans for heading south had been abandoned for now and nothing further had developed. Guiltily I trudged back to the Rue Ravignan and found Guillaume obliviously engaged in exalting poor Inspector Pernicieux, whom I now believed he meant only to ridicule.

A meal was ordered from an excellent restaurant where we occasionally dined, and several of the gang were enlisted to decorate the little Spaniard's studio, where the fête would take place. The services of a noted cabaret performer who produced very simple tunes by means of loud gaseous emissions released in tempo and on pitch from his rectum were secured, as were those of several more conventional musicians.

At last the great day arrived, the Saturday of the banquet for the painting Inspector. I had sufficiently recovered my health and self-confidence to share in the festive mood. There had been no visits from Moorish assassins bent on revenge, and our two shifts of guardians were discreetly efficient and quietly abstinent. I paid a second visit to Pierre, received word that Darlington appreciated my cooperation, and, on a whim, left word that I would like to meet with Darlington to discuss the Cirque Mediano. Oblique, yet provocative, I thought.

Back at Frédé's in the sunshine I finally told Guillaume that I had been approached at the reception by American and French intelligence agents interested in his activities.

"Wonderful. And you agreed to work with them?" he asked, undismayed and betraying little surprise.

"Well, yes, I did. I'm sorry I didn't tell you sooner," I excused myself. "I had little choice. It was either that or lose my visa and be sent home."

"Of course. Poor Clayton." He grinned and actually seemed pleased by these new attentions. "And what have you reported to them?" I told him nothing, but that I felt I should tell them of Boppe and Vogel and the clowns. His face tightened and he shook his head.

"If you wish, you will do so, but I think that is a mistake, and quite unfair to those gentlemen of the circus who have already been and may again be of great aid to us. As for me, tell them all, I care not. I have nothing to hide." His enthusiasm in this statement was so genuine that I found myself once more believing he was as innocent as I. My anticipation of the evening's entertainment increased.

In late afternoon the crew met in motley at the Bar Fauvet to commence drinking, Père Frédé having closed his doors in honor of the occasion. He was with us himself, white beard billowing. Lolo was hitched to one of the elms along the way. The sun moved in stippled patches across the faces at the table: pale Max, eyelids drooping and an incisive grin across his face; peasant Paul, his face already flushed with wine; Marie with her cat, bursting spontaneously into song with Guillaume gaily at her side, telling everyone once more the greatness of Pernicieux—priming, prefacing, and propagandizing all at once.

Catherine sashayed over to our table. She was wrapped in a sarong and nothing else, an unhappily bucktoothed and thin-cheeked Sorbonne *philosophe* in tow, he muttering about Bergson while Catherine dazzled me with her mouth and the tip of her tongue. Apolline was nowhere. A half-dozen others dawdled by the tables and hung over the chairs. I thought I detected our watchdog across the street by a kiosk decorated with an abundantly arabesqued poster. It was not a comforting sight, and I drifted out of the conversation into my own recurrent obsessions.

Suddenly Guillaume asked the time. Though the low sun still shone in our faces we discovered it was past eight. The Inspector was expected at nine.

"It always amazes me how early it gets late here," I quipped, though whether this was a function of attitude or merely latitude was never explained to me. Guillaume grinned and led us back up the street to the Place Ravignan.

The banquet hall was a loft studio with thick beams

from which Chinese lanterns had been suspended, colored candles burning precariously close to the rice paper. Garlands were festooned from the beams. A map of Europe and a collection of Negro masks adorned one wall, and at the far end of the room hung a large canvas of Inspector Pernicieux's. A reclusive acquaintance who played piano in a Montmartre cabaret began performing one of his lyrical, deceptively simple pieces. Immaculately groomed and dressed in burgundy velvet, like his tones, he coaxed an evocative, smoky mood from the old piano. As we filed into the studio those who had not previously seen any of the Inspector's underwater wonderlands gathered round enraptured.

"Why, this is wonderful," proclaimed Marie. "This is life. This is the essence of what makes a man a man."

"But not a woman a woman," retorted Guillaume, and Marie whirled on him, then laughed and agreed. His hands swept the air. "Marie is a new woman, to be sure," he said. "But she is not so foolish as some of these women." Faces turned to him. "She is conscious of the profound difference between men and women," he concluded. "And that is all."

Marie shook her head with amused resignation. She took her cat from a chair and, draping it across her shoulders, where it appeared quite comfortable, said, "Puss poses for all the women's faces in my paintings." The cat mewed, and we heard a great roar in the street. It began frightfully loud, then approached and grew louder, accompanied by a screeching across the cobbles and a howl from the cat as it leapt from Marie's neck and scurried beneath a crate.

We crowded at a small window overlooking the *place* and I saw the source of this great din, now growling hungrily beneath the stunted plane trees by the fountain. It was a sleek, white two-seater Bugatti racing

style automobile. The roof was retracted and its goggled driver hulked over the wheel, one hand on the bulb horn, his long black hair flowing from beneath a wide white hat. "*Olà,*" he cried. Waving, he roared in a circle around the tiny *place,* scattering dirt and stones and bits of shrubbery. Concerned faces appeared at doorways and windows. After completing his circuit he parked near the top of the square and the engine hammered to a halt as he hopped onto the pavement. He wore knee-high boots with dark trousers ballooning over them and a tight vest beneath his open coat.

"It is Tommaso," Guillaume announced. "Come from the Abbaye at Créteil for the banquet. We are in for it now," he added.

Tommaso was a hurricane invading our sea, as he pummeled Guillaume on the back, hugged Paul and Père Frédé, clapped the fragile Max across his shoulders, and shadow-boxed around the little Spaniard. The two exchanged a few punches and then embraced. Tommaso did not greet any of the women.

Paul, a motoring enthusiast, engaged Tommaso in a technical dialogue on his Bugatti, something about overhead camshafts and dual pistons.

"Internal combustion speaks eloquently of the future," Tommaso thundered. "Power and speed. We must move and move now." He flourished a long cigar and lighted it. "Where is Père Ubu tonight?" he asked. "Where is my mechanical *débauché?*"

"He won't be coming," Paul said soberly. "You must not go to see him. It is too horrible."

"Yes, he is ending," declaimed Max. I envisioned the black-caped figure with the crooked cane careening down the street on the evening I met Guillaume.

"It is no longer amusing, merely pathetic," said Max drily, and Paul became angry. "It is nothing to joke about," he said. "A man is dying at age thirty-four." Max opened a copy of *La Revue Blanche* and stared blankly at the page.

"Ubu has taken the great leap into the vacuum of total creation," said Tommaso. "He cannot die, he can only explode."

Tommaso had a scar, a saber slash carved in his cheek like a badge of false bravado. Suddenly he rushed over to the velvet pianist and began banging on the keyboard with his fists. "Noise, make some noise, you feeble *passéist* clown," he sneered. "Forget your sweet harmonies. Let me hear sirens and engines in your hands, the crashing of machinery, gunfire and combustion."

The pianist abandoned his instrument, and Tommaso, tossing his hair and bellowing in Italian, raged over it with his elbows.

As nine-thirty passed and the Inspector failed to appear, Guillaume grew alternately whimsical and anxious and sent out for more wine. It arrived and was quickly consumed. Finally, near ten o'clock, the door was opened tentatively and the guest of honor stood before us.

"So sorry, my dear Guillaume," he said. "Préfecture business, you know. A nasty little case which would not solve itself. Could not be helped. But here I am."

The Inspector tended to trot rather than walk and he stepped eagerly into the room. Carrying a cane, he was dressed in a dark three-piece suit, very prim and proper and crowned by a satin ascot and wide, flattopped beret tilted jauntily upon his head, which gave him a comic appearance.

"Ladies and gentlemen," Guillaume proclaimed. "May I present the latest discovery of the new school, the last great genius of the old century, that *primitif* without equal, Inspector Guy Pernicieux of the Paris Préfecture."

Amidst tumultuous applause Marie and Catherine

and the other women kissed the blushing Inspector repeatedly, and Tommaso sent him reeling with a belt across the back. When he had recovered, I nodded my welcome and shook his hand.

"And have we been up to any mischief lately?" he asked me with what almost appeared to be a wink. "No more midnight seances or visits to the circus, eh?" I shook my head, wondered how he knew about the circus, but dismissed these thoughts from my mind.

Pernicieux was conducted to the head of the table—actually several doors set on sawhorses and laid with an array of mismatched china and cutlery—where he sat in his wide beret beneath his own canvas. At first he could not overcome his embarrassment at all the fuss, and he ingenuously asked people's opinion of his work. After listening to the lavish praise, he said, "No, but what do you *really* think?" and received a sarcastic retort, which left him unsatisfied. Max offered to provide whatever opinion the Inspector wished to hear, but he did not know. The line between mockery and adulation was thin, and grew thinner as the spirits flowed. Somewhere in that fastidious and skittish personality which had labored for nearly three decades on cases of diminishing importance and canvases of dubious artistry nestled a bud of sincerity and zest for the creative life which bloomed in this environment. Seated before us Pernicieux was renascent, brilliantly transformed. It was a glorious sight to behold, even if a little bit ludicrous: this trim little man fairly glowing as one after another of these young artists, drug users, pornographers, bohemians, decadents and dilettantes, wastrels and wags, anarchists, every conceivable antithesis to what his outward life represented, welcomed him and congratulated him on his paintings, "his courage, his purity, and his sense of grandeur," as Guillaume expressed it.

"Yes, I have made a very careful study of fish and

crustaceans," he explained to Paul, who did not mock nor poke fun at anything. "From books I have learned the length and number of the scales, the position of gills on certain species, the arrangement of the suction cups on the tentacles of an octopus." Marie began giggling. "It is all quite mathematical and precise, as I am sure you can appreciate from your own work," he added.

"But have you explored the fourth dimension?" queried the Spaniard with a curling smile. "You must go beyond your Euclid."

"My good fellow, the fourth dimension?" replied the Inspector. "Why, I have only just mastered the first three."

Guillaume explained. "We are seeking a new space in which to situate objects. That is what Pablo means."

"I didn't know there was a fourth dimension," he insisted.

"The fourth dimension represents the immensity of space eternalizing itself in all directions at any given moment," said Guillaume. "It is what endows objects with plasticity, what makes them true to life and not mere depictions of life."

"One must not imitate what one hopes to create," said a voice, the inevitable conundrum drumming upon the puzzled Inspector's head.

"I'm not quite sure I understand," he said as I entered the fray in hopes of clarifying matters.

"It is like watching an object from a speeding railway coach. It seems to grow larger and then smaller, yet in fact it has not changed. Or a row of telegraph poles as one passes, which appear to move across the horizon when we know they are standing still."

"You must learn to paint scientifically," added Paul.

"If you mean I must paint in little dots, no thank you," responded the Inspector. "I think this fourth dimension is just another of the clever notions which you devise over coffee to confound the rest of us. What is the necessity of it?"

"But it is not contrived," I burst forth enthusiastically. "It flows quite spontaneously."

"Not unlike the wine," said the Inspector, and his glass was refilled. He looked at Guillaume. "But what has my work to do with your theories? I am clearly not part of your way of thinking and never shall be."

"But you are, you are, and you don't even know it," said Marie, coming over and kissing his cheeks again. "That is what is so wonderful."

The Inspector was too flushed to argue with this pert young woman. "I am a common man with common tastes," he asserted. "A humble inspector at the Paris Préfecture with a weakness for *frites* in paper and a young Beaujolais. Nothing more. You imagine me as something else, and I believe you, Guillaume, would endeavor to create me into something more if you could."

"Not at all," Guillaume countered. "I need not create you. That has been accomplished by some mysterious force far beyond my control." Laughter swept the room, and the Inspector's eyes darted over the faces, searching for reassurance that they were not laughing at him.

"You have studied the dimensions of fish for your paintings, is that right?" Max enunciated slowly. He drew himself close to Guy Pernicieux, who nodded suspiciously. "Have you ever studied the forms and shapes of human thought?" The Inspector shook his head firmly, sipped his wine, and smiled hopefully at Marie. "Yet this has been done," declared Max. "Let me show you."

He displayed a large picture book of what appeared to be photographs.

"This book was published just two years ago." Max slowly turned the pages as he spoke. "It is called

Thought Forms and was compiled by the theosophists Annie Besant and C. W. Leadbeater. And that is precisely what it is. Thought forms."

Pernicieux placed his pince-nez high on the bridge of his nose. I peered over his shoulder and found Catherine close beside me, also ostensibly examining the thought forms.

The pages of the book bore cloudy, abstract, multicolored forms, rather like full-length haloes, overlaid on photographs of individuals. Or, I thought, like the cloud from which Sébastien had emerged that night at Madame Orgueil's.

"The subject's thought is reflected in the form which emanates about him in some characteristic shape and color," Max elucidated. "Here we have the anger of a London tram conductor." A carmine and magenta cloud, tinged with green, rather elongated. "Here the reflections of a young girl upon viewing the sea." This one was fluffy and pastel. He continued to turn the pages and tell us what we saw.

"This is all very remarkable, to be sure," admitted the Inspector. "Most remarkable. But how were these . . . thought forms recorded?"

"That we do not know. Only C. W. Leadbeater understands the process."

"And he, I suppose, is loath to reveal his secret?" the Inspector asked.

"It would be like trying to explain the fourth dimension to you, Monsieur Inspector," Tommaso sneered. He raised a fist toward the flinching Inspector, then burst into laughter. "Coward. War is the world's only hygiene. The time has come for the bourgeois philistines to accept on faith the artistic visions we present to them," he roared. "And that is all," came Guillaume's coda, putting an end to the discussion of thought forms. The

Inspector appeared relieved but unconvinced. I felt a soft hand on my thigh.

"Oh, Clayton, I remember."

"Do you? How conscientious."

I felt renewed yearnings for Catherine, and ridiculous jealousy at the thought that this fellow, this critic for *Gil Blas* or whatever he was with his protruding lips hanging off his thin face, this narrow aesthete, could possibly be the nightly recipient of the wild passions I had known that night with Catherine. Now, as she ogled me so confidently and so brazenly, I felt hostile yet unable to resist. I swept my mouth across her rich hair and down the side of her neck.

"We must visit Max's together. Tonight. Soon," she whispered.

As she swung her curls past me and dipped her head, I noticed Guillaume and the wild Italian across the room, conferring quietly. Tommaso nodded. Then they crossed to the window and he pointed toward the car and spoke animatedly. Guillaume became suddenly quite excited and laughed. Then the Italian began to laugh, but all I could hear was his coarse laughter across the room while the rest of the dialogue was in silent tableau, like a film. They shook hands and Guillaume turned away. I felt a twinge in my stomach and a hand on my hip.

"Oh, but everyone is *here*," I teased Catherine.

"Yes, I know," she smiled warmly, and the dark eyes swam through the smoke haze like one of C. W. Leadbeater's subjects having a thought form, scarlet and crimson. The approach of Monsieur the Critic interrupted this heated exchange.

"We were discussing the *élan vital*," he announced haughtily.

"I see," I said.

"Oh, but Mathieu." Of course, the name had to be Mathieu, a name I would always associate with a mother's voice calling her eight-year-old son across a playground. I had often wondered what happened to these Mathieus after pubescence, if the process required them to change their names. But no, here was a full-grown Mathieu. "Mathieu—" Catherine drooled over the long diphthong, and I felt a trifle ill. "This is the young American I told you about." She touched my arm lightly and leered.

"Ah yes, the one who sleeps in the cinema," he sniffed.

"That wasn't the only place I slept that night," I told him and huffed off as Catherine merrily mouthed "Max's" and Mathieu mirthlessly pursued his endless tangent. But I nodded and knew I would meet her at Max's.

The fartist had begun his unique rites. He performed a variety of popular tunes and displayed remarkable control. People began dancing to these musical outbursts. Paul and one of the girls from up the Butte pitched and veered in a bizarre mechanical dance that somehow fit this most human of instruments.

Now the fartist commenced "The Marseillaise," a bit haltingly, for I believe he was running out of steam. The crowd grew still. Tommaso honked loudly and pounded the piano top. Inspector Pernicieux rose, the color glowed in his cheeks, and I thought I could detect his head tripping along with the meter of the anthem.

By the end of "The Marseillaise" most of the audience was in hysterics, but Inspector Pernicieux's eyes had begun to glisten.

"And France *is* great," he said solemnly. "When I began my career I was involved in the preventive measures taken against the Boulanger demonstrators. People bent upon destroying France under the banner of saving her. But she shall be saved. The great Louis Lepine directed those operations. I was with him at Les Halles when he stepped between the strikers and police lines in his bowler hat and morning coat and told us: 'Do not attack these honest men.' The strike ended. We have only to remember our common humanity as Frenchmen and all things are possible."

"Bravo, bravo . . . *Vive la France,*" came the chorus of esteem, while Paul and the little Spaniard restrained Tommaso, who felt little common humanity for anyone. Guillaume drew me aside.

"I told you there would be trouble, and all I wanted to do was give old Pernicieux a joyous evening. Just look at him. Did you hear that patriotic drivel?" He seemed excessively ardent but as soon as we stood out of earshot of the others his face grew pensive.

"Apolline is here. She is waiting for you at Max's."

Delightful, I thought. Wouldn't it be cozy if Catherine arrived at the same time and we could arrange some sort of perverse *ménage*. Then the memory of Apolline jolted these lascivious thoughts from my mind. This was no joke.

"We depart tonight," Guillaume said simply.

"Depart?" I knew instantly this was no joke either, but pretended I did not, hoping to fool myself.

"Yes. Everything has been arranged. We will take Tommaso's Bugatti. We will be sought on the trains. This will be safer."

"Take it where? Do you mean—"

"Yes, of course that is what I mean. Tonight, with the Inspector right here, on the case, as you say. We will drive off in Tommaso's car and disappear."

"And drive to Morocco?" I gasped. "Oh boy."

"To the south of Spain, or as far as the white machine takes us."

"Going the inconspicuous route as usual?" I asked.

"Yes. One must always outreach the common imagination and then one becomes invisible. And that is all." He smiled recklessly, but tension flashed on his fleshy face. Perhaps it was my own reflected there.

"So. You must travel light, Clayton Peavey. Fresh linen. A hat. Nothing more. It will be warm in the south."

That much I knew. "But what if . . . I mean, if I'm not ready to just . . ."

"Of course you are, my friend. You're not going to let me go alone, are you?"

"Maybe I won't let you go at all," I said. He laughed and put his hand on my upper arm. "Go to Apolline," he said. "She awaits you." With those words he left me.

Like underdeveloped photographs, my doubts were flushed too soon from their fluid and remained blurred and indistinct. Guillaume, with his infallible instincts, had planned well. I had no time to send a message to Darlington, and the Inspector was beyond fulfilling his official duties. I had to go; God knows, I surely wanted to go. I was caught.

Catherine eyed me as I slipped out the door, and I felt my stomach jump and knot: caught again. I shook my head, a meaningless gesture by this point, and descended the rickety stairs toward Max's, hoping Catherine would be delayed and would not burst in on us.

Outside the frenzied chaos of the studio—that chaos with which Guillaume chose always to surround himself—I felt a warm flush on my cheeks and pitched awkwardly down the darkened halls. Dim light shone beneath the door at Max's. Apolline was sitting on a floor cushion by a low lamp, her eyes half shut.

"You are here," I said.

"I am here, now and then, but not for long." She

opened her eyes, my inscrutable waif, her omnivorous eyes. "That's physics, actually."

"What do you know about physics?" I asked.

"Nothing. What do you know about Morocco?"

"More than nothing. Enough to know better."

"Better than who?"

"What? Oh. No one."

"So many know so much but understand so little," she breathed, and I waited. "Yet some who don't know already understand."

"Yes . . . I . . ."

"That is you, Clayton. You do not know why you are going to Morocco and you fear it, yet you must go. I will think of you. Often."

"You will. But why? I should think—"

"Stop."

I stopped. I dropped beside her, desperate to take her hand: even with ordinary girls I have always been reduced at such tender moments to the gawking and stalking approach with its inevitable awkward frustration. Apolline smiled, always testing me. But could I doubt?

"You are true," she said. "I will miss that." She lifted one fragile arm, the skin nearly translucent over the web of blue tributaries, and touched my cheek with a cool fingertip. I turned my head to kiss her fingers, but the pale, thin hand was gone with only the fragrance of her skin left for me to taste. I listened fearfully for Catherine's footsteps in the hall but heard nothing.

"Life is within," she said. "All good things, all that is real lies within." Her arms curled against her chest as though clutching at her heart and she shrank into the floor. I hung over her a moment, utterly hesitant, understanding for the first time the essence of doubt, the struggle between instinct and thought, the struggle being waged *always* within this tiny girl who lived totally within her mind. I wanted desperately to hold her forever and to stay with her in that corner of Max's dark studio.

Then she took my hand. Hovering over it, she gazed into my heart pulsing across the back, then gently turned it and glanced for an instant into the palm. She shut her eyes and dropped my hand quickly. Quivering, she looked up at me, her eyes wide with bewilderment. I no longer could see her with my eyes but perceived her with my heart. I understood that her silence was not mystical lucidity but simply incoherence. She was lost. In that instant a bond of affection for this dream girl was born. I was suffused with a sense of wonder and joy I had never experienced. And I did love her.

"Part of me wants you so much . . . Apolline." She had turned away. "But most of me feels I already have you."

"Yes, I feel it too. The rest is not necessary. It would only detract."

"But I don't understand. Why is it so strong?"

"Why must you always ask why, poor Clayton?" She shook her head. I heard footsteps on the stairs. "Go. Go because you must, though I do wish you could remain. Go quickly."

"There is so much I want to ask you."

"But there is nothing I can tell you." She lapsed into silence with only her transparent purity to speak for her.

I rushed from Max's studio, staggering into Catherine in the narrow hallway, pushed her aside wordlessly, and climbed back to the roistering above without ever looking back.

The wine was not exhausted, nor the levity diminished, but the meal had never arrived and it was near midnight. Someone had been sent to the restaurant but not returned. Père Frédé sang Norman duets with Marie. Paul belched genially.

I moved furtively to my valise, stuffed a few things from it into a double strength of burlap, slipped in a sketchpad, and set my wide-brimmed hat on top of this packet. I looked up to find Guillaume, his arm around Tommaso, watching me from across the room. Catherine had returned and was dancing wildly and obliviously with her pathetic Mathieu.

The Inspector had passed out beneath one of the Chinese lanterns, his whiskers well wetted and the guttering candle in the lantern dribbling wax on his beret. It ran across the wool and formed a thin tail where it dripped off onto the floor.

I learned later that the dinner arrived the following evening, someone having mistaken the date when ordering it.

XI

"This is madness," I said.

"And madness," replied Tommaso, taking one hand from the steering wheel and poking me as he made his point, "madness is the beginning of creation, the spark of divine intuition. Madness is life."

"Make him watch the road," I said, and Guillaume laughed.

We were crammed together in the passenger seat of Tommaso's Bugatti, our small satchels stashed between our feet. I sat on Guillaume's abundant lap.

"Apolline told me to go with you," I informed Guillaume. "Somehow that makes me more secure in my decision. I don't know why it should."

"She confuses you?"

"Everything in our relationship is contradictory. She confuses me yet lends clarity to my convictions. She arouses me yet empowers me to resist her. She makes the physical side of life seem so trivial."

"Both sides are important," Guillaume assured me. "You *are* confused."

"I am confused about what you expect to find in Morocco," I responded.

"We will find the answers to all our puzzles. We will find Sébastien's murderer."

"But the danger—"

"Is greater here in Paris waiting idly for our fate to come to us. Better to go out seeking it."

I sighed. "Of course, the most sensible thing to do would be—"

"Common sense must be banished," Tommaso shouted, accelerating through a sharp corner. The cool damp air rushed over my face and I shut my eyes a moment and began to feel dizzy. I swallowed and nudged Guillaume.

"Can't you make him go slower?" I implored him.

"*Hah*. Tommaso only goes faster. Never slower."

I shut my eyes again and clung to the seat. After a few moments we slowed, made a turn, and crept carefully down a side street. Even rows of small brick and stone houses hid behind little yards and black grate gates.

"Where are we going?" I asked.

"To my mother's," Guillaume replied. "To say goodbye."

I barely concealed my amusement. He shook his head solemnly as we pulled up to the little house and motioned me to come with him, either for moral support or as witness to a potential altercation.

After several moments, with a great cursing and shuffling, her hair curled and snooded, the Countess appeared in a long dressing gown fraying at the hem.

"Ahhh, Guillaume, what do you want? Have you lost your key?"

"No, Mama. Clayton and I are traveling south tonight. We may be gone some weeks."

"Some weeks? What do you mean? Where are—"

"I am not sure. But we must travel south."

"And you've come here to upset me and watch me beg you not to leave, is that it?" She was becoming herself again. "Well, I shan't do it." She began to cry. "Go. Be gone, villain."

"No, no, Mama. I've come to reassure you that I am quite all right, that no harm has befallen us, that we are safely out of Paris."

"Wonderful. I am reassured. I am very content that you should rush off like a fool." She turned from him, but he caught her shoulder, forced her to face him, and spoke with a sincerity I had never heard before.

"Would you have been more content had I simply disappeared?" he asked her. "Would you?" She shook her head and fell sobbing on his shoulder. He embraced her while I shifted from foot to foot. Tommaso honked and gunned his engine. The Countess looked up aggrieved.

"But you are a fool, Guillaume," she said. "You are such a fool."

Guillaume nodded and took her hands. "Yes, Mama, I know. It is our little secret though, eh?" She started to smile, then recalled her maternal anguish and waved him away.

"At least I shall have that nice Inspector to comfort me. He does care for you, you know? And he'll find you, too."

"Not in his present condition, he won't."

"Why, what have you done to him? . . . Guillaume . . ." At this sign that her agitation was returning, Guillaume dropped her hands, kissed her cheeks swiftly, and turned to go. She threw herself on his back and he remained, comforting her silently for a few moments.

"Be careful," she whimpered. He nodded dutifully, kissed her wet cheeks once more, and extricated himself from her grasp. With a wave we were off.

Tommaso raced through the outer suburbs and along the river Marne to Créteil, where he lived in a communal artist's colony called the Abbaye, dedicated to "the imposition of a universal aesthetic ideal by a vanguard of artist/rulers."

Invited in, we drank a quick glass of clear, fierce-burning Italian anisette. Tommaso smashed his glass.

Guillaume did likewise and looked at me. I tossed my glass against the hearth.

"A good voyage, my friends, and good hunting. Enjoy my little monster," Tommaso said as he turned over his Bugatti and we drove off.

Mercifully, Guillaume drove with caution and respect for his own life. He was correct about the danger, for as soon as we left Paris my head cleared. As I stared up into the night and the lights of the sky rushed past I felt a rising sense of relief from the tension which had gripped me. Despite the gaiety, Paris had become claustrophobic and oppressive. In the open spaces of rural France my feeling of well-being grew. As Guillaume had correctly predicted, although everyone along the way noticed our sleek white sports car with the curling exhaust pipes and rounded grill, no one was looking for it. Local police waved as we passed through their towns.

Although Apolline's words and the ever-increasing distance from Paris shored up my confidence in our undertaking, my questions over Guillaume's deeper involvement in the affair persisted. As we drove I asked him about our search for the *saltimbanques* and the mask. He told me he had placed "discreetly worded inquiries in each of the journals suggested by our friend Vogel" and that by the time we returned they should have elicited a response from the Zorns.

"In the meantime," he told me, "I'm confident we'll learn something of our acrobatic friends, even in Morocco."

"I'm far less sanguine about all this than you," I told him, but I could feel the tension easing from my face as we sped south, stopping now and then at a country inn, for a picnic beneath a stand of willows and juniper near Poitiers, or to pick fruit in an orchard at

Angoulême. There were no Moors—though there would be plenty where we were headed—only lush meadows in the spring sunlight, yellow mustard fields, and the world rolling past the little white Bugatti.

"Let's just keep traveling," I suggested to Guillaume, half-seriously. "You can show me Nice and Italy. Let's forget Morocco for a while." His response was a firm face and unwavering eyes.

We crossed the border into Spain at the coast and, ominously, the car immediately broke down in the fishing port of San Sebastian.

We stayed there several days, sleeping in an unpleasant hotel, eating squid and mackerel, drinking red wine, and trying to coax a variety of confounded Spaniards into helping us repair our infernal machine. When this finally proved impossible we wired Tommaso of our plight, abandoned the Bugatti, and boarded the train for Madrid. From thence we took trains to Sevilla and on to Algeciras for the ferry ride across the straits to Tangier.

In Algeciras I briefly fancied going to the British consulate at Gibraltar, informing them of my identity, and scotching the whole operation, but I could not bring myself to do it.

On the ferry I stood by the bow and breathed the sweet salt air. A lingering image of Apolline that last night floated through my mind. I saw her rise from her cushion, willowy and numinous like one of the Inspector's mermaids. Deep in the calm green sea beneath me I saw her eyes and recalled the sense of awe and wonder I felt at that moment when I understood that I would not touch her and that it did not matter.

I lifted my head and turned my sights south where the cliffs to the west of Tangier harbor came into view through chiffon mists. I dreaded to think what raging maelstrom lay beyond those cliffs, yet I would have been nowhere else on earth at that moment than precisely where I was.

And so the dauntless duo came south and arrived on June 21, 1907, in the international city of Tangier.

XII

Everything slowed as we traveled south. When we reached Morocco time stopped altogether.

At customs a French-speaking official instructed us not to venture beyond the "international zone of Tangier." Our passports were stamped accordingly.

Immediately beyond the customs house we were accosted by young men and boys offering, in several languages, to supply whatever our dissolute hearts might desire. Some revealed samples of their contraband in the folds of their *jilabas* while others stood back and pierced us with the languid stare I would grow to know so well during our sojourn in the land of the Moors.

An old man in a fraying brown burnoose, mud-splattered along its unraveling hem, grinned and gazed glazedly at us with bloodshot eyes that seemed fluid within the sockets—slick red marbles which rolled about as he wavered before us. He nodded and stared but did not pursue us. Several young boys dogged our footsteps into town. Guillaume forced his stout frame forward relentlessly, and I waded after him bearing my notebook under one arm and fending off these agents of vice and pleasure with the other.

Tangier stretches over two hills rising from the port and bay just within the lip of the straits of Gibraltar. Before us lay the slanting rooftops and pocked facades of the medina or old section of town. To its left, upon the next hilltop and farther down the beach, we saw the tall white buildings of the European quarter. There we found rooms in a comfortable, unpretentious hotel overlooking the harbor.

The European community in Tangier was highly agitated over "events in the south," as nearly all forms of political activity—colonial and internal, military and diplomatic—were described. Apparently a full-scale uprising had begun among the Berber lords of the high Atlas beyond Marrakesh. The Sultan Abd el-Aziz, a young prince of continental tastes who dwelt in the seclusion of his palace at Fez, was being called to accounts by a large segment of his people. Europeans had been slaughtered in several locations, and a well-known British military adviser to the Sultan had been kidnapped and was held for ransom by a warlord in the Rif mountains south of Tangier. The revolt was assuming the characteristics of a holy war and had accordingly aroused intense passions among the tribesmen and *fellahin* of the countryside. This, in turn, made the position of any foreigner in Morocco ambivalent at least and often decidedly dangerous.

No pink British ladies hugging Baedekers could be seen along the tree-lined boulevards of the European quarter, and the diplomatic community no longer sat placidly sipping aquavit and planning equestrian events. In the half-deserted cafés on a sultry evening one glimpsed the frightened faces of a podgy French civil servant, a severe German merchant, or a morbid and befuddled Spanish physician waiting for the afternoon press to bring reports of the latest atrocities.

Finding the company of this wan, forsaken lot alternately unnerving and boring, we sallied forth once or twice a day into the swirling market plaza atop the town, where donkey loads of dates and oranges were spread on dirty blankets and flies clung to blackened sheep's heads hung over charcoal braziers on which skewers of mutton and goat roasted. Despite the heat the local inhabitants wore full-length *jilabas*. The men were hooded and the women veiled with only eyes and nose visible. Many of the younger boys had tossed back their hoods to reveal tiny wool skullcaps. They hunkered down in the doorways and passed thin-stemmed pipes filled with *kif*.

We repeatedly encountered the wobbling old man in the frayed burnoose whom we had seen staring at us the first day at the docks. He grinned amiably like a stubby stalk of bleary-eyed asparagus, and recognition gradually led to exchanges in broken French. Guillaume befriended him and, by default, he became our dragoman, our guide to the old quarter.

His name was Abd al-Malik. Unlike the clusters of Moors who stood croodling at the corners and stared at us with drooping, deceitful eyes, he did not look through us as though we were stone. He was content to show us about the city for minimal pay.

He introduced us to a hashish bar with brightly painted walls and a band of musicians toodling incessantly upon pipes or banging out percussive rhythms on stringed instruments, drums, and hand cymbals—a constantly changing and never ceasing musical agglomeration surrounded by enormous hookahs and cups of mint tea. This Moorish music, discordant and lacking the modalities familiar to an ear schooled on Mozart and Beethoven, filled the streets of the medina. One could never escape it. It was as thick as the flies or the smell of sweat and hashish and lamb stew which swam around us in the bright primary world of the dirty old bar. Guillaume had always been scornful of drug users in Montmartre but here, in its native element and attended by the insatiable Abd al-Malik, he indulged endlessly in the *Cannabis indica* for which Morocco is so justly noted.

Nearly two weeks after our arrival in Tangier, Guillaume insisted we move to a small hotel crumpled amongst the serried structures of the old part of the city on a narrow slanting street indistinguishable to me from all the other narrow slanting streets. Here, he felt, we were more likely to find a clue or to make contact with someone who could direct us *to the mountains*.

As days passed and Guillaume smoked, I sat at the window of our stuffy little room and sketched scenes of the medina. I found the angularities and sun-drenched pastels of the city an inspiration for my work. Following lunch I often took a couple of puffs on the big hookah at our regular bar and then sat in the shade in the plaza or returned to the hotel and spent the afternoon drawing and dreaming. Some of the notions I had absorbed during those months in Paris emerged in the perspectives and shapes on the pages of my notebook. Lines extended beyond their normal end points and transected at impossible angles; the features on faces became mobile, shifting about on the head like pieces on a chessboard.

One afternoon as I sat lost in my drawings in the plaza outside our bar Abd al-Malik appeared suddenly before me. Grinning and pointing excitedly up the alleyway which led off the square, he called Guillaume out of the bar. Communicating as he always did in a series of grunts, aborted French phrases, and wavering gesticulations, he announced a spectacle about to take place in the plaza. I set down my sketch pad and waited.

A small procession passed before us. Several native boys in what appeared to be friar's robes—they were certainly not *jilabas*—waved palm fronds to part the milling crowds and allow the passage of a peculiar character: a European, short and fearsomely thin with slicked-back hair, a crooked nose, and a bushy black mustache overhanging tight, unsmiling lips. He wore knee breeches and riding boots and a short coat, buttoned to the neck.

As he strutted across the plaza he waved familiarly and tossed several gold coins toward the mendicants he passed. The scramble for these coins was savage.

"What in God's name is that?" Guillaume asked.

"Fritz," said Abd al-Malik. "Is German, wealthy man. Fritz Amgott. Long time Tangier."

We watched Fritz until his little entourage disappeared down a narrow side street.

"What a ridiculous character," I mused to Guillaume. "That should be today's high point, don't you think?" But Guillaume was puzzled or distracted. With unusual agility he slipped through the crowd and began talking excitedly to a lad who had recovered one of the gold coins. After a lengthy bargaining session he produced sufficient douros to entice the coin away from the boy and returned with it to our table.

The coin was inscribed in a Gothic script I could not decipher, with two crossed forks at its center.

"What do you make of it?" he asked me. Abd al-Malik became quite excited and several of the musicians emerged from the bar to examine our souvenir.

"You must tell us more about this man Fritz," Guillaume insisted. A pipe was passed and Abd al-Malik, in his languorous and disjointed style, informed us of the popular legends surrounding Fritz Amgott.

He was of a wealthy German family, his father a friend of the Kaiser's, but he had displeased his father in some way and been banished to Tangier many years ago. After his wife's mysterious death he had become increasingly eccentric. He bought young boys. The uses to which he put them, though not explicitly elucidated by our storyteller, were apparently severe. Each month on the night of the full moon he held candlelit ceremonies with his vassals on the beach. Of the coins Abd al-Malik knew nothing except that Fritz used them to bribe local officials and occasionally tossed them to beggars. Over the years he had become in Tangier an accepted figure, never leaving and never changing.

Guillaume was fascinated by this tale. We had lingered for so long in an unproductive state of ennui that I could hardly blame him for grasping at this first scrap of the unusual.

"Where has Fritz gone now?" he asked.

"Down to beach. I show you."

Abd al-Malik led us through a series of winding alleys and paths, out of the central medina and onto a terrace overlooking the Atlantic. Hovels and caves and straw lean-tos dotted the steep cliffs running down to a long strand of sandy beach. Paths fit only for mountain goats descended from the casbah walls along these cliffs. Far down the beach we saw the waving palm fronds and the stern master with his boys.

"Can we reach that stretch of beach?" Guillaume asked.

Abd al-Malik grinned his imbecilic grin. "There is way. Through casbah, beneath walls. Tunnel."

We choked on the stench of dead animals and sewage in the tunnel, but the passage was mercifully brief and issued us forth in a brisk sea breeze halfway down the cliffs. From there we negotiated a narrow path to the beach.

Fritz and his entourage had disappeared down the beach where the cliffs were carved with caves and grottoes. Tall rocks stood along the shore. Guillaume wished to follow the lost procession, but Abd al-Malik refused.

"Fritz no good man," he explained. "Is only one God and Mohammed is his prophet. Some men believe Christian God. Fritz believes nothing. Not Allah, not Christian God."

We spent the remainder of the afternoon bathing in

the breakers and taking shelter behind a large rock when the western sun became too intense. By the time we retraced our steps up the cliff and through the stinking tunnel I had nearly forgotten why we had gone to that beach. But Guillaume did not forget.

For several days we returned to that state of pleasant detachment from all continuity yet concentrated engagement in each moment afforded by our prodigious consumption of hashish. We searched the bazaars and shops for masks similar to the one worn by Sébastien. Our occasional sorties into the European quarter indicated that nothing had changed. Returning from the European sector one evening I was convinced we were being followed, but nothing ever came of it.

On the day of the full moon in July, Guillaume reminded me that Fritz would be holding one of his ceremonies that night and insisted we return to the beach and observe him. I expressed my usual prudence but he assured me it would be an amusing diversion and nothing more.

The long afternoon left me nearly insensate over my mint tea in the busy main square of the old city. We dined on wrinkled black olives, raisins, and stewed turnips with couscous grain. Two hours before dusk we set out.

After passing through the tunnel beneath the casbah walls and trekking down the steep path, we reached the beach and sat for a few moments squinting into the final glimmerings of the sun setting over the Atlantic. Then we walked down the beach in the direction the procession had disappeared the week before.

It seemed we would be unrewarded in our search for an evening's entertainment, and I had begun to view with growing trepidation the moonlit ascent of that narrow path and passage of the foul tunnel back into the medina. We had never prowled far from our hotel after dark. I suggested that we turn back while some deepening green remained in the sky, but Guillaume assured me the full moon would provide all the illumination our homeward journey required. Ill-comforted by this allusion to full moons I trudged along the deserted beach; the warm sand squished through my toes and ran across the tops of my feet.

Suddenly Guillaume raised his hand and motioned me to halt. From the next grotto, behind a jagged rock perhaps thirty feet high, came a faint light and a droning chant in high boyish voices. We moved stealthily to the rock and peered around it.

The grotto's entrance was marked by an arch of palm fronds. Beneath this stood a monstrous bronze assault cannon, aimed seaward, with a pyramid of eight-pound balls piled beside it. The cannon was guarded by a pair of lads in the habits of a Franciscan brotherhood.

Within the grotto itself, hollowed by sea and wind into a semicircular chapel with small prayer niches cleft in the rock face, stood a chanting choir of a dozen boys. Candles burned on ornate Gothic candelabra. These boys also wore monk's robes and had daubs of red smeared on their cheeks and foreheads.

The depths of the grotto had been meticulously steened in brick and painted white. In this glowing mew of reflected moon and candlelight sat Fritz Amgott. He was dressed in a corsetlike military tunic decorated with iron crosses and stars, epaulettes over his shoulders, and a spike-topped German helmet on his head. He sat in his knee breeches and tall black boots on a fan-chair throne of bent reeds. His face bore a cold, imperious expression. His eyes avidly followed his coterie through their paces.

We remained for some moments hidden behind our rock and observed in utter stupefaction the scene unfolding before us. My inclination was to giggle and be gone, but Guillaume pulled me back into the cliff shadows and slowly we edged forward until we could see across the grotto.

The chanting ceased and the boys commenced crawling about in the sand on all fours. A terrified urchin of about ten, wearing only a cloth tied at the waist, was brought in and kowtowed before the master on his throne. Daubs of red were applied to his face, his loincloth was stripped away, and he was made to crouch naked before Fritz.

The candles were extinguished. By moonlight the man rose and approached the cowering boy. Fritz drew a switch from his belt and snapped it across the boy's face. When he cried out he was whipped again, but this time he swallowed his pain and remained silent. The switch was applied to his buttocks until red lines crisscrossed the brown flesh. Fritz then grew tender and caressed the boy's shoulders. He drew him up by the armpits and kissed his forehead, then knelt so that they were at the same level and fondled him.

In that instant I heard an intaken breath behind me and the sound of feet rustling the sand. Turning toward Guillaume, I saw his eyes widen as strong fingers gripped my arms and I was cudgeled twice upon the head.

We were quickly surrounded by several Moors whose hoods totally obscured their faces. They had come upon us silently and now forced us against the cliffs, tied our hands with thongs, and pulled blindfolds over our eyes. We were slapped about to subdue any inclinations we might have towards resistance or flight, and then tossed down in the sand.

The commotion of our scuffle with these masked Moors had disrupted the service. I heard the confused voices of the boys' choir and above them the brittle tones of Fritz calling out for them to resume singing and screaming instructions in German and Arabic.

I thought I heard him say, "take them to your master, take them away from here." The choir's dirge began again as a knee crunched into the small of my back and my face was forced down into the sand. The cudgel fell once more against my skull and I gagged on a mouthful of sand and something warm and wet in my throat.

XIII

My memories of that night consist solely of sensations: my eyes remained blindfolded, my mind numbed by the gnawing fear that each pair of rough hands clutching at me would be followed by the cool slice of steel at my throat. Unable to think clearly, I inhabited a world of sounds, smells, and tactile impressions as we traveled by a variety of conveyances from the beach at Tangier to the encampment where we found ourselves the next morning.

Clattering hooves and wagon wheels provided a syncopated background for the voices of our abductors and the occasional whimper or groan from Guillaume, who lay beside me in our cart. The Moors' words came in short bursts, half-swallowed glottal closures and gruff plosives—more a series of grunts and snorts than a proper language. None of them addressed us directly in French or English.

Distilled throughout the night was the smell of our wagon, of our abductors in their wool cloaks, and brief waftings of countryside fragrance. These penetrated the strong aroma of brine and dust in the cart, which had been used for hauling fish or seaweed at Tangier, I surmised. My head rested on wool, probably a folded *jilaba*. Its reek of human sweat was so heavy I tried for some time to shift my head or hold it aloft. Finally I sank onto this vile pillow and accepted its meager comfort. Each jolt or bump pummeled my kidneys and shoulders and I was repeatedly slammed against the side of the cart, scraping my elbows and forearms, in which I found dozens of little splinters the next day.

And so the night passed: we were slung over shoulders and hauled up the cliffs; forced to stumble blindly over rocky, uneven streets; prodded when we tarried and dragged across the ground when we fell. Finally we were transferred to a donkey-drawn cart for the remainder of our journey. Several times we halted and I heard voices raised in argument. When I tried to call Guillaume, strong fingers seized my shoulder and a harsh monosyllable communicated the message to be silent.

I sensed that one or two of the company wished to be done with us immediately while the others, a prevailing majority I was thankful to note, felt it their duty to deliver us somewhere, presumably to a superior.

I spent the first half of the journey trying with my tongue and lips to clear the sand from my mouth. This was a painstaking process without water or the use of one's hands, but slowly the saliva came and I worked the sand over my lips and let it run down my chin. I dared not spit for fear of losing the precious saliva, and so, like a dying man in the desert, I recycled the thick moisture again and again until gradually my scraped mouth was cleared of most of the grains of sand.

Shortly before dawn we rested and the blindfolds were removed. I was permitted to rinse my mouth with water and moisten my eyes and chafed cheeks.

We stood in the foothills of a low mountain range. The rising sun cast its first reflected rays across the mountaintops behind us. A long rocky basin dotted with small patches of dark trees disappeared in a pale pastel haze in the west. A single narrow wadi roadway led back down the hills and westward into the distance.

We had stopped in a green valley where almond and carob trees grew by a little spring. The almonds were in fruit and one of the company picked and husked a few, using his pointed brown teeth to pull away the outer shell. He tossed the almonds to us and we ate. The meat was tender and sweet and its juice ran down my throat like exquisite nectar. I had never tasted a fresh almond before. The sweetness of the nut and the glorious sunrise colors glimmering up over this surprisingly verdant land dipped in the dew of dawn filled me with tranquillity, despite our precarious situation, and I felt ready to slump down beneath a carob tree and drift into a pleasant sleep. The brilliant intensity of dawn evoked in me a sense of the beauty of life, even as it was lived by these brutal savages, even at this unlikely moment. The world turned from indigo in the west to lavender and coral while the cragged mountains above us tore into the pale sky.

Our captors spread rugs on the earth by the spring, then bowed toward the rising sun in the east, muttering their prayers. They disregarded us entirely, but I don't know where we could have run. There was nothing to do but watch their morning ritual and be thankful for a moment's respite.

When we set out again we were allowed to sit up in the cart and the blindfolds were discarded. I could not imagine why they had been kept on at night. We slowly ascended a narrow rock path through low chaparral and a prickly stubble of hedge. Far away I heard a jackal or coyote howl, and overhead a flock of kites circled, black dots above the mountaintops.

Rounding a bend I felt the morning sun flush in my face, and then we dove down a narrow defile between sharp rock faces. This emerged in a widening gorge, perhaps a creek in spring, now parched and pebbled and lined by dried oleander. The cart rocked unmercifully.

Suddenly we were in a little valley. A small encampment was pitched along its eastern wall among stunted oaks, almonds, and carobs. Thin wisps of smoke drifted over a half-dozen tents and a pair of semipermanent wood structures, and several men tended the donkeys and horses hitched to one side of the encampment.

A pair of ambassadors came out to meet us. They were of darker complexion than our captors and wore small knit caps while our guards' headdress was a wound turban. After a brief consultation a tall man with a trimmed dark beard emerged from the larger of the wood structures. A single eyebrow stretched across his forehead, like a crease from endless pondering. He had a quiet manner, an almost sad expression, but a cruel mouth within his beard. He did not smile but commanded instant respect. He wore a white robe and yellow slippers with curled, pointed toes and flattened heels.

This man examined us and asked in French our names and nationalities. We answered him, and nodding, he dismissed us, and we were taken to the smaller wood hut. Already the sun had entered the valley. Its heat struck my shoulders and neck and drew out some of the pain and fatigue residing there. Without a word our abductors shoved us into the hut, slammed the door, and were gone.

A figure lay sleeping on a reed mat in the corner. It was a man cloaked in a tartan kaftan, unlike anything I had seen worn by a Moor, with a linen shirt drawn over his head and a pair of English hunting boots set neatly at the foot of his mat. Pale feet and long toes extended from the tartan kaftan, and I thought I saw a single eye open briefly when our escort brought us in.

"Well," I said to Guillaume, "here we are in the mountains." He did not share my lightheartedness.

"I ache all over." Guillaume grimaced. "Last night was horrible."

"Yes," I nodded. "But we could be dead."

"Mmmm," he groaned and wiped gingerly at his puffy face. "I guess they want to torture us first. I would rather be dead than endure any more trips like last night," he said.

"Goodness, you do exaggerate a trifle, chaps," came a voice speaking English from the folds of the tartan kaftan, and a thin, mustachioed, freckled face appeared. "If they'd meant to do you in they'd surely have done so by now." He sat up and stretched.

"Then you don't think they intend to kill us?" I asked in English.

"I shouldn't guess so," came the reply. "When they want to kill you they make short work of it. None of this touring about the countryside, you know. Besides, those didn't look like any of Raysuni's lads who brought you in. Berbers of the High Atlas if I'm not mistaken." He smiled and stood up.

"But isn't this the Atlas where we are now?"

"Oh, hardly. These are the Jabala mountains, just a small range in the Rif running east to west below Tangier and Ceuta. The Atlas are far to the south." Guillaume groaned, but the man chattered along quite amiably. "I must say this is a jolly surprise of a morning. Cellmates, and English-speaking ones at that." He came forward, hand extended. "Harry Maclean's the name. Sorry, but you caught me unawares."

We shook hands all around; Guillaume grumbled a greeting in French and collapsed in the corner.

"Your friend seems a bit done in," Maclean commented, and I nodded. "Don't meet many Americans in Africa. Certainly not here at Raysuni's."

"I suppose not," I said. "But who is this Raysuni?"

"Why, he is your host, as it were, your captor and your master so long as you remain within his purview.

Moulay Ahmed ben Mohammed al-Raysuni is a *sharif*, a descendant of the Prophet so they say, through Moulay Idris, the patron saint of Morocco. Actually he's a brigand, a cattle robber, a murderer, an intriguer, and a fakir of immense proportions."

"But what can he want with us?"

"I haven't the foggiest, my dear fellow. I don't know who you are or what you know, but you must be worth something to him or you'd be dead long since."

"What sort of something?"

"That depends on what you know and who you are. Don't you understand what's happened to you?"

"I guess I don't."

"You've been kidnapped." I puzzled over this. "And where there is a kidnapping there is a ransom. Mind you, when Raysuni nabbed your countryman Ian Perdicaris a few years back he received twenty thousand pounds and the governorship of the province of Tangier in ransom." I gaped at this. "Quite true, quite true," he continued. "But then Perdicaris is a man of substantial wealth and influence here, while you two are, if I am not mistaken, newcomers. Frightfully puzzling, isn't it?"

"And you?" I asked. "Do you work with this Raysuni?"

"Work with him, ha. Oh, quite. No, lads, I've been kidnapped as well and held for two months now. That's right, you look surprised, but Raysuni is a stubborn beast. He wants power in the Rif, and things are not so simple as they were when he took Perdicaris. Not so simple at all. You see, I was sent by the Sultan to negotiate with Raysuni, being familiar with him and trusted by both sides, insofar as any non-Moslem is trusted. But Raysuni had other plans, and when I arrived at the meeting place, dressed as you see in my best tartans, he whisked me off to this dreadful camp and it has been my home since. Best prepare yourselves for a long summer in the mountains unless you have some valuable information or service to render." I stared and shook my head. "Not the fanciest digs, but I'm well looked after. Would you care for some tea?" I nodded. "And for your friend as well? Chin up, old chap, I'm at this two months now and none the worse for it. Shed a few pounds I don't doubt, but not much else. You'll find Raysuni a most obliging host. He even had some of my own tea brought in from Tangier. Well then, have a seat and I'll brew the tea. We'll have to share a cup, I'm afraid, but one can't have everything, can one?"

Guillaume roused himself and we squatted around a small fire while Harry Maclean heated water and poured it over tea leaves he had taken from a small leather pouch on a belt inside his kaftan.

"Tell me the circumstances of your abduction and perhaps I can find a clue as to what's afoot."

I described our surveillance of Fritz and his boys on the beach, our sudden attack by the hooded men, and the long night's passage to Raysuni's encampment.

"Oh dear, Fritz. Poor Fritz. A nasty bit of business, that one is. Surprised the Berber lads ventured near him. A very superstitious lot these Berbers: show them a lame leg they'll call you a prophet, but fool around with little boys and they'll stand well clear. Evil spirits. Spooked, the lot of them. Mind you, they'll engage in that sort of horseplay themselves, but for a Christian, who is well on the way toward damnation as it is, to fool about, well, there's not much hope. No, I rather doubt your Berbers have to do with old Fritz. It is quite a puzzle, isn't it?" He seemed thoroughly pleased by the puzzle and the diversion it provided him. While we drank our tea from the shared cup he ruminated over possible reasons for our abduction and told us something of his own circumstances.

He had come to Morocco in the 1880s as military adviser to the father of the current Sultan, taken a liking to the country, and remained as a permanent fixture of the British mission and personal representative at the Sultan's court, to which he apparently had full access. This, however, carried little weight with Raysuni other than in bargaining over the ransom for his deliverance. I did not mention the reasons we had come to Morocco. Maclean's expression when I told him we were tourists displayed irony and amusement—but not a shred of belief.

"Come now, you don't expect an old Morocco hand like myself to believe that. Surely you know the situation here. Europeans are leaving, not arriving, and those who stay behind should consider themselves fortunate to be kidnapped by Raysuni rather than torn apart by the frightful mobs of tribesmen rampaging about the countryside. No, Raysuni, scurvy brigand that he is, is at least an educated man. He is familiar with international politics and knows the value of human life on the European market: where it is, I must say, a good bit dearer than on the Moroccan exchange." He chuckled over this and poured another cup of tea.

We drank our tea in silence. I was thankful for Maclean's companionship and the opportunity to converse in English and I busied myself picking the slivers of wood from my hand and forearm. Guillaume toyed restlessly with his torn shirt ends and steadfastly declined any offer of friendship.

"I suspect your friend is a bit peckish after the all-night trek," Maclean offered with a kindly glance. "A bowl of their porridge should help, and that will be along shortly." Guillaume scowled at him and glanced meaningfully at me. "Well, lads, be as mysterious as you wish, but I think I might be able to extend a hand, so to speak, if you'd at least take me partially into your confidence. I know a thing or two about Morocco."

I was prepared to touch upon our interests and the events in Paris which had led us south, but Guillaume spoke first.

"And what possible good can you do us? You are a captive yourself and have been for, what did you say, two months now?"

"Quite right."

"And you seem rather nonchalant about your condition."

"Hah." Maclean loosed a shrill, whistling laugh and covered his mouth. "Nonchalant? Hardly that, not even resigned. But after two months one gets used to most anything. Now the first few days were quite ghastly, what with half Raysuni's lads wanting to do me in, and me stuck in a damp little hole without a change of clothes, covered with vermin. But Raysuni is a sensible chap and treats me well enough. And I know there are people working for my release. Only Raysuni is demanding so much. He's grown obstinate as his situation grows more untenable. There's not much poor Lousy can do."

"Lousy?"

"Sir Gerald Lowther. Our man in Tangier. We call him Lousy, though he's really not at all. Quite a decent fellow. They call me Qaid Maclean, though I'm surely no *qaid*."

I was about to ask what a *qaid* was when our breakfast arrived: a millet porridge served with sour milk and garnished with raisins. My spirits had lifted when Maclean returned to the subject of our presence in Morocco.

"What I cannot figure," he exclaimed after I had revealed a few essentials of our adventures in Paris, "is why they should kidnap you. What possible ransom can they exact? Now, I am a valuable bit of baggage, and no doubt of it. But you two? Rich uncles back in the States perhaps? You're not related to a family of arms manufacturers, are you? Raysuni's always alert for a fresh supply of guns and ammo." I shook my head. "Pardon my saying so, but you surely cannot know anything of value to these Moors. It must lie with the Berbers who brought you in. I think you'll find that Raysuni's is merely a waystation for you. Perhaps you'll reach your Atlas mountains yet."

"We'll be dead before we ever reach the mountains," lamented Guilaume.

"Really, Guillaume," I interjected. "Whatever did you expect when you came down here? You act as though all is over. From what Harry here says we should take heart that we've survived this long and may well be on our way to the Atlas."

"I suppose you are right, Clayton Peavey," he said. "But I hate this feeling that things are out of my control. We are no longer acting, we are being acted upon."

"I felt that way in Paris."

"But I didn't. Normally I rely upon my instincts to guide my actions, but here those instincts have utterly abandoned me. Events don't make sense, and I feel lost."

"Well, that makes two of us, if that is any comfort to you."

Guillaume shook his head forlornly. Had our danger been less palpable his vacillations between reckless enthusiasm and simpering complaints would have been quite ridiculous. As it was, my empathy overshadowed my amusement.

"It bothers me not knowing what people are saying," he continued. "And from their eyes you can never tell what these Moors are thinking. It is as if we were surrounded by creatures of a different species and not men at all."

"Oh, they are men all right," said Maclean. "But in a sense you're right, they are of a different world. More different than you can possibly imagine. And totally unpredictable because of it."

"And that is the frightening part," Guillaume agreed with him.

"No, my French friend," said Maclean in a flat, phlegmatic tone. "The frightening thing is that mercy toward one's enemies is weakness to the followers of Islam. You may receive your due, you may for one reason or another be treated kindly or even released, but you will never, never receive mercy. Don't expect it, don't ask it, don't beg for it, as that is the surest way to get your throat cut. Bear that in mind and you may just survive your visit to this embattled land."

We remained that day and through the next night in our wood hut with Qaid Harry Maclean. Guillaume hunched glumly on the floor, his fat legs splayed and his face filled with a look that said something had gone terribly wrong with his well-laid plans. His self-pity annoyed me. In time Maclean's good nature and plucky self-possession neutralized these hard feelings and eased even Guillaume's malaise. When our evening meal was served, much of the pain and fear of the previous night's ordeal had vanished. Maclean described the weakness of the young Sultan and his fondness for European toys and inventions, which Maclean had been among the first to provide. This had created suspicion in the eyes of his people that their divine lord—for the Sultan was as much a religious as a secular leader—had been corrupted. Pretenders had sprung up all around the country: Raysuni was a mere brigand and a minor problem, but another man in this region was calling himself Moulay Mohammed (the Sultan's idiot brother, long since locked away in a fortress in the south) and traipsing about the countryside on a she-donkey performing conjuring tricks and arousing the people. He had gained control of substantial parts of the northeast.

"But the real danger lies in the south," Maclean explained. "It is rumored that the Sultan's true brother, Moulay Abd el-Hafiz, is organizing an insurrection with the support of the great Berber *qaids* of the Atlas. Should that occur, Abd el-Aziz will be in a most difficult position. You see, none of the other pretenders could receive the sanction of the *ulama* of Fez, without which a sultan cannot rule. Abd el-Hafiz just might. And that would undo all our efforts over the past ten years. Hafiz is an independent man, a fervent Moslem, and will not tie himself to any colonial power." He leaned back and sipped his tea. "Yes, the days are gone when we could play cricket in the Sultan's palace at Fez. I remember when the first bicycles arrived. Aziz is a child, really, and he bought a dozen of everything. There was a Scottish dentist at the court that spring. He and I organized bicycle polo games. The Sultan wobbled about on his bicycle while slaves took the ball from the rest of us and placed it where he could give it a good whack as he rode by. What that foolish man didn't bring to his court: grand pianos, theatrical costumes from Covent Garden, a hansom cab, printing presses, a passenger lift for a palace with only one floor. All of it purchased and then set aside to rust or decay."

"No wonder his people have grown tired of him," I said. "It sounds as though he is ill-advised."

"Yes, I suppose he is, but Morocco must come up through the centuries. She must enter this twentieth century and recognize the changes in the world. None of us can remain what we once were." He gazed at me, in his eyes a soft glow of nostalgia for the days of Empire fading, and said: "Nothing can save Abd el-Aziz. When the outrages began it was said, 'Our sultan does not know.' They continued and now people say, 'Our sultan does not care,' or even 'There is no sultan.' Soon there will be another."

The next morning we were awakened before dawn and led from our cell. We left Maclean asleep in his tartan kaftan without so much as a goodbye.

A pair of donkeys and a group of eight mounted warriors awaited us. I could not recognize our original abductors among them, for now they wore long white hoodless robes and turbans in emerald green knotted about their heads. Several carried obsolete muzzle-loading Bouchfers, and the leader had a shiny new Remington rifle strapped across his back.

Raysuni padded forth in his yellow slippers to see us off. He smiled mockingly as we rode forth from his bleak encampment in the Rif valley.

For ten days we traveled along the base of a gradually ascending mountain range. To our right the submontane bluffs and gullies diminished into an ashen haze over the wide interior valley of Morocco. We could see small scattered villages and clusters of nomadic tribesmen far in the distance below us.

I had endured many a humid Washington summer but I had never known such a dry, searing heat. Our abductors proceeded at a steady clip, and we, poor horsemen that we were, tried unsuccessfully to keep pace. By the third evening I could barely sit down. Guillaume's agony exceeded mine: he had sores on his thighs and rump and eventually had to be strapped to his donkey like a piece of luggage for fear that he would pass out and fall off.

As we progressed south and the mountains loomed higher above us we passed groups of tribesmen whose complexions were paler than those in the north. Respectful representatives came out from the villages to speak with the leader of our pack, and groups of young men came down from the nearby hills, many of them armed with ancient rifles of dubious utility but ready for war. Throughout this journey I saw troops of mounted warriors heading south to join the Sultan's brother at Marrakesh. Several times haggard bands of soldiers attacked our caravan. Our white-robed escort repulsed these attacks, killing those soldiers who did not flee.

On the fifth day the heat grew worse and I clung deliriously to my donkey. Our captors rode far ahead, making no effort to guard us. Surely an effort to escape would have meant instant death either from the elements or from some less benevolent group of Moors. I had begun to look upon our escort as protectors and realized our only hope for survival lay in reaching their ultimate destination.

One afternoon we passed a slaughtered soldier by the road. His body was beginning to discolor and swell beneath the sun. A piece of fruit had been wedged in the man's mouth, both his eyes gouged out, and his fingerless hands staked to the ground. Jackals or vultures had disembowled him. One of the Berbers called our attention to him, pointing and laughing as if to say, "That's what you'll look like soon enough."

Toward evening of the following day we began to climb into the central massif of the Atlas, which now towered far above us. My eyes itched from the dry heat and some of the peaks appeared to be snow-capped, even in midsummer. I tried to rub this mirage from my eyes but it persisted.

We worked our way up a rocky trail through mountains utterly devoid of vegetation. Hundreds of small boulders were scattered over this bare landscape. We crossed a saline sea and followed a saline riverbed that ascended sharply through a narrow gorge. Needle-pointed spires of rock towered two hundred feet above this river of salt. Vultures, ravens, and kites circled the spires like birds of prey over some haunted medieval church.

As the setting sun at our backs turned the mountains from ocher to pale rose to lilac we stood beneath two great peaks. One of our guards, in apparent awe himself, pointed and named the place. "Jebel Ghat," he croaked and waved his hand through the air. The shadows and heat waves shimmered around his hand as it passed dreamlike before me. Then my eyes strained through the dwindling light to make out what stood on a tall bluff beneath the peak of Jebel Ghat, at the gateway to the pass over these mountains. Slowly I focused and my mind cleared as I realized this was no desert illusion but a great fortress, filling my field of vision, turreted and bartizaned with countless crenellations running along its balconies like missing teeth in a fell smile, rooftops at a dozen different levels and hundreds of arched windows and doorways facing west into the setting sun. A few cork and carob trees stood beneath the fortress walls, and tufts of desert grass trembled in the warm breeze blowing down the bluff.

We approached this fortress quickly and several mounted sentinels came out to meet us, dressed in white with turbans and carrying gleaming Winchester repeaters. As we approached, the dimensions of the fortress, though dwarfed by the mountain peaks all around, astounded me and I wanted to rush to the wall and touch its pink surface with my hands to convince myself it was real. Above us on the turrets and watchtowers a few heads observed us crossing the bare plain before the fortress.

At the double gates, bossed in brass and arched

more than twenty feet tall, armed sentinels stood attended by mammoth black slaves. The doors swung open and our captors escorted us into the casbah of Telouet, the eagle's nest and seat of power and authority for Qaid Madani al-Glaoui, lord of the Atlas.

XIV

Inside the gates of that vast citadel our escort delivered us to a brace of menacing guards dressed in long white robes sashed in scarlet. Their heads were shaved except for single side-queues which fell almost to one shoulder.

We were tethered together and led like a pair of hobbling, aged donkeys through the passageways and atria of the palace. Many of the delighted and amused inhabitants stopped to watch our pitiful progress through their city. Several times Guillaume collapsed, nearly dragging me down with him, and the spectators laughed and applauded. He was rudely jerked to his feet by our guards. And so we passed into Telouet.

A bustle of activity swept all around us: soldiers cleaning and preparing weapons, artisans repairing crumbling sections of the walls, slaves hauling rock blocks on sagging carts, women bearing water jugs and baskets of food across mosaic floors. This intensity contrasted sharply with the universal lethargy I had observed throughout Morocco. It suggested a state of preparedness or a moment of crisis. Harsh calls from the crowds thrummed on my thick head and nightmare apparitions swirled before my clouded vision: oval faces broken in laughter, the icy stares of turbaned warriors, donkeys braying, and the unending maze of half-crumbling, half-constructed walls and mismatched architectural styles. High above us on the crenellated battlements, lookouts stood starkly outlined against the evening sky. On a tall platform I saw a tremendous bronze Krupp cannon, aimed through a deep machicolation down the valley, a redoubtable presence which must have filled any enemy with awe and made this fortress even more impregnable. There could be no rear attack from the east, where the peaks soared upward thousands of feet.

With the laughter of our tormenters ringing about us we were led down from the main level of the fortress along crumbling steps on which Guillaume was unable to retain his footing. I was blinded in the dark but felt a stony coolness at my neck which eased my delirium and slightly clarified my swimming thoughts.

Along a narrow corridor grilled openings dropped into deep dungeons where I could imagine prisoners, perhaps myself, languishing for years: I heard their voices echoing up out of the depths, out of the past. The architecture became coldly elemental as we descended and at last a low door was opened to us. We were untied and shoved into a small dark room with a single window, no more than a foot across, high up near the ceiling.

Guillaume fell prone on the dank stone floor and lay motionless while I leaned against the wall. As my eyes adjusted to the light I noticed a shape on the floor across our tiny cell and for a moment recalled Harry Maclean. Something in the posture of this shape told me it was no chipper British cellmate to amuse and inform us on our predicament.

Closer examination confirmed the horrifying validity of my impression. It was a man's body, not long dead, a pool of coagulating blood spread beneath it. He had been mutilated and brutally flogged across his back, which was turned to us, then decapitated and left in our cell. I crouched against the wall and retched drily till my stomach felt it would burst. The body was naked, but he had been so severely flogged that strips of his linen shirt had been beaten into the flesh, which had closed over them, and still clung to his bare back. I crawled over to Guillaume and fell into a delirious sleep against him.

I woke to find Guillaume twitching feverishly beneath me. His left hand clawed his face, and when I tried to shake him awake his convulsions grew worse. In despair I began to weep; there was nothing else to do. Sitting between a dying Guillaume and the unmentionable form behind me I clutched at myself, shivering in the moist dungeon, and tried to take what little stock there was to take of our situation.

We had arrived in the Atlas, of that there was no doubt, in a mountain fastness comparable to the palace of a thousand and one nights, though I dreaded that I should spend even one night beside that rotting corpse and the unpleasant creatures it would attract from the depths of the fortress. I imagined rats gnawing at my toes and abruptly slipped past consciousness, numbed to the terrible sensations. I sat, eyes open but unable to focus my mind long enough to complete a thought.

Like the faintest fading sun of hope I heard Harry Maclean's words: "If they meant to kill you they'd have done with it." No, they wanted something from us. But what could we possibly give them? In gloomy resignation I slumped against Guillaume, wiped the congealed spittle from his parched face, and tried to rouse him with a word. He twitched a single convulsive twitch down the length of his body and lay still. I caressed his face for a moment, then sank into unconsciousness at his side.

I don't know how long we lay like that, but each time I drifted out of sleep it seemed days had passed, my body screamed so for peace. Finally the door to our cell was opened and a man with a flat smile and few teeth behind it entered. He brought water, which he splashed on our faces, and a dish of ground root, whitish and bitter to the taste, which he forced us to eat. When he returned in a few moments the food had revived me considerably and Guillaume also was sitting up, pale and dreary, but alive.

Again we were tethered together and led through the underbelly of the mountain fortress, then upward to ground level. It was night (perhaps the same night we had arrived) and the feverish activity had not abated. Groups of mounted men were deploying in the central courtyard while others stood inspecting several Gatling guns and fastening small emerald insignia to their white cloaks. Many of the men went bareheaded within the city and the single side-queue seemed the common, though by no means universal, hairstyle. The women mingled freely with the men, wore brightly colored dresses, and went unveiled, in sharp contrast to Tangier.

We were hauled into the palace chambers over blue and green mosaic fields through guarded hallways. I thought I heard running water, though I saw no fountain. The interior of Telouet was a mishmash of Islamic styles with bizarre superannuated European objects incongruously displayed—a golden chandelier, a Gothic German clock obviously inoperative, a Flemish tapestry. These grotesque, inappropriate items leapt out at me as though imbued with a living force, like my own, wishing to escape from this place.

Through a winding passageway and double set of doors we entered a tall vaulted room. Colonnaded in black marble along one side, it was illuminated by hundreds of thick candles. Black slaves knelt near the doorway, half-clothed odalisques lounged on a low divan, and several distinguished men in long rich cloaks stood quietly at the room's end. Before them a tall, thin man in an elaborately wrapped turban sat serenely with his hands folded in his lap. His slanting, heavy-lidded black eyes stared across at us. I could not suppress the recurring impression that I was in someone else's fairy tale, that this was not really happening to Clayton Peavey, and I believe this detachment enabled me to control my fear.

Our guards kowtowed before the man with black eyes and pushed us to the floor, where we remained, face down, for some moments while they conferred with their master. One of the distinguished elders motioned us to rise and approach the throne. We did so, haltingly and awkwardly, still tethered together like animals.

At closer view the man seated on the throne had an almost ascetic pale face and delicate features. His mouth turned down sharply beneath a narrow mustache. He appeared fierce yet intelligent, and his dark eyes gazed at us without rancor but with a kind of vague annoyance which was matched by the impatience in his deep voice. He spoke to us in excellent French.

"You have come far to visit me at Telouet," he said. "Monsieur Malaimé and the American, Monsieur Peavey." He touched his mouth with an extended forefinger and eyed an aide, who scurried off into the shadows. "As you may have observed, we are quite busy just now. A most inconvenient time for guests. The war of purification has been declared. The old blood feuds will be set aside in the cause of Islam, for the *amazigh* are roused from their long slumber. Soon we shall come down from the mountains and reclaim the land of Moulay Idris from you and your countrymen and their despicable underlings at Fez." His thin lips curled down as he spoke and he seemed to taste the displeasure thoughts of these enemies brought him. His lids lifted and once more he gazed on us with cruel amusement, a touch of annoyance, but no real malice. "So what am I to do with you? Scheming intruders in our land." He paused a moment. "You should not die too quickly, I think. That would not do at all. You must be made to regret deeply your intervention in matters that are of no concern to you, that are far weightier than you could imagine in your foolish play in Paris." My astonishment at this statement drew a reaction from him. "Yes, Monsieur Peavey, I know a good deal about your activities, remarkable as that may seem to you. More than I ever wished to know. I am not isolated, though my casbah may appear remote to you. I understand your European meddling in my country quite well and I know your evil intentions for us. But Abd el-Hafiz and the great *qaids* of the south have declared the holy war, and we shall lead the *mujahudin* against those who have lost the blessing of Allah, and vanquish them, and restore the power of grace to our lord the Sultan. But perhaps you do not wish to hear these things?" I opened my mouth to speak but only a feeble croak emerged from deep in my ravaged throat. The man laughed. "You see, there is no God but Allah and he does not wish the infidels to speak in the presence of Madani al-Glaoui." At his name many of those in attendance kowtowed again, but I stood my ground and managed to scratch out the words: "Why have you brought us here?"

"Why have you come?" He grew angry. "Interfering and delving into our affairs. I brought you here so that I should know where you are. I would have preferred to see you in a shallow grave beneath the sun, but I must consider the needs and desires of others, on whom I still depend for certain necessities in our struggle. The circumstances at this moment remain unclear, and so it was suggested that you be kept alive and held in detention." He rubbed his temples and the heavy-lidded eyes narrowed. "Something does not fit and we must find the missing piece before you can be dispatched. So that is what we shall do. But now I shall let you return to your friend below, for he awaits you."

We began to hobble toward the door when he called

us back. Staring very hard at me, he said: "Tell me what became of the dancers with the mask and you may earn some measure of relief."

For the first time I sensed a vague awareness kindling itself within Guillaume. He raised his head and fixed Qaid Madani al-Glaoui in a frightened but perceptive gaze. Then he shook his head. "Think on it. Life in these halls can be far more unpleasant than a swift death."

Outside the throne room a soft breeze blew out of the mountains, ruffling the emerald banners atop the turrets of the great casbah. We were hurried below ground level, where everything was still and the light and heat no different at night than they had been at midday.

In our little cell a weak moonbeam struck the dried blood puddle which earlier had spilled directly beneath the dead man. He appeared to have slid further into a shadowed corner of the room, though this was hardly possible. Something in the body's posture startled me.

Guillaume leaned against the wall and stared blankly, as though worried not for his life but pondering the final words of the Berber chief and the incredible fact that what he wanted from us was information regarding the *saltimbanques* and Sébastien's mask. As we silently considered the implications of this I heard a slight movement behind me and the horrible corpse in the corner began to roll over. I shrank against the wall, prepared for a vision of death, a ghost, for anything but what I saw.

"What a ghastly spot," said a dry, scornful voice. "I say, no time to lose, lads. Let's be off."

XV

So it was in the depths of the casbah at Telouet, in a cell from which no escape seemed possible, that we first encountered Timothy Daunt.

He was a spare, sinewy man, freckled and fair but deeply burnished by long exposure to the Moroccan sun. He moved in a crouch across our little cell—his movement lithe and agile.

"We meet at last," he said without irony. "I reached Tangier shortly after your rather abrupt departure. Picked up your trail south of the Rif. You are much sought after, my young friends." A small bundle materialized from behind him and he unrolled two white linen *jilabas*. "You'll want to jettison your old togs and wear these, I think."

His astounding presence in that dungeon, and his blithe, confident manner, left us both gaping and speechless.

"Well, get on with it," he said. "This has all been quite neatly arranged, but the timing is a bit tricky. When the guard comes with your evening gruel we'll have our one chance to escape, and I intend to take it."

"Who are you?" Guillaume asked him. "What are you doing here?"

"I am your savior, monsieur," he said, introducing himself. "And I'm here, as any good savior, to lead you out of the darkness and into the light."

"Another Englishman," muttered Guillaume. "I can't move."

"Well, you'd bloody well better move," snapped Daunt. "Unless you prefer to be left here for the Glaoui's dogs to nibble on."

I finally regained my voice. "But how did you get here?" I asked. "And why are you—"

"Why am I risking my neck for your sake? An excellent question. I assure you I shall be rewarded for my part in this crude farce. Besides, it serves my purposes to be here." He paused and glanced at the door to our cell. "I entered Telouet disguised as a warrior from a neighboring tribe. I have friends within the fortress, though your warder is not among them. That's why I had to impersonate your wretched fellow inmate just now. But we simply must forgo the niceties until later."

"I don't understand this," complained Guillaume, and his head drooped onto his chest.

"You needn't understand. Just pull yourself together, slip into this nice hooded cloak, and be ready when the man returns with your supper. I have a cart waiting just down the mountain. We can discuss these matters there."

I helped Guillaume change clothes and we hid in the shadows at the back of our cell until we heard the guard's approach. When the door opened Daunt slipped a thin cord around the man's neck, and in a matter of seconds he lay strangled on the floor. We locked him in the cell and crept down the dark hallway deeper into the caverns of Telouet. Daunt was obviously familiar with the layout of the fortress, and he led us swiftly through a series of narrow, twisting passageways. I brought up the rear, urging Guillaume forward and listening anxiously for the echo of following footsteps.

"This will be a bit sloppy but it will have to serve as our private exit," Daunt explained in a whisper. He knelt by a low drainage sluice coated with a moist, mossy slickness. It was pitch black inside and we crawled down the slanting, slippery surface for about fifty yards. The moisture oozed through my *jilaba* at the knees and I cracked my head once on an overhanging stone.

The drainage sluice emptied into a dry moat running along the outside wall of the fortress. We huddled in the opening while Daunt peered left and right.

"We must wait for the sentries to pass," he cautioned us. My skull throbbed where I'd struck it. I clenched my eyes shut and helped Daunt support Guillaume, who tottered on his haunches and nearly fell out the end of the tunnel. Soon a pair of sentries passed along the far lip of the moat. When they had progressed beyond hearing we dropped out and clambered on our bellies across the ditch and up its far side.

"Just fall in behind me and keep your hoods up," Daunt told us, and we marched like a trio of guards in our white *jilabas* along the moat around Telouet. At the end of the fortress we turned and slunk along a narrow ledge between the sheer walls and a long slope of stone and shale. Daunt urged us down this slope and with a great clattering of loose stone we staggered down the hill, shale slipping beneath our feet in the darkness.

Guillaume pitched forward on his face and moaned in pain. Daunt scrambled back to him and together we set him upright. Blood flowed freely from his forehead into his eyes, and he lunged blindly down the last section of slate slope. In the distance I heard a hyena call. I glanced back at the crenellated smile along the top of the wall, but no sentry had heard our noisy descent.

"Well done. Not far to go now," Daunt told us as we paused panting at the edge of a bluff of hard-packed dirt and scattered brush. We edged sideways for several hundred feet, just within the shadow cast by the walls of Telouet.

"This is the tricky part," said Daunt, though not once during the escape did he seem genuinely fearful of failure. "We'll be exposed crossing this bluff. Do you think you can run?" he asked Guillaume. We wiped the blood from his face and eyes. A long, ragged gash ran up the center of his forehead, but he seemed to hear and understand Daunt's words and he nodded. "It's about a quarter mile to the cart but they'll have a clear view of us once we step out of the shadows. Luckily I arranged a new moon for this little escapade."

I could not imagine Guillaume running and pictured him sprawled in the middle of the bluff with gunshots raining down on him. Daunt's jaunty cockiness did little to raise my confidence. When he saw a sentry pass along the wall he gave a signal and we scampered among the brush and boulders across the bluff with our cloaks billowing around us. I stayed behind Guillaume, who lurched forward, constantly about to fall on his face but impelled by some force which kept him upright.

Behind a large rock, hidden from Telouet, we found a small, open cart, drawn by a single donkey and driven by a man in a dark cloak. He nodded to Daunt and we loaded Guillaume into the cart. A rug was thrown over us and we set out.

After a few minutes our driver threw back the rug. We were beyond range of the fortress and our escape from Telouet had been a success. Guillaume's head still bled, and Daunt tore a strip from his *jilaba* and wrapped it around the wound. He looked back toward the fortress, now no more than a square dark cloud looming among the crags of rock. No pursuing hoofbeats broke the steady clip-clop of our donkey along the road. Satisfied at last, Daunt leaned back against the wall of the cart and smiled.

"That seemed rather easy," I said.

"You would have preferred armed pursuit and obstructions?" He laughed at me.

Guillaume had passed out and was turning pale. We covered him with the rug. For about two hours we jounced along in the open cart. Daunt and I exchanged particles of conversation, laying the groundwork for a dialogue which would continue over several days, sparring lightly like two prizefighters not sure who has the more telling punch.

"I have visited Telouet before," he told me. "The war preparations served me well, for there are many warriors gathering from the surrounding mountains and I had little difficulty entering the fortress. Of course, I have friends within Telouet. Surely you have not already developed such respect for my facility that you believe I could enter and leave that fortress on my own? It was *arranged.*" He paused for effect. "I believe I even had the tacit agreement of Qaid Madani al-Glaoui for your escape. He was not altogether happy to have you as his guests just now."

"So he told us. But what is a *qaid?*"

"A *qaid* is a chief, a general, a master, a tyrant. Temporal power in the Atlas has consolidated recently into the hands of three great *qaids:* the M'touggi, the Goundafi, and the Glaoui. But the Glaoui are the greatest. They have dominated the mountains since they received the blessing of the Sultan Moulay Hassan some fourteen years ago . . . and a nasty 77-millimeter Krupp to go with it."

"But that fellow Maclean called himself a *qaid.* Surely—"

"Maclean? Good heavens, you've seen Sir Harry?"

"Yes. We were held overnight with him at a place called Raysuni's."

Daunt shook his head and chuckled. "Remarkable.

You lads manage to run up against the most unlikely situations. Walter Harris will be drooling for your story if I get you out of here in one piece."

"But this man Maclean?"

"Harry Maclean is court jester for the present Sultan. He came to Morocco as a military adviser to the Sultan's father, so they call him Qaid Maclean. But his time is past. The years of the *commis voyageurs* and the decadence at Fez are ending. It is the warrior princes like Madani al-Glaoui who hold the future of Morocco in their hands. Maclean is one of those people who tend to live exclusively in a glorious past. He has for as long as I've known him, and few Englishmen have been in Morocco longer than I. Harry accepts the present very dubiously, if at all, as an experimental model being examined for defects which he and his lot have the prerogative to reject if it displeases them." He gave me a keen, hard look which seemed to exclude me from his scornful judgments. "But that is not the case, is it?" I shook my head.

"And Raysuni, what about him? Maclean said he had kidnapped him."

"Yes, yes, but Raysuni is also a sideshow, living in the past when he could bargain with the Sultan. But the Sultan no longer has anything to give him, and Raysuni is ignorant of the international dimensions of Moroccan politics. Madani al-Glaoui is not."

"And what are the 'international dimensions of Moroccan politics'?" I parried his phrase, even adopting, as I often instinctively do, a slight British accent when speaking to him. I don't know if this is due merely to my liking for the care and precision with which the English use our language or is a self-conscious effort to ingratiate myself with an unfamiliar people. It seemed to amuse Daunt.

"You are a clever fellow, Peavey," he told me. "Much cleverer than I had expected. I shall enlighten you in the valley of the Ait-Mugri."

We had descended from the barren crags and boulder strewn bluffs beneath Telouet into a small valley. In the waning moonlight I saw patches of pine, twisted cork, and olive trees and three clusters of mud hovels on rock outcroppings spaced along the valley. We approached the central settlement, and several men with shaved heads and side-queues helped us carry the unconscious Guillaume into one of the mud huts.

We remained that night and for two days in the village of the Ait-Mugri, whom the conversant Timothy Daunt explained were a Berber tribe owing fealty to the master of Telouet but also under the protection of an aged marabout, a *sharif* like the Sultan's family descended from the Prophet, and therefore unassailable even to the power of Madani al-Glaoui. We were safe and could remain there unmolested until Guillaume recovered.

My injured companion displayed amazing resilience. As he convalesced and I rested and talked with Daunt, a strangely contemplative peacefulness overtook me. The dense, hanging stillness of this wooded valley, the heat waves rising from the packed earth, the dryness in my nose and throat became, rather than mortifying discomforts or counteragents to mental acuity, harmonious mollifiers which drained the stress of our recent abduction and left me unnaturally, inexplicably clearheaded.

The women of the Berber tribe, who shared a large measure of responsibility and authority in village life, ministered to us with gentle attention. This familiarity and ease between the sexes was at once startling and refreshing among Moors. We were befriended first by the children of the tribe: lovely girls with silken skin in shades from terracotta to pale fawn, boys with round faces and knotted side-queues who demonstrated stick tossing games and played native instruments for us.

The first night a young girl bathed Guillaume's head and two large red ants were applied to the wound. Their mandibles clipped over the gash and they were then neatly decapitated by a native nurse and the wound thus stitched. When I objected I was told the mandibles would weaken and fall out at about the time more conventional stitching would have to be removed.

While shaving Guillaume's head for this operation the girl offered to shave mine as well, and I accepted impulsively. We were given little wool caps to protect us from the sun. Perhaps my impulse was based upon subtle calculation, for after our adoption of the tribal hairdo the normal xenophobia of these mountain people disappeared and we were treated almost as members of the tribe. I have no doubt that Daunt, who spoke their dialect and with whom they were already on friendly terms, facilitated our integration enormously.

For two days we sat in their tiny village beneath the forbidding Atlas peaks. We ate sour milk and millet porridge, dried turnips and olives, and even a few striped rock squirrels which the Berber lads caught and roasted for us. Squirrel could never have tasted quite so good. As we recuperated we talked to Timothy Daunt.

"I came to Morocco in 1891 with the mission of Sir Charles Euan-Smith. Salisbury sent Sir Charles to conclude trade agreements with Moulay Hassan. That's the present Sultan's father, the same man who gave the Glaoui his Krupp. Euan-Smith was ill chosen for the task and the mission was a total failure, due in part to the intrigues and press campaign waged against it by the French. The same sort of avaricious behavior which has continued to this day." He glanced at Guillaume, who said nothing, being the least likely Frenchman to support the colonial policies of the Quai d'Orsay. "Be that as it may, Sir Charles beat a hasty retreat to the west counties, and I remained. I was sick of England, and from the very first I found something in this land which appealed to me. No ghastly layers of pretense and polish and well-mannered Victorian propriety. The Moors can be a cruel and difficult people, but they are what they are, and that can be quite useful once you've learned to recognize it."

"And what have you done here all these years?"

"Oh, quite everything. I've been a journalist, a trader and merchant representing a number of London firms, a translator and tour guide, a teacher of English, a cartographer, and an occasional subaltern with the British consulate."

"In other words, a spy," I said.

"Oh, hardly that, just versatile," he retorted forthrightly, and gleefully rubbed his knobby hands together. "I think you read too many novels, Clayton. No, nothing so romantic as that for old Timothy Daunt."

"Then how did you come to rescue us from Telouet?" I puzzled aloud. "Surely that was not the work of a cartographer and tour guide."

"No, it was not. But it was work for which I was uniquely qualified. As I told you, I have access to Telouet and have visited there before. And I am just sufficiently lacking in sound judgment or the desire for self-preservation to attempt it. The ideal combination, you see."

"But who commissioned you to do this?" I continued my cross-examination.

"No one *commissioned* it. Your governments will be pleased to have you back, of course; but I acted on my own."

"And what led you to Telouet?"

"You did."

"I don't understand."

"Apparently not. Let me try to explain." But his explanations did more to obscure than to clarify matters and were filled with the most captious and contradictory tales of international cartels, French penetration, German animosity, Islamic fervor, famine, monetary crisis, decadence, debt, internecine tribal strife, and—through it all—British helplessness to keep things on an even keel. I very soon lost interest in what he was saying. Guillaume, however, still grouchy, insisted on arguing.

"First you tell us it is the French who are trying to control Morocco, then that the Germans are behind the uprising, and all the time you claim to be the true friend of the Moroccan people. Yet clearly you are working for something larger. What is it?" he said.

"Being anti-French," Daunt taunted him, "is an old habit for me and easily fallen into. Nothing personal, you understand. Anglo-French hostility has been *the prime fact* of international life for many years. What with Fashoda and the rest even the recent *accorde* has left us in a state of suspended animosity, shall we say, but not genuine friendship. As for the Germans, while many of my countrymen admire them, I have seen enough of them in person to doubt that they will remain allied to anything other than their own inflated egos for longer than it suits them." As he launched into this tirade he rattled a handful of nuts and tossed them, like punctuation, into his mouth. "The important thing in life is not loyalty to one's bloody country. They're all the same, governments, and constantly changing." A nut here. "Who is Mr. Campbell-Bannerman to me? Not a damned thing. Never met the blighter and I hope I never do." Another nut. "My creed is loyalty to myself. To the standards I set for myself and no one else. That's why I stay in Morocco. Because I am allowed that freedom here, and I can do it straight out and not be bothered with a lot of condescension and obfuscation and excuses as I would be in Europe or Britain."

"But there I think you are mistaken," Guillaume told him. "Things are changing rapidly in Europe. It is a new century."

"But the same old world, I'm afraid. Thank you, no."

"It will never be the same old world again." This was a subject on which Guillaume often held forth, and he embraced it eagerly in the face of Daunt's scrupulous skepticism. "The changes today are elemental. In the past they have been mere surface alterations on the same, enduring substance. Now time, space, and matter itself are being re-examined."

"I see," scoffed Daunt. "And the conclusions?"

"Have not been reached. It is a dynamic process in which Clayton and myself and many others, artists and scientists alike, are engaged. Much has changed since you left Europe, Monsieur Timothy."

"And I have followed those changes with avid interest, though from afar," he replied. "Yet on my few visits to dear old England and the continent I have encountered the same enveloping claustrophobia of Victorian mentality which denies nature and veils reality." He paused a moment. "Here these things are not hidden."

I remarked that the veil seemed a rather pronounced aspect of Moroccan culture and pointed out that Queen Victoria was dead.

"Oh, is she?" he smirked. "You don't say? I hadn't heard."

I shrugged but his discreet smile reassured me of the strengthening bond between us. I was enjoying our leisurely dialogue with Daunt and felt deeply indebted to him, but I could not overcome my suspicions or bring myself to confide in him about our involvements, past and present. I took this opportunity to return to the subject of most pressing interest to me. "Why," I implored him once more, "did you miraculously appear in that dungeon at Telouet?"

"I seem incapable of convincing you that I am my own man. It suited me, that is why. I wanted to meet you chaps, having heard so much about you. I wanted to visit my old friends the Ait-Mugri here and to see the extent of Madani al-Glaoui's war preparations."

"And?"

"As to the latter, they are quite extensive. As to you two, I am not disappointed."

"I don't believe it is as simple as that," sulked Guillaume.

"That is your prerogative. But tomorrow you will have other matters to consider, for I think we must leave the Ait-Mugri. Monsieur Guillaume is well enough to travel, is he not?" he asked in French.

Guillaume nodded and I inquired were we not safe there? The village tucked in its little valley seemed so secluded, and our days there had been so idyllic, that I was reluctant to set out again into the surrounding chaos.

"No, it is not that. Madani al-Glaoui will not violate the domain of a *sharif*. You must understand that the power of religion remains stronger here than military might. Let me tell you a story to illustrate this point." He was always telling us a story to illustrate some point, parables and pieces of half-fact, often combatively recounted in a style doubtless acquired in his public school debates, yet always tinged with that ironic civility which he could not totally discard. "About four years ago an Englishman named Cooper, a newcomer to the country, wandered near the temple of Moulay Idris at Fez. Moulay Idris was the founder of the current dynasty and is the patron saint of Morocco. His temple at Fez is no place for Christians. A tribesman leaving the mosque was so enraged to see a non-Moslem within the consecrated area surrounding it that he killed Cooper and took refuge in the temple, where the saint would protect him. He should have been safe there, but of course there was an uproar in the European community at Fez. Pressure was applied to Abd el-Aziz and at length the tribesman was enticed from the temple with the promise of saintly protection. He was then executed at the Sultan's order. This should never have been. It was a disgrace and a direct challenge to the religious elders who rule Fez and to the sanctity of Moulay Idris. So you see, the Sultan Abd el-Aziz has quite lost contact with his own past and his people. His extravagance and indulgence in the European toys provided by Maclean and his cronies is a minor cause of the disaffection of his people. Incidents such as the one I have described touch them much more deeply. He does not want to hear of their abject conditions or their discontent. The last time I spoke with him—this was several years ago now—he said to me an astonishing thing. He said: 'I am weary of being Sultan.' But even I understand that being Sultan is not something one grows weary of. It is like being English or being a man: it is a condition, not a role. When I heard that, I knew Abd el-Aziz was done for in Morocco. He has only survived with the constant financial and military support of the French. Now even that will not suffice."

"But how," I asked him, bringing the subject back once more to my personal concerns, "does all this relate to us?"

"I merely wished to say that Madani al-Glaoui does

respect the religious traditions which Aziz has forgotten. He would never, for any reason, violate them. Certainly not for you two, in whom he has only a passing interest."

"Which is something else I cannot make out," I persisted. "What is his interest in us?"

"That has me puzzled as well, I'm afraid. I don't know why he abducted you in Tangier, but I think it is your very irrelevance which troubles him. He can't place you in his scheme of things, and that is an unfamiliar feeling for the Glaoui. He suspects you of meddling, but is not quite sure where or why."

I had not revealed the circumstances of our abduction to Daunt, and I ceased my questioning at this point. He did not seem impatient to force my tale from me. I took several strips of dried, glazed turnip and chewed thoughtfully, drifting off into the valley's somnolence.

"But we must leave the Ait-Mugri, and the sooner the better. Travel can only become increasingly perilous." He took a turnip strip and sucked on it. "I have been thinking a great deal about our safest course when we leave this valley. I had hoped we might go to Marrakesh. It's only a day's journey, but that is the provenance of the Hafiziya rebellion and no place for foreigners."

"Wasn't it there that Dr. Mauchamp was killed last spring?"

"You are well apprised on these matters, Clayton." He continued to outline his thinking, his voice drumming like the insect hum as evening settled over the valley. A fragrant breeze rustled the olive trees. "Casablanca, which is on the coast and somewhat north, would have made an excellent port of escape. But it is in a virtual state of siege just now with marauding bands of tribesmen. The French have shelled the town and a force of legionnaries under General Drude are the only thing standing between order and wholesale slaughter. And so, I suppose, we must make for Fez, which is perhaps best. It is my favorite city in Morocco, the ancient capital and location of the Sultan's court. There is still a large European community there. I think we can unravel a few questions and see you safely on your way from Fez. But it will be a full week's journey. Are you prepared for that?"

"I am prepared," I admitted, "though I'd be happy to remain here. I am not anxious to become further embroiled in the internal affairs of Morocco. But you spoke of an escape port. I get the feeling you are conducting us out of Morocco."

"What are the alternatives? If you remain you will be taken captive again and this time your captors will be less patient and less merciful."

"But we have not yet learned what we came for," Guillaume interjected.

"And what was that?"

"Don't you already know?" I baited him.

"No, Clayton, you remain a mystery to me. I observe and I listen, but I am beginning to feel that the mere application of deductive logic will be insufficient in determining your business in Morocco. Inasmuch as you are resistant to direct questioning—"

"There you are correct for once, Monsieur Timothy." Guillaume was a self-righteous zeppelin, overinflated by the heat, bursting at the seams where the red ant mandibles ridged along his shaven pate, his dark eyes exaggerated, the whole head mammoth now without hair. "Deductive logic will not suffice," he said and offered us the long-stemmed pipe. Yes, these Berbers were acquainted with the properties of the *Cannabis indica* found in the foothills of their mountains, and Guillaume was not averse to indulging. Daunt forbore on the grounds it gave him "a wretched headache." I found that hashish stimulated my mind to a point intolerable in the rendering furnace of midafternoon. I smoked as dusk edged along the sands in umber and auburn, rising upward to the jagged peaks ready to prink that portly zeppelin with his keen yet loving eyes, in whom somehow anything was forgivable. "I always follow my instincts," he intoned. "Not my intellect. This has stood me in good stead many times."

This was rubbish, as I reminded Guillaume. "And in hot water, as well, more often than not."

"Don't you mean hot sand?" he bantered back, coughing on a lungful of smoke.

Daunt laughed. "You know, despite your suspicious natures, I truly enjoy talking with you two. But you can't recognize a friend when he sits before you. Rather amusing. I find your attitudes positively bracing, if such a word can even be spoken in Morocco in midsummer. The only other speakers of English one encounters down here are all sods across the century line somewhere, back in Victoria's England which I left behind, though I jolly well doubt it's changed, despite"—he bowed to Guillaume—"your prodigious pronouncements on the liberalization of values and even human hearts and minds. And I still insist that instinct is useless if not shaped, in part, by logic."

I watched Timothy Daunt wringing his knuckly hands: bronzed with the freckles turned almost to the color of liver spotting, strong, sinewy hands and forearms reaching from beneath the folds of his white burnoose. I felt—and I could sense by his playful repartée that Guillaume had begun to share my feelings—a strange, symbiotic attachment to this man with his detached, ironic perspective and the critical self-assurance which I sensed lay at the heart of his remaining for sixteen years in this tantalizing but utterly alien land—even more alien for him as an Englishman than for me from that land across the sea with its endless frontier and barren flatlands. We were quite dissimilar. Duant and I, and as for Guillaume they could not have been more different both emotionally and physically, yet there existed a mutually beneficial and satisfying rapport. Oddly this rapport did not stimulate trust, even for the man who had saved our lives. But had he really risked his life to save ours? I wondered.

"I admit," he addressed Guillaume and the question of instinct, "that taken to its ultimate extreme total logic leads to total cynicism."

"And it is there you have arrived?" Guillaume pressed him.

"No, I think not." But it occurred to me that perhaps he had.

"Then it is where you are heading," Guillaume concluded.

Abruptly Daunt tacked, his spindly body turning on his haunches. "Yes, I suppose that is where I've arrived after all. And that's why I don't give a bloody bother whether you know why I've plucked you from Telouet or whether you care."

"I think it's quite simple," I declared and he glanced at me with mordant curiosity. "It is because you are ready to die at any moment. So you do always exactly what you want."

"Oh, am I? How charming. And this makes it possible for me to go trotting in and out of Telouet at the slightest whim. Well, I tell you I am not ready to die at any moment and certainly not for you lads. Not a whit of it, thank you."

"Oh, but you are," I told him and took the pipe.

"Well, sport," he teased me, "I can see you are a likely prospect."

"For what is that?" I asked.

"Just wait. You'll see if I am not right." He left it at that, adding only: "The difference between you two, the crucial difference, is that you always ask why while monsieur never does. It is that simple."

Thus enlightened I reclined on the rolled mat behind me and drew slowly on the pipe. A girl of the village, pale with slanting green eyes and a flat nose, her skin rich and glistening, brought a pot of *asidah,* the barley porridge which was the basis of every meal, and with it a special treat: dates and almonds. She poured water from a clay ewer over our hands, and then we attempted to imitate Daunt and the villagers as they scooped mouthfuls of the white glue on two fingers and with a quick turn of the wrist stuffed it into their mouths. I felt the distinct need of a bib, despite our hosts' good-natured indulgence.

That evening tribe members from the two extended family clusters situated across the valley and at its far end came to the outcropping of mud huts where we had convalesced. Even the old marabout Tayyib appeared for the festivities.

The girls of the tribe stood bareheaded around a blazing fire in loose, brightly colored skirts. They remained motionless, arms limp at their sides, entranced as a drumbeat and the first strains of a wood flute sounded. Almost imperceptibly a nervous tremor ran through the body of one girl and then another. Their arms rose with the tremor into an outstretched position and it exited at their fingertips. The movement seemed disembodied from the girl, flowing as the illusive spirit of the music entered her in this most visible fashion.

The quickening drumbeat was joined by several instruments, and the dancers came alive with a sudden swift movement of their feet and shoulders. After a few beats of soft stomping they froze back into immobility—Berber goddesses in amber marble, statues that returned to life as the music repeatedly drew the dance from their bodies and finally conquered them entirely, the resistant bodies succumbing in a dizzying whirlwind of movement. Many of the older people sang along with the music, a monotonous chant resonating across the still canyon.

"This is Morocco," I said to Guillaume, and he nodded. "This is why we came."

"Yes, it is a long way from the boys on the beach at Tangier."

Daunt overheard our exchange and missed no opportunity to pry. "What's that? Boys on the beach at Tangier?"

"Yes, Fritz's boys, the night we were abducted." The words slipped out so easily, three days of conscientious caution washed away in a moment of injudicious candor. But once initiated I rushed headlong into further indiscretions. "You probably even know the man. Fritz Amgott."

Daunt frowned. "Old Fritz, eh? A nasty bit of business that one is." He used the precise term of disapprobation employed by Maclean in describing Fritz. Perhaps there was yet some lingering likeness between our two English acquaintances. "Yes, I've had my eye on that old boy for some years now. Hmmm. Fancy that." He seemed more amused than concerned and gazed back at the dancers. The music had intensified and the dancing with it. "How did you happen onto Fritz?" he asked casually.

"We weren't *onto* him," I explained. "Our dragoman told us of his night rituals after we saw him in the medina. We were watching him on the beach when the Glaoui's men grabbed us."

"Is that so?"

"But why have you had your eye on him, Timothy?" Guillaume asked. "Not your sort of fellow, I wouldn't think."

"Not at all. Our former man at Tangier, Arthur Nicolson, suspected Fritz of involvement in the lucrative arms-smuggling business. 'Suspected' is an understatement, but we never could prove anything. His family are in munitions back in Germany, as you may know. Aligned with the Mannesmann brothers and the French firm of Schneider and Company, actually an Alsatian firm, but that's Germany now, so you see." He threw up his hands. "Anyway, that lot are certainly involved with the Hafiziya uprising, and probably Madani al-Glaoui as well, not to mention Raysuni and a number of other brigands festering like little sores in the mountains around Fez."

The music had reached a frenetic pace, and Daunt had to shout to make himself heard.

"So Fritz is in armaments, you say?" I called out to him.

"Yes, the production of gunpowder. All fits in quite nicely. Constant supply keeps the rebels forever in his debt, gets rid of obsolete weapons and surplus for the family, gives the French a packet of headaches in the bargain, and forces my own countrymen into the unenviable position of having at some point to make a choice. Gunpowder supply is quite the key, I think."

I was no longer listening to him, for something had struck me and I was staring at Guillaume. My heart suddenly beat in time to the music, which had reached what had to be its ultimate frenzy, the dancers nearly disassembling before us, the musicians pounding and slapping at their instruments while the rest of the tribe shouted the chant.

At last Guillaume noticed my persistent stare. He

gazed at me while the music drowned all thoughts from our minds, the crying of the night creatures and the wind consumed in this wailing torrent of sound.

Suddenly it ceased. The dancers, without exception, froze with the final drumbeat and the crowd whimpered instantly to silence. High up the Atlas the wind sang through a breach in the jagged peaks, a thin monody in counterpoint to the lives of the Ait-Mugri.

In the rapt silence I spoke softly, yet incisively, to Guillaume.

"I just remembered something Darlington told me the day we were released from the Santée: that traces of gunpowder were found in the hollow mask worn by Sébastien. Traces of gunpowder," I repeated.

Guillaume's dark eyes pierced me for an instant, a look requiring discretion and analysis. Daunt had also turned with a quizzical expression in his hazel eyes. But he did not question me further and seemed not to have heard or understood the implications of what I said.

I was not sure that I understood them myself.

XVI

Daunt roused us before dawn the next day. We ate our *asidah* and set in a store of dates and nuts for the trip north. We were given pentacular copper badges bearing Koranic inscriptions which Daunt explained carried some of the *baraka* (or blessing) of the local *sharif*. They would protect us from robbers and other troublesome tribesmen we might encounter on the road to Fez. Thus fortified, we set out.

Daunt's plan was to proceed in the shadows along the eastern side of the valley and upwards to the summit during the morning hours. We would rest during the heat of midday and cross the pass near nightfall. He believed the greatest danger of an ambush by Madani al-Glaoui's warriors lay in the immediate vicinity of the valley of the Ait-Mugri. Once we crossed that barrier in darkness, and traveled as far down toward the flatlands as our strength would permit, we would be relatively safe.

At the crest of the valley I glanced wistfully back at that place I knew I would never see again. Then I turned and followed Daunt's bouncing head down the mountainside. The night was calm with a few distant cries of jackals and hyenas. We passed through stands of pine and cork and wound along a rocky riverbed overgrown with oleander. The Glaoui were apparently otherwise engaged for we met no resistance. Late in the night beneath a crescent moon Daunt agreed to rest for a few hours, but insisted we set out again before dawn.

We traveled along the base of the mountains on

horses hired by Daunt the next morning. Far out across the plateaus we saw dust storms, nomads with their camels, and mounted regiments of soldiers moving south and west. "It is the massing of the *haraka,*" Daunt told us. "All the local militia are gathering for the holy war to begin soon at Marrakesh."

We passed a small village recently razed by fire. The blackened husks of the buildings leaned into the dry winds, already beginning to merge back into the sand out of which they had sprung.

It was not until the third day that we confronted a ticklish situation: a half-dozen ragged, hostile characters whom one might have labeled highwaymen in another time and place, two of them armed with old muzzle-loading rifles, surrounded us on the road. Daunt's use of a few carefully chosen phrases of Arabic and the flashing of the pentacular copper badges dispersed the ruffians without serious incident.

Each evening a mountain outpost or tiny Berber hamlet would come into view like a mirage just when we thought we could go no farther on our horses, and each time we were welcomed by the tribe and departed refreshed the next morning.

Late on the morning of the eighth day we mounted a low hill through cedar forests and saw the ancient walls of Fez below us. The sprawling medina (many times larger than that at Tangier) rolled and twisted through the hilly basin in which the city is built with scores of minarets dotting it like cactus quills. After the peace in the valley of the Ait-Mugri and a week in the rugged mountains the sounds and smells of Fez instantly burdened me with the tumult of Morocco in revolt.

We found that in his absence Daunt's Fez had fallen subject to the same chaotic discord as the rest of the country. Bedraggled soldiers prowled the streets like vicious dogs, many of them deserters from the Sultan's army on their way south to join the pretender. Bands of starving youngsters jostled us while others, too weak to do more than hold out cupped hands, cringed against the walls of the crowded streets with pitiful eyes, swollen bellies, and legs that widened at the ankle like palm stumps.

Daunt led us rapidly past the Sultan's palace and through the Jewish sector to his own residence on a narrow roadway just outside the medina by the Blue Gate. He left us there while he went out to reconnoiter the situation in the capital.

Daunt's "digs"—as he referred to them—were cool and comfortable: low-ceilinged plaster walls and tiled floors with a defunct fountain in the center of one room. An arched passageway opened onto his sleeping quarters, where low divans and cushions covered half the floor and a stunted writing table sat amid a litter of newspapers, books, crumpled and slashed pieces of writing paper, and overflowing ashtrays. He returned after three hours with a packet of fruits and grains and a disheartening tale to tell.

"The situation is deteriorating quite rapidly," he said. "The *maghzan*"—this was the national administration—"is in total disarray, the Sultan's orders are no longer carried out, and only a handful of incompetent, self-seeking men remain loyal. There is talk that the Sultan and what remains of his court will leave the city for Rabat and there prepare for a confrontation with his brother. If that happens, Fez will be plunged into total anarchy and it will be no safer for you here than elsewhere."

"So we must hide again until it is safe to flee?" I said.

"It seems," complained Guillaume, "that all we

have done since we came to this country is either hide or flee. There is never a time for action."

"Quite so, old sport. There is little time for anything. I'm afraid the Moors respond to European blood rather like sharks, and now that the first blood has flowed, well . . ."

"So we must sit here, under your benign protection, and await our execution?"

"Not at all, my dear Guillaume. We must devise a plan of escape."

"But we have gone to great lengths to reach Fez," I grumbled. "And now we are trapped here and must once again escape. I think Guillaume is right."

"Right about what?" asked Daunt, but he received no answer.

My expression of support had encouraged Guillaume to assert himself. "I am tired of it," he said. "I thank you for rescuing us from that cell in the mountains and bringing us this far, but there is still a large European community here and I think it best we go our separate ways now." Daunt raised his eyebrows.

Guillaume was finally emerging from the dense fog which had surrounded him since the night of our abduction. I had attributed it to physical strain, but his personality had been transformed as well. He had become yielding and receptive, whining like an old woman one moment and drawing into himself the next. In the vacuum created by his weakness I had turned to Daunt, and he had, with the added connivance of the language barrier, come between us. Now I felt this subtle personal drift reversing itself.

"Who among us is not tired of it?" Daunt chastised him. "And we shall grow wearier still. This chaos, this disintegration of society, will become commonplace and widespread. It has begun in Morocco because the fabric of society is weakest here when confronted by European ways. I believe it will become the prevalent condition of our age."

"I disagree with you entirely," Guillaume countered. "The future is not chaos but a new ordering of life, to conform to the real nature of the universe which we are at last free to perceive."

"I regret that I am somewhat less sanguine about our prospects than you, Monsieur Guillaume," Daunt understated himself facetiously and smiled at me. "I have less faith than you in humanity . . . in what is sometimes called human nature."

"Then you are not worthy to be called a man."

"Indeed? Yet when I observe men I see Moorish cruelty, French pride, German egoism, and British myopia. Hardly the stuff on which faith is built."

"You are being rather unkind, don't you think?" I told him.

"And you are a kindhearted chap, Clayton. And so remain something of a fool in this world." I stared at him. "Though I am confident you shall at length overcome your foolishness."

"I don't know if that is a compliment or not," I muttered.

"It is close to one," he replied.

I thanked him, but added that I agreed with Guillaume that we were on the verge today of a total revolution in the life of man.

"But what you silly revolutionaries fail to grasp," he said, "is that civilization is not a continuity and therefore revolution is not a culmination. Rather it is a violent breaking off. And as such, if what you say is true, the chaos will be all the greater afterwards." I had no rebuttal to this argument. I could see Guillaume formulating an answer and searching for the words in English to express it when Daunt addressed himself to the practical present. "In any case, I hope you will accept my invitation to remain here for at least a day or two, until I can arrange safe passage for you out of Morocco."

"Then you shall not conduct us yourself to the customs house?"

"I think the personal phase of my custodianship has ended. I have pressing business in Fez now that the walls of the sultanate have truly begun to crumble."

So we remained cloistered in Daunt's digs. Evenings we climbed several narrow flights of steps to the roof of our building and surveyed the city. We could see the tall, arched blue tile gate not far away, leading down into the sprawling medina. Behind us wooded parkland surrounded the fabled Qarawiyin University, a seat of learning dating to the period of the Cordoba caliphate and the ascendancy of Islam from India to Iberia. Beyond that stood the walls and towers of the Sultan's palace, a low building nymph-pink in the sunset, with even rows of palms and sentries before it.

Directly below us in an open plaza merchants and farmers from the countryside spread their wares on blankets. The plaza had a carnival atmosphere with snake charmers, magicians, acrobats, and dancers who leapt about in a crouch while black men from the south beat big drums with curved sticks. A clown in a bright spangled outfit with a tasseled hat sold drinking water from brass cups. Hooded figures lay on the ground by open fires, hands reaching out for mercy no one could afford to extend. For us there could be no participation in this world; only detached surveillance from our rooftop and Daunt's endless cigarettes and stoic observations on what might be and what might have been.

On the third day of this frustrating captivity, made all the more frustrating by our host's unhindered comings and goings, Daunt informed us that we had been invited to a dinner with several longtime European residents of the city at the home of one of the *ulama* of Fez, where we would be quite safe and might discuss our flight.

"What are the *ulama?*" I asked.

"They are the educated, religious elite of the city, to whom all parties, even the Sultan, must look for guidance and approval. They are wavering toward accepting the pretender, and this has disastrously curtailed Abd el-Aziz's ability to rally his forces. He cannot survive desertion by the *ulama.*"

"But why are they deserting him?"

"A curious thing is happening in Morocco," he explained. "For the first time temporal and spiritual power have joined forces in rebellion. The great *qaids* of the Atlas, Berbers and nonreligious leaders, have joined with a member of the Alaouite dynasty, Abd el-Hafiz. This alliance is unprecedented. It has already gained the blessing of some of the *sharifs* of Tafilalet, the ancestral home of the dynasty in the desert beyond the High Atlas, and with this the *jihad* is launched and Aziz's fate sealed."

Daunt warned us that we would be observed specimens at the dinner, but Guillaume and I readily agreed this was far better than remaining hidden away. Two hours later we set out together for the home of the *ulama* Idris al-Jalil.

For the first time we passed through the Blue Gate and descended into the medina. The Moors seemed unable to assess these two young Christians with their shaved heads, wool Berber caps, and well-worn *jilabas.* We followed Daunt through an unending maze of intersections and crisscrossing alleyways. One felt that, unlike the medina at Tangier where simply by moving continuously downhill one could eventually reach the bay, in the rolling medina at Fez one could wander endlessly without finding a gate, forever doubling back upon oneself and being drawn deeper and deeper into the tangled web of streets. Donkeys laden with blankets and skins—for the recent drought, while creating food shortages, had been munificent to traders in the skins of dead animals—waded through the human sea. We had to flatten against the walls as they passed. I felt callused, carbuncular hands at my ankles, literally trying to pull the shoes from my feet or, I imagined, to draw me down into some underground inferno, and I began to appreciate Daunt's reluctance to allow us out in the city. The disorder was overwhelming, the poverty more severe than anything I had ever conceived, a fearful degradation of humanity which made our dreams in Paris seem vain and absurd—the idle considerations of foolish children.

Daunt led us out of the bustle of the wider avenues —just wide enough to allow the passage of a pair of laden donkeys. I gagged on the fumes rising from the dyeing vats and then we turned down a narrow dirt path along a peeling plaster wall. The door at which we stopped was plain and unmarked, without name or number or any indication of what lay inside.

Within that drab doorway dwelt a magnificent humility (there is no contradiction here) of decor and spirit. A respectful black slave ushered us into a still courtyard, galleried on three sides. We waited by an emerald-tiled fountain in the shape of a six-petaled flower. I was struck by the stark contrast between the exterior street life and interior home life of the Moors: the oppressive tumult of the medina could in no way lead one to predict the cool, self-contained composure of this home where only the gushing fountain could be heard. I wondered whether a corresponding contrast existed in the people, whether their gruff exteriors concealed an inner life of delicacy and reflection. For one evening, at least, this seemed to be the case.

From the central courtyard we were conducted through a series of symmetrical arched passages into the dining room. The ceiling and walls were carved in dark wood, not elaborate scrollwork but simple, repeated geometric patterns. A low divan along the walls was spread with colorful cloths and cushions, and a gleaming silver tea service sat upon a low table at the room's center.

The other European guests had arrived: Philip Kassel, the German consul at Fez, monocled and stout with a firm handshake; Urbain Bienfait, a photographer at the Sultan's court with an aquiline nose and elongated limbs, dressed in buff linens and twirled mustaches; and Daunt's English compatriot Egbert Dotson, a medical doctor and recently appointed member of the Debt Commission. Condolences had been sent by Monsieur Fabarez, agent of the powerful French firm Compagnie Marocaine, who had left Fez for the coast on business.

Daunt was momentarily disturbed by this news. We chatted with Egbert Dotson, a busy little man with narrow lips and squinched brow who was altogether too staunch to fit my notion of a middle-aged British doctor.

"Dottie has tended many of my little maladies over the years, haven't you, old boy?" Daunt teased his friend amiably.

"Yes, a doctor must engage a broad practice in this land. I have been midwife, surgeon, dentist, and chemist during my years here." He smiled thinly and furrowed his tall brow as though not quite convinced of something. At this moment our host entered and we were seated for the evening repast.

Idris al-Jalil was not a "man of religion" in any sense of that phrase familiar to Europeans: he had none of the gentility, professional compassion, or preachiness of a pastor, nor the haughty grandeur of a bishop; neither was he a saint or a mystic. Rather he was a scholar—he even bore an odd, unsettling resemblance to Professor Stallwarts—for the foremost characteristic of the *ulama* was scholarship of the Koran. It was to this that Idris (whose name recalled the founder of the first Moroccan dynasty and was, second only to that of the Prophet, the most revered name in Morocco) had devoted most of his life.

We sat on floor cushions around the table and were served by the household's women. They wore kerchiefs on their heads and ankle-length robes, but went unveiled within doors.

A slave girl brought a basin and ewer of water which she poured over our hands. Daunt explained to me that the Moorish custom of eating with the hands was based on the simple fact that cutlery had the day before been in someone else's mouth, while one's fingers went only into one's own mouth and were intended for this purpose. A sensible enough theory though not so easy in execution, as my awkward dribblings attested throughout the evening.

We were served small cups of lemon verbena tea. The slave waited for us to finish and then twice refilled our cups. All the movements of our host were delicate and precise, obviously stylized yet somehow quite natural.

A rich stew of what tasted like mutton, though I was informed it was camel's flesh, was centered on the table and surrounded by flat breads, salt, capsicums, and piquant powders. The scents of orange and almond wafting from the stew mixed with a subtle incense and the lingering fragrance of verbena in a heady concoction.

Idris began the meal by dipping bread into the stew and tasting it; he was followed by the chief guest, the German counsul Kassel. The dinner conversation, which was conducted simultaneously in four languages (English, French, German, and Arabic), touched upon little of significance. Everyone was aware of the situation raging around us, but within the *ulama*'s home we felt insulated from that madness. One could neither hear nor smell the medina which encircled us so closely.

Idris al-Jalil apologized to Guillaume and me for the state of affairs in his country and suggested we had chosen an unpropitious moment to visit Morocco. "For myself," he said, "I have always tried to cultivate the friendship of those Europeans who I believed were not here to take from my country. You can see I have many foreign friends. This is quite rare for a man in my position."

"And it has caused a bit of talk along the back corridors of the palace," sniped Bienfait beneath his thin nose.

"That is nothing," replied Idris. "Those whose respect I value do not consider such matters. They see beyond them."

The stew was replaced by a plate of wrinkled black olives and artichoke hearts. We were served couscous grain on silver plates and each given three skewers of tiny bits of meat and liver. The remaining gravy from the stew was ladled over the grain.

Daunt showed me how to scoop the couscous into a ball on the back of my thumb and transfer it to my mouth with a half turn of the wrist. I was rapidly absorbed by the task of consuming this wonderful feast.

"We are most honored to be your guests," Guillaume told our host. "And you may be certain we have come here without any intention of *taking* from your country."

"We are only seeking to understand certain things and set to rest a problem we encountered in France," I added.

"Yes, I know you are seeking, but not to take. Mr.

Daunt has spoken most highly of you. I wonder if I might be of assistance in your quest?"

Inconsistency is a sign of the amateur in any profession; in sleuthing it is a particularly grievous fault. Lulled by the embalming atmosphere of the *ulama*'s abode, the fountain's flow, and the fragrant stew, and undismayed by the eager faces which turned upon me when Idris posed his question, I began at the Place St. Sulpice and followed through the Santée and the circus and the seance at Madame Orgueil's and finally our abduction by the Glaoui warriors, visit to Telouet, and rescue by Daunt. At the mention of the Glaoui, Idris looked concerned. The others were far too well entertained by the European aspects of our story, of which Guillaume aided in the recounting by a series of witty asides and corrections, to concern themselves with what had transpired in Morocco. Kidnappings and threats against Europeans were commonplace here. My single precaution was to omit mention of whom we had been engaged in observing at the moment of our abduction.

"I cannot imagine any connection between the great *qaid* and this affair of yours in Paris. A most puzzling tale," Idris said. He glanced at Daunt and added: "Perhaps someone wishes to use the uprising of the Hafiziya to some greater purpose." Daunt nodded and I was about to question our host when a servant entered and addressed first Idris and then Kassel. Soon another German was shown in: a stiff, bristling major with wide cheeks, a flat, coarse voice, and a high collar.

"Pardon my intrusion, Herr Konsul," he began and bowed to the host. He was nearly breathless, either from excitement or the struggle through the medina crowds, and stammered through his message. "The *maghzan* . . . that is, the loyal administration . . . there is a decree . . . and from the local police as well . . . they can no longer guarantee the safety of Europeans in Fez and . . . and they have requested that all foreigners leave the city immediately. . . . A crowd has gathered outside the Blue Gate, threatening anyone seen entering or leaving the city. I myself was fortunate. . . . It is rumored that the Sultan has already left the capital for Rabat."

"Nonsense," said the French photographer with an authoritative air. Kassel waved for his underling to continue.

"The German community has assembled at the consulate and awaits your presence there. All of us . . . them . . . wish to leave the city."

"So the end is coming." Kassel seemed not entirely dissatisfied by this turn of events. "No longer can any foreign power police this nation. We must let the flood currents settle where they will."

Kassel apologized to his host for the unseemly intrusion of political reality onto our dinner, but Idris al-Jalil agreed that it could not be helped. As soon as Kassel had departed the rest of the company eagerly began a discussion of these events.

"Is that not just like a German?" demanded Bienfait. "For all their proud talk, they are the first to abandon a sinking ship."

"And shall you wait until the water is at your ears before realizing your feet are wet, Urbain?" queried Daunt. "This ship's sunk."

"We must all reflect quietly upon the meaning of these events," said Idris al-Jalil, "and withhold our accusations. Though I knew it would finally come to this, I am sorry to see it. I had hoped . . ." His voice trailed off and he folded his hands in his lap and lowered his eyes.

"I shouldn't be surprised," muttered the graceless Bienfait, "if the Germans were behind the entire uprising in the south. They are forever seeking ways to jeopardize French interests."

"And to wreak havoc with the Entente Cordiale as well," commented Daunt.

"Well, it does seem," I offered my one bit of knowledge on the subject of international diplomacy in North Africa, "that the French have continually overstepped the stipulations of the Act of Algeciras and violated Moroccan integrity without consulting the other powers. Perhaps the Germans are merely—"

"I quite agree with young Clayton," Egbert Dotson interrupted me. Daunt was outwardly pleased by my sentiments, though I could not imagine why, while Bienfait gave me a condescending and horrified look, as much I suppose for my obtrusion into the argument at all as for the substance of my remarks. "You know my feelings on this subject, Timothy," Dotson continued. "The growth of modern Germany may be highly inconvenient to Great Britain, but it is inevitable, it is an established fact, and it is *not an inherent threat* to our country, notwithstanding Admiral Tirpitz and his dreadnoughts."

"It is a threat because of Germany's intentions toward France," replied Daunt.

"Or France's intentions toward Germany. No, Timothy, I think our greatest national interest lies in establishing and maintaining friendly relations with both France and Germany. This inevitable European war appears to be a French conception."

"Monsieur Dotson!" Bienfait could no longer restrain himself. "I cannot permit such statements. I cannot permit them," he repeated. He performed an elaborate series of facial twitchings, lip pursings, eye rollings, and cheek suckings with accompanying sound effects.

Guillaume, who had remained silent throughout this debate, watched him disgustedly and said, "I am French and I fear Monsieur Dotson is correct."

"You see," Dotson exploded at this unexpected support. "Deny it if you will, Urbain, but France is reverting to the traditions of the Second Empire." This remark elicited further harrumphs from the distraught Bienfait. "Whenever France feels herself strong enough she immediately attempts to assert world supremacy."

"Gentlemen, gentlemen, please." Idris al-Jalil emerged from his thoughts and brought the discussion to a halt with a raised hand. "We are all under a great strain. You will want to make your own preparations for departure, I know, but let us not disrupt what may be our last friendly supper together." He signaled the slaves to bring rinsing water and tea.

"You are quite right, Idris al-Jalil," Daunt agreed, but he insisted upon having the last word. "Foreign intervention in Moroccan affairs has been botched and bungled by all nations with equal zeal." He eyed Idris thoughtfully and added: "But I think you may find in Mr. Dotson's sentiments the answer to your question regarding the puzzling affair of my two young friends here." Though I questioned him about this later that evening and wondered over it many times, it was years before I fully understood the implications of this remark.

We rinsed our mouths with scented water which we spit into a ceramic bowl. A soapy basin was brought for our hands, followed by a ewer of cool water for rinsing. A brass plate of incense chips perfumed the air. Thus mollified, we were served mint tea and small honey cakes. The three-cup ritual with the tea was repeated, and so dinner concluded.

"This unexpected development has provided us with a perfect opportunity for your passage to Tangier," Daunt observed as we stood in the fountain courtyard and prepared to depart. "The confusion attending a mass exodus of Europeans from Fez will allow you to disappear among the crowd quite naturally. You will not travel alone but with a large group, and Dottie shall see you as far as Tangier."

"Really? But you and he seemed to be on opposite sides just now," I said.

"Oh, Dottie is a bit, isn't he? We have our differences, but I trust him. . . . Dottie, old sport, do you think you could watch over my two charges on the flight to the coast?"

"Why of course, Timothy. But you?"

"I shall find my own way to Tangier. I must speak with Fabarez first." He smiled at his friend. "A rather good go-round we had just now, what?"

"Call it what you will, but I still hold to my views that—" Dotson was off again, but Daunt silenced him.

"Yes, yes, Dottie old chum, quite so, but we'll neither of us convince the other. Now, how are we going to make our way home tonight? And what are the arrangements for tomorrow?"

They discussed alternate ways out of the medina and debated their relative advantages. It was agreed that we should meet the following morning in the grand square before the Sultan's palace. Our host strolled into the courtyard to bid us farewell.

"We shall not meet again like this," he said somberly and with a touch of nostalgia in his voice. "The self-purification has begun, and there is no place for any of you in it." He straightened as he spoke. "The cleansing and unifying spirit of true Islam must be severe in order to be just. This is the way of Allah. It is written and it will be so. . . . Yet I say to you farewell, my friends, and may your passage home be a safe one."

We emerged into the narrow dirt pathway and climbed through the crowded streets of the city. I detected no change; the languid stares which greeted us at every turn were neither more nor less hostile than before.

Still we skirted the Blue Gate, exited through a smaller portal, and there took leave of Dotson. We could see the angry crowd outside the Blue Gate as we slipped down the side street to Daunt's digs. Once inside he wedged a board against the door, lighted a cigarette, and settled into deep thought.

Hours and many cigarettes later, with Guillaume dozing on his mat, Daunt and I conversed by gas lantern.

"I believe that through the combination of your friend's intuition and your own curiosity you have stumbled onto something, Clayton. I hope to tell you more about it in Tangier, after I have made a few private investigations. We must work together on this."

"Then we should await word from you in Tangier?"

"Yes. I shall reach you there, I guarantee that."

"Do you suspect this Amgott of involvement in the death of the *saltimbanque* boy in Paris?"

"Oh, I don't know about that; it seems rather far-fetched. I don't doubt that Fritz has been supplying the rebels with gunpowder. What else he may have in mind could be very much more important."

"What do you mean?" I pressed him.

"I don't quite know. I fear the Germans have grown bolder since their success two years ago when the Kaiser visited Tangier. Fritz may be part of their plans, or he may be operating on his own."

"I only wish I knew to whom *you* owed allegiance. You claim to be independent, yet you often display great patriotism toward England."

"Is that not natural?" he asked.

"It is, but I still feel you have an ulterior motive for your interest in us. And that your services can be bought for the high bid."

"Rubbish. You don't believe that. If you do you are

more of a fool than I thought." He lighted a cigarette and coughed. "Venality is the most heinous sin. Far worse than anything Fritz could do, for he at least believes in himself. Whatever I may be, Clayton, I am not a venal man." I believed him, and I think this showed. He took a piece of paper and pen from his little writing desk, spread the paper on the floor, and began drawing a design on it. "Now I want to give you a couple of tools. This first is quite useful and really very simple."

He drew a grid and beside it a large X.

"This is a crude cipher which I may have occasion to use in writing to you regarding this matter." I observed him intently now. This cryptography lesson confirmed my belief that he was more than a cartographer and tour guide. He nodded. "There are nine squares in the grid plus the four quadrants of the X, precisely thirteen areas. By placing two letters in each section of the cipher and dotting the second letter so that it is distinguishable from the first we create a way of encoding messages."

Here I must resort to graphics. He filled in the letters from A to Z in order, left to right in the grid and clockwise around the X, thus:

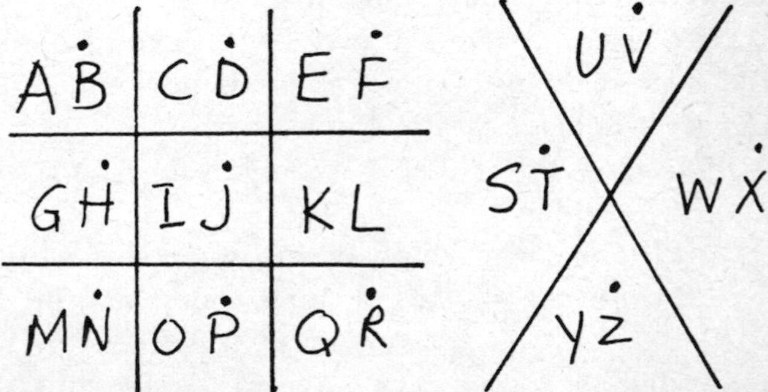

"Now, if we wish to write my name it would appear like this." He drew the five symbols:

"The code can be made more complex by commencing at some arbitrarily determined point in the alphabet, by altering the starting point with each message, or by taking the letters at intervals of three or five rather than consecutively. Do you understand?" I smiled and nodded. "Good. In your case let us start with the letter C, since that is the first letter of your first name and this is your first cipher. Then let us proceed at intervals of three, so the second letter is F, the third I, and so forth. Fill in the squares as I have, dotting the second letter in each square." I did this. "Now you understand how this works, don't you, sport? Because you cannot write it down like a school assignment and refer to it later. This is important, Clayton."

I assured him that I understood, that it was indeed quite simple, and that I looked forward to receiving his messages.

"Well, I hope I can deliver them in person. But one never knows. Here, I have something else for you."

He opened a narrow drawer beneath the table and withdrew a small knife with a curved bone handle inlaid with pearls, its blade sheathed in leather.

"This may prove useful in ways you cannot even imagine," he told us.

"Well, I'm not much good with weapons," I apologized. "I've never stabbed a man, not even in self-defense."

"And I hope you won't have to. Accept this as a memento of your visit to Fez, and keep it with you until you are out of Morocco." He clasped my arm fondly. "You'll see, Clayton. This sort of life, once you have a taste for it, gets in your blood. You simply cannot quit." I smiled and he stretched his thin arms high over his head and yawned. "But tomorrow we both have difficult journeys." He indicated the slumbering figure across the room. "Guillaume is smarter than we. He will be rested for the ordeal."

The next morning Daunt accompanied us to a point near the Sultan's palace, where four dozen somber Europeans had assembled for the flight to Larache. There we would board the French freighter *Du Chayla,* bound for Tangier.

"You sure you'll be able to make do on your own?" Egbert Dotson asked Daunt, but his only answer was a grimly determined face that said he would make do far better in this Islamic mayhem on his own than with a motley collection of terrified Christian infidels.

We shared another round of goodbyes as the caravan prepared to depart. Daunt shook my hand and resumed our dialogue from the previous night as though it had just broken off. "I see it in you," he said, "for all you may believe you are meant for something else."

He turned to Guillaume. For an uncomfortable moment the animosity, the teasing, and the disputes between them were remembered, and then forgotten. Guillaume gripped Daunt's sinewy hands in his soft ones and smiled earnestly.

"Thank you, Monsieur Timothy," he said. "I believe you are a man of this century after all, though you may not know it." From Guillaume this was the highest praise.

Daunt acknowledged it and then, still gripping his hands, he asked: "What I still cannot understand is how you latched onto Fritz in the first place. What made you follow him to the beach?"

"Instinct," replied Guillaume.

XVII

The crossing from Fez to Larache, while but two days' journey and made in the company of a large number of Europeans less prepared to bear the strain of such a journey than we, was nevertheless as trying as any of our Moroccan travels, leaving aside that horrendous blindfolded night in the cart to Raysuni's.

Within hours of leaving the capital, violent dust storms forced us to halt. We huddled together in a barren sink until the winds abated. When we set out again, coated with a fine pestling of silt and sand—our eyebrows weighted with it, cloaks impregnated, nostrils starched—the dust storms pestered us all the way to the coast. I feared for the older members of our party.

Throughout this journey, and the comparatively pleasant day upon the French freighter *Du Chayla* which conveyed us from Larache to Tangier, Daunt's friend Egbert Dotson proved an excellent and informative traveling companion, if a trifle oversolicitous in his doctorly manner. He circulated cheerfully, taking pulses and peering into bloodshot eyes for signs of heat stroke or doling out the water supplies.

When we reached the port of Larache, dwarfed on the shore by the French ship in its tiny harbor, Guillaume and I plunged into the sea and emerged wet and wonderfully refreshed. We did not see the sense in Dotson's admonition against this until the water dried, leaving a sticky coat of salt on our skins with no way to rinse off.

On board the *Du Chayla*, safely off Moroccan soil

and out of reach of Berbers, Moors, or any other heathens of evil intent, we drank chilled beer and talked. Dotson told us he understood that Fritz Amgott, in whom he gathered we had taken some interest, was an eccentric outcast but not an innately evil man and certainly no intriguer.

"Timothy tends to imagine plots where they do not exist," he explained. "Fritz is no longer associated with his family's armaments business in any way. I don't think they'll have him. But I am not surprised at your tale of little boys on the beach. That is not the most offensive rumor one hears of that man."

"You seem partial to Germans in general," I coaxed him, playing the detective and hoping to unearth additional morsels about Fritz.

"Fritz Amgott is not a German. That is, he is a sick man, and there are such men of all nationalities. As to my partialities, I merely believe that England and Germany must learn to live together. Any other course is suicidal, and I fear, if you'll pardon my saying so, Guillaume, that the French government is eager to embark on such a suicidal mission of revenge."

"But the Germans are not eager for this?" I asked.

"I see no evidence of it," he said. "You will note that while France has increased her interests in Africa and elsewhere the victorious German military has been quiet for nearly four decades."

"That's hardly comforting," Guillaume said, but the subject was dropped. Dotson's attentions were required elsewhere on board, and we two bristle-headed intrigants returned to our private musings.

As soon as we left Daunt we became enclosed once more in our mystery and in our sense of pursuit and apprehension. So long as we remained with him he had shouldered this burden for us. His mood of sarcastic levity was contagious, even in the most trying circumstances, and his ironic perspective on both past and future tended to discount the seriousness of our situation. Apart from him we had only the turmoil of Morocco and our yet-unfulfilled quest.

Rapidly we resumed our former relationship. My teasing of Guillaume, which I had rather enjoyed—perhaps out of revenge for the times I had been teased in Paris—ceased. His brooding made me restless, wondering what he knew, though it had become quite apparent that I knew far more than he and was quicker to assimilate new information. He had only his blasted instincts, and they could not answer my questions.

In this state we arrived in Tangier, where the *Du Chayla* would dock for two days awaiting other refugees from the hinterlands before departing for France.

Most of us were lodged in a hotel in the European sector which had been set aside for this purpose, though some of the party stayed with friends in villas outside town. The zone of Tangier remained, and would remain throughout the worst of the troubles, the last inviolate bastion of Christian contamination in the land of the Moors.

A Monsieur Regnault came to lecture us on our bravery and on the certainty that Abd el-Aziz would weather the storm, order be restored, and the brigand Hafiz quashed. Not many believed him. Someone mentioned a report from the south that Hafiz had dispatched six thousand troops and fifty Krupp guns to the Shawai district and received 1.7 million rounds of ammunition at Mazagan. Hardly a brigand in the Raysuni mold.

Regarding our friend Raysuni, Dotson escorted us, not without due precautions, to the villa of Walter Harris, for two decades Tangier correspondent of the London *Times*. There we retold our story, meticulously edited for publication, to the absolutely awestruck and elegantly mustachioed Mr. Harris. He pressed us for details of Qaid Harry Maclean, whom we reported was happily sipping black tea in the Rif mountains. He could hardly believe our visit and escape from Telouet, and he grew hostile at the mention of Daunt's role in this.

I felt thoroughly uneasy throughout our two days in Tangier, despite the outward calm in contrast to the chaotic conditions at Fez. Our bizarre appearance with shaved heads and Berber caps drew frequent icy stares and seemed to put a fright into the superstitious Moors, who could not quite decide where we stood.

I was uncertain where I stood on the matter of Fritz. Was he somehow connected with the death of Sébastien? Was that the answer to the wraith's riddle posed at Madame Orgueil's? And if so, who was the pale man, and what was his relation to Fritz? Should we hope to locate him, seek him out, attempt to descry further information? Or should we avoid him dreadfully well and hope he could not find us? The latter course appealed to me, and when Guillaume wished to venture into the medina looking for Fritz I asked what we should do when we found him. Better to wait for Daunt and let him take care of it.

But Daunt did not appear. The evening of our departure arrived without even a message. In desperation I succumbed to Guillaume's entreaties and we set out to look for him.

For the last time we crossed the great market plaza atop the city and began our descent into the medina.

A runty man with a deformed hand blocked our way down the main thoroughfare, his twisted extremity held out to us for alms. We edged around him down a side alley which I thought I remembered doubling back into the main square halfway down the hill. Two hooded men followed rapidly behind us.

This side street did not lead safely into the open but

burrowed deeper into the medina. Our two shadows stayed close behind us. I glanced at Guillaume with his enormous bald head and wide, roving eyes.

Then we saw him. Not Daunt, but Fritz. He lurked on a balcony at a second-story window two or three streets from us, half concealed behind the sash. Only his bushy mustache and one shadowed eye showed, but I had no doubt it was he. I looked back to find our two tails had stopped and were looking up at the balcony. Before withdrawing behind the shade Fritz nodded once. Two more Moors materialized on our left, and we began to run. Footsteps clattered down the pavement behind us.

I remembered to move downhill, and we kept descending, doubling back, and slipping through narrow passageways, trying to reach the broad central corridor somewhere to our right. Somehow we managed to elude our pursuers, but when at last we emerged in the open roadway dissecting the medina, they had taken another path and preceded us there. They were now a full half-dozen: filthy, loathsome, scowling creatures in dark *jilabas.* Several wore turbans in emerald green, and they awaited us at both sides of the plaza outside our old hashish bar, from which the discordant strains of music issued. Daunt would not appear miraculously to rescue us this time. He had been waylaid, perhaps by these same villains. Our long junket through Morocco would end precisely where it had begun.

I scanned across the rooftops toward the balcony where Fritz had appeared but could not locate the place. Behind me I heard a voice, shrill and piercing, uttering censure and commands at once, but I could only sense the tone, not understand the words, for the voice spoke not German but Arabic.

At that moment a donkey passed before me bearing two huge sacks of spice. I smelled the bright fragrance through the burlap. Seizing Guillaume's hand, I pulled him with me behind the donkey, as though we might use it to fend off the assassins awaiting us where the road narrowed.

When the donkey stood before them I drew out the small bone-handled knife Daunt had given me in Fez and slashed the burlap. With my other hand I thrust upward so that the spice fanned out in the faces of the two villains on our right. Then quickly, in the confusion, I repeated this procedure, rent the other sack with an upward sweep and flushed the brilliant ocher spice into the faces of those on our left.

The owner of the donkey whirled on us screaming, but Guillaume bowled him over with remarkable force. We leapt over him past the blinded and befuddled Moors. As we raced downhill to the docks, I heard pursuing footsteps but did not look back.

At the docks we forced our way through the crowds milling along the quai and out to the customs house, where groups of forlorn Europeans stood with their trunks and string-tied crates boarding the *Du Chayla* for passage home. Still I heard pursuing footsteps and a voice, but this voice called my name.

In an anguish of heat and chest-constricting pain we reached the customs officer and, unable to speak, motioned backwards at the voice and footsteps, trying to communicate our danger. Finally I turned to face it.

It was not Fritz's henchmen nor Madani al-Glaoui's warriors who pursued us across the docks at Tangier. It was our old dragoman, Abd al-Malik, and as he tottered toward us calling my name he raised his fist, waving my old sketchpad above his head like a flag of surrender.

He reached us and was shoved roughly away by the customs officials, but I rushed to him, took the notebook, and thanked him. I explained to the officials that he had been our guide and was returning something of great value to me which I had never expected to see again. I took the few remaining *douros* from my pocket and held them out to him. To my astonishment he refused. This was so unlike him I offered them again. Still he shook his head.

"Already paid," he said, as though he knew far more than one might have guessed. Nonetheless, when I continued to offer the coins and repeated my thanks, impoverished pragmatism got the better of whatever other powerful force was at work and he accepted. The whistle sounded, the final boardings began, and before I could ask who had paid him to deliver my notebook we were swept up the gangplank and on board the *Du Chayla.*

A few moments later we loosed our moorings and I stood aft, watching the wake crest out behind us and the white hills of Tangier shimmer in the evening sun as we passed through the straits and headed out to sea.

I still held the notebook, the only of my original possessions to have miraculously survived my visit to Morocco, and I began thumbing through those sketches I had made of the city weeks before.

Guillaume stood beside me, the sea breeze in his watery eyes. He removed his wool cap and pointed at his head. I saw that somewhere in the rush down the hill and our escape his red ant mandibles had fallen out. His wound was healed and we were safely out of Morocco on our way back to France.

I had begun to close the notebook when, on the inside front cover, I noticed the cipher marks and realized who had paid Abd al-Malik and how my notebook had come back to me, though the saving of it must have been that kindhearted old man's doing.

The marks appeared as follows:

I shall leave it to my readers to decipher this message, bearing in mind that the sequence of letters begins with C and proceeds by intervals of three (thus F, I, L, etc.) from left to right across each line of the grid and clockwise from the leftmost quadrant of the X, the dotted letters following those without dots in each pair throughout the code.

Perhaps this little entertainment will keep you busy while we set sail, and when you have done you will find that we have safely arrived in France, and then you may turn the page. . . .

XVIII

"So you finally decided to play our way," Colonel Judd Struck rasped with his impeccable flair for the fresh phrase.

I sat with Darlington in the Colonel's office at the American embassy in Paris, Daunt's coded message and my translation before us on a desk, awaiting the arrival of the man from the Troisième Bureau who, Darlington assured me, could answer my questions far better than he.

Guillaume and I had reached Paris at the end of the first week of September and I had gone directly to the embassy. I clearly had no choice in the matter; my involvement was in an affair of far-reaching implications and I owed it to myself, as well as the interested powers, to be forthright.

"The faulty grammar in the first line," I was expounding my personal exegesis of Daunt's message, "this phrase 'God am Satan,' makes the reference to Fritz Amgott quite explicit yet discreet, as though encoding it were not enough. This implies that the danger of detection is great and not, we may presume, by Moors." They nodded. "At least we know Fritz is the devil in this business." I paused. "And I think that 'Satan' here must be taken quite literally: not merely a bad person but the *root of all evil*. In other words, something more than selling used weapons and ammunition to Moroccan rebels is implied. Something far fouler than that is the work of a true Satan, and I do not think Daunt would use the word thoughtlessly. Do you agree?" I glanced up.

"Maybe," allowed Colonel Struck, and Darlington nodded.

"The clue to what that greater evil might be lies in the second line, the phrase 'Check Glautsch.' Who is Mr. Glautsch?"

"That's where our friend from the Trojan Burrow can give us a hand," said the Colonel.

"I hope so," I replied. "The name means nothing to you?" I scrutinized Darlington, who shook his head.

"My, my, you've grown most perspicacious in your travels," he told me, and I smiled peavishly. The Colonel frowned and tried to conceal the fact he hadn't the vaguest idea what perspicacious meant. "I hope you will not be resistant to what is so obviously your *métier* in life," Darlington added.

"And what is that?" I asked.

"A line of work which, though you may not have chosen it, has quite clearly chosen you. You have the most marvelous facility for serendipity," he exclaimed, and again the Colonel examined his well-chewed fingernails.

"You mean intelligence work, I suppose. Daunt said the same thing, but I don't know."

"I cannot speak for your Mr. Daunt, but you are so well suited to the task. Beneath your deceptive simplicity —and I admit you had me fooled when I first made your acquaintance in those appalling circumstances last spring—lies a keen observation of all around you."

"Perhaps I should be a novelist," I quibbled. "They too utilize keen observation."

"But no, this is a much more useful trade," Darlington went on humorlessly. "You should not waste your talents in that other profession." I studied him attentively. "At least," he continued, "I pray you will complete your education this fall and seriously consider the life now open to you."

I was about to counter this when the door swung open and Ambassador White ushered the black-suited and unsmiling Monsieur Sirot from the Troisième Bureau into the office. Hands were shaken all around.

"Glad to see you've made it back from that madness down south," said the Ambassador. "And brought us a prize as well, I understand."

"Yes, sir," I snapped and trod once more over the ground I had covered with Darlington and Colonel Struck. When I reached an impasse at the name Glautsch we turned to the man from the Troisième Bureau and awaited enlightenment.

"So who is this man Glautsch?" urged the Colonel, filling the silence surrounding the somber Sirot. He did not look up, but the thinnest crease of a smile flickered across his lips.

"And who is this man Daunt?" asked the Ambassador.

"The question," replied Sirot, "Is not who but *what* is Glautsch."

"What?" I asked rhetorically.

"Yes, Monsieur Peavey. If I am not mistaken the reference is to Armand Glautsch and Company."

"I don't quite understand—"

"If you will allow me to explain," he modulated. "Glautsch is part of the cartel of firms recently conjoined into the Compagnie Marocaine. They have been influential in securing large loans from the French government to the current Sultan, placing him substantially in our debt."

"I see. And what is the business of Armand Glautsch and Company?"

"That is a trifle difficult to say. Before its absorption

in the Compagnie Marocaine it was one of several subdivisions within Schneider, a giant of French commerce and one of the largest arms manufacturers in Europe." I gulped but did not interrupt, though his lengthy pause invited it. "The history of Glautsch over the past four decades is somewhat problematical. It was originally a French chemical firm but now has fallen into German hands. I understand several of its factories and control of its day-to-day activities are jointly shared, and that certain plants are wholly operated by the Germans."

"But how can that be?" I asked. "A French firm in German hands?"

Monsieur Sirot from the Troisième Bureau smiled now, at last, and replied tartly: "The firm, monsieur, is Alsatian."

Back in Montmartre little had changed: everyone was returning from summer holidays or visits home, and our adventures and deeply bronzed appearance with just a frizz of hair were cause for countless conversations.

Paul, the sturdy Breton whose straightforward manner so appealed to me, told me that Apolline had become ill shortly after my departure, given up her role with the touring company, and spent the summer convalescing with her mother in Provence. She was expected back in Paris that fall; he did not know when. I was distressed by the news of her unspecified illness and recalled with renewed ardor my feelings at our parting.

The little Spaniard had taken a smaller studio on the top floor of the old building, and had brought back with him from the south a large mysterious canvas. He remained hidden away with what Max called "this work of madness" and admitted only a select few to his atelier, all of whom emerged pale and speechless or filled with superlatives.

Paul had summered in Great Britain and told many amusing tales of that country. He was working on a canvas entitled *England Burning,* which juxtaposed several typically English scenes with bits of bedclothing material called "Non-Flam." The *Times* advertisement, which he had affixed to the canvas, proclaimed that "Non-Flam permanently resists fire—hence coroners recommend it." This charming message provoked no end of anti-British jokes. Guillaume noted, "Today one can use any material in art; certain Italians, I understand, have even used *merde,*" but Paul demurred at this suggestion.

Following my interview at the embassy, where no further information of note was disclosed, and in the absence of word from the *saltimbanques,* I began seriously considering a return to Cambridge for the fall semester and the eventual attainment of my baccalaureate degree. With this in mind, sailing arrangements were made and Guillaume, utterly crestfallen at my cruel desertion, reluctantly planned a farewell banquet. He assured me I would be back sooner than I thought.

We journeyed one day to the Paris Préfecture on the Île de la Cité in search of Inspector Pernicieux. Approaching from the Pont Neuf I gazed along the quai where I had sat pondering my future after being barred from Madame Adelaide's. Two wet dogs and a pair of boots had been set out to dry in the sun. We strolled past hunched men at stands selling old coins and medals, through the *porte cochère* and up the broad stairs into the Préfecture.

Inspector Pernicieux was on a case. We left our names and a brief message inviting him to my farewell fête. The desk sergeant recognized our names and offhandedly informed us that our murder case had been solved.

"Oh, really?" Guillaume exclaimed. "And who was the murderer?"

"Some Moor," replied the sergeant with a shrug. "Well, I'll tell the Inspector you were here."

With this surprising—but then again not so surprising—piece of information tucked in our spinning heads we stepped back into the warm September afternoon, had a brief chat over Mutzig beers at a café, and decided to walk to Montmartre. I whistled as we ambled up the Boulevard de Sébastopol, and Guillaume crossly requested that I be silent. My "mindless frivolity" disrupted his thoughts. I was pleased to see him back to normal after his Moroccan deflation.

Our conjectures varied on that walk but all eventually reached the same point: we could not see how any Moor could have killed Sébastien. Neither of us even recalled one at St. Sulpice that day. While providing further confirmation of the entirely Moorish orientation of the crime, the police report did nothing to clarify their connection to the *saltimbanques*.

Up the Butte we climbed. Sunlight filtered through the limbs of tall elms hanging over red mansard roofs, and a child's face peered through a tall dormer between green shutters. I smiled up at her and she waved.

As we shut the front door at the Rue Ravignan I heard Max calling us down the corridor, and we went to his room. He was nibbling at a fried egg which he had cooked in an old sardine tin. The smell of sardine oil, frankincense, and lingering ether nauseated me; I could barely remain in his little cell.

Max congratulated us. Word had come down from on high—that is, from the top atelier now inhabited solely by the little Spaniard—that we would be allowed an audience before the "work of madness." Thus honored, we mounted the steps with some trepidation.

I do not intend to digress from the unraveling of the mysteries which had confounded us over those six months, but what I beheld that afternoon was so impressive, has remained so vividly in my memory, and had such a profound impact upon my state of mind and my future, which in turn contributed to that very unraveling from which I digress, that I must describe it in some detail.

The studio was dark with a single large canvas set beneath a skylight. The other canvases were turned to the walls as though afraid to face their master. It was hot as a Turkish bath and the artist wore a scarf tied at the waist and nothing else. His small body was tanned and firm. Day-old rice and tomatoes lay coagulating in a dish with a single sleeping Spaniard curled on the floor beside it.

In the painting itself—five presumably female figures arranged about a bowl of fruit—the artist had abandoned all the old devices—the illusions of *trompe l'oeil,* local proportion, perspective, and foreshortening—and chosen to express what Guillaume once called "the grandeur of the metaphysical." One felt that the nudes were observed from all angles at once, or that several views over a period of time had been superimposed on the canvas. It was baffling at first, and quite ugly. There were elements of Negro art in it, and much geometry, but it possessed something more, and I instantly understood why Max dubbed it a work of madness.

"It is like swallowing kerosene in the hope of spitting fire, to paint like this," I said.

"Yes, but it is not madness," Guillaume replied. "It is supreme courage, total confidence in one's vision. From this moment on, painting is to be a science." He paused. "And this is its governing equation."

"So he has taken refuge in this monstrous equation, in his intricate crystals and perfect geometry where he is untouchable, inscrutable. It is still self-destructive."

"Not so; but it is desperate," he admitted and stared reverently at the painting. I shook my head and inspected once more the faces with noses at once full face and in profile, the almond-shaped arms, the impossibly twisted hands and necks: these unfeminine, disjointed, grotesque figures. Perhaps this was the implication of all our splendid talk; and perhaps I too was not prepared to face it. I wanted to cover my eyes or turn away, but the canvas would not permit it.

"Do you not see what he has done, this genius who walks among us?" The Spaniard grunted and turned his back to us at these words. "He has turned our words and abstractions into fact, into a canvas which expresses all. He studies an object as a surgeon dissects a cadaver." I agreed that the figures had a distinctly cadaverous character. "No, no, much more than that." Guillaume was not listening now. The words formulated in his head and rushed forth impulsively. "It is the difference between painting with a mirror held up to life or painting diagrams of life, diagrams which reveal the non-self-evident forms and truths and reality. This is his diagram of life."

"And what does he call this diagram?"

"Everyone suggests a different title," Guillaume explained. "And he settles on none. I would call it *The Philosophic Brothel.* Max claims one of the figures resembles his grandmother and that it should be called *Max's Grandmama,* but that is too silly."

"It is hardly a silly painting," I commented and wiped the perspiration from my face. Still staring at the canvas, I addressed the flexed, muscular back of its creator. "But, señor," I asked him with astonishment, "what is it you seek?"

The dark back twitched. He whirled and gloated over us with brilliant, accusative eyes, haunting eyes which burned with something between hatred and a love so impassioned as to be more frightening than any hatred.

"Seek?" he roared at me in his lilting Spanish French, the tendons standing out in his neck. "I do not seek. To search means nothing in art. To find is the thing. The intent of my painting is not to show what I am seeking but what I have found." But what horror had he uncovered, I thought to myself; what was it he had found?

We retreated from his stuffy studio with a single backward glance at the barbaric figures on the canvas and the sleeping Spaniard in the sunlight by the plate of rice.

"Someday," I told Guillaume on the stairs, "he will be found hanging behind his own canvas."

"Nonsense," he answered me. "He is entranced. He is the instrument of his art, the medium by which a divine form expresses itself. It is magic, but not in the old sense of a clever magician who contrives and conjures. This is pure magic which flows naturally and without connivance or preconception. And that is all."

I was so troubled by what I had seen and the vague implications taking shape in my head that I could not sleep that night nor consider my still-unresolved questions regarding the *saltimbanques*.

I recalled something Daunt had told us in Fez: that chaos would dominate the new century, that the great advances in science and human thought would not forge a new order with greater understanding but lead deeper into chaos, discontinuity, and holocaust. Of course, Daunt meant chaos in political terms, social chaos, but I freely extended the metaphor to apply to the Spaniard's painting. It was brilliant, it was revolutionary, and it was undoubtedly the first work to encompass all the theories regarding primitive art, the new geometries, and the fourth dimension which we had discussed so fervently that spring. But the result was horrifying, such a distortion of beauty that I feared not only for its creator's sanity but for anyone forced to live in a world where such things might become, if not commonplace, at least an accepted vision of reality. When that happened so much would be lost, so much that I treasured, familiar things which comforted me in the vast, incomprehensible, sometimes unendurable world in which I lived: order and logic and reason itself, and justice, and compassion, respect for the past and joyful anticipation of the future, a belief that despite all the complexities surrounding one the effort to understand was not a vain effort, that it brought if not wisdom and comprehension at least a sense of peace and belonging, a personal ordering of one's affairs, and that it was this, this vital context in which we rational creatures lived, which permitted us to love one another and to develop convictions and values and to pursue our lives' ends, knowing that we might die before they were accomplished, but with an abiding sense of hope and purpose in the pursuit itself. With this destroyed, as it was in the Spaniard's canvas, anarchy would reign in society and confusion in men's minds, and I could conceive of nothing to replace what would be lost. All men would be mad and madness itself would be nothing, a mere joke with which the forces of this horrible, uncontrollable nature, this unleashed monster, would toy mercilessly in their hilarity.

I had met a true artist, and in the presence of his disturbing work of undeniable genius my own feeble gropings seemed less than art, an excuse for self-indulgence, a total delusion regarding both my own talent, or lack thereof, and my disposition. I was not fit to compete with a man who would swallow kerosene in the hope of spitting fire; I did not really wish to spit fire. But to paint more conventionally, to disregard what I had learned, to doodle and sketch cartoons and be clever and arch as I had done so contentedly for so long, this too was a vast self-deception, a cheap venality with which I could not live. Drawing was a satisfactory recreation, something into which I could always escape to amuse myself, but it was not and could never be the obsession of my life nor the controlling factor in shaping the way I lived and what I hoped to achieve. I had not considered my life in this light before. I had done what pleased me and been satisfied, but my confrontation with the blinding vision and overpowering conviction in that canvas produced within me the need to find such things in my life, to give it a meaning as profound and compelling as his. In despair I realized that my art could never do this.

In this state I lay awake through the night, alone, into a bright autumn morning. What I had experienced in Morocco, though not at the forefront of my thoughts that night, may have primed my soul for this conversion, this loss of faith in my art. I resolved that I should use my sudden perception of the unleashed monster, my privileged position as it were, to help fashion a buffer, a balancing force which might protect and restore sanity, and with it the capacity for love and work, to mankind faced with the sundering reality implied in that painting. I recognized that my initially halfhearted decision to return to Harvard was now the only one I could make. I would not become an intelligence agent as Darlington suggested, much less a diplomat of the more pedestrian sort my father envisioned, but would broaden myself, explore my real nature, and gain access to places where I could most usefully employ what I felt to be this special secret I had uncovered.

Inspector Pernicieux called on us in Montmartre two days before my farewell fête. He heartily welcomed us back to Paris and sat in the dappled shade at our table outside Père Frédé's, where he drank three glasses of red wine. He was positively jaunty and seemed fully ten years younger than when we left; he told us this was due in large part to Guillaume's encouragement in his painting. He had new confidence in that and, consequently, in himself. As for the night of his banquet . . .

"That is really what I've come to discuss." He regained the officious air of old, his pince-nez set loftily in place. "Your behavior on that occasion was utterly inexcusable and I cannot forgive it. Nevertheless, it was my curious good fortune to fall asleep in the studio. The next morning I awoke to find two extremely menacing Moors prowling the Place Ravignan. Considering the likelihood of their connection with the death of Charles, I had them arrested—and then the remarkable coincidence." He paused for effect. Guillaume and I exchanged dubious glances: we had learned much about coincidence. "One of these Moors carried in his pocket a palm-size tube and several needlelike darts. Experts at the Sûreté examined the tube and determined it to be a small dart gun. The needles had been dipped in a deadly poison. I demanded that the body of the *saltimbanque* lad be exhumed, and when it was . . . you recall the curious lumps we found on his side which we assumed to be the bite or sting of an insect? Perhaps not. They were in fact puncture wounds inflicted by two of these tiny poison darts. Faced with this evidence, the Moor confessed to the murder of Sébastian Zorn." He smiled broadly. "Case closed."

"That explains the vision of Sébastien pierced with arrows at Madame Orgueil's, does it not, Guillaume?" My partner was slightly dazed by these disclosures. He slowly nodded while I explained to the Inspector the details of our vision of the wraith St. Sébastien on the night of Charles' death.

"Most remarkable. I have always believed clairvoyants to be no more than charlatans and fakirs, but perhaps there is something to this spirit business after all."

"There is one thing more, Inspector. We know how the boy was killed and by whom. But we don't know why. Why should this Moor want to kill the young acrobat?"

"My dear Clayton," he reprimanded me. "You would never make a good detective." His opinion of my qualifications differed sharply from others recently voiced. "One seeks motives for unsolved crimes, not for those which have been solved and in which there has been a confession. What difference does it make why he killed him?" He snorted and bristled and poured himself a fourth glass of wine.

I scanned Guillaume's face for recognition of our mutual thoughts. It did matter why, and for the answer to that question we could not turn to the American Embassy, nor the Sûreté, nor even the Troisième Bureau. I pictured the expression on the face of a flushed, bejowled clown in the Place St. Sulpice; an expression which said, "I know, at this instant, you are not guilty," and eyes which searched the crowd for the real murderer. Arbogast Zorn could tell us *why* but, to Guillaume's immense disappointment, there had been no response to the advertisements he had placed in the trade journals of the *banquistes*. The *saltimbanques* either did not wish to be found or had not seen the advertisements; in either case we were no closer to locating them than before we set out for Morocco.

Some things never changed in Montmartre, and this being Thursday we were all going to the Cirque Mediano. Since my sleepless night of introspection earlier in the week I had drifted listlessly through "our" activities, biding my time until the day of departure. This final visit to the circus suddenly excited my interest. While enjoying the festivities we might again question Darius Boppe about the Zorns. I invited the Inspector to accompany us.

"No, my young friends, I cannot. There is always work to do, and for those of us who must labor for a living there is little time. I am engaged in an exciting new canvas. I hope you will come to see it before you depart, Clayton." I promised him I would try and reminded him of the farewell fête two days hence.

"Oh, I shall be here to bid you adieu." He smiled affably, swiping the droplets of wine from his mustache with a swish of his forefinger. "By the way, Guillaume," he confided, "I find your dear mother to be a most generous and kindhearted woman. You should pay as much attention to her needs as she does to yours. Not that I would interfere, but speaking as a man of some experience, and as a father." He stopped speaking. Rising, he popped his bowler onto his head and trotted off down the hill. Guillaume was left somewhere between rage and hysterics over his parting comment.

"Well, I must speak to Mama about that," he mused. "I believe the Inspector is smitten, Clayton Peavey." Though he spoke in jest his eyes were cold and defensive.

A few moments later such thoughts were abandoned as all the gang, even the fire spitter himself, cavorted from Père Frédé's past Sacré Coeur down the steps of the Butte and along the Boulevard Rouchechouart to our regular weekly session at the Med.

XIX

That evening at the circus was totally unlike my first visit there. No Moors lurked in the shadows, no apaches slept on deserted benches. Along the boulevard open stalls were heaped with cheap clothing, and evening crowds still jostled at the curb. All was brightly lit, vibrant with activity and good cheer. I expected little more than a few hours' diversion for my franc.

The performances at the Cirque Mediano were highly entertaining. A brass band blared beside the ring, the *forains* shouted from their booths, equestrians galloped about, and acrobats performed on bicycles and tightropes. Our group, numbering nearly a dozen, shouted wildly when the clowns appeared dressed in their ill-fitting clothes and huge shoes.

Darius Boppe was in whiteface with his eyebrows plucked pencil thin. He wore a white skullcap with three holes through which clumps of bright orange hair protruded. When Guillaume caught his chocolate eye he looked distressed to see us and managed to avoid further troublesome glances. Apart from sudden bursts of nearly violent hilarity, Guillaume was brooding and distracted, redolent with instinctive foreboding.

At the intermission we congregated by the long bar. Boppe approached and exchanged with Guillaume that formalized greeting I had heard before: "The time has come for the clowns to be masters." Neither of them seemed to believe it.

He motioned us to the end of the bar.

"I hoped to avoid this meeting," he said. "But I

knew that one Thursday you would come again to the *cirque*. And so you have." Guillaume stared at him and said nothing. "They are here at the Mediano. They have seen your advertisements but could not risk answering them. They wish to speak with you, though I have vehemently discouraged such a meeting."

"You mean, the Zorns are here—"

"Yes," he said, holding a finger to his bright red lips. "*La Famille Jollicorps*. They wait for you in their tent on the waste grounds. Come."

Before we could reply he turned and slowly made his way toward the performers' entrance to the ring. We left the gang chatting and drinking at the bar and followed Darius Boppe out back.

Behind the main wood structure of the Cirque Mediano, bunched in among railroad tracks, vans and carts for hauling circus equipment, and all manner of tents, were the living quarters of most of the performers. Smoky dark, it smelled of hay and urine (for the animals were quartered here as well), of bubbling stew and theatrical cosmetics.

Beyond the humor and gaiety and brilliance inside the circus, life on the waste grounds was drab and imbued with the familiar lassitude I had observed in Darius Boppe on our first meeting. One almost felt the aching muscles of the gymnasts. The abandoned smiles of the clowns were tossed to one side like dirty wrinkled costumes or broken props.

Outside the Jollicorps' wagon their old horse was being watered by a thin man who kept his back to us as we pushed aside the shaggy curtain and stepped inside.

A black pot hung simmering over a low wood fire, and on a bench beside it sat the woman with the mantic eyes, her long fingers darning a child's tutu. Across from her on an upturned barrel sat Arbogast Zorn, the massive clown, drinking his soup from a bowl. A drum top on his knees served as plate for bread and a chunk of cheese. He was dressed in a long, dark robe, tied clumsily over his bulging stomach. When we entered he glanced up, set down his bowl and the drum top, and stepped forward into the half-light before the fire.

"And so at last," he said. "Coco said you might come this night." He shook our hands. The firmness of his prolonged grip was gentle and restrained.

"We have searched very far for you," Guillaume whispered. Something in the shadowy solitude, at the very edge of misery, required whispers and justifications.

"You have searched for us?" Arbogast Zorn asked.

"For some reason, some understanding of what happened that day," Guillaume explained.

"We have been to Morocco," I added.

At this the old clown shuddered. "Ah, then you already know much of what I might tell you."

"We have learned many things." Guillaume selected his words carefully. "Many small parts which remain scattered."

"We hoped—" I began.

Zorn stopped me. "You hoped I might bring these parts together for you?"

"Yes," I nodded.

"I can. Perhaps I will." He glanced at Boppe. "My comrade has advised me not to reveal the things I wish to tell you. But I feel you deserve to know. Learning that you have been as far as Morocco, I believe this more firmly." Boppe began to leave the wagon, but before he departed Arbogast Zorn added: "You must understand. We have spent many years building something of which you inadvertently became a small part. This cannot be endangered for any reason. Too many lives depend upon it. If I felt I could not trust you to honor my confidences, you would not be standing here now. We are adept at remaining hidden when we choose. Do you understand?"

We both nodded while Arbogast Zorn regarded Boppe, almost as if asking permission to continue. With a slight tilt of his head Boppe acquiesced and silently withdrew. As he stepped from the wagon the lank man who had been watering the horse entered.

"My brother Gaspard will sit with us," said Zorn. The man, whom I recognized as the harlequin father of the children, did not sit but leaned against the supports of the canvas canopy and rolled a cigarette in thick yellow paper. There was no sign of the children, and the gaunt woman continued darning her dreams.

"What I cannot understand," I questioned the old clown more confidently with Boppe gone, "is why the Moors wished to kill your boy. It's incomprehensible to me, this vital connection on which all the rest depends."

"Yet it is quite simple. I shall explain. But please make yourselves comfortable, if you can, in our poor home. I wish all things to become clear to you. But for that I must go far back, many decades, before Sébastien's birth. When you have heard all of my story, then, perhaps, you will begin to understand."

We hunched along the splintered floorboards of the wagon across from the fire, and Arbogast Zorn began his tale.

"I have some great need to tell all of my story, and I believe you two young men have come to me so that I might unburden myself. It was no coincidence that placed you in the Place St. Sulpice that day. Of that I am certain. There are always reasons." He rested his thick hands on his knees and leaned forward with a long intaken breath, precondition to the great sigh which followed.

"I was born in the village Thann on the eastern

slopes of the Vosges mountains above Mulhouse. My father, and his father before him, carved wooden rollers for printing designs on the calico tissues of our region. For many years we pursued our craft and served as local troubadours, passing the legends of Thann from generation to generation and occasionally taking to the streets with the musicians and other performers to celebrate our traditional festivals. But the performers of the Bas-Rhin no longer attend the festivals.

"The first uprooting occurred when I was a boy. As the textile industry grew, the demand for artisans like my father decreased. He was forced to move down from the mountains into the city of Mulhouse. There he found a job in one of the great mills along the Rhine.

"Still, we enjoyed our life there. Mulhouse was organized for the good of its workers into clean, gas-lit Working Men's Cities. Each family owned its own home, and a worker's association guaranteed the general welfare.

"I should explain that Mulhouse had long been among the Swiss cantons. In sympathy with the principles of the Great Revolution we joined the French Republic in 1798. This was a happy union.

"At the time of the German attack in the war of 1870, I was a young man and Gaspard only an infant. I eagerly joined the struggle to protect my homeland. My father died in that struggle, and many of my friends died as well. I saw my home overrun, churches and factories and libraries burned, the spirit vanquished from our land. I watched helplessly as Mulhouse was torn from France and made part of the new *Kultur*, the Reichsland.

"Our conquerors called us their long lost brothers, but treated us as enemies. Peasants were terrorized. Old men and children were imprisoned for disrespect to the Kaiser's image.

"When the day of choice came I knew I must leave my home if I was ever to see it whole again. I could not spend my days and years in the broken corpse it had become. We were given this choice: by the first of October in 1872, if we wished to leave our homes and families, our jobs and friends, we could do so; if not, on that date we would become Germans.

"My mother refused to leave. She told me she had died with my father and would not abandon his body there. She died six months later. And so I set out with Gaspard, who was but two years old, and a neighbor from the Working Men's City at Mulhouse.

"That day is etched upon my memory for many reasons. Every moment in the crossing of the mountains, our passage above Thann and down onto the plains of Belfort, is as clear to me in all its horror as on the day of our flight. The trains overflowed with fugitives, many clinging to the rooftops. Swarms of refugees filled the roads, their households piled on wobbly carts, all knowing it was better to have nothing and remain French than to keep all and be German. I particularly remember one very old man, bedridden, swaddled in a great quilt atop an old cart. We walked beside him for several hours and parked our cart near his at the outskirts of Belfort, beyond Bartholdi's Lion. We remained there several days, seeking for what we did not know. On the fourth day I secured train passage to Paris, where I hoped to find work. The old man, drained by the crossing of the mountains, was dying. He thanked God he would die a Frenchman. Those were his words, spoken in a weak voice filled with indomitable pride which echoes within me to this day.

"There was no work in Paris. Many Parisians were openly hostile to the refugees who had come seeking a new life there. Gaspard and I camped in our cart by the

Seine. I thought we would starve that first autumn in Paris. But when winter came the first miracle came with it. That miracle lies all around you. It was the circus.

"I had never considered my knowledge of Alsatian songs and comic tales anything more than a recreation. Something to keep the past alive in my heart. During the first harsh winter in Paris several of us with similar backgrounds realized we might employ these assets where we could not use our hands and backs in labor. We were young, dedicated above all to the recovery of our homeland, but resourceful and not without humor. So we formed a troupe of clowns and began performing. Four of us at first, of whom I think you have met all but one. Of course, the deeper intentions and goals of our comic brotherhood were not to establish a circus and entertain, not merely to achieve a livelihood and hide our faces with makeup. Yet the role served us well, and in 1873 we founded the Cirque Mediano. We created a community for ourselves around which others in our unhappy circumstances might congregate.

"But we remained refugees in a land besieged by refugees. The societies set up to deal with Alsatians in Paris did not think highly of circus life. There were other, more essential vocations. I was young and strong and could be of use in the colonies. And so, two years after the birth of the circus, Gaspard and I were resettled in Algeria.

"Over a thousand Alsatian families were resettled at French expense in Algiers and Oran. We were told we were 'farmers who could tame the Algerian wilderness and make it forever French.' For several weeks we lived in tents awaiting our assignment to the free holdings. Finally we were given two oxen, fodder, and seed and dispatched to our arid, inhospitable farms.

"As I was unmarried I shared my homestead with

another man, a friend of my father's from Mulhouse whose wife had died the first winter in Paris. Shortly after his arrival in Oran he married an Algerian girl, and a daughter was born. She and Gaspard grew up together on that barren farm outside Oran, where we lived for nearly twenty years.

"I might have married too and settled peacefully on my homestead. But I had discovered the possibility of something greater in Paris, and nothing could distract me from it. My father's friend raised Gaspard as his own son and by 1880 I had become disillusioned with this quiet, useless life. I moved to the city, where many young *colons* had gone. There I met soldiers and legionnaires in the bars. I decided to join the Foreign Legion, to prepare myself for the inevitable struggle to regain my homeland.

"The Foreign Legion had little of the glamour or glory associated with it in those days. Algeria had been colonized for fifty years. I served uneventfully for three years at a small outpost on the borders of the Sahara near Gerryville.

"I love France and shall always love her, but I do not love what France has done in Algeria, nor what she is setting about doing in Morocco. My view of life changed in the Legion. It was at the time of the revolt of the Ouled Sis Cheikh confederation. We were dispatched into the desert to quell the rebellion, but we had underestimated it. A group of us were caught in a sandstorm in the small, isolated valley of the Chott Tigri. The name still horrifies me. Chott Tigri. We were cut off from the other troops and ambushed there by several thousand Moslems. Nearly all our battalion was massacred. I pretended to be dead and lay several hours beneath the desert sun, suffering from head and leg wounds, curled between the bodies of two dead companions and half covered by swirling sands. I believed I would die in that spot. My mind and spirit crossed many bridges during those hours, bridges backward through my past and the life of my people in Alsace, and bridges which I could not distinguish but which seemed to lead forward from that place into something fine and great. The rebel tribesmen returned to Chott Tigri. I lay in my shallow grave watching them decapitate and mutilate the bodies of my comrades. Watching my death approach. Before they reached me another battalion of legionnaires arrived, repulsed them with a volley of gunfire, and descended into the valley. I was rescued and hospitalized in Oran. When I had recovered I quit the Foreign Legion and returned to the farm where my brother was living.

"I remained there, bored and unhappy, playing at being a farmer, always waiting to move toward the great end I had foreseen for myself beneath the sun at Chott Tigri. Gaspard and the daughter of my father's friend were the most intimate of companions all their lives. As these intimacies will lead to experimentation at a certain age, when the girl was fourteen she became pregnant. The father was furious. He threatened Gaspard and me, but the native mother calmed him. They were not blood relatives and they insisted they loved each other. They were married and Sébastien was born, but the father refused to let us remain on his land. I went briefly with the young couple to Oran, then to Algiers. From there I communicated with my old circle of clowns. The Cirque Mediano was thriving and we would be welcome back in Paris. And so, in 1893, after eighteen years in Algeria, we returned to France.

"We remained at the Mediano until the first year of the new century. Those were the happiest years of my life. Two more children were born to Kasia and Gaspard, and we all immersed ourselves in the life of the circus. Sébastien was tumbling and doing acrobatics as soon as he could walk, and Claudie also began performing when she was practically an infant. Little Thiébaut took naturally to animals from an early age. I was content, surrounded at last by my true compatriots and bound by our desire for revenge. We found joy in the work we did in Paris, the pleasure we brought to children, and the forgetfulness of sorrow we brought to each other in our baggy clothes and painted faces. That, too, was part of those happy years.

"I wished desperately to visit Alsace again during this time. Darius had done so once. The dangers for a refugee, should the Germans catch him, were very great. Those were the years of fearsome repression, the Blood and Iron regime of Prince von Hohenlohe-Schillingsfurst. No one from France was allowed into Alsace without a special passport, nearly impossible to obtain. French was removed from the street signs and even from the tombstones, as though they could reclaim the dead as well for the Reichsland. During the nineties this repression broke the spirit of my countrymen. Those who remained in the homeland began to seek autonomy under the Reichstag, to accept the annexation and forget our past. Only a few fanatics still clung to the dream of revenge. It was simply too dangerous. The best of Alsace, its future leaders, had been lost in the emigration. A new generation had grown up since 1871, without living memory of the past, born under German rule and less inclined to resist it.

"Back in Paris we plotted and schemed and prayed for the day of recovery. But by the beginning of the new century it seemed all was lost. 'There is no injustice, no reason to recover Alsace and Lorraine,' said many in France. Others admitted the injustice but felt the balance of power in Europe was too delicate to be endangered. I will not bore you with their lies. As for the Germans, they said it was all 'a misunderstanding.' There was no question of Alsace-Lorraine.

"I became restless in Paris, making the people laugh, growing fat, and watching Alsace fade from the hearts and minds of all but a few old men like myself. I could not bear it. So Gaspard and I took upon ourselves a more active role, that of couriers for the resistance movement based at the Cirque Mediano. We became a traveling family of *saltimbanques. La Famille Jollicorps.* This was an ideal cover for our travels, allowing us easy passage across all but that one inviolable border. We carried documents and secret messages from Spain to Holland and Brussels, from Paris to our brothers in Italy, to the independence movements in the Balkans, and even into Germany itself.

"Once more I was doing something to free my homeland. I found peace for my heart in the constant travel and in the sort of danger which had once drawn me to the Foreign Legion.

"As couriers we crossed paths with many groups fighting for freedom in many places, within Europe and in the colonized areas of the Mediterranean. So it was that three years ago, in Amsterdam, I was contacted by an Englishman recently returned from Morocco. He knew of our work as couriers and introduced me to his friend, an educated Moor of some standing in Amsterdam, a merchant and importer of African crafts. We spoke of my experiences in Algeria and his anxiety over the activities of France and other European powers in his country. I sympathized with his fears and shared his hopes for the continued independence and sovereignty of his people, just as he shared my hopes for the recovery of the lost provinces. We agreed to aid each other. *La Famille Jollicorps* would serve as continental couriers for his movement, and he would provide protection for us.

He also promised to supply weapons to the Alsatian movement when we needed them.

"Again I must repeat, and you must understand, there were many such pacts. Many people came to us for help and we, in turn, in time went to them. When it concerns the freedom of an oppressed people one does not ask many questions. One simply follows one's instincts. Our association with the Moors began in 1905, at a time of crisis in their land. We carried coded messages into France and Brussels for them. On two occasions I delivered messages to the Moorish merchant in Amsterdam. I was reassured by his presence in their organization. The Moors with whom we regularly dealt were ruffians, and inspired little confidence, but this man was different. I never again saw the Englishman who first introduced me to these Moors.

"We transported messages and other items for them in a hollow mask we had been given for this purpose. Sébastien took an immediate liking to the mask, which he always wore around his neck like an amulet. He claimed it would bring us all good fortune. And I was foolish enough to allow this.

"We had been involved with the Moors for two years when I began to suspect something sinister in their intrigues. I don't know what it was that first alerted me, but one knows when one has been involved in this sort of work for as long as I have. Sébastien denied my allegations. He liked the Moors and smoked hashish with them and played their native instruments when we met at our encampments outside Brussels and Amsterdam. Since he was born in Algeria and raised in Paris, Alsace was for him only an abstraction, a ghost. Yet all the more powerful because less real and less tangible. He was totally absorbed by the life of courier for a movement which he did not even begin to understand.

"You may recall that shortly before the incident

which began our acquaintance the English King Edward VII visited Paris. There was a flurry of activity among the Moroccans at this time. I saw a decoded message which indicated that a plan was afoot to assassinate the King during his stay in Paris. One of Sébastien's Moorish friends even boasted of this. I recognized that the assassination would be blamed on the French and would serve to alienate the two countries and undo the good that had been done with the Entente Cordiale. I could not understand why the Moors should wish to do this. It was of no advantage for them to kill Edward VII. It would not bring freedom to Morocco. The more I puzzled over it, the more a frightening prospect formed in my mind. I recalled trivial elements in our association with the Moors—bits of dialogue, odd references, messages indiscreetly revealed. All of them pointed to one nation, one power in Europe, for whom this assassination and the ensuing discord between France and England would be of the greatest benefit. The Germans.

"With that realization I knew we must end our relationship with the Moors. I did not reveal my suspicions but created an elaborate tale of our doing special work for the Alsatian movement. While speaking of future cooperation, I refused to deliver the coded messages relating to the assassination and a packet of explosives which accompanied them. The Moors were very displeased. But Sébastien was absolutely irreconcilable. When he understood that I suspected we had been duped into serving, albeit indirectly, our German enemies, he raged uncontrollably and said many things he should not have said in the presence of the Moors. He threatened them and revealed certain of my private thoughts to them. The situation was far too complex for Sébastien. He did not know what he was doing.

"For several days, to my horror, we were stalked by

these Moors. Then, on that afternoon in the Place St. Sulpice, Sébastien was killed.

"You can imagine my grief for having permitted his involvement in this intrigue. I do not know if the Moors killed him as a warning to us or because they felt they must answer the challenge in his threats. I have since learned that the Moors themselves had split. Many of them were dupes like ourselves without any knowledge of the German connections of their movement. They felt double-crossed, while those who had known felt betrayed. My brother's son was the victim of their confusion and discord.

"Of course, I immediately recognized your unfortunate involvement in this case. Half the Moors believed you had killed their trusted courier. The other half saw you as scapegoats for their own crime. I wanted to help you, but did not know how. I feared for my life and the lives of my brother and his family. I also feared a breach in our own organization by the Moors. This danger was most terrible of all. Our usefulness to the movement would be ended. So we fled that night, and throughout the summer we continued moving across Europe. At last we heard from Darius of the formal resolution of the murder case and the arrest of several Moors.

"After Sébastien's death the idea of continuing to serve as couriers became intolerable to me and to his parents. I think we have returned to Paris once more, perhaps to stay at the Mediano. Our days of travel, at least mine, are finished.

"But the hint of a conspiracy between England and Germany frightened me. If the Germans succeed through some ploy in bringing England to their side in the coming war, Alsace and Lorraine may be lost for yet another generation. This is an incidental consideration for the British, but not for France nor for the Alsatians. We have endured the Romans, the Huns, the Vandals, the Prussians. Alsace remains Alsace. Our soil has been sullied and our spirit crushed, but the words spoken at Bordeaux in 1871 and the spirit embodied in them have enabled us to live through nearly four decades of migration and oppression. Perhaps you know the words to which I refer."

He stopped speaking. In the silence I met his gaze and heard my voice repeat the words I had seen on the little plaque in Clovis Vogel's shop.

"N'en parlez jamais; mais pensez-y toujours."

"Yes," he replied softly. "Only tonight I have spoken of it far too much. Far more than I have ever spoken of these things before."

He bowed his head and rubbed his hands together between his legs as though a chill had run through his sagging flesh. We remained seated around the low, growling fire for some time; the only sound was the movement of the needle in the long, dark fingers of Kasia Zorn.

"But these Moors followed us," I said at last. "They killed a man in Montmartre looking for us."

"They believed you had killed their messenger. At least some of them did. And they may have been hoping to recover the mask."

"Ah, the mask again. But why do they want it?"

"That I cannot tell you. But they *do* want it."

"Didn't you recover the mask from the police?" I asked hopefully.

"No. The mask disappeared from the Préfecture and the police could not account for it. I think they knew what happened to it but refused to say." He shrugged, apparently less concerned than I with the fate of the mask.

"The Troisième Bureau," I said beneath my breath. The ensuing hush in the little wagon seeped across me like a cool mist, turning what had come clear indistinct. The long-nosed face in dark wood floated through the mist, a single salient eye watching me, challenging me with its continuing enigma. But this was not the only remaining unresolved puzzle.

"I hesitate to ask more of you," I confessed, "but I must ask one thing." Arbogast Zorn looked at me ruefully. It seemed the exertion of telling his tale and the unstinting struggle over four decades would crush even this massive man. "What do you know of Armand Glautsch and Company?"

He was surprised and puzzled by my question.

"Glautsch? I think it is an Alsatian firm. What should I know? There is a plant outside Mulhouse, in Ottmarsheim, where I believe chemicals are manufactured. I really don't know."

"I think there is some connection between this firm and your Moors," I said. Again the ambivalent silence settled over the wagon. I turned to Guillaume. "This explains the vision of Sébastien at Madame Orgueil's."

Gaspard and Kasia Zorn had remained silent throughout Arbo's long recounting of their lives. When I mentioned their son I felt upon me two pairs of wistful eyes.

"What vision have you had?" Kasia's dry lips trembled and the needle slipped from her fingers onto the floor.

I described our visit to Madame Orgueil's and the wraith pierced with arrows who told us that his murderer lay *in the mountains*. She was overcome by my account and brushed the tears from her cheeks. Her husband remained silent and immobile.

Arbogast was particularly interested in the pale man. When I described him the old clown leaned back on his barrel and shut his eyes.

"Where is the girl?" Guillaume asked suddenly.

"Who? Claudie? She is sleeping with her brother." Arbogast gestured toward the back of the wagon but did not open his eyes.

"Might I see her?" Guillaume hesitated. "I . . . I should like to see her again."

We followed Gaspard across the wagon. When he slung back the strings of curtain separating the sleeping and living quarters a shaft of firelight illuminated a tiny wood bed where two small figures were curled beneath a patchwork quilt.

Claudie lay on her back with her face turned into the faint light. Her thin bare shoulders were exposed and one hand clutched at the covers as though modestly trying to hide her naked shoulders. I suppose one could have found in her face that curious and fascinating mixture of child and young woman which reveals itself in girls of a certain age, but to me, seeing her asleep with her brother Thiébaut, hers was the face of a child, truly angelic, with a fragile beauty, and only the long, dark fingers—so much like her mother's—to gainsay this image of innocence.

Guillaume's reverent expression and the hint of a tender smile on his lips said that he saw much more than a sleeping child in a tiny bed. He obviously detected some delitescent power within Claudie, or some power which he would create and set there, something hidden from the rest of us: a powerful aura, glimmering in the drab darkness of the *saltimbanque*'s wagon.

Outside the wagon came the pitter of passing footsteps and a horse's neigh. Claudie swiveled her slim shoulders, twisted her face away from us, and flung her hand back across her brother's body. The vision drifted from Guillaume's eyes.

"We will help you," he told the old clown when we

had gathered again before the fire. He lighted a cigarette and drew deeply on it. "We *must* help you."

"Very well," Arbogast assented. "Though I think you can do little for us."

"But you must let me." Guillaume rushed forward, overpowered by the passion within him. "You must let me give her the opportunity she deserves. You must let me free her to become what she can become."

Arbogast Zorn was more amused than put off by Guillaume's urgency. "My good man, I don't know quite what you have in mind." He glanced at his brother. "She is a lovely and talented child, I agree, but given to uncontrollable extremes of mood. These have worsened since her brother's death. And your association with that trauma. I don't know, monsieur. Nevertheless, we shall be staying in Paris, for some months at least. We will be pleased to receive you again, and you may speak to Claudie about whatever plans you have for her." He smiled as a thought occurred to him. "In a way, she is a Parisienne; she was born here. Perhaps she will thrive here."

"That is all I ask. The rest she will do herself. In return I shall endeavor to help you end your days of suffering and exile, and achieve your proper destiny as you envisioned it in the sands of Chott Tigri."

"I appreciate your sympathy. But I think our martyrdom must be ended by powers far greater than yours." He gripped our hands between his thick fingers for a long time. Before we took our leave, he said: "Do not repeat to anyone what I have told you this evening." And he added, "The time has come for the clowns to be masters." That simple phrase was replete with new meanings for me now. "Be very careful if you step into our lives again, messieurs. Your chance involvement has ended. If you advance knowingly into this web, you will be forever entangled. Forever."

Guillaume nodded solemnly, and with the trance-like melancholy stare of Kasia Zorn clinging to the backs of our necks we descended from the little wagon into a mild Parisian night.

XX

The next day Guillaume and I began drinking before noon: reliving our adventures, celebrating our successes, and relishing the curious dichotomies in our personalities which had bound us together over six months. Sitting in the sycamore sunlight at Père Frédé's—where the *patron* regaled us with free drink and sang Ronsard sonnets to harmonium accompaniment—I was handed an envelope bearing the seal of the American embassy.

"Well." I set Darlington's letter on the table. "It turns out Armand Glautsch and Company has been an affiliate of Amgott Woffen und Munitions Fabriken since immediately after the annexation of Alsace-Lorraine. Our old friend Fritz, you see." Guillaume glanced at me vaguely. He still viewed our Moroccan escapades as little more than exotic material for a series of poems and essays. I continued reading from the letter. "The interlocking company relationships with Schneider and Amgott remain a bit muddled, but it is clear that certain operations of the Amgotts' were transferred to the main Glautsch plant near Mulhouse in the 1870s. Fritz himself worked there for several years before beginning his travels, which ended in Tangier." I looked at Guillaume, and he nodded. "Relations between Papa Amgott and the Wilhelmstrasse remain quite cordial, Fritz notwithstanding. Ordnance experts at the Quai d'Orsay believe the chemical facilities at Ottmarsheim have undergone certain renovations since 1871."

"Fascinating," Guillaume said with apparent disinterest as he refilled his wineglass.

"But it is, Guillaume," I contended vainly. "The assassination plot against the English king which precipitated Sébastien's death must be subsumed in some broader intrigue. The link to Glautsch is the key."

"But where is the link?" he grumbled. "I still don't see it."

"I don't know yet. But someday I'll find it, and then we can destroy the evil responsible for Sébastien's death and God knows how much more sorrow and misery endured by those poor people."

"We?" Guillaume smirked. "A noble crusade for you, Clayton Peavey. But we have discovered what we sought. We found the *saltimbanques*."

"Perhaps that is enough for you, my friend. Not for me." I recalled Daunt's words—"it gets into your blood, this life"—and Darlington's belief that I had grown "perspicacious," and I knew that, better without Guillaume than with him, I would someday confront Fritz Amgott.

Today, though, was for celebration; for endings, not beginnings. We drank all afternoon, and Guillaume arranged for us to dine outside Montmartre at a small bistro he had frequented in earlier days. We could be alone there and talk.

"I have invited Marie to join us after dinner," he told me. "She has a little surprise for you."

"Does she?" I replied. Something in the lascivious twinkle in Guillaume's eye and the warmth of the wine inside me suggested that were Timothy Daunt to create a cipher for my surprise it would commence, like mine, with the letter C, and for the same reason.

We were dreadfully drunk by the end of our dinner and sat blithering over our cognac, the velvet gentleman coaxing bittersweet phrases from his piano, when Marie appeared in the doorway of the little bistro and proved my guess correct. Breathing sensuality, Catherine glided into the room and flopped down in the chair beside me. She wore a clinging gauze gown, decolleté, with a rose attached at her bosom and a chartreuse turban entirely encircling her head.

"Isn't it a splendid outfit?" said Marie. "She's working as a mannequin for the incomparable Paul Poiret. Iribe will be drawing her tomorrow for his collection."

I praised Mousieur Poiret's latest creation. "But what has become of the divine Mathieu?" I chuckled to Catherine. She cooed "Clayton" in my ear and pressed against me, her hand on my thigh, her head on my shoulder.

We drank another round of cognac. Then, as it was nearly closing time, we found a fiacre and squeezed into the seat with the girls on our laps for the ride through another balmy evening back to the Rue Ravignan.

"You look so funny with your little scar," Catherine told Guillaume. She insisted on touching the pale lines where the ant mandibles had been. Our hair had grown in an even stubble all over our heads. Guillaume, with his big lips and high scarred forehead, looked more like some grotesque clown at the Mediano than an ordinary person on the street. I think this suited him quite well, lending a physical dimension to his deep-seated belief that he was indeed a cut above the ordinary, an exception to the common moral codes and practicalities of daily life.

"The old worlds are disappearing forever," he was saying. "Men are flying through the sky, dancing before our eyes on suspended screens, speaking to us from little boxes, rushing past us in carriages without horses. Everything is new and everything is possible. And the artist must sacrifice everything to this truth, to his vision and to the deeper reality he alone comprehends."

"Bravo, Guillaume," Marie congratulated him, though not without the sardonic edge with which she so often welcomed his proclamations.

I was about to engage in a little drunken discourse on this subject, but Catherine clapped her hand over my mouth. We were lounging comfortably in Guillaume's studio amidst candles and mirrors and jasmine. Through the open window a soft breeze wafted across us. Unwinding her turban, Catherine shook loose her waves of dark hair; my own constraints also unwound as the tresses fell over her shoulders. As I embraced Catherine and rolled on top of her, the door behind us opened noiselessly and a phantom whom I assumed to have disappeared entirely from my life hovered in the doorway.

"I was told you wished to see me. I have come far but . . ." She was frightening; frightened yet intimidating in her soft, aloof manner and the sudden hurt in her wide eyes. "But I see I am disturbing you." She turned to go.

"No. Apolline, no, I—" I leapt from Catherine and rushed after her, impulsively taking her cold hand. In horror she whirled, withdrew her hand from me, and held it trembling against her flat breast.

"You would violate me as well," she said.

I wobbled, I wavered. Had I tried to move I might well have staggered, but with bloodshot eyes I beseeched her to stay.

"You smell of it," she said coldly, and I covered my mouth compulsively with one hand.

"I did wish . . . I do wish to speak with you again. And to thank you for—" She shook her head and gazed at the floor.

We stood frozen until she raised her eyes and stared into me and through me. Her brief look was gone before I could answer. It was devoid of emotion: neither anger nor fear nor love nor regret. I was merely another element in the void surrounding her.

"No, Clayton, you have changed. The thing I held sacred in you is lost. I only imagined it . . . just like all the rest. . . ."

I shook my head and heard Catherine giggling behind me.

"No," Apolline said. "I see it in your eyes. Do not lie to me as well. You are lost." She pronounced the words carefully, like an incantation, and cast me one last ineffable look. "Lost . . ."

The word shivered out of the darkness behind her as she turned and slipped silently into the hall.

For a moment I hung in the doorway and watched her recede into the darkness. I felt my optimism—all my lusty anticipation of a night with Catherine and my confident resolve to return to Harvard—tumble away from me and turn to dust at my feet. I glanced back at Catherine, giggling and goggle-eyed on the bed, mocking poor Apolline. Then I bounded down the stairs after her and out into the moonlit *place*.

She stood waiting beneath a stunted plane tree, weaving in place. I stopped running and walked to her, drawn across the *place* by her powerful, obscure magnetism.

"You're *so* crazy," I said with a tender smile which admitted we were both a little crazy.

"Yes. If you choose to see me that way, I am."

"What, more metaphysics? Don't you ever get tired? Don't you ever want to speak directly, to feel and say what you feel?"

"Yes, yes, I do want that, Clayton." She broke down —momentarily. "But it is so hard. I . . . I am afraid." She withdrew a step.

"Don't be afraid of me. Please, Apolline. I won't

touch you. I don't even want to because I'm afraid you'll shatter if I do. I understand. Really I do. I feel something for you that I can't identify. I'm afraid to call it love, because it's not that. Maybe it is. It's nothing like what I feel for Catherine."

"How can you feel *anything* for her?" She grimaced at the thought and covered her mouth with the back of her hand.

"Because those feelings are part of life. For the rest of us, they are. It's not ugly or bad. It can be very beautiful."

"It is all in how you see things. The nature of things is determined by our act of observing them in constant transformation. You see me only as what you have made of me."

"I don't know what you mean by that, but I do know this: when I see you with my eyes I see something frail and trembling, something small and frightened; and when I see you with my mind I get lost in your words and your riddles and see just vapor or nothing at all. But when I see you with my heart, that is when I truly perceive your inner self. The part of you that for one moment last spring and for one moment just now reached out to me. Now it's looking for excuses to escape, ways to convince you that I have changed and you were wrong to reach out. You just want a reason to draw further away from what is right here in front of you, real and tangible and offering you a chance to live and grow. I *am* offering that, my dear sweet Apolline. I know it's mad to be saying this, but I want to be someone you can trust, and I believe you think I might be."

She regarded me intently as I spoke, kneeling on a low bench with my head at the level of her face. It made no sense, yet I felt mysteriously compelled to articulate my pathetic proposal. But she saw neither the sincerity nor the absurdity in what I said.

"No," she said at last. "You are the same. You cannot distinguish between what you feel and what is real."

"But they are the same thing. Don't you see that? That is how we know what is real."

"Not for me," she said as she drew away once more. "It lies in how deeply you see. You are still at the surface, Clayton. I cannot come back for you. I cannot come back."

She walked down the humped Place Ravignan, her arms limp at her sides, a slack and wispy frock barely inhabited by a small morsel of human flesh. Beneath the stunted plane trees and silver maples she glanced back; then she descended the steps into the next street and disappeared from sight.

I knelt a moment on the bench, befogged and befuddled, until I heard Guillaume call from the window. Then I trudged back to the studio. The precise dichotomy between spirituality and sensuality, the absolute contrast between Apolline and Catherine, made each more intensely real, a more perfect personification of her unique trait. As I fell into the arms of sensuality, ready to give myself over to our last night together, I realized that Apolline's haunted appearance and her pathetic accusation that it was I who was lost merely confirmed the futility of remaining in Paris and the good sense in my resolve to return home and pursue a life actively involved in affairs of the world. Perhaps something in my own inexperience, in my inhibitions and shock at unabashed sensuality such as Catherine's, drew me to Apolline's innocence and the safety she promised. At the same time, unlike her, I knew I must confront this in myself. I had not so emptied myself of instinct and physical delight that I could follow her down the hill into whatever endless dreams she wished us to inhabit together. I wanted to follow her, but only to bring her back and I knew that was impossible, as futile as trying to paint like the Spaniard or turn myself into a spy like Timothy Daunt. I was simply too damned sane, too much aware of myself at each moment, too fond of asking why and too likely to find some answer to that question.

Back in the studio I allowed myself to be teased from this confused condition by the sympathetic jests of my friends. The frolicsome foursome resumed its games and soon enough I was being seduced by Catherine.

Each time we made love during that night I felt, by the violence and passion of the act, that I could obliterate images of Apolline which still flitted about the periphery of my mind, judging and censuring me, not for my pleasure in Catherine but for something else, for a change I had only begun to sense in myself yet which I believed she had truly seen, fully developed, in an instant.

"Do not torture yourself," Guillaume counseled me later. "She lives totally within her mind, in an essential spirit world where you cannot join her, Clayton Peavey." He smiled. "And that is all."

She did not grace my farewell fête, of course; I hardly expected it. The rowdy, drunken party lasted through the night. I managed to corner Inspector Pernicieux early in the evening and probed him about the fate of the *saltimbanque*'s mask. He was evasive in a good-natured way.

"Still harping on that silly mask, Clayton? Let me just say that the mask left the Préfecture under obscure circumstances which suggest that certain agencies of the French government did not wish it to be returned to its previous owners. But truly, that is all I know of it." It was certainly all he would tell me.

Two days later I set sail from Brest, bound for my studies and the new career which beckoned beyond them. I abandoned Paris still unattained, my mind unsettled and many questions unresolved. I knew I must take charge of my affairs in a realistic and mature manner, and that is what I set about doing. On the voyage I consoled myself in the knowledge that I had a good topic for my senior thesis, one even Professor Stallwarts would approve: "Gun Running in Morocco and Its International Implications." I felt certain I would someday take a less academic interest in this subject again.

By early October the crisis in Morocco had passed. The rival sultans glowered at each other from a distance, but Abd el-Aziz had deserted Fez and would never return there. In January of 1908 his brother Hafiz marched north with his German guns and was proclaimed sultan by the *ulama* at Fez.

By then I was hard at work on my thesis and already growing tired of repeating my wondrous tales to my housemates. If I had given up, as Apolline believed, and returned to the fold, becoming like all the rest, it was out of my resolve to improve this wretched world. Even if the conviction formed by viewing the little Spaniard's canvas —that I must use my secret knowledge to protect the world from a general madness welling up around it— had already begun to dissolve, at least I knew enough to recognize this and to divert my energies toward more achievable goals. That, in itself, was a concession I would have been loath to make not long before.

During my final year at Harvard I corresponded frequently with Guillaume, the following year somewhat less, and then I lost touch with him altogether. I continued to hear of his exploits in the literary journals and art reviews and of the success of the school of painters who called themselves Cubists, but I believed that part of my life was gone forever.

I did not see Guillaume again for nearly four years.

Book Two

I

In May of 1911 I was back on the Rue du Sommerard, less than a block from Madame Adelaide's. I could claim that some perverse affinity for the cyclical ordering of events drew me there, but in fact I had come to Paris on special assignment for the State Department and it suited my purposes to appear a foreign graduate student arrived for the summer session at the Sorbonne. Finding a room on my old street was coincidental.

Several years older, with wire spectacles and a mustache, and quite conspicuously without my portfolio and sketchpads, I was unrecognizable to Madame Adelaide when we passed on the street, as we did from time to time that summer.

By one of those curious conjunctions of events which haunt my life, three apparently unrelated incidents of international significance occurred during my first week in Paris: on the Saturday, May 20, Kaiser Wilhelm and his wife completed a state visit to London, where they were well received by the public and the new royal family (Uncle Edward having passed on the previous spring); the next day a large French expeditionary force under General Moinier arrived in Fez, delivering the Sultan Abd el-Hafiz and his tottering government from a three-month siege by local tribesmen and at the same time occupying the city themselves; and on the following Friday, May 26, a sham constitution for an autonomous Alsace-Lorraine was passed in the Reichstag. In a single week I saw the evidence, provocation, and side effects of the last desperate effort to fashion an Anglo-German accord in the inevitable upcoming war.

This was a subject in which I had no little interest. The prospect of such an alliance had been the innovative conclusion to my senior thesis, and had earned for me a *magna* which nothing in my previous academic career warranted, and even coaxed Professor Stallwarts into announcing that I was "redeemed, my boy." It had also attracted attention in certain diplomatic circles in Washington. When I returned there I found my reputation had preceded me. I was no longer Adam Peavey's recalcitrant son but the author of a unique and bold premise which had either not occured in these circles or been abandoned by them.

Rather than belaboring and obscuring this point, let me quote briefly from the conclusion to that celebrated thesis:

"Germany confronts a predicament which only a Teutonic accord can mitigate. The Triple Alliance has been faltering since its inception: Austria, looking constantly over her shoulder into the Balkans, and Italy, unsure of herself at home and embroiled in conflicts with the Ottoman Empire, are fragile and uncertain partners in the face of an encircling two-front campaign against France and Russia. Only through a German understanding with Great Britain can the French be induced to restrain their desire for revenge and a balance of power maintained.

"Similarly, for Great Britain such an alliance, in addition to satisfying an historical Anglo-Saxon aversion to things French, would disassociate the British from the necessity of taking part in a costly war which her French allies desire but which she does not. Furthermore, arrangements could be made for sharing the seas with her German rivals and for the joint development of dreadnoughts and U-boats and the new naval weaponry, and acceptable settlements made regarding the Baghdad Railway and the economic penetration of North Africa.

"The initial subject of this inquiry is the apparently isolated Islamic insurrection in Morocco and foreign involvement in it. Given the avaricious actions in Morocco of the Quai d'Orsay, the French banking consortium, and the Compagnie Marocaine, no locale could be more logically selected for forging an Anglo-Germanic accord than that battle-torn country just entering the international financial and political playing field of the twentieth century. This has been and remains the goal of all German actions there—to play upon the age-old British antipathy to France—and the secret negotiations for such a settlement are in fact taking place, with the price tag to include a wide range of international and domestic issues, including Africa, the Near East, the high seas, munitions supply, and the fate of the occupied German territories of the Reichsland.

"The Entente Cordiale notwithstanding, Great Britain remains the only unaligned nation in Europe today, and her alignment with Germany is vital to avoiding a bloody confrontation and the probable dismantling of the German Empire. Nothing less is at stake, from the German viewpoint, and no other solution to this dilemma is feasible."

A bold statement to be sure, but supported by extensive research, my personal experiences in North Africa (used with the judicious discretion of any good academician), and several startling revelations regarding the activities of the firm of Armand Glautsch, the premise held, the *magna* was served, and I embarked upon a new career—one for which, I admit, I had acquired a thirst I could not quench.

I entered Philander C. Knox's State Department at

the time of the great reorganization of 1909 and was installed in the newly established Division of Information: where I gathered, analyzed, and dispensed that most abundant product of our federal bureaucracy. Behind this paperwork edifice I quietly awaited the chance to pursue my true interests. In the spring of 1911 the opportunity presented itself.

In Paris I had a new contact, the plumping and somewhat dandified Darlington having been retired to a suitable sinecure and poor Colonel Struck mercifully returned to native soil. The man's name was Derrick Underwood and he was precursor to a new breed of diplomats who would emerge after the war. No longer the aquavit-sipping, dog-breeding equestrians of the old century who wished for nothing more than to appear European, Underwood was only a few years older than myself, hard and tough, an expansionist and one of TR's bully boys, trained at West Point, with a firm broad jaw and clipped nails. He believed, and informed me, that this was America's century, that European squabbling would weaken the old empires and a new one, an empire of gold, would emerge. He relished being an American. Despite his self-righteous staunchness and an aggressive edge which I found unsettling, he was undeniably bright, far brighter than Darlington or the Colonel.

Having established myself with Underwood and settled in the Rue du Sommerard, I naturally sought out Guillaume.

I already had an inkling that Montmartre had passed; Père Frédé was dead and we had moved across the river again, to Montparnasse. The Butte swarmed in late May with second-rate conmen and third-rate artists plying their wares to the beguiled tourists at first-rate prices.

The Place Ravignan was verdant with spring, the

old fountain with its allegorical figures still bubbling, but the low, battered building appeared deserted. Studio doors swung open on the hinges, the breeze rattling their flimsy frames.

Max alone remained, a *memento mori* of that other time, winnowing down the rickety hallways like a figment of his own imagination. He was but one of the ghosts. Success had come—the first collective cubist show at the Salon des Indépendants that spring, though prompting much critical abuse, had been a sensation—and with it had come change. The old optimism was gone, the struggle over, the war was coming. We could feel it. . . .

I found Max in his cell on the ground floor. The oil lamp burned at midday and the smell of ether was frightful. He was supporting himself against the wall with one hand, drawing zodiacal configurations in pink Chinese chalks on the flaking walls. He welcomed me as an old friend. Pouring an absinthe which I could not refuse, he described the affairs and exploits of the gang over the past four years.

The little Spaniard had broken with the cubist school at the first signs of acceptance and taken a handsome three-room apartment on the Boulevard Clichy. I was relieved to hear that he had never shown the canvas of *Max's Grandmama.* Paul had endeared himself to Benois and was designing for the Ballet Russe, now in its third season in Paris. Marie was entrenched in the artistic life of the left bank; Catherine a leading fashion model and paramour to the great and near-great. And Apolline? I asked timidly.

"Gone," he said, shaking his head, the word rushing like a wind across barren plains with terminal implications I would not suffer to understand until later.

"Yet you remain?" I challenged him.

"Yes. And I have been published. I too am a success, can't you see?" He passed a frail hand across his worn black coat and regarded me with his great gloomy eyes. "I pass my days forecasting the apocalypse into which we are all so eagerly rushing. I am a mad beast." He laughed, but I did detect a hunch in his shoulders, a half-crouch and the use of his forearms almost like legs, and a continual guttural spluttering in the long silences which broke his more cogent conversation.

"As for Guillaume, the eminent man of letters, he no longer visits me here on Monday nights. He is too busy." The eyes carved me briefly and rolled back into their prune-black hollows. He hunched forward onto all fours and sniffed at me. "Seek him at his mother's," he said, crawled back to the wall, and recommenced his astrological scrawlings. I set down my unfinished absinthe and departed.

I found Guillaume's mother living in the same little brick bourgeois house in Auteuil, and of all the renewed contacts I was to make in Paris that summer she seemed least changed and most unabashedly pleased to see me. She insisted that I remain for dinner.

"It is so charming of you to pay me a visit. Not many of the young people nowadays bother with mothers."

"Not at all, madame," I replied. "Though to be quite frank I came here today hoping to find Guillaume or at least learn his whereabouts."

"Ah." She grimaced and her hands trembled very slightly. "Let us not speak of that rascal or I shall have one of my fits. And you needn't be *so* honest, Clayton. You must learn to allow old people their little self-delusions. But then candor was always your way, wasn't it?" I shrugged as harmlessly as I could, tugged at the corner of my mustache, and tried to look sympathetic. "I'm only sorry Guy won't be dining with me this evening. He would be so pleased to see you again. But this is not his night."

"Guy?" I asked, only half believing.

"Yes, yes, the Inspector. We've become good friends. And since Jules died two years ago we have our loneliness in common. He is a widower, you know." I nodded. "We dine here together on Thursdays, and on Sundays he takes me to a little restaurant in Charonne where he has been going for many years." She paused in the warm glow of this thought.

"And what has become of dear Inspector Pernicieux these past four years?"

"Oh, he is quite the celebrity now. 'The Painting Inspector' he is called." She laughed.

"Yes, I read of the retrospective of his hidden works at the Salon des Indépendants two years ago. A great success."

"Yes, he is very happy with all the attention. It has even boosted his stature at the Préfecture, though I don't see why it should, those silly paintings of his. He gets what he calls 'better cases.' But he will be retiring soon."

"What does Guillaume think of your friendship with him?" I asked, recalling past jealousies.

"Oh la la." She shuddered and again I noticed the trembling in her hands, the only sign of aging. "He is content. You see, he is credited with having *discovered* the Inspector, so he looks upon the whole affair as very much in the family. He has the oddest doting manner with Guy. But he carefully avoids coming to visit me on Thursday evenings, that much I've noticed."

One thing had not changed with the Countess and that was her consumption of drink. By the time dinner was ready her cheeks had grown florid, her speech torrid.

While the same *ecce homo* watched over us she regaled me with stories from her past.

"Our religious background is very strong, for you see I grew up within the Vatican itself. My father fled Poland at the time of the troubles there and served as Papal Chamberlain under Pius IX. Guillaume's father was of the Benedictine order, though sadly fallen, and I was just a child, a foolish child who believed so many things. We moved to Monaco, he studied at Cannes, and then we came to Paris a dozen years ago, around the time I met Jules." A moment's somber reflection flushed across her face. "But I am boring you. Please, have some more wine." She refilled my glass and her own as well.

"Not at all, I find it quite fascinating," I replied.

"He was never the same after that year in Germany and his infatuation with the English girl. It seemed to break his spirit and alter him. He used to be a sensible, enterprising boy. But after traipsing about after that girl, to London and elsewhere, he became . . . ridiculous. It was then he took that silly name Malaimé." She shook her head. "I suppose for a poet it is a good name, but as a mother, I—"

She had broken down, her prolixity faltering into sentimentality. I edged her on as gently as I could.

"Is Guillaume happy now? I know he is widely read; he too is a success, isn't he?"

She blinked at me. "Oh, he is as capricious as ever. He has broken with Marie again, and this time I believe it is the end."

"Really?"

"Yes, yes, I disliked her at first, I know that's what you are thinking. It's true. She is what they call 'a new woman,' one of those who have forgotten the difference between men and women in this world and the difference in our appointed lots. But I have grown to accept her over the years. And she knows how to manage Guillaume, which is more than any of his other young women could do. But now, just when it seemed they might finally marry and settle down to a more sensible existence, he has broken it off. I had even begun imagining grandchildren." She sipped her wine. "At first I thought it was another of their spats. They have always had the most violent quarrels, as though they needed them to remain together. But I fear this time it is something more."

"Why, what has happened?"

"Oh, it's this whole business with the girl. He is obsessed by some young dancer whom he is trying to place with the Ballet Russe. And she just a child from what I understand. It is all too foolish, and too pathetic. Please let us not discuss it any more, Clayton."

She clasped her plump trembling hands. I gave an obedient nod and dropped the subject. I hardly needed to ask who this child dancer might be. The prospect of seeing her again delighted me.

Late in the evening the Countess gave me an address in the Rue Henner where Guillaume had an apartment, but she told me that he spent his days at the rehearsal halls of the Ballet Russe, admiring his young protégée and writing poetry.

When the time came to depart she embraced me, beseeched me to talk some sense into her son, promised to remember me to the Inspector, and invited me to attend one of their Thursday suppers. I apologized for the uncertainty of my own schedule but assured her I would make every effort to join them. She offered her cheeks to my kisses and with the scent of her musky cologne and pomades teasing my sinuses I stepped from her stuffy little sitting room and returned to the Rue du Sommerard.

Unfortunately it was well into June before I could

contact Guillaume. For several days after my dinner with the Countess I was engaged in a dreary assignment for the State Department which required a great deal of research in the National Archives and Bibliothèque and a totally unrevealing surveillance of a Russian diplomat on a mission to Paris. I am afraid the department still mistrusted my fascination with internal European affairs and felt my services to be most useful in the sort of research at which I had demonstrated my skills at Harvard and not the field work in which I was anxious to become involved.

I continued to follow events in the south with keen interest. On the first of June, under the influence of the occupying French forces, the Sultan Abd el-Hafiz broke with his Grand Vizier, Madani al-Glaoui, and the powerful Glaoui clan were cast out of the government. It was a portentous event for the Moroccan crisis of independence and the grand designs which I suspected were dependent upon it.

I reported my inconsequential findings, and my more significant premonitions, to Derrick Underwood, who duly recorded them without comment. At last, on June 10, I made my way to the Châtelet Theatre where the Ballet Russe was in its final preparations for the opening of *Petrouchka*.

II

The first hint of what would long be remembered as the blistering summer of 1911 smothered Paris on that Saturday as I crossed the Petit Pont before Notre Dame and traversed the quai to the Place du Châtelet.

I was perspiring freely and rested a moment by the fountain at the center of the *place*. The spouting mouths of lappeted sphinxes at the base of a column in the fountain sent a fine refreshing spray across my face. Behind me was the Théâtre Sarah Bernhardt and before me, beneath a green mullioned roof and flanked by scarlet advertisements announcing the opening of *Petrouchka*, the Théâtre Municipal du Châtelet.

It was cool beneath the tall arched roof, and the marble floored foyer was deserted at midday. I walked into the main auditorium, where carpenters and riggers were assembling sets for the performance. A frightening curtain hung upstage: a dark-blue winter skyline of St. Petersburg, with stars and black, batlike creatures flying up into the night with red flaming mouths. Before this backdrop small wooden stages and booths were being constructed.

I spotted Paul immediately. Helping hoist a flat, he was still the sturdy Breton with a stevedore's build beneath somewhat citified attire. I called his name from the front of the proscenium and he peered blankly at me a moment, then suddenly rushed forward.

"Clayton, my God, I hardly recognized you. What brings you to Paris? Come to see the ballet, have you?"

"Not exactly, Paul, but I'll try to attend."

"I hope so. It is going to be fabulous, if we have everything ready in time. I've done some of the work on the sets, you know?"

"So I heard. Actually I was looking for Guillaume. I was told I might find him here."

"Ah, Monsieur Malaimé, is it? Yes, yes, he is quite the patron of the Ballet Russe." Paul seemed amused and slipped me a brief aside. "And setting himself up for the great calamity once more, I suspect." He straightened and glanced back at the workmen awaiting his directions with a piece of scenery. "He is in the small rehearsal hall downstairs. The first dress rehearsal is tomorrow, and some of Benois' decor was damaged on its way from Petersburg. I don't know how we'll be ready for the opening Tuesday."

He directed me downstairs and returned to his labors.

The rehearsal studio was a converted buffet in the theater basement, unventilated and stifling. The floor was covered by worn, dirty carpets on which many of the dancers sat or lay, stretching and unlimbering for the afternoon rehearsal. As I entered the room they began their floor exercises.

I stood unnoticed at one end of this long room, occasionally catching glimpses of my reflection in the mirror at the room's far end between rows of dancers crossing before me. Despite the heat many of the dancers wore woolen leggings, ankle warmers with cut-out heels in pastel hues, pantaloons, and shabby loose-fitting tunics on their upper bodies.

A pacing, imperious director stood by the piano, his voice snapping out the count "*cinq, six, sept et—*" as the echoing piano filled the room with right-hand jingles and a thrumming thwack in the bass. It was answered by the flick and patter of slippers across the floor.

Even from behind I recognized Claudie, if only because she was so much smaller than the uniform dancers of the Russian corps. Her body appeared unchanged, still nearly breastless, frail arms flittering about her head in pirouettes that were, even to my unschooled eye, less precise than those of the other dancers. But equally apparent was a briskness, an energy and alacrity with which her movements were imbued, and this too in contrast to the others. When she turned toward me to retrace her movement across the floor her sharp collarbones rose and fell as she breathed like fanning wings beneath her fine, thin neck.

The Russian ballerinas, all of whom had no doubt been at this for a dozen years or more, yet were only a few years older than Claudie, eyed her with a mixture of awe, jealousy, and contempt.

Guillaume sat near the piano on a low stool. A small notebook was open in his lap, a pen in his hand. Several Russian men in ill-fitting dark suits clustered behind him. At the moment I first noticed him his eyes were shut.

The men around him had a distinctly distracted yet manic intensity. These were not the big, brawling vodka swizzlers one met at foreign-service functions or at the Quai d'Orsay, but all thin and restive. They looked like a collection of reprieved Raskolnikovs; pale drawn faces with all of Raskolnikov's potential as yet untapped. Such were the male dancers' faces as well, and only one did not have that quality. I recognized him from the photographs: Nijinsky, who had that winter been dismissed from the Russian Imperial Theatre for appearing before the Dowager Empress without trunks over his tights, the man who had reminded France that there were also male dancers. He was seated on the floor, adjusting his slippers and woolen anklets. When he rose the movement was fluid but lacked the magic I expected as he swept across the room with the same mechanical precision as the others. It was only the soft delicacy of his features and the depths of his slanting eyes that distinguished him.

At length one of the reprieved Raskolnikovs in the funny suits noticed me. When I explained to him that I did not wish to disturb their rehearsal but had business with Monsieur Malaimé, indicating Guillaume, his expression changed from officious to merely impatient. He nervously fingered his trouser pockets while we spoke, as though searching for a lost note or making certain his wallet had not been stolen. Suddenly Guillaume was distracted from his reveries. His eyes opened wide when he saw me there, hirsute and in seersucker, pointing at him and arguing with the nervous Russian.

He rumbled across the room to me, his movements like those of a great lumbering bear amidst the lithe figures around and reflected behind him in the mirror. He was noticeably heftier than before, softer and less healthy, with his hair combed forward across his forehead to conceal the red ant scar.

He shook my hand and kissed both cheeks in a greeting decidedly more Russian than French.

"Just look at you, just look at you," he kept saying.

"I am," I told him and gestured toward the mirror across the room. He laughed loudly, and the Russian who kept checking his trouser pockets cringed. But Guillaume clearly was tolerated here, for whatever reasons. I was led to a station by his stool, where we resumed our watch of the floor exercises.

"You look well, Clayton Peavey, with your mustache and self-assured air. But however did you find me here? And how long have you been in Paris?"

"It hardly seems to be kept secret where you spend your days," I replied

"But of course," he said, a hint of annoyance showing in his face. "I find this an ideal environment for creation. The sound of the piano, the movement of the dancers. I must show you my series of dance poems."

Claudie crossed before us. As she turned at the far side of the room to walk back to her starting position she tossed a brief smile over her shoulder at Guillaume, almost flirting but with joyous affection and pride in her eyes. Guillaume beamed his adulation back at her, and I wondered why Diaghilev ever embraced the singular notion of having this untrained girl in his company. Could it have had to do with the pervasiveness of Guillaume's personality, not to mention his persuasiveness? Or perhaps with Paul's having worked on the decor? Or, most likely, it was that Diaghilev—this genius at spotting and developing genius in others—sensed something in Claudie Zorn which was unique and might be molded and utilized in the eccentric, dramatic dance he was creating with his company in Paris.

The music ceased, the Raskolnikovs conferred by the piano, and the dancers drifted to the far end of the room, discarding scarves and leg warmers, changing slippers, fanning themselves.

"Yes, yes, I cannot begin to tell you how wonderful it all is," Guillaume rhapsodized. "When I took her to see *Les Sylphides* in the Russians' first season she was overwhelmed. It was a revelation to her, something she had been waiting to discover. She has embarked upon this path over the past two years with total dedication. And now this wonderful opportunity in the fair scenes. She will be dancing with the Ballet Russe, next week, at the Châtelet. For twenty seconds the attention of the Shrovetide revelers will focus on Claudie. Even Nijinsky will look up, and all of the Châtelet audience will suddenly behold, in those twenty seconds, a potential for movement they had not even previously considered. Oh, Clayton, it is all too wonderful."

"Good heavens, Guillaume," I stammered. "Do you really believe all that?"

He was arrested midflight, his arms suspended above him in the air in a very awkward arabesque. He stared at me for a moment, puzzled and, I feared, hurt.

"No," he replied with a laugh. "I am merely composing a review I shall write of that performance." He smiled broadly, and I laughed with him.

At that moment the door opened and two men entered. One was dapper, formally dressed, with a thin black mustache, plump cheeks, and a smug smile. The dancers fell silent. He raised a single eyebrow in their direction, while his other eye and mouth inclined toward the man at his side, who had a wispy mustache over large, sensual lips, a lopsided bowtie, and a monocle—a dumpy, crumpled, totally unpreposessing little man. I recognized the plump-cheeked man by the white highlight in his black hair. It was Diaghilev.

"That is the composer of the music for *Petrouchka,*" Guillaume identified the other man. The two were obviously arguing about something, for the impresario looked much put out and the composer extremely apprehensive as they crossed the hushed room.

"They have been having a terrible time with the orchestra," Guillaume whispered in explanation "Everything conspires against the production. The musicians laugh at the score in rehearsal, call it unplayable and unmusical. Many of them have walked out a week before opening. But he is a genius. They laughed at him last year, but when *The Firebird* came into performance the consonance of the music and choreography was instantly apparent. It was a miracle which transcended the difficulty of the music and made it accessible to the most musically illiterate members of the audience."

"Guillaume, you're not working on your review again, are you?"

"Well then, Clayton Peavey, it really is you returned to Paris." He gripped my arm in utter delight. "You will dine with us this evening?" I raised my hands in surrender. "You moved to Washington and I lost track of you," he mused. "I suppose that means—"

"I am not an artist, Guillaume. Not a great artist. I never was. I sketch now and then, as a release from the tension . . . and the boredom of that other life, but—"

"But it is what you are suited for, eh? Perhaps."

With the arrival of the master, tension in the rehearsal hall had mounted. Now the composer sat at the piano and began work with Nijinsky and one of the Russian ballerinas. It was time for Claudie and the others to move to another room where the crowd scenes would be rehearsed.

She came to Guillaume and smiled shyly, her eyes at once petulant and grateful. When we were introduced she furled her brow and said: "Of course I remember you." Her ambivalent tone left me uncertain whether she harbored unpleasant memories or was happy to see me. I looked for reassurance into eyes which denied the girlish enthusiasm and freshness of her physical presence; eyes not sad but moody and observant; eyes which I believed saw Guillaume as he was, but eyes which loved him too. I found no reassurance in those eyes. She turned abruptly and left us to reminisce while she rehearsed.

We left the Châtelet in late afternoon and walked out the Boulevard de l'Opéra. Claudie walked brisky before us beneath the trees of the Boulevard Haussmann. A thin lavender scarf was tied around her hair, which had been gathered into a bun. The breeze blew the ends of the scarf up over her head, forming wobbling rabbit ears on her shadow which danced between us along the sidewalk.

"So that was the Ballet Russe," I said later. We sat in a café midway from the theatre to Guillaume's apartment. I was sipping a beer, Claudie was drinking her second soda, but Guillaume, despite the heat, drank espresso and smoked continuously. "And that was the famous Diagh and the Nij," I said, tossing out a line I had been saving for just the right occasion only to discover this was not it. Guillaume gave me a blank look, Claudie giggled, and Guillaume frowned. I sipped my Mutzig.

"Wait till you see him perform, you will not be so glib," he snapped at me. "He is a masterpiece."

"I will always be glib," I informed him. "It is a permanent affliction whose seizures we must learn to live with, rather like epilepsy." And I grinned peavishly.

"It's only your insecurity," Claudie told me and quickly gazed off through the branches of a maple tree beside our table. Guillaume obviously derived immense pleasure from her sharp tongue.

Guillaume's apartment in the Rue Henner was respectable compared to the studio at the Rue Ravignan; two rooms plus a small kitchen, the long sofa and table in the front room strewn with his books and papers, worn copies of *La Phalange,* stale overflowing ashtrays, and half-drunk glasses of *porto,* the walls crammed with drawings and sketches by his celebrated friends. The back room was filled by a huge canopied bed piled with cushions. The bed was surrounded by multicolored silk scarves, toe shoes in descending stages of disintegration, flowers in various stages of wilt, bits of ribbon, brooches and pins and feathers and pantaloons, tiny bodices and tunics, chemises and all manner of underclothes, rumpled gypsy skirts in purple and chartreuse—the entire wardrobe of his young protégée. It was clear whose room was whose, and I wondered whether Guillaume might not sleep on that well worn sofa. A thick blanket was folded at its foot. When I made suggestive remarks Guillaume was evasive about the exact nature of their relationship. At one point he mentioned that the Zorns lived in "one of the lesser arrondissements" and implied that Claudie might dwell in such an inhospitable place herself.

He suffered from such odd instances of petty bourgeois diffidence in the midst of his bohemian disorder. It was a trait he could never cull from his personality. He told me proudly that his naturalization was nearly complete, and spoke of how soon poets of the new school might be accepted as members of the Académie Française. Four years earlier this would have been anathema to him, a condemnation rather than an honor. When I mentioned his breaking off from Marie and my dinner with his mother, he laughed wildly, uncontrollably, and dismissed it as nothing.

"Yes, now I am a confirmed bachelor," he boasted.

"Then it really is all over between you and Marie," I pushed him. Claudie pretended to ignore our conversation.

Guillaume shrugged. "Nothing is ever truly over. The ache in the heart remains; we never know what mischief it will work. She knows me too well for me to break loose. But I shall." His eyes flashed with resolve to extricate himself from this unhappy triangle, but I could see a shaken emptiness in those eyes, as though in casting off Marie he was losing a trusted balance in his tumultuous life and was not sure the perching bird to which he had attached himself would take him along on her flight.

That bird wore out moods and dispositions with a

rapidity that was bewildering to me, for whom the changes and flippancy, the puerile demands and tender commiserations, were merely something to be observed and not a constant source of self-doubt or exaltation as they obviously were to Guillaume.

We ate together—each of them cooking one course in the meal, she an omelette, he a rissolé—and the afterglow of the wine and remembrance, even with the sharp edge of Sébastien's death hovering over us, brought us closer together. Claudie and I laughed together at Guillaume's posturings and proclamations, but in her laughter, as in her eyes, was a sensitivity toward Guillaume which said, "Yes, we two know that Guillaume is a big goose, his head in the clouds, but he is kind, and creative, and believes fervently in me, and I love him." It was a pleasure to be in her company, and I could see how Guillaume had become so infatuated.

After dinner he performed an elaborate pedicure on her tired and knobby young feet. He applied a rose petal unguent with soft cotton swabs, while she lounged on the sofa, one moment toying with his thinning hair or tracing the ant scar with a slender finger, which annoyed him, and the next holding out her arm and assessing the arc of her hand. She combined the focus on self necessary to any creative artist with mere childish self-absorption in an exhilarating, yet frustrating manner.

"You know, it is truly a miracle that Monsieur Diaghilev has allowed me this little part at the fair." They were always speaking of miracles. "All the other dancers are so much farther advanced than I." She seemed genuinely humble, not fishing for the compliment which Guillaume quickly provided.

"But you have your gift, Claudie. Your passion. That can never be taken away or modified, it can only be improved upon by training. Serge sees that. The others do not have it."

"Some of them do. I still think it's not fair."

"Of course it's not," I agreed. "But you would hardly trade places with—"

"I would not trade places with any girl in all of Europe," she exclaimed joyfully, and the muscles in her neck flattened as she broke into a wide grin. When she grinned her eyes closed and her face became like that of any excited young girl.

"Claudie's great charm, as you can see," Guillaume was saying moments later, when she had gone out of the room, "lies in her total freedom from pretension or display, her joy in the impulse of each moment in her life. This is what gives her the freedom and passion to dance as she dances. Her happy spontaneity has even infected the Russians. During rehearsal earlier this week, when the showman plays his flute to animate the puppets, Claudie was literally entranced and wandered out into the open center of the stage, magically drawn there by the music. This was unplanned, out of place, but Fokine has decided to keep it in the choreography. They are all so charmed by her. Yet she is totally unaware of the rarity of her talent."

"But she'll not be for long if you continue to extol her for it and preach over her and cosset and pamper her like a doll. She will turn unwholesome, like a piece of fruit left too long unplucked."

"But she is not unplucked." He grinned, rewarding my curiosity at last, as our terpsichorean delight reappeared from the bedroom. She had shed her day's clothing and worse just a soft silk peignoir, further evidence of Guillaume's largesse. Beneath it a pair of boy's linen trousers with drawstrings at the ankles deprived us of a view of her legs. He completed the pedicure and we drank more cognac.

"I shall give you tickets to the opening next week, of course," he told me. "You are staying alone in Paris?"

"Yes, but perhaps two tickets would be better than one."

"But, of course. You have . . . a friend?"

I really had nothing in mind but assented to his insinuation.

"I'm glad you'll come to watch me dance," Claudie said softly with a small smile. She tossed her unbound hair back across the sofa arm and shut her eyes.

"You remember our dear chum Madani al-Glaoui?" I asked when I had stopped staring at her.

Guillaume thought a moment. "You know, I can barely remember that episode. I recall Daunt and what came after, but the kidnapping and journey to the mountains were like a dream to me. I have only the vaguest images of them, nothing I could call a proper memory."

"Nonetheless, you know who I mean. He's had a falling out with the Sultan and been booted out of the government. Should stir up all the old troubles down there."

"Yes, really? I don't follow such affairs as closely as I should. I rather understood we had taken things in hand in Morocco."

"So your government seems to think. The Quai d'Orsay acts as though a protectorate were already established. I think there will be severe repercussions both in North Africa and on the continent before that comes to pass."

"Oh, this is all so difficult, Clayton. I am too tired to solve the problems of these haggling nations. We have more important things to do here in Paris." He nodded at Claudie, who was dozing on the sofa as he rubbed her feet. "But it is time for sleep," he said. "Come, angel, you must rest and renew your strength for tomorrow." He picked her up and carried her toward the bedroom. I took this as a signal to depart. "No, no." He waved for me to stay. "We shall talk further, only the child must rest."

He stepped into the bedroom and for a few moments I heard the sounds of pillows and coverlets being adjusted, yawns and whines from Claudie, Guillaume's shushing and soothing, and the click of a light kiss.

"Do you see the Zorns often?"

"Yes, quite regularly. *La Famille Jollicorps* still performs at the circus—Gaspard and Kasia and the boy. Arbo has aged a great deal since they settled in Paris. He appears at the Mediano now and then, but is less active than before."

"And . . ." I hesitated. "What of his . . . other activities?"

"The lost provinces remain lost. Nothing has changed."

"I thought not. I should like to see Arbogast Zorn again."

"He will attend the ballet on closing night. Come then, if you wish. Come every night with me, if you wish. I don't care."

"I shall certainly do that," I said without indicating exactly what I meant.

"It is a great shame what has happened to all of us." Guillaume stretched out on the sofa, his head back and eyes shut, his cognac cupped between soft hands.

"Why, what do you mean, Guillaume? I thought everyone had found success."

"Success? But things become spoiled so swiftly. Like what you were saying about fruit. The new schools become more dogmatic than the old, books are written, rules established, cliques formed, criteria set, and all the joy and fun of creating these things is lost. And what happens to us who stated the new precepts? We are cast aside and forgotten, or must declare our opposition, or be made use of and merely tolerated, or be mocked and relegated to the status of elder statesmen at the age of thirty-one. Martyrs and saints." He coughed. "In no case do we receive respect. That is why I say it is a shame."

"There is something to be said for involvement in matters of more universal concern. One can indulge one's fancies and the mind's diversions for only so long." But I think he missed my meaning, for he replied:

"What can be more universal than love and art and creation?"

"Hatred and tyranny and destruction are equally widespread, I'm afraid."

"Oh, Clayton Peavey, open your eyes. Did you not see her dance? And you speak of tyranny and destruction as power. They have no power, no power like life."

"And yet death—."

"We cannot think like that and survive," he said and lighted a cigarette. His dark eyes stared at me; mocking, pitying, and encouraging me all at once. Then he let his eyes slip shut. "To live is to be forever engaged in the pursuit of the unattainable. Anything less is to be only half alive."

I left him there, the cigarette dangling from his lips, the cognac cupped between his hands, a thin trail of acrid smoke rising over him, with his books and papers strewn about him on his roost, and life not fifteen feet away, on the other side of the wall, in a room full of pillows and scarves.

III

I attended the opening of *Petrouchka* with a piffled Guillaume and Claudie's parents and her brother Thiébaut. The seats and walls of the Châtelet Theatre had been refurbished in bright red upholstery, which heightened the Russian drama of the event. Nijinsky and Karsavina were brilliant as the awkward puppet and doll-like ballerina, and the difficult music with its spasmodic changes did achieve a consonance with the choreography as Guillaume had predicted.

Claudie Zorn shone brightly for her twenty seconds in Scene IV, during which she performed a combination drawing on elements of classical ballet, gymnastics, and her own peculiar talents. In the context of the Shrovetide fair it was quite suitable, though I preferred her entranced straying across the stage in the opening scene, which seemed more expressive of her character. Backstage I congratulated her and departed, promising to return for the closing on June 20, when Arbogast Zorn would be in attendance.

I awoke before dawn on the twentieth and could not fall back asleep. For half an hour I lay in my bed and then, as the first light began to fleck the sky, I gave up hope of sleep and drew a chair to the window to watch the sunrise.

This insomnia was unusual for me, and I attributed my restlessness to the prospect of seeing Arbogast Zorn that evening. Events in the south and on the continent had proceeded much as I expected. The Spanish had established a foothold at Larache (ostensibly "to protect Spanish citizens there," but obviously in protest of French encroachments) and Herr Kiderlen-Waechter had demanded compensation for the occupation of Fez—the first step toward an imminent German thrust. I anxiously looked forward to speaking with Arbo Zorn about these affairs and learning his reaction to the Alsatian constitution recently passed in the Reichstag.

The first brief heat wave of the summer had broken in storms the previous evening and shoots of sunlight pierced the dark clouds of morning, glancing off the spires of Notre Dame in the distance. Across the street from my room was an elementary school. Crude children's paintings in bright primary colors hung on the walls, and moisture condensed on the slanting roof around sheaths of tin chimneys with tops like Chinamen's hats. I felt the deepened sense of awareness which often accompanies sunrise and sunset, with the rapid transfiguring of all around us from the light and the first appearance of life in the streets.

I was startled by the sudden appearance of a Moorish street sweeper beneath my window. He shambled down the Rue du Sommerard pulling a thatched barrel and a broom made of long, stiff reeds. He was almost black and wore a tall wool cap. Outside my building he paused and looked up. I watched him discreetly from behind the sash as he moved off with his cart.

I felt uneasy seeing this man. All my past anxieties were roused by his presence and I began imagining that I had awakened early for the purpose of seeing him. This was an ill omen for the new day. For some time I pursued this line of thinking and must have dozed off when I was again startled, this time by footsteps on the stairs and my concierge's firm knock at the door. She had a mole on her chin and smelled of wine, even at this hour.

"This package came for you in the early post, monsieur," she said, handing me a small packet wrapped in brown paper. "I'm sorry to bother you, but I thought it might be something important." She gawked at it, obviously hoping for a hint as to its contents, but as I hadn't a clue myself she withdrew unsatisfied.

The package was quite light, without a return address, and posted the previous day in Paris. Inside were three small envelopes, each filled with a fine-grained powder—one red, one yellow, and one ocher—and a folded, typewritten letter. It read:

> My dear Clayton-
>
> Here are the medications I promised you when last we met. I regret exceedingly that I could not deliver them in person, but other responsibilities have required my departure from Paris. I only hope they will provide you with some relief. They are quite highly regarded by the native doctors, though I do not doubt western medicine would look askance at such remedies.
>
> For the best results follow this method of application precisely. First sprinkle the ocher powder across the affected area and rub it in lightly with your thumb. Next make a thick, water-base paste with the red powder and apply this evenly over the entire surface of the affected area. Let this dry for five to ten minutes, or until the red paste has hardened and will crack and flake off. Once all the red flakes have been removed, take a small brush of the sort found in a lady's toilet and dust lightly over the affected area with the yellow powder. This should provide the desired results.
>
> I do hope this cure is of some use to you and that it has not arrived too late, as it concerns a situation

of the utmost delicacy to us both. I have many fond memories of our first meeting and hope we shall have the opportunity to converse again in the near future.

Please believe that I am and shall remain your most humble servant—

Dean Timmons

I had not the slightest doubt as to the identity of Dean Timmons, but sat puzzling over the letter for some moments, at a loss as to the affected area to which I should apply the wondrous powders. At last I decided, inasmuch as the sender could have no knowledge of the state of my anatomy or the contents of my room, that he must have intended that I apply the powders to the letter itself.

Next I faced the problem of the lady's toiletry brush. I located a pharmacy on the Boulevard St. Germain and anxiously communicated my need to the sleepy-eyed girl who was opening the shop. Her expression as I hurried off with my purchase betrayed a less than complimentary opinion of my personal habits and hygiene.

I returned to my room, spread the letter on my writing desk, applied the ocher powder, made the paste, and spread it across the page, though not without some lingering fear that I had totally misinterpreted the meaning of the letter and was destroying it. But it was altogether such a Daunt-like device I could not believe myself to have erred.

Unfortunately inexperience or haste caused me to mix the paste far too thin and I had to wait more than half an hour until it dried to the flaking stage. When I tested one corner of the sheet I smeared the paste and left a dark red stain. In a fury of impatience I paced my room until at last the flakes began to curl across the page and delicately, with trembling fingers, I shook them off. The letter was unchanged, coated with a faint reddish haze and nothing more.

I applied myself to the toiletry brush and carefully dusted the letter with the yellow powder. To my great relief and excitement my surmise proved correct. As soon as the yellow powder touched the page a new message began to appear, written top to bottom in the cipher I had learned in Morocco.

When I was satisfied that all the encoded symbols had emerged from their invisible ink, I set about translating this second message, which read:

> Chaos commencing. Satan on continent. German mobe. Desperate. Meet me, Wednesday, early Calais express, first-class carriage, compartment with seal Belgian Ambassador Baron Guillaume. Enter, do not knock. Daunt.

At last, I thought. All my premonitions were correct. Then I recalled the Moorish street sweeper and my heart missed. I examined the letter for further directions or clues, briefly considered destroying it, then folded it neatly and placed it in my waistcoat pocket.

I was thrilled, like a child who had been awaiting a particular Christmas present for months and at last the great day arrived. I would have to inform Underwood of what was afoot, but I would tell and not ask him about meeting Daunt on the train. Nothing short of incarceration would keep me off that train.

The only thing odd about Daunt's clever palimpsest was the train compartment seal in the name Baron Guillaume. For a moment I thought perhaps this was all some kind of elaborate joke. Then I recalled that the new Belgian Ambassador in Paris was, indeed, one Baron Guillaume, and I assumed that Daunt was making use of diplomatic immunity from disturbance and border checks to ensure the privacy of our meeting.

The prospect of another twenty-four hours' wait was sheer anguish, the evening at the ballet irrelevant, and the function I would be attending that afternoon at the embassy utterly intolerable. But the chance to see Arbogast Zorn and probe him on his understanding of affairs before my meeting with Daunt was certainly propitious.

The crisis had come at last. The French cabinet was floundering, Foreign Minister Cruppi making unctuous remarks about "the humiliation of withdrawal" from North Africa, and then those two words of greatest impact: *German mobe.*

The great sundering was upon us, and I would get to play my own small part in it.

IV

"This is a surprise seeing you here today, Clayton."

"I assure you, Darlington, I would not be here if I could possibly help it."

"If you can't help yourself, my boy, no one else can help you," he sniffed sententiously with a snide smile and sidled off into the crowd on the arm of a bosomy French countess in whose company he was seen far more frequently than suited decorum.

This embassy function celebrating the Ambassador's fiftieth birthday was peopled by the standard allotment of diplomats, warriors, socialites, and general parasites. The Dom Pérignon flowed freely, but I abstained, caught up as I was in serious considerations. Politely I bore the amenities, all the time seeking an opportunity to meet privately with Underwood and escape.

The only conversations of interest focused on the imminent demise of the French cabinet of Prime Minister de Monis. This talentless collection of ambitious neophytes and political compromises had come to power in March and floundered for three months. Now, faced with a Moroccan crisis, challenges from the Wilhelmstrasse, the pressures of the *parti colonial* and jingoist French press for more swift and decisive action, and its own vacillations, it was about to collapse.

A deputy foreign minister was engaged in a heated dispute over the "police action" in the south. His adversary was a short, volatile man identified by Darlington as the new Navy Minister.

"We must maintain the dignity of the French position and ensure respect for international conventions," the man from the Quai d'Orsay was saying. "Surely that is the goal of all civilized nations."

"It is our duty to establish a protectorate, and you know it," agitated the Navy Minister. "All *true* Frenchmen know it. If the Germans are not ready to accept that, we know the consequences."

"But, monsieur," protested the other. "One must not unnecessarily aggravate the situation."

The Navy Minister grunted and turned my way. I recognized him as former Foreign Minister Théophile Delcassé, a product of the Midi known to be fond of quoting Gambetta and Racine at cabinet meetings who had been removed from office following the first Moroccan crisis in 1905. He had returned to the cabinet in a less powerful role, but still exerted considerable influence over the press and public and remained a rallying point for the *parti colonial* and all proponents of expansion.

"Why such concern over German sensitivities?" he demanded. "Soon you will join Monsieur Jaurès in proposing surrender as a means of keeping peace. We must keep face as well; that is the correct way to maintain the peace. We must stand up for what is right."

"I do believe, Monsieur Delcassé," replied his frustrated adversary, "that you look forward to war." The man was mildly miffed, and Delcassé jettisoned him in disgust. I had enjoyed this performance—it always amused me how, despite their physical proximity, it was a long way from the Quai d'Orsay to the Rue St. Dominique where the War Ministry was located. I marked for future reference this outspoken advocate of *revanche* and potential ally in my campaign against Fritz Amgott.

As I prowled the marble floors of the embassy, my neck pinched behind a bowtie and my head buzzing with thoughts of the letter in my pocket, I was repeatedly shaken by the fear that when I opened the letter the ink would have turned invisible again, the message disappeared, and Underwood would be laughing in my face.

Several times during the dreary hour I was thus preoccupied my gaze was attracted to a handsome fellow whom I had not seen before in Paris. He was extremely young, baby-faced and elegantly caparisoned, and had a permanently wry, irreverent expression with which I instantly sympathized. He appeared as bored as I. Noticing this kinship between us, he appoached me.

"You do not drink the excellent champagne?" he asked.

"No, not today," I replied brusquely, ready to withdraw.

"James Cornelius." He extended a hand of introduction. "And what brings you to the womb today?" he asked with the same ironic smile I had detected from afar.

"I *work* in the womb," I told him.

"Pity," he replied. "I am on holiday myself. I do love Paris."

We continued our conversation, and I found my spirits so much improved by his company that I was prevailed upon to take a glass of Dom Pérignon. For the first time since morning my thoughts strayed from Daunt and his message.

James and I quietly ridiculed every guest who crossed our field of vision. He was intelligent, witty, and shrewd in his judgments of people whom I knew but who were mere faces in the crowd to him. He was far more worldly than his youthful appearance suggested. Impulsively I invited him to make use of my second ticket for the ballet that evening.

"Oh, delighted to accompany you," he said.

"Charmed. In San Francisco we are not often exposed to such high culture. We have only the High Jinks and our cufflinks." He flashed a cufflink with a diamond owl set in gold.

"Most peculiar," I acknowledged, though the cufflink meant nothing to me, and I returned the owl's gaze unenlightened. "So you live in California?" I inquired.

"Yes, yes, the old buzzard owns the state, so they say."

"The old buzzard?"

"My father." He shrugged.

"Rather an odd appellation for one's father, don't you think, James?"

"Not, my dear fellow, if one's father is seventy-two years old. Not so odd at all."

Though I was intrigued and would have liked to pursue our conversation about this seventy-two-year-old buzzard who owned the state of California, I managed at last to make meaningful eye contact with Underwood, who was watching me talk to James. I made my excuses and soon was in Derrick Underwood's office downstairs.

"That was quite a look you gave me back there, Peavey," he said.

"I have something important to tell you." Unfolding the letter from Daunt, I was relieved to find the palimpsest intact.

"That young fellow you were talking to, that Cornelius, he is rich rich," Underwood informed me. He peered at the pink letter with the cipher running down it. "What's this?"

"Do you remember that British spy Daunt I told you about—the one I met in Morocco four years ago?" He nodded and I expanded upon that adventure's details, many of which had seemed irrelevant before, and stated my beliefs regarding the message in the letter.

"But who is this Daunt really? How are you certain you can trust him?"

"I'm not certain, but he did save my life, and there is something about him that makes me feel he is on *our* side." Underwood was invariably comforted by the predictability of a world divided into sides.

"Well, I don't know." He stiffened as he always did before issuing instructions. "We'll have to clear this upstairs and also see what the Brits have to say about your Mr. Daunt."

"That's an excellent thing for you to do tomorrow while I'm on the train, Derrick. When I return we can put our two halves together and—"

"Who said anything about your meeting him on the train? I think we should investigate first. And if there is a German mobilization, how is he alone privy to that fact?"

"I don't know, but there is no time to go through proper channels with our embassy and the British. I have to be on that train tomorrow morning."

"Do you *have* to be?" His voice rose. "And who has determined that to be your duty, may I ask?"

"I have determined it, and you'll not stand in my way. This could be the most important piece of intelligence I gather in Europe this summer. More than that, it could be—"

"It could be a trap. It could be a blind lead. It could be a diversion. It could be any number of things." He was fuming now, his wide jaws set and flexing, his small eyes contracting. "I'll not have someone for whom I am responsible—"

"I take full responsbility for my actions. Tell them I tied you up in your office and disappeared."

"Peavey, this is ridiculous."

The door to his office opened without a knock. We

both whirled and Underwood reached inside his coat for the revolver which I knew he kept there. But it was only Darlington.

"Yes indeed," he said. "I saw you two slip away at the same time. Thought I'd find you here. Seems I've arrived just in time to prevent fisticuffs. You really should be more discreet, you know; your voices are audible up and down the hallway."

"No one should be sneaking about in the hallway listening," I snapped at him, but he was already ogling the letter on the desk. He recognized the cipher from four years past and made the logical assumptions.

Once he had been briefly informed of the content of the message and my intention to meet Daunt on the train, he proved a willing arbiter to our dispute and, for once, took my side.

"No, Derrick, this Daunt may be a bit balmy from too long in the Moroccan sun, but I think at the very worst it is a wild goose chase for Clayton and he will simply waste a day, which he does often enough as it is. But at best, as Clayton says, it could be quite a significant piece of intelligence."

"And you will vouch for this man Daunt?"

"Well, I can hardly do that, Derrick, but I will support you should anything untoward happen to poor Clayton. I'll say that I prevailed upon you against your better judgment and all the rest. Is that sufficient for you?"

Underwood grudgingly accepted this and I thanked Darlington for his unexpected support.

"But I insist on sending someone along for support," Underwood said. "Just in case."

"No, no, that's exactly the wrong thing to do," I argued. "Daunt would spot it immediately. He's a professional, I tell you."

"Yes, I think it best to wait a day before involving anyone else in this business," Darlington concurred. "Why create a fuss over what might well prove to be nothing?"

"That I cannot do." Underwood would brook no further breach in his authority, though Darlington's suggestion made good sense. "I must report this entire unconventional episode at once."

"Very well, report it. But please hold off your hounds," I said.

"Besides," Darlington reassured our reluctant accomplice, "the man has use of the Belgian diplomatic seal on his carriage compartment. That lends him some credibility, don't you think?"

"I suppose it does. I'll have a word with Baron Guillaume about that as well. Perhaps he can tell us who this Daunt is."

In uneasy accord over how to proceed, we adjourned our meeting and made our separate ways back to the assembly hall, which was bubbling and buzzing as vapidly as ever.

James Cornelius must have noticed my increased distraction, but he restrained himself from questioning me about it, thus further elevating him in my estimation. With far less apprehension than I first felt upon realizing I had invited him to accompany me to the ballet, I arranged to call for him at the Hôtel Ritz, where he was staying, wished the Ambassador my heartiest felicitations for a second half century, and returned to the Rue du Sommerard to prepare my wardrobe for the ballet that evening and my mind for what lay beyond.

The ballet was splendid, Nijinsky outdid himself, and I found, despite my preoccupation, that I observed more closely and appreciated more keenly the artistry of the Russian company on this second viewing of the program.

No one in our box appeared cognizant of my state of mind. Guillaume occupied himself with apotheosizing Diaghilev, Fokine, Claudie, Nijinsky, Karsavina, Stravinsky, and the rest. James was as much taken by the Zorns as by Guillaume or the ballet itself and had little time for me.

Gaspard and Kasia Zorn silently watched the performance in their pensive manner and awaited Claudie's appearance in *Petrouchka.* Their presence in a box at the Châtelet Theatre was incongruous. Thiébaut, now sixteen, had grown remarkably like his dead brother: wiry-strong with fierce dark eyes, a defensive streak which could be easily aroused, and visible disdain for the crowd with whom we mingled during intermissions at the mezzanine bar.

Only Arbogast Zorn was aware of me. Once or twice I observed him watching me during *Schéhérazade,* but after the first intermission he sat dozing, his head drooping onto his broad chest. He had aged many years since Sébastien's death, growing resigned to the passive life in Paris. He had also lost weight so that his skin hung empty where the flesh had been, his ruddy jowls like the wattles of an old rooster.

At the second intermission, following *La Spectre de la Rose,* I pried him loose of the others for a brief private exchange. All around us the Boni de Castellanes flitted and sipped, but Arbo Zorn gazed through his patina of weary displacement and ignored my comments about the ballet and the circus.

"You are searching for something, Clayton," he challenged my equivocations.

"Searching? Excuse me, I—"

"Something you believe I can help you find."

"Yes. In a way."

"In a way, then, what is it?"

"I . . . well, let me ask your opinion of this recent business in the Reichstag."

"The constitution is a hollow sham, if that is what you mean. It will harden the resistance of those who believe in the freedom of Alsace and Lorraine. I believe a European war is coming soon, and in that war the Germans will be crushed and our homeland restored to us. What else can I believe?"

"But these beliefs, are they merely your personal hopes or is there something which makes you believe as you do? Are you only speaking with your heart?"

Arbo Zorn was silent. I felt him dwindling before me, slipping away like an elusive seer who has spoken once and refuses to speak again. At last he spoke.

"You are correct. These are my personal hopes, nothing more. I shall never return to Alsace. Perhaps Thiébaut. Perhaps . . . We Alsatians are the preterite of Europe. We have been passed over again and again, cursed, left homeless. This constitution will not rouse but placate. It will serve its cruel purpose. Hansi has been imprisoned, the people are brutalized past hope. Already the other nations of Europe are pointing and saying, 'Ah, but you see, the Alsatians are content to become an independent state within the Reichsland.' Already we are losing ground."

"I believe," I told him, edging closer and speaking *sotto voce*, "that the Germans are luring the English away from the Entente Cordiale. And I believe that the price for whatever they have offered the English is the abandonment of the lost provinces."

"Yes." He was absolutely indifferent, as though submitting to my words.

"And I believe that this scheme, this accord, has something to do with the chemical plant near Mulhouse about which I once asked you." A small voice within me whispered "No," but I could not stop what I had begun. "The Glautsch plant, do you remember?"

The patina lifted for a moment and his eyes came alive. He nodded.

"Are you still . . ." I hesitated.

"Yes. Some things remain unchanged."

"Then perhaps you can inquire for me among your sources. See what you can learn about the operations of that plant. Anything at all may be of use. Ask Boppe, I don't know who else. Whatever you think best. Will you do that?"

"I will. And you, you will come to see me? At the circus?"

"Or at your home, wherever you wish. I must leave Paris for a day or two. Do not tell anyone about this, but act swiftly, for I fear a crisis is at hand," I cautioned him who had lived his entire life with caution. "When I return I may know something more and I will contact you."

"Very well," he said. "But the bell has sounded. We must return to our seats."

"I would not impose this upon you if I did not feel it to be essential."

"Yes," he said quietly. "I know that." Slowly he made his way through the mezzanine bar and out among the brilliant red seats of the Châtelet, this dowdy old clown in his frumpy suit with his wattles waggling as he went.

Much relieved by my conference with Arbogast Zorn, I was now absorbed in the evening's final offering, *Petrouchka*. Only the appearance of the puppet Moor disturbed me; it seemed my life was perpetually plagued by Moors.

Stravinsky's music, on this second hearing, enthralled me: the bustle of the fair was perfectly reflected in the shrill score, contrasting themes interrupted by the impatient drummed stamping of the crowds and the lovely flute cadenza which animated the puppets. When Nijinsky came to life in his floppy collar and checkered pants he was no longer the man I had watched in rehearsal. This was his third leading role of the evening, in itself an astounding feat. An expression of transcendent joy, of ecstasy shimmering at the edge of every movement, glowed on the grotesque chalky features of this awkward puppet trying unsuccessfully to attain humanity. While the technique and energy of all the Russian company was stunning—they seemed to perform effortlessly the most wonderful combinations—few of the other dancers possessed this transcendent passion. Karsavina did and, curiously enough, so did Claudie Zorn in her brief solo.

When the fourth scene commenced and the revelries of the fair again commanded the stage, Guillaume nudged Arbogast Zorn awake. With a wistful expression he watched these masqueraders, walking bears, and gypsies—one might even have said *saltimbanques* in another time and place—as though he saw not a staged ballet set in nineteenth-century Russia but something alive and real and familiar. Claudie appeared in a twisted posture on a raised platform, then gracefully unreeled from her contortion and crossed her platform in a series of brisk pirouettes and *jetés*, culminating in a leap into the air and an indescribably soft landing to the accompaniment of a single ching from the triangle. A slight gasp escaped some of the audience, and Arbogast Zorn smiled and touched his flushed cheek.

As the final scene was played out he was asleep again. We were all left suspended by those four ominous plucked notes which end the ballet without resolve, as the ghost of Petrouchka appears over the stage, laughing at the puppet master, the crowd, at all of us. Old Zorn was jarred from his slumber by the tumultuous applause and stood with the rest of us cheering long and loudly for his little niece, or for the ballet, or for whatever it was he had been dreaming during the evening.

Guillaume insisted that we accompany him backstage into the crowded dressing room to congratulate Claudie. The Zorns seemed far more at home backstage than they had in the plush box.

Guillaume circulated familiarly among the dancers and spoke briefly with Diaghilev.

"I am going with the company to London," he announced. "I must see them triumph everywhere."

"Have you nothing better to do than trail about after this ballet company?" James Cornelius asked Guillaume.

"No, sir, I have nothing better to do. If you must find a vocational niche into which you may stuff me to satisfy your poor mind's seeking after reasons, call me a publicist for the Ballet Russe, for I assure you the articles I write will exalt this company in the eyes of many readers."

"Quite," replied James, convinced of Guillaume's passion, whose source now appeared at the dressing-room door, dressed in an old gypsy skirt and a clinging silk blouse with ballooning sleeves, her hair drawn back in a lilac scarf.

We all paid our compliments. James and I kissed her hand. Young Thiébaut said something which made her giggle and punch him, and she and Guillaume exchanged embarrassing looks of mutual gratitude and affection.

"Claudie understands intuitively the great maxim of all creative artists," he told me.

"And what is that, Guillaume?"

"That above all the artist, the painter, the dancer, the poet must contemplate his own divinity and create in his own image. And that is all."

"And for those of us who are not divine?" James attempted to puncture the proclamation.

"Count your dollars, sir, if that is all you are fit for," Guillaume dismissed him.

Guillaume suggested a particular café which he favored across the river near the Place St. Michel, but the Zorns wavered, Claudie admitted to fatigue, and my thoughts had already turned to my morning assignation with Daunt. The proposal was rejected.

"Well then, it is better so," Guillaume consoled himself. "We all must rest," and he glanced at Claudie, who bathed him in her most enchanting glow, enough to melt the iciest heart.

We said goodnight in the backstage jostle. James thanked me and wished me well on my enterprises, whatever they might be. I shook Arbogast Zorn's hand and looked briefly into his eyes, but no words passed between us. Then I shook his brother's hand and leaned forward to embrace Kasia. As I bobbed forward, kissing first one and then the other of her drawn cheeks, I heard a voice, her voice I presumed, though she had barely spoken to me before, close at hand yet distant, a soft, fey voice whispering in my ear like those four ambivalent pizzicato notes which ended *Petrouchka* yet left it unresolved and incomplete, saying:

"You . . . must stop . . . him."

V

I nearly missed that train.

A fierce yellow sun hung low and blinding in the sky, funnels of steam rising off the river like the dawn's breath of the city. My taxi was caught in the snarl of morning traffic, and I had to dodge through the crowds beneath the great vault of the Gare du Nord as the whistle of the departing Calais express sounded. I managed to leap onto the rear of the last carriage halfway out the platform.

I quickly located the compartment bearing the seal of the Belgian ministry. The window was curtained. I hesitated a moment over the instructions—"Enter, do not knock"—but finally turned the handle and stepped into the compartment.

Daunt was alone, a cigarette clasped between two knobby fingers. He slouched in the seat with his back to me, staring out the window.

"Turn the latch, would you?" he said without looking round. I locked the door and dropped, panting, into the seat opposite him.

"You certainly are casual about all this," I ventured. "I might have been—"

"Yes, who might you have been?" he said, at last turning his thin, freckled countenance my way. His eyes flickered across my face and back to the window.

"Oh, I don't know," I muttered and breathed deeply. He was silent for a moment.

"I certainly am glad to see you managed to locate the affected area," he said.

"Yes, that was a bit confusing at first. I compliment your device."

"Don't. You'll never guess whom I saw on the platform just now, boarding this train."

"I won't even try. Who?"

"Your old mate Guillaume, with a lissome lass on his arm, surrounded by what looked to be the Russian Ballet with full equipage. Quite a coincidence, eh?" He smiled at me with an irony which said we both knew better than that.

"An awkward coincidence, I think, if he sees me on the train."

"Perhaps not. We shall find some way to make use of him." He paused and stubbed out his cigarette before turning from the window to face me. "You're looking quite well, Clayton, mustache and all."

"Yes, I am happy. You look . . . the same. I didn't think you ever planned to leave Morocco. What brought you—"

"One thing at a time, please. There is nothing left for me to do in the south. Morocco shall be a French protectorate before the year is out, if I am not mistaken. Events on the continent demand my attention now. Satan has bestirred himself."

"So your note implied. A German mobilization? Do you really mean that?"

"That was, perhaps, a slight exaggeration. But only very slight. The Germans want to excite world opinion and instigate a crisis. I'm not certain how that will be accomplished, but when it occurs their mobilization shall be far more efficient than ours."

"But what makes you believe that? What do you know?"

"My visit to the battlefields at Metz twenty years ago convinced me of the superiority of German preparedness." He smiled and lighted another cigarette. "Do you remember in Morocco when I said you were an excellent prospect, that you would get a taste for this life, but you were oblivious to my meaning? I was right, wasn't I?"

I stared at him, my mere presence in that compartment ample affirmation of what he said. I tapped my foot.

"Yes, right you are, down to business it is, though I am truly pleased to see you again. It was an unexpected blessing to learn you were in Paris, for you can supply confirmation of a significant piece of information." I waited anxiously while he gazed at me with total composure; immune to the attacks of excitement from which I still suffered. "Very well," he continued at last. "It concerns Fritz Amgott, of course. I have you to thank for first alerting me to the extent of his involvement in certain wicked affairs. I have watched him closely and made a number of inquiries over the past four years. I think he is at the heart of a cabal which seeks to rend Europe apart. Have you seen one of these before?"

He pulled a small valise from beneath his seat, opened one of its compartments, slid away a false bottom, and withdrew two folded sheets and a small velvet pouch. He set the pouch on the seat beside him, unfolded one of the papers, and handed it to me.

It was the "Third Futurist Manifesto," a long diatribe on the coming turmoil and the perfect state which would evolve from it. "War," it said, "is the father of all things," and "the perfecting synthesis of progress." It bore the signatures of several Italians, an Englishman named Heneage Filch, a Frenchman, and Fritz Amgott.

"So he is a madman," I said. "That much we already knew. And a cabalist. And a futurist. I know the term, I think. But this hardly means—"

"Indeed, were he merely a madman on the fringe of society I should hardly be concerned with him myself.

But as you know from your study of the House of Glautsch, its deep involvement in all areas of Moroccan life, and the Amgott family's controlling interest in that firm, he is not on the fringe at all."

"I understood Fritz had been disinherited by his family."

"That is what they wished us to believe."

"But what has Glautsch to do with futurism?"

"Nothing in itself, but the Glautsch chemical works has been redesigned and converted over the past two decades. Leading German scientists have gone to Mulhouse to develop the melinite explosive process and today Glautsch is the largest producer of gunpowder in Europe. Only the American firm of Dupont can rival its capacity."

"I see."

"Not yet, you don't, sport, but you will, and your eyes will open wide with wonder when you do. Let me show you another item I have gone to great lengths to secure."

He unfolded the second paper, a slightly blurred photographic reproduction of a letter addressed to General Helmuth von Moltke, the German Chief of Staff.

"How is your German?" he asked.

"Not bad, but perhaps you would translate."

"Better that I simply tell you the gist of this letter concerns a Herr Sturm. You notice the references to him. Sturm is a sobriquet for Fritz Amgott. This letter, from Count Metternich, the German Ambassador in London, informs General von Moltke that Herr Sturm's negotiations have proceeded satisfactorily and that when the moment for action arrives their 'silent understanding' will hold."

"And the 'silent understanding' is an Anglo-German accord?"

"Precisely. An accord, I speculate, whereby the Germans agree to curtail the production of dreadnoughts and the new undersea vessels—the contract for which is in the hands of the Amgott Munitions Fabriken in Bremen—and further to supply the British with gunpowder and explosives in the upcoming war at a price unapproachable by Dupont or Vickers or any of the domestic British firms. The savings to Britain could be in the millions of pounds. In return the British will accede to the German claims on the provinces of Alsace-Lorraine, abandon the French in Morocco, and support Germany in the great war."

"But who in the British government could be involved in this?" I spluttered.

"That is something you may be able to help me determine."

"I?"

"Yes, but let me explain everything before I tell you exactly what I want you to do. We have less than an hour. My carriage switches at Amiens. I will be going on to Brussels for a very important meeting with the Belgian Foreign Minister, Monsieur Davignon, while you will be continuing to London."

"Oh, I will? But—"

"Your skepticism over British collusion in such a scheme is surely exceeded by my own. Mind you, we British have looked to Germany before in our search for a reliable continental ally. It was the first nation to which Chamberlain made overtures after Fashoda, you may recall. You may *not* know of the secret military conversations which have been carried on between the English and French since the signing of the Entente Cordiale, or of the secret articles of that treaty. Preparations for a joint British-French mobilization are nearly complete, and when the English press speak of the 'coming war with Germany' they may be a bit bold but they are on the mark. The Teutonic Accord shall fail."

"Then why this meeting, and why must I go to London, and what's your great concern?"

"Simply this, Clayton. The temptations of the German offer are vast. You know that my countrymen have no great love for the French or concern for the recovery of Alsace-Lorraine. Many Englishmen fear that French imprudence, particularly regarding the situation in Morocco, will incite German action. This will place them in an awkward bind, forcing them to choose one side or the other. This is precisely what the Germans want. If the French do not handle the delicate Moroccan crisis exactly right they may well lose their British ally. The days of splendid isolation are over, but the new and permanent direction of policy is not settled." He broke off to light another cigarette, and I noticed that his hands trembled slightly as he held the match. "A German agreement regarding naval production is vital to continued English mastery of the seas. But most important, and this *must not* be underestimated, is the enormous economy to be derived from the gunpowder deal which only Fritz Amgott can offer. That is the element which makes the German accord less hopeless than it might appear. What is needed is provocation, a French action which will give the British government the excuse it needs to break the Entente Cordiale and turn, for the greater security of all Europe, to a Teutonic Accord. Perhaps even a triple Teutonic Accord."

"You mean my country as well?"

"Quite so. The French would be in a pretty pickle with just the bumbling Russian bear for an ally. They would have to swallow their pride, forsake the lost provinces, abandon the Moroccan venture, and do nothing. Either that or engage in a suicidal war."

"Then this is a critical moment."

"Yes, Clayton old chum, it certainly is. The crisis in Morocco, and the unseemly French intervention there, has provided the Germans with the opportunity to bring all of their plans to fruition."

"But what has futurism to do with any of this? Surely it is a small sect and not a matter of state."

"In itself, you are correct." He coughed into a curled fist and must have been in pain, for his knuckles stood white and clenched as he composed himself. "Excuse me, just the moist air. They are a sect, and their philosophy is abhorrent to me and to most of my countrymen, but they must not be dismissed lightly. The futurists prefigure a dark shadow of evil awaiting us in the coming war. A horror which all our fine new techniques will merely serve to make more terrible."

"You are not answering my question, Timothy." My impatience was turning to sympathy for my old benefactor; I had begun to wonder whether he was being evasive or was, himself, confused.

"Must I spell it out for you? You are such a deucedly literal-minded chap, Clayton." He smiled. "I surmise that the group of futurists in London to which Fritz Amgott is party is in fact the focus of the secret negotiations. And that is what I wish you to find out. Nothing less than that."

I sat for a moment, stunned by this glut of information and the extremely significant assignment he had entrusted to me.

"But why me? Why can't you do this yourself?" I asked eventually.

"I am known by certain persons and could not make the necessary surveillance. And I have more pressing business in Brussels, as I told you. The Belgians must be warned. It has long been assumed that a German mobilization would mean a sudden strike from the east, through Lorraine. But one must never forget Clausewitz's precept."

"And what is that?" He seemed to have regained control.

"That the heart of France lies between Brussels and Paris. I have heard rumors of a secret memorandum written by Count von Schlieffen at the time of his retirement as Chief of the German General Staff five years ago. In it he stated that German strategy must focus on a swift and decisive victory over France. Such a plan depends on a lack of British intervention and a thrust on Paris from the north, through Belgium. Military intelligence indicates the majority of German divisions have been moved north of Metz over the past few years. This can mean only one thing. German arrogance is apparently so great they believe they can violate Belgian neutrality in this highhanded manner. One must never underestimate that arrogance. That has been the fatal mistake of many diplomats and generals over the past fifty years. My first task is to warn the Belgians of the Schlieffen plan."

The train had stopped in Beauvais. I stood by the window and watched the porters load luggage at the first-class door. I used the time to order my thoughts, seeking for the salient in the abundant detail. When we had begun moving again I sat opposite Daunt.

"I have so many questions I don't really know where to begin."

"Don't apologize for your bloody questions. The best measure of intelligence is not knowing the right answers but asking the right questions," he said and looked at me with donnish self-satisfaction.

"Why should I trust you?" I began. "Whom are you representing? Why have the normal channels of communication not been used? But let me start with the most obvious question, which you persist in ignoring: What exactly do you propose I do?"

"You are clear-headed despite all my meanderings.

That is why I placed my faith in you and took a great risk by asking you to meet me today."

"And . . ."

"I want you to go to a house in Berkeley Square in London. I will give you the address. Stay in the park, engage yourself as inconspicuously as you can, and watch that house. Note the people who come and go, observe the lights and movements within the house, try to identify the owner."

"But who is the owner?"

"He may be the Englishman Heneage Filch who signed the futurist manifesto, though that is not his correct name. They hold meetings at his house. But I think, if my conjectures regarding your past adventures are correct, that you will recognize this man when you see him. I pray you do."

"And that is all?"

"It is possible you will see Fritz. In that case we have more time than I thought. I want you to telegraph that single word—'Time'—to a postal box I have rented at the main Paris post office. You should also leave word with Jacques de Lalaing at the Belgian embassy in Belgrave Square. He knows of these arrangements. I shall be back in Paris by July 1 and shall contact you then."

He took the small velvet pouch from the seat and opened it, removing a dark, leather-covered object about the size of a box of wax vesta cigarettes.

"This is for you to record your observations." He handed me a tiny camera.

"Is this real? It isn't a toy?" I wondered.

"Not at all. It is called an Ensignette. You will find it fits perfectly in your waistcoat pocket. I assure you the photographs it takes are every bit as good as those from a larger model." I turned the Ensignette around in my hands, unable to believe such a small device could make photographs. "Do you carry a handgun?" Daunt asked me quietly.

"No," I said firmly. "But I still carry that little knife you gave me in Fez," I added, proudly displaying it to him.

"I am most honored, but I'm afraid that mayn't do you much good now. You would do well to consider a more formidable weapon."

"Thank you, no," I said.

"Do not be obstinate, sport. I am only thinking of your safety."

I swallowed thickly and tugged at the corner of my mustache.

"This is all so irregular," I complained. "Why have you contacted me in this manner? Whom are you working for?"

Daunt laughed—a brusque, chilling laughter which did little to reassure me. "I am working for the British government, of course. Whom did you think? My department was created after Crimea—F.O. originally. Five years ago we were moved along with the Secret Service to the War Office under Lord Haldane. Hardly affected me, really. As for my peculiar method of contacting you, I could not very well allow myself to become bogged down with American imbeciles who have little understanding or concern for this affair and would have been quick to assign some more experienced agent to it. As for the French, I do not trust the current flimsy administration for a moment." He spit a speck of tobacco from the tip of his tongue. "I doubt they will survive the current crisis and I hope they have been replaced before the German thrust occurs or all of us will be in grave difficulties. I should not be surprised to find a new cabinet in power by the time you and I return to Paris. But our work is more important than a change of cabinets. You know the

Kaiser visited London recently?" I nodded. "There is talk of a royal marriage."

"Yes, but surely you don't think—"

He shrugged. "It is an extremely tricky business. And only you, Clayton, can confirm the identity of Mr. Filch and with it the extent to which Fritz and his cohorts have penetrated high levels of the British government with their wretched intrigues."

"Only I?"

"That is correct. You must be vigilant in your observation of the house in Berkeley Square. Remain late into the evening, until you are certain all guests have left. The house is located on a mews at the north end of the square. This affords several different angles of observation. I'm dreadfully sorry I cannot be more explicit about what I expect you to see, but it simply must be so. There *is* a reason."

"Oh, I don't doubt that. But you know, you could very well be sending me down this mews merely to keep me distracted while you make mischief elsewhere."

Daunt coughed drily. "I have never been enamored of displays of glib, outspoken stupidity, so please forbear, Clayton. I shall lose all my confidence in you."

His knobby hands knuckled his temples while severe hazel eyes stared unflinchingly into my face. I felt foolish, shrugged, and admitted I trusted him, though I did not see why I should for all his "shenanigans." He laughed over the word.

"Yes, it has been a dreadfully long innings, this," he said, relaxing. "But I think we shall have a new batsman soon enough."

Still reeling from the responsibility which had suddenly devolved upon me, I sat in silence and considered those aspects of the business left unclear.

"What is happening in Morocco now?" I asked. "Why the falling-out between the Sultan and Madani al-Glaoui?"

"You needn't concern yourself with the Glaoui anymore. I'm afraid poor Abd el-Hafiz found himself caught in the same political vise as his brother: foreign creditors and revenue agents on one side and rebellious Islamic tribesmen on the other, with no way to please both and no way to survive without doing so. A cooperative dyarchy is unworkable in Morocco."

"So you believe the French will establish a protectorate?"

"I believe that is their intention. Whether they succeed depends in large part on the disposition of the British and the success of those seeking a Teutonic Accord. I am not exaggerating when I tell you that our enterprise is part of an effort to save civilization as we know it. The chaos you witnessed in Morocco four years back is coming to Europe. This will be the greatest war since 1815, Clayton. Our futurist enemies promote this possibility for their own warped reasons, but you and I have the chance to thwart them."

"You've certainly become quite the patriotic idealist since I saw you last."

"There is no time now for cynicism. No neutral stance remains. We must make our choices *now,* you and I, all of us."

For the next quarter hour we spoke of other things, reminisced of Morocco, and devised variations on the cipher to ensure the safety of future transmissions between us. As we neared Amiens I recalled Guillaume's presence on the train and questioned Daunt on how best to deal with this: avoid him, lie to him, confide in him?

"Well, you certainly cannot confide in him. Trying to avoid him when you reach the Dover ferry will be impossible. Best approach him. Tell him you're going to London for the coronation of George V. I don't know."

"Oh boy, I certainly wouldn't want to miss that."

"Doubtless not. In any case I think your waggish friend will carry on in oblivion. He might even prove useful in London, should you need a cover for your lengthy visits to Berkeley Square. You must be careful to observe but not to be observed, you understand."

"Yes. That troubles me."

"The coronation crowds will help. Just carry a Baedeker and ask foolish questions in American. That should suffice."

"You are mocking me."

"Jesting." He lighted another cigarette and stretched his legs.

"But how am I to know when I have seen what it is I am to see, since I don't know the owner of the house or exactly what you expect me to discover there?"

"You will know, old sport. Believe me, you will know."

The train drew into Amiens. I unlatched the door, slipped the Ensignette into my waistcoat pocket, and shook Daunt's hand.

"I shall contact you in Paris as soon as I receive word in the postal box. Good luck." He gave me a sharp nod as he closed the compartment door behind me.

The latch clicked and I walked numbly along the corridor and crossed into the next carriage, which would continue to Calais and the Dover ferry. It was filled with dancers.

VI

If one has never passed a professional dancer in a narrow corridor let me say that it is a sublime experience, and one I enjoyed many times as I sought a seat on the train and tried to avoid an immediate confrontation with Guillaume.

These dancers possessed an instinctive aplomb—in both senses of that word, composure and balance. When they turned sideways to allow my passage I dared not touch their slim shoulders or waists, so strong was my sense of their need for an encompassing space which they occupied alone with their perfect bodies. I found the men's bodies quite as attractive as the women's.

At the end of the third carriage I reached the entry to the diner. Realizing this was where I was most likely to meet my loquacious friend, I doubled back and located a single seat. I clambered across several sets of knees and finally situated myself and tried to take stock of my position.

The train was rushing me, quite outside my control, toward a vaguely predetermined fate in London. I had no will; Daunt was on his way to Brussels, leaving me no reference, no one with whom to confer or to ask the dozens of questions whirling through my boggled brain.

I could turn back at Calais, return to Paris, report all this to my superiors, and be done with it, but as in the past I could not be satisfied with a retreat. Not only was my curiosity too great and my instinctive faith in Daunt too strong, but my belief that I was part of a larger scheme (and had been since that day in the Place

St. Sulpice four years earlier) forbade my turning back, as Daunt had known it would. I would send Underwood an infuriating telegram from London and he would have to suffer a sense of powerlessness for once. I assured myself it would do him good.

Daunt's persistent mystification annoyed me. His unwillingness to reveal exactly what he expected me to see aroused feelings of ill-ease, feelings that I was being made use of and observed. These feelings increased on the ferry and the train from Dover into London. For the moment I examined my Ensignette (a magical little gadget if it worked) and pondered Daunt's admonition to acquire a firearm.

I boarded the ferry at Calais and made my way to the top deck at the prow to watch the continent recede. Soon other sentimentalists joined me, among them Claudie and Guillaume. He wore a bright striped scarf while the young dancer was in a bizarre outfit of multiple scarves, vestlets, and dangling brooches, her gypsy pants flapping in the breeze. They did not notice me at first, half turned from them as I was, and I edged near them along the rail so that I could overhear their conversation.

"The morning light is marvelous at sea, don't you think, my darling?" he said.

"Oh yes, it is so beautiful," she exclaimed and swung by her hands from the railing, scarves billowing around her as though she might take flight, her cheeks pink and eyes moist with the brilliant reflected light and sea spray. "Sometimes I think it does not matter at all whether I become a great dancer, Guillaume, because what is truly important is that I see all the world with my heart and keep my eyes open to the life around me, all the time. Like the light on the sea today."

He turned to reply but looked past her shoulder into my grinning face.

"Man loves the light above all else, eh, Guillaume?" I repeated one of his old maxims.

"Clayton Peavey. Whatever are you doing here? But how wonderful."

"Yes, isn't it? I decided the coronation would be a cure for my boredom."

"Ah, indeed." He eyed me suspiciously. "And not a word last night. A little secret agent business, is it?" I shrugged. "Well, no doubt you are on the trail of some international criminal, eh?"

"That's right, Guillaume," I humored him. "However did you guess?"

"I am glad you'll be with us in London." Claudie instantly assumed I would be their companion there. "We shan't be doing *Petrouchka* because Monsieur Diaghilev feels it might frighten them." She and Guillaume laughed over this appraisal of the straitlaced British. "But I shall be doing *Prince Igor* and perhaps *Carnaval,* so you will have a chance to see me dance again," she added with charming immodesty that was somehow excusable, as though all the world could have no greater pleasure than to watch her dance. I told her I would be delighted to see her dance again if my duties in London permitted.

We moved to the buffet for the Channel crossing. As we approached Dover I noticed a man in a dark double-breasted frock coat. I had observed him on the prow when I first encountered Guillaume and Claudie. He was standing by the bar, holding an empty beer glass which he occasionally lifted to his lips. When I rose to go outside he set down his glass, turned up the collar of his frock coat, and followed.

I whistled cheerfully beside Guillaume, squinting through the bright sunlight of midafternoon for my first glimpse of England. It suddenly occurred to me that this was June 21, the first day of summer—exactly four years to the day since he and I stood upon another ferry, heading south from the European continent.

While I must disclaim the possibility that I subscribe to cyclical theories of events or that I am a symbolist—much less a novelist, for whom coincidence must always, to be believable, thwart the protagonist, and must certainly never be so gratuitous as this—I was struck by this conjunction of dates, this anniversary, as it were, of our first adventure together, and I could not help believing that Guillaume's presence on the train that morning was indeed destined to be of some use to me in London.

Even though he did not understand what I was about, and despite the ominous presence of the man in the Prince Albert frock coat above us on the bridge, when I saw the white cliffs come into view in the distance (and they really were white) I rejoiced that we were together again.

VII

It was three days before I could act upon the promise of aid and companionship inherent in Guillaume's presence on the ferry.

London had contracted a severe bout of coronation fever. I braved coronation bunting and coronation pudding, coronation ascots and coronation derbies. John Young had produced a special coronation bitter and the Darracq company offered, for only £295, a fifteen-horsepower coronation model automobile. There were endless coronation banquets to be attended and coronation biscuits to be munched: Huntley & Palmer's offered its Royal Sovereign Biscuit and Macfarland Lang proclaimed that its Coronation Biscuit should be in every loyal household in the kingdom. Peek Frean and Company, alas, was being struck by its obviously disloyal employees and had no biscuits at all for sale.

I found all this fascinating, if a bit out of proportion, since we all knew that power lay not at Buckingham Palace but with Mr. Asquith and his fellow Liberals along Whitehall. June 22, the exalted day itself, was cursed by a warm, persistent drizzle, but this could not diminish the size nor enthusiasm of the crowds in the streets.

I paid my first visit to the house overlooking Berkeley Square in midmorning. It was located not on a proper mews but on Jones Street, the shortest street in London—so my hansom driver informed me. The house was large, of flat gray stone, Victorian in simplicity, shunning both Gothic and Classical tendencies, and embellished only by a bit of Regency ironwork over the windows and along the balconies on the second floor and a pair of oval windows on the third. The door faced discreetly onto little Jones Street between wide jambs with attached columns beneath an arched transom. It was most tasteful and unimaginative, rather like the park itself with its crusty plane trees and circular and intersecting paths.

Following my perfunctory appraisal of the house in Berkeley Square, I joined the throngs along Piccadilly and worked my way toward the hub. The roads were cleared of all vehicular traffic at dawn, yet I was repeatedly halted at police barriers and prevented from proceeding past the Mall. There I managed to glimpse the reprehensibly ornate coronation carriage on its stately procession from the royal palace to Westminster Abbey.

The afternoon was spent toasting the new king and enjoying the festivities, which induced the normally reticent Englishmen to turn vociferous for a day. Bonfires and illuminations dotted the hills around the city, and the pubs remained jammed into the muggy evening.

At eight o'clock, dulled by the beer and the crowds, I returned to Berkeley Square and stationed myself on a bench near Jones Street. No one came or went, the lights remained dimmed, and when I began dozing I abandoned my reconnaissance for the day and returned through streets still dense with activity to the room I had taken in Russell Square.

The following day was overcast but hot. I set out in late morning, guidebook in hand, and found a place beneath the tall plane trees lining the paths of the park. This time I was rewarded by the arrival at the house of a hansom cab, from which a tall gentleman emerged. The door was opened by a formidable footman and I managed a peek into the opulent, mahogany-paneled interior of the house. It looked invitingly cool and dark in there, and I grew wearier and more uncomfortable. I moved to a different bench and from this angle made a noteworthy discovery—the last oval window on the top floor, overlooking Jones Street, was of stained glass, as though the owner had a small chapel at that corner of the building. I recorded this with my Ensignette. At noon I found a pub off Regent Street, where I enjoyed my first bangers in several years and swilled down two pints of ale. Returning to the shade of Berkeley Square, I was soon asleep.

When I awoke the sun had broken through the clouds and was slanting across the rooftops directly into my face; I was soaked with perspiration. I moved once more and gazed blankly at my Baedeker. But throughout that evening and most of the next day I saw nothing of interest. Carriages deposited or picked up single individuals, formally dressed and apparently British, men stepped onto the balcony overlooking the park for a breath of air, but I recognized no one and rapidly grew bored and anxious. Perhaps I had come too late.

In search of a way in which to occupy my time during this fruitless surveillance, I located an art supply store in Charing Cross Road and purchased a sketch pad and charcoal. The next day was cooler and I sketched the houses, the gnarled trees, the little tin-roofed pagoda structure at the center of the square, and a few old men sleeping on benches.

The excitement fostered by my conference with Daunt had withered in the heat, and I began to question my presence in London. In this state of mind I decided to call upon Guillaume that evening and confide my mission. There seemed no harm in this; he might even join me in my vain wait.

That third evening activities at the house quickened

and an event occured which ensured that Guillaume would be eager to join my watch.

Shortly past suppertime a light breeze was stirring the trees overhead as a carriage brought two guests to the door. One was a fair-haired gentleman with a distinct Savile Row cut to his trousers, the other a heavy-set woman of advanced years with a black lace mantilla shielding her face. This was the first woman visitor I had seen—not surprising if this was a futurist meeting place, for the futurists scorned women as much as they scorned peace, love, and morality, each of these being symptoms of weakness. In her haughty bearing and the partial glimpse I caught of her face beneath the black lace mantilla, something was vaguely familiar, though I could not place it.

Following her arrival two more carriages came in rapid succession. I could see heads bobbing about in what must have been a drawing room on the second floor. A man, perhaps Heneage Filch himself, stood briefly at the balcony with the woman, pointing out to her objects around the square. His hand was raised before his face and I could not see either of them clearly in the half-light of dusk.

Soon a faint glow illuminated the stained glass window. I crossed to the end of the mews for a closer look. From an open window next to the stained-glass oval came a flickering light—either a gas jet or candle but certainly nothing incandescent—and I thought I detected a low droning.

While I was straining to hear this sound a hansom pulled hurriedly up before the house. Being at close range I pretended to be taking pictures of the street with my Ensignette. The new visitor stepped from his cab: a large man in a wide-brimmed white hat, long dark hair to his broad shoulders, with a tightly belted jacket and striped trousers. At the doorway he glanced back, and I saw the scar slashed across his cheek. It was Tommaso.

The Ensignette clicked, he looked up, I turned quickly away, and the door slammed shut as the cab clattered out of the mews.

This was inexplicable and totally unexpected. I could hardly believe this was the same man who four years earlier had given us his Bugatti for our trip to Morocco, nor could I imagine how he came to be visiting that house.

I sat on a bench and waited, but all I saw was the flickering light. An old man in a threadbare coat sat near me on the bench and asked for a cigarette. I told him I had none and moved away, but he remained on the best bench for observing without being observed and refused to depart. I recalled Daunt's words to remain late into the evening, so I stayed until past midnight, thankful now for the unseasonable mildness. The old man did not leave his bench all this time. His presence irritated me.

At last the guests began leaving. I could not come close enough to confirm the identity of Tommaso or inspect the familiar looking woman as she departed. Nor had I been able yet to determine the mysterious owner of the house. When I was quite certain all the earlier arrivals had retired I collected my sketchpad and walked across the park. Glancing back, I saw the old man still sitting on his bench, awake and waiting.

"What an hour to come calling, Clayton. Have you gone mad?" Guillaume blinked at me with bleary, brandy eyes and gathered his dressing gown over his nakedness.

"I apologize, Guillaume, but when I explain I know you will forgive me."

"Very well, then, come in," he said, and I did.

Hearing no sweet adolescent pinings from the darkened alcove which housed the bed, I surmised that Claudie was not staying with Guillaume at the Waldorf. This surprised me.

"I know, I know, it's awful," grumbled Guillaume, lighting a cigarette and slopping a bit of cognac into a glass. "But the maestro says she must rest. We were fortunate to find rooms here ourselves, with all these foreign dignitaries in town for the coronation. She is rooming with two of the Russian ballerinas in Bloomsbury."

"Can he do that so arbitrarily—just place her wherever he wants?" I asked, for a moment distracted by Guillaume's misery.

"Oh yes, it's his company. And Claudie abides by whatever he says. She worships him. He has grand plans for her, you know."

"But that's wonderful." I pretended to ignore his transparent jealousy.

"Oh, I suppose it is, only at times I do not trust Sergei. He is so self-centered, so single-minded when it comes to his company. And he influences everyone he contacts. They are already planning Claudie's training and developing roles for her for next season. She is his . . ." He broke off, at a loss for the word to express what he felt.

"But you cannot possess her *totally*, Guillaume," I protested. "Is this not what you wanted for her?"

"She possesses me," he said. "Totally."

"It's not the same, my friend, and I'm afraid you cannot make it so by sheer force of will."

"I see less of her here than I did in Paris. It's ridiculous. I want to show her London, and she has no time. I feel like an outsider," he pouted and drew deeply on his cigarette. "But London depresses me. It always has."

"And why is that?" I asked, now totally engrossed in

his problems and entirely forgetting the reason for my visit. "I thought you were looking forward to coming here."

"I was. I had forgotten."

"Forgotten?"

"Little Annie, the Rose of Hildesheim. Do you remember? I told you, I'm sure."

"One loses track of—"

"Yes, of all my stories. But this is true. The British governess I met in Germany. My first love. I followed her to London as a suitor. She was not unwilling but her father distrusted me. A cold, pious man he was, in a cold, pious house. Finally he sent her off to your country, since I could not follow her there. London has seemed an uninviting place to me ever since. I always have a sense of helplessness here, and of foreboding."

"I think, Guillaume, that your problem, if I may call it that and be excused a bit of unsolicited advice, lies in the fact that you select some poor, unsuspecting girl, like this governess, and invest in her all the magical poetic powers, the sublime love, of your own imagination. You see her as you wish her to be, not as she really is. It is a pattern which foredooms all love affairs to failure."

"I think you have never been in love, to speak like that."

"But one must try to see one's beloved as she really is."

"Let me tell you something, Clayton—and I say this soberly and without emotion." He sipped his cognac and wiped his lips, composing his thoughts without ever taking his eyes from my face. "I try to control it, but I find that I have scorn for nearly all my fellow creatures. They are a shallow, stupid lot, and few do I meet for whom I feel respect. You I rather like because you are clever and irreverent and honest. But you lack the gift for creation, that spark which distinguishes a few of us. This sounds like utter artistic arrogance, I know, but it is something one lives with, something I have discovered in myself and in a very few other people I have met. It cannot be denied. It is that rare quality which communicates itself to others not through the power of personality but through great art. And Claudie has it. She is the only woman I have known who does, the only one who measures up. The rest I mock, but her I respect and admire completely. She is no governess and never will be. She is my equal, and for that I love her with a love I have never known before. Do you believe what I am saying?"

I gazed at him for several long seconds, then replied that I did believe him. "But Marie is your equal," I added. "Did she not possess—"

"She is like you, Clayton Peavey: clever, glib, bright, imaginative, cheerful, all these wonderful things. But she lacks that other essential quality."

"She is not a genius and so you rejected her?"

"I rejected her? Oh, Clayton, if you only knew the truth of that. No, all the women I love end by rejecting me. From the English governess to Marie, they have all rejected me."

"Perhaps they did not care for your scorn."

"No, it is because they misunderstand. I am ill-loved. I have tried to love them, truly I have." He downed another gulp of cognac and looked at me with his muddy rivers of remorse. "I love too deeply and suffer for it. This is the lament of the ill-loved, my friend." I shook my head. "And now my dearest, my sweetest angel, my little protégée as they insist on calling her, she will end by rejecting me as well. I know it. It must be. I shall be left with nothing but my sweet misery, my hopeful regrets."

When Guillaume resorted to oxymoron and other

cheap rhetorical devices I recognized that his brief flight of contradictory self-revelations was over and that we would soon be swatting the aphorisms in the air. I awaited the inevitable "And that is all," so appropriate here, but it did not come. This in itself was tribute to the depth of his feelings for Claudie. Nonetheless, I turned the subject, at long last, to my own affairs. I told him of my meeting with Daunt, my surveillance of the house in Berkeley Square, and the appearance that evening of Tommaso. He was not surprised by any of it.

"Yes, I understood Tommaso was in London. You say Daunt told you they were futurists at this house. That is Tommaso's cause, most certainly. There is to be a Futurist Ball at the Dudgeon Gallery next week. I have the invitation somewhere. Nevinson and some of the others. I don't know." He searched vaguely for the invitation. "But the futurists are poets and artists. And Tommaso hates the Germans, as he hates all systematic philosophies. I scarcely see them as evil or even political."

"Don't you understand? It is a cover. Tommaso may not know what is really going on there. Perhaps this man Filch has a spiritual hold over Fritz Amgott."

"Oh really, Clayton Peavey, I can hardly believe that." Guillaume laughed.

"But you don't know. When I saw Tommaso this evening I decided to ask you to join me tomorrow, to help me. That is, if you can spare the time."

"I am bored and miserable in London. I should rather enjoy playing at being a spy again for a day or two. It will surely not be so dangerous as Morocco. After all, what harm can befall one in Berkeley Square?"

"I would not be so sure of that, Guillaume. In any case, I will be glad of your company. Somehow I feel this affair always has and still does concern you."

"Then why did you not tell me of it sooner?"

"I wanted to tell you on the ferry. But I couldn't. I don't know why."

"So you see, we hold each other in high regard yet withhold our full respect. You are no artist, and I . . . I do no accept the priority of this affair which you make the center of your life, and so you do not completely trust me."

"Perhaps that is so. But you will join me tomorrow, even if only for your vicarious delight?"

"Yes, and we shall see what we can espy of these nasty futurists in Berkeley Square." He stubbed out his cigarette and took my hand to seal our agreement.

It was perfectly still and blazing hot by nine the next morning. I walked from my hotel past the steaming produce stands around Covent Garden and along Aldwych Crescent to join Guillaume at the Waldorf for coffee. The thick air settling over London inhibited breathing and stung my eyes.

Almost immediately upon our arrival in Berkeley Square a hansom cab pulled up before the house and a figure emerged: a rail-thin man with a stiff high collar and black tie, wearing a top hat and carrying gloves and a cane. He mounted the stoop and half turned to address his driver. Through the haze across the park I gazed over the bushy mustaches and crooked nose into the monocled eye of Fritz Amgott.

I pulled out my Ensignette but caught only a rear view of his top hat disappearing into the house. This little prologue to the day convinced Guillaume that something was afoot. At that moment in Berkeley Square a transformation began in Guillaume. I detected it at first only as enthusiasm—an awakening of patriotism and devotion to the cause of France as he imagined it, personified by the Zorns and threatened by Fritz Amgott.

This sense of mission gradually replaced his self-absorbed malaise.

We took up posts with opposite views into Jones Street and sat for some time. I noticed the same old man in the threadbare coat who had asked me for a cigarette the previous day. Perhaps he was an idler with nothing better to do than lounge in Berkeley Square, but somehow I doubted it.

Twenty minutes after Fritz's arrival an elegant two-horse carriage drew into the mews and a stout man in a chesterfield stepped from it. I could not recognize him from my vantage point, nor could Guillaume. His private carriage remained parked outside the door.

Shortly past noon the door opened. I positioned myself with Ensignette in hand and this time I was doubly rewarded. Fritz stepped forth in full view, and beside him the stout, distinguished man with the private carriage. Again the Ensignette clicked. I thought Fritz glanced up, though he could not possibly have heard the sound; then he and the other man mounted the private carriage and set out together.

Having an accomplice to watch over the house, I decided to follow the carriage and to use this opportunity to cable Daunt that single word "Time," as I had promised to do should Fritz appear in London.

I managed to hail a hansom, and we pursued the two-horse carriage down Oxford Street and along Hyde Park, where Fritz was let out at his hotel. I leaned out and called up to my driver. Waving a silver crown in his face, I prevailed upon him to continue following the carriage. It proceeded along the Mall past St. James Park, then doubled back down Whitehall. We nearly lost the scent when one of the new double-decker omnibuses cut between us and the carriage, but my skillful driver maneuvered around this hulking, fuming goliath. He was as stunned as I to see the carriage turn between the Horse Guard sentries posted at a narrow, dead-end alleyway off Whitehall and deposit its passenger at the door to No. 10.

I posted my cable and rushed back to Berkeley Square to find Guillaume smoking and chatting with the old man on the bench. Finally prying him loose of this likely counteragent, I conveyed my latest astonishing discovery and he informed me that nothing further had transpired at the house. This was the state of affairs through the afternoon. We lunched in shifts. By early evening we had resumed our watch, and Guillaume grew once again bored and dissatisfied.

Shortly before eight the procession began. Fritz returned in evening dress accompanied by another man, shorter and adorned with distinctive German braiding and a conspicuous iron cross. They were followed by a second carriage from which issued Tommaso, respectfully leading on his arm the plump, elderly woman with the black lace mantilla whom I had seen the previous evening but could still not identify. As Guillaume gaped at Tommaso, I clicked my trusty Ensignette, and they entered the house. A third carriage deposited one more guest, a trim Englishman with ruffled hair in a crumpled corduroy suit. Shortly thereafter their meeting began.

As before, the oval stained glass window was illuminated and I detected the flickering light of candle or gas; and again I thought I heard unison voices repeating a litany of some sort. The haunting sound made my stomach twitch, for fear that at this moment of truth something would go amiss.

For two hours I stood quite still opposite the house, oblivious of my lack of security, filled with a dreamlike aching, my eyes dulled by the spectral light of the evening, Guillaume seated on a bench not far away.

Finally the windows flew open on the balcony and Tommaso appeared at the Regency grillwork. He stood a moment looking out, his long dark hair hanging around his face like a sinister aura. The light brightened behind him and another man stepped onto the balcony. It was the same man I had seen the day before describing the square to the woman.

This man edged forward and gazed out with the light behind him, a penumbral presence rising out of my past, then turned so that he was silhouetted in profile.

It was so difficult to be sure; I wanted desperately to see his hands, which might have verified all, but they remained hidden. I glanced at Guillaume, who had come up beside me, and his eyes reflected my own disbelief and the dawning of recognition. Somewhere far away the wind whistled in my ears, though it was perfectly calm in Berkeley Square.

At last the man turned and withdrew a step. The light fell on his face—the thin mustache, the heavy lidded eyes—and now I was sure, and I realized instantly who that familiar looking older woman was.

I snatched out my Ensignette in the vain hope of recording permanent confirmation that what I was indeed seeing was the pale man from Madame Orgueil's.

VIII

After sighting the pale man we saw nothing during two more days at the house in Berkeley Square. Realizing that their work was finished there, and mine with it, I left Guillaume to his "sweet misery and hopeful regrets" in London and returned to Paris on the last day of June. A new French cabinet had been installed under Joseph Caillaux, exactly as Daunt had predicted. But there was no message from Daunt at the Rue du Sommerard.

On July 1 the German gunboat *Panther* occupied Agadir, a small port in southern Morocco, reportedly for "the protection of German citizens endangered there" but clearly as a direct challenge to French encroachments at Fez. The storm had broken; and the heat with it, though not for long.

Buoyed by these confirmations of Daunt's predictions I rushed to the embassy. It was a Saturday: Underwood was out of town for the weekend, Darlington had been suddenly recalled to the States, and no one else knew of my activities. I could do nothing but wait until Monday. The weekend papers reflected my anxiety over the mounting crisis as they asked the question on everyone's mind: "Could this mean war?"

This was apparently not the question on Derrick Underwood's mind. When I located him early Monday morning he was annoyed by my long absence and unimpressed by my prognostications of doom.

"But Daunt told me ten days ago this would happen. And I *saw* Fritz and the pale man in Berkeley

Square. We are failing in our responsibility to the French government if we don't go to them with this information." My voice grew shrill. Underwood wrinkled his brow and appeared inclined to wring my neck. He fiddled with his stickpin and cuff buttons instead.

"I hate to discountenance your commendable efforts to save Europe, Peavey," he told me, "but I've been round this whole business with Ambassador White and with the Brits. Your man Daunt is something of an independent operator, though apparently a loyal member of their service. I don't know what he's on to, but it is of no great concern to the British government, so I don't see why it should be to us."

"I want to talk to the Ambassador," I said firmly.

"That, I'm afraid, is out of the question."

"Why?"

"He can't be bothered with your futurists and pale men and Teutonic Accords."

"Why not let him decide that?"

"He has. Besides, do you know what day tomorrow is, Peavey? Do you?"

I was too blinded by frustration to discern what he was driving at. "No, what day is it? What difference does that make?"

"Tomorrow is the Fourth of July, Peavey. Ambassador White is not in the embassy this morning, and we are all preparing for a rally in the Place Etats-Unis tomorrow. I hope you'll come."

"Christ, Underwood, you don't seem to understand what is happening in the world. Do you read the papers?"

"Do you believe them?"

"In this instance, yes. Daunt told me—"

"Oh, Daunt, Daunt, Daunt. I am tired of your Mr. Daunt."

"I'm sorry, but I want you to arrange for me to meet

with someone at the Quai d'Orsay, and from that Troisième Bureau too, as soon as possible."

"And if I do not arrange this meeting for you?"

"Then I shall have to go over there myself and make a mess of all your proper channels and punctilio."

"And make a fool of yourself in the bargain." He gave me his most condescending look. My fury rose: his petty objections and jousting simply made no sense, and I told him so.

"Very well," he said. "I'll see what I can do, if that will placate you. Relax, Peavey, you're overinvolved. Will you be coming to the fireworks tomorrow evening? I'll save a place for you."

"Damn your fireworks," I shouted indignantly and stomped out of his office.

In the ivory sunlight I stood outside the embassy puzzling over the resistance and hostility I had encountered there. I felt disoriented and at a loss, as though something were missing inside me, and I could not regain my sense of equilibrium until I had found it. But I knew not where to look and so began walking, aimlessly but swiftly.

On the Rue du Louvre I passed the central Paris post office. I went on a whim to the rows of glass-cased boxes and found the one Daunt had reserved for our messages. Through the glass I saw the folded blue envelope bearing my cable from London. He had not yet returned to Paris and had never received my message.

This disturbed me even further, and I dawdled by the river, tearing maple leaves along their spines and searching the gray waters for direction. All the time a sense of urgency slashed at me, shredding first one feeble resolve and then the next. Again I began to walk.

I knew where I was going this time and soon stood

in the Place St. Sulpice. Back to the beginning, hoping to see forward from that vantage point; but everything remained clouded, and the heat of midday fettered me in its leaden grip.

Several boys were playing soccer in the *place*. One of them kicked the ball into the second level of the tiered fountain. He had to wade in to his waist to retrieve it. Above him, at the center of the fountain, sat the four clerics, looking out as stonily as I looked in; one of them had a brown scab of pigeon droppings down his forehead. When the booming bells of St. Sulpice rang noon, the square quickly emptied and I walked away from the river, through the Luxembourg Gardens toward Montparnasse.

In a daze I trudged the broad, tree-lined Boulevard Raspail, bumping into people, seeing nothing except the pale man, Fritz, Daunt on the train, and lurking behind these, as I imagined them, the great smoking chimneys of the Glautsch chemical works on the Rhine, surrounded by spike-helmeted German soldiers marching toward France.

I heard shouts, voices raised in argument, and a deep voice at my shoulder crying *"Guerre, guerre."* A bearish, bearded man with red eyes was distributing broadsides topped with the bleeding word *"Guerre."* I realized I was standing before the Café de la Rôtonde, filled at the noon hour, as always, by syndicalists and mystics, vagabonds and bohemians, geniuses of all nationalities and all ages come to share their genius over coffee while glaring across the boulevard at the German millionaires and rich aesthetes who populated the rival Dôme.

The tables crowded out onto the sidewalk, and sneering waiters pushed past me with trays held above their heads, a precarious perch of glasses and coffee cups jangling as they went. For a moment I debated entering this jungle, having a *café crème,* and listening to the conversation. I was about to turn away when I noticed someone pointing and waving a newspaper at me. When he stood I recognized Paul, our sturdy Breton, and shambled over to him without any show of enthusiasm.

"Hello, Clayton." He was pleased to see me. "Everything all right?"

"Is it so obvious?" I asked.

"Well, you look a bit down. Come have a drink with us. I'm with someone who should be able to cheer you up." He led me by the arm to a table against the wall occupied by two young men whom I might have known and a woman with her back to me. When she turned—straight dark hair framing a square face, the button nose and irreverent grin in place—I recognized Guillaume's Marie. She kissed me warmly.

"Marie and I are planning to work together on a ballet decor next season," Paul explained. Napkin sketches covered the table.

"Really?" I paused, trying to accept this opportunity to distract myself in idle talk. "I've just come from London. Guillaume is there now with the ballet."

There was a moment's strained silence; for Marie, I realized, talk of Guillaume was not idle.

"How is he?" she asked softly.

"I'm surprised you still care, the way he's treated you."

"Of course I do," she said, and her bright little eyes caught mine and persisted in the sincerity of this remark. "I do."

"To be frank, he is in a terrible state. All his usually boundless enthusiasm for life has been sapped. He speaks of his scorn for all men."

"Things are not so heavenly with his little angel?"

smirked one of the young men at the table. All Paris, at least all of the Rôtonde, knew of Guillaume's infatuation.

"Do not speak of things you cannot understand, Patrick," Marie chastised the young man, who adopted a look of contrition tinged with mockery. Marie turned to me with compassionate eyes. "That is the problem, though? He is not getting on with the girl?" she asked bravely.

"What else could one expect?" said Paul, and I nodded.

"It's not her fault, of course," I explained. "He expects so much from their relationship and forgets his own work. That's the worst part. He is concerned only with the ballet."

"She is a very sweet girl," said Marie, wrinkling her nose. "We must help him, Clayton. You and I."

"I think you might be able to help him, Marie, except he is too proud to recognize this. But I . . ."

"Oh, but he loves you, Clayton. He spoke of you so often the past four years. I think he respects you because you two are so unalike yet you do not try to hide the differences."

"Well then, what are we to do?" I asked, flattered to hear that Guillaume "loved" me. I was moved by my own affection for him and by the depth and constancy of Marie's.

"I want nothing for myself, you understand. I am not jealous," she said, and I believed her. "We are just friends now, and that is enough. But we must help him remember what he is, so that he can go on living as he must live, actively at work. We must show him that he has not thrown away his past through this attachment. He has added to it."

"You're wonderful, Marie," I said. "He doesn't deserve you."

"But he does." She laughed. "That is precisely the point."

We determined to arrange a meeting, perhaps a dinner at his mother's (with the Inspector too, I suggested), when Guillaume returned from London. The prospect pleased Marie. My own thoughts quickly returned to the world at large, and I fell silent.

"What's troubling you, Clayton?" Marie inquired. "You're not your old carefree self at all." She put her hand on my arm.

"How can I be? It's this war business. I'm frightened."

The two young men tittered, and they all looked at me curiously until Paul spoke. "There'll be no war. It's a lot of talk. And I don't see what concern it is of yours, anyway. It's not *your* war, after all. If things get knotty you can sail home, can't you?"

I shook my head. It *was* my war, I thought, and I could not tell Paul how personally I took the events occurring in the world that week. It was my war and Daunt's.

"Goodness, what a mood," he said. "Why not have lunch with me? Just the two of us, old friends, and Marie if you'd like." Marie shook her head. Before I could protest Paul had tossed off the last of his aperitif, set his straw hat on his head, dropped a few sous on the table, shaken the hands of the two, and kissed Marie.

"Do not forget our plan for Guillaume," she reminded me as I kissed her cheeks. "And Paul, give her my love, poor thing," she added as he led me down the Boulevard Raspail to a small restaurant with checked cloths and bowls of fruit on the tables.

* * *

Throughout the meal Paul kept up a pleasant banter on his work with the ballet, his misgivings over the affair of Guillaume, Marie, and Claudie, and other subjects which he guessed might ease my preoccupation. He ate heartily and with great pleasure. I barely tasted my food and could not follow his conversation. All I heard was the laughter.

It was laughter which normally would have been comforting in the cozy restaurant with its rich, sweet smells; the sort of laughter which makes you smile though you do not know its source, merely to hear others so gay. It came from the kitchen and continued through most of our meal: an old woman's cackling, a girlish giggle, a man's coarse guffaws, but above it all the old woman's wild cackling and half-swallowed comments on whatever was so funny. When our waitress brought each course from the kitchen she could barely contain the smile tugging at her cheeks, which Paul returned with his eyes. But the laughter did not amuse me, and I wished it would stop. It became like a torture, trying to shut it out and follow Paul's rambling conversation while still distracted by my graver thoughts. At last Paul caught my attention. He was describing a play for which he had designed the sets.

"It was Apolline's last role in Paris," he said.

"Apolline?"

"Yes, the poor dear. You were quite close to her once, weren't you?"

"I was . . . that is . . . I have often wondered about her."

"As a matter of fact I am visiting her this afternoon. It's my day."

"But I didn't know she was in Paris. Max said she was gone."

"Ah, then you don't know."

"What?"

"She is in Paris; but gone, as Max says. She is in a private sanitarium in the Bois des Vincennes. I'm afraid she has become even more distant. Spends most of her time reading physics texts she can't possibly understand and doodling the equations on a slate." He looked into his plate.

"I should like to see her," I said. "Do you think I might come with you today?"

"It's not likely to cheer you up."

"I don't need cheering up. I need direction."

"Well, she surely can't provide that. The poor thing cannot even direct her own life, much less someone else's."

"Nevertheless, I would like to come with you," I repeated testily, and added: "If that is permissible."

Paul hesitated. It seemed his reluctance—voiced only out of consideration for my sensibilities—confirmed in me the absolute necessity of seeing Apolline. It was not that I wished to see her, nor could I specify the reasons for my sudden need to visit her or my expectations for that visit. But I felt certain that I must see her—a familiar certainty out of my past—in order to awaken that part of my mind and soul which existed only in her presence and to see what it could tell me about my current dilemma. I cannot say whether it was intuition, superstition, frustration, or boredom—or some combination of these and the heat and my inability to silence that damned laughter—but an obstinate determination must have risen into my face, already pink and puffy from the wine, for Paul noted my hostile expression and shrugged it off.

"Oh, I'm sure it is permissible," he said. "You are an old friend. Perhaps she will be glad to see you, if she even recognizes you." He paused to allow me one last chance to reconsider, but I rejected it with fierce eyes. "Fine, fine." He rapped my arm. "I told my friend Georges I would stop by to see his new canvas, if you don't mind. It's on the way. You might find it interesting. And how is your work coming along?" he inquired.

I shook my head.

Paul's friend lived in a sixth-floor walkup off the Rue Mouffetard. The little studio was unbearably stuffy, and my head whirred with my usual midafternoon, post-lunch torpor.

I was not prepared for what I saw there. It was quite a large canvas which the young man—pale and sharp-chinned with thick spectacles and sinewy forearms—claimed was a violin. The instrument had been fragmented, broken into a great number of pieces, and these had duplicated themselves and been scattered at random about the canvas. This had been fractured into a series of dissecting planes on which the scattered fragments of the violin—a tuning peg, a bit of scroll inlay, a section of string, part of the neck or the curve of the body—took rest to form a new violin structure. Other musical notations, clefs and notes and rests, were added to the design as though the instrument were playing. The whole thing was arranged on planes formed by brief dark slashes of pigment, and little rectangular daubs of white had been added about the periphery. I gazed for a long time at the floating, disembodied pieces and felt a tightening in my throat.

"It's beautiful, don't you think?" Paul asked me, and I leaned against the wall, wearily wondering what beauty had come to. "Because it is so real," he added.

"It's all broken in fragments. Like the world, it's coming apart."

"And like some people, too," Paul mused.

"Your friend looks a bit dazed," the painter said, and they offered me a glass of tepid water. I accepted it and endured their dialogue regarding the violin, which I could not look at again, until we departed.

I insisted upon boarding a steamboat for the trip through the heat of midafternoon to the Bois des Vincennes. I stretched out with the river breeze in my face while Paul described a composer in Vienna who was doing the same thing in his music as Georges with the violin: breaking apart the formal structure, disregarding tonality in this case, in order to achieve a greater freedom of expression.

The steamboat deposited us at the Porte de Charenton, near the juncture of the Marne and the Seine. We strolled into the Bois beneath tall wych elms and chestnut trees, past a lake in the shape of a figure eight. At the center of the lake were two small islands with weeping willows whose lush branches hung almost to the water level. Ducks and swans navigated between the drooping branches.

On pebbly patches of dirt adjacent to the lake old men were playing at *boules*—the ideal game for this muggy weather, I thought. I could become mesmerized watching the concentrated way the men crouched, then the stylized turn of the hand for the delivery of the big steel *boule*.

We followed a narrow path away from the lake where the bois was more densely wooded with elms, conifers, and maples. The path crossed a single carriageway lined with neat topiary hedges. This circled a broad lawn to a marble-faced building which I took to be the sanitarium.

It was an elegant old chateau, domed and porticoed, with tall palladian windows and wings each side of the central dome. It reminded me of the Petit Trianon at Versailles (only the pink marble was missing): a magical structure hiden in the woods which one chanced upon so suddenly and unexpectedly. Several elderly patients were maundering about in the gardens, thoroughly distracted but apparently quite harmless.

We found Apolline alone in a room, seated on the floor beneath a skylight, bathed in the rays of the hot sun and dressed in a thin shirt and shorts. Her hair was hacked unevenly and she had lost weight, if that were possible.

"Hello, Paul," she said and gazed at me a moment; but when recognition occurred she seemed neither surprised nor particularly moved by my presence. "Oh, Clayton," was all she said.

She was surrounded by several thick tomes, opened to pages of equations and diagrams. These were her physics texts—an odd direction for her mysticism to have taken. Folded papers and journals were piled about her on the floor and on the rungs of an open étagère. She held a large slate on which were drawn a variety of incomprehensible symbols.

"She's frightfully thin," I whispered to Paul.

"Yes, she is suffering something called anorexia. At least that is the diagnosis of this unconventional doctor from Vienna who has taken an interest in the case. It means—"

"I don't eat." She smiled. Her teeth were not all there, and her dark eyes appeared even larger on her hollow face—haunted and haunting.

"You remember Clayton," Paul coached her. "I hope you don't mind that I've brought him to see you."

"I can see, I'm no child, and I know who he is," she lilted. I regarded her as though she were that ghastly violin, broken in fragments before me.

"She has an odd way of speaking, sort of singsong," Paul explained, talking about her in the way people speak of children or sick people, in their presence, as though they were inanimate objects incapable of hearing or responding.

He was right about her speech. Throughout our visit she spoke only in anapests (short-short-long phrases), out of which she constructed, apparently without thinking, whatever she wished to say. This gave to her speech an oddly pleasant lilt, as though she were actually singing. I have retained the original meter in my translation of her words (for she spoke in French, of course), as the effect of her rhythmic patterns on me was more forceful than the substance of what she said.

"Do you like these books?" I asked her, at a loss for what else to say. "You don't understand physics, do you?"

"But I do, but I do," she replied. "Measure change not by what has been changed but by what has remained still unchanged." She beamed and drew on her slate.

Paul shook his head and talked to her of life outside the sanitarium and about their old friends, but she seemed uninterested in his feeble defense against her madness.

"Delta t." She pointed at the slate. "This is change. Delta t, delta t," she sang, and I edged closer to her protective ring of books, trying to make out this delta t. She shrank in her sunny circle but held up the slate for me to see. "Delta t," she repeated. "What remains still unchanged. What remains still unchanged." She spoke it like a question and a definition all at once, and the phrase stuck in my head. I could not shake it loose, though it made no particular sense to me.

"It's too hot," she observed flatly and removed her blouse, tossing it onto the floor across the room. Her ribs showed and she had no breasts, just very pink nipples and the slightest sag of flesh where her small breasts had been. She was indifferent to my stare—she was hot so she discarded her shirt—and it occurred to me that this disregard for appearances was characteristic of a small child, a madman, an idiot, or a genius; but what combination of these she was I could not decide. I persisted in my belief that she was more than a madwoman.

"The doctors encourage her reading and scribbling," Paul explained. "I suppose it is better than some things she might be doing."

"It is quite bizarre," I agreed.

"Inwardness, that is life," she said. "Inwardness. What remains still unchanged."

We remained, not totally unchanged, for two hours, while she doodled and rambled in her lilting cadence. I was rendered utterly enervated in her presence, my faculties as atrophied as her pathetic body. The anapests swam through the warm air beneath the skylight, and her thin, chalk-smeared hands erased the slate and drew over it new equations with less meaning than the last.

"What we see has been seen, has been changed by our sight." She directed this at me, as though I were more receptive than Paul, who had probably heard it all before. "It is changed by our gaze, by our thoughts, by our lives." She lifted one frail hand: "Where we are," and pointed with the other. "Where we go. Not the same. Not unchanged. Delta t measures change. What remains still unchanged."

She fell silent, and for several moments we sat awkwardly. She rose and wavered across the room to her shirt, which she slung about her neck like a scarf, then she started to swoon, perhaps from sitting so long in the sun.

"Time to go," she said and smiled endearingly through tight blanched lips, a little lost waif's smile missing several teeth.

She walked with us to the portico and stood leaning

against one of the columns, as straight and pale as the white marble. Like an orchestra conductor she waved us off into the bois. I looked back, waved, and blew her a kiss from the edge of the pines, but either she did not see the gesture or it meant nothing to her, for she turned away and withdrew into her marble cloister in the woods.

"Can they do nothing for her?" I asked, and Paul shook his head. "And her parents?"

"Her father is dead, and her mother would rather she remain in Paris, where she wishes to be. So the mother purchases her own freedom from that disturbing presence and rewards Apolline with the comfort and freedom she enjoys here. It is very sad."

"Very sad," I concurred, my own anapestic coda to our visit with Apolline.

I left Paul and returned to the Rue du Sommerard hoping, as I hoped on each return to my room, for a message from Daunt. There was none. For twenty minutes I sat on the bed. It was still quite warm and I was restless, so I walked out to a café in the Boul' Mich' and sat for a long time over a *pastis*.

I knew from my reception at the embassy that I must take charge of my own affairs, but without further word from Daunt I could not decide how to do this. While French President Fallières and Queen Wilhelmina dithered obliviously in Amsterdam, the evening papers screamed, "War Imminent." James Gordon Bennett's *Paris Herald* usually restrained itself to naming names and reprinting the letter from the "Old Philadelphia Lady" about centigrade/fahrenheit conversion, but even it had taken up the cry.

Surprisingly, the English had not protested the German incursion in Morocco. This left France isolated, threatened, with few alternatives, and unable to make the next move. From Berlin came only Bethmann-Hollweg's renowned sphinxlike silence, in apparent anticipation of British acquiescence to the establishment of a foothold at Agadir. Let the French draw their own conclusions.

As I sat in the café, Apolline's phrase ran through my mind: "What remains still unchanged." I did not understand her delta t—that part of my education had been woefully neglected—but the words clawed at me, insisting that if I pondered them, or simply allowed them to roam long enough through my weary brain, they would provide my dispensation and tell me what to do. I was not disappointed.

At length the words assumed a different sound, the phrasing altered slightly, and I heard them through the buzz of the lobby at the Châtelet Theatre, in an old clown's voice: "Some things remain unchanged."

I rose quickly, paid my tab, and hailed a cab. Now I knew what to do, and it was obvious, of course. The final link, the one remaining piece of evidence to be verified, drawing Fritz and the pale man, the Teutonic Accord, the death of Sébastien, all of it together and silencing my remaining uncertainty about the truth in what Daunt had told me. One simple verification.

It was near the end of the evening's second performance at the Cirque Mediano. I stood by the bar, drinking a beer and watching Darius Boppe. When he concluded his act I raised my hand to him, fearful he would not recognize me. But he had already seen me and advanced on me with that steady look of enduring lassitude in his chocolate eyes.

"So you come on *this* night," he said, shaking my hand. He seemed absolutely unchanged, as though he would go on forever.

"I wondered if Arbogast—"

He held up his hand to silence me. "Follow me, then." He led me to the living quarters of the performers, back among the tracks and animal cages, the simmering stock pots and cast-off costumes, where we had first gone to hear Arbogast Zorn's tale four years before.

In a long room in what appeared to be a converted railway carriage, I found Zorn and Clovis Vogel and a younger man seated around a gas lantern. Vogel was hunched and grumbling through a three-day beard. He looked more wretched and slovenly than I remembered.

"They all want ridiculous prices," he complained to Arbo Zorn. "These patrons have no respect for art, only for money." He spit into a cup between his knees and eyed me blankly. Zorn rose and welcomed me, a faded cutaway Zouave jacket parting over the bulge of his belly.

"You have returned from your mission," he said. "And returned in terrible times for us all."

"Well, I'm thankful to hear someone believes with me that war is at hand and times are bad."

"But of course, we are deeply troubled," said Zorn. "We have gathered tonight to discuss what must be done."

"Perhaps I bring you more troubling news," I said. I drew from my pocket two pictures I had taken with the Ensignette: one of Fritz at the door to the house in Berkeley Square; the other, in the darkness, from a distance, of the pale man. "Do you know either of these men?" I asked and the pictures were handed around. None of them knew Fritz, which was to be expected, but I waited breathlessly as the picture of the pale man passed from Boppe to Arbo Zorn.

He held it and turned it into the light and squinted at it for a long time. His face grew grim and weary. He shook his head and studied it again.

"It is so difficult to tell. The picture is not clear."

"It was night," I told him. "But who?"

"I cannot be sure, but I believe this is the Englishman I met years ago in Amsterdam. The one who began our unfortunate association with the Moors. But how do you come to have his likeness today?"

The last link. The wraith had spoken quite literally, notwithstanding Madame Orgueil's facile obfuscations, which now also seemed predictable. The finger had pointed that night at the man who was, in a very real sense, Sébastien's murderer. There seemed no doubt that he was behind the plot to assassinate the former English king and therefore likewise involved with Fritz, as Daunt had suspected, in the Teutonic Accord and plans for a war against France.

I explained all of this—my own interpretations, my difficulty in finding an ear at the embassy, and the role of Daunt—to the sodality of clowns gathered that night behind the Cirque Mediano. When I told them Britain might renounce the independence of Alsace their pessimism deepened. They realized the urgency with which action must be taken to save the lost provinces—always their first objective—and to save France itself.

"For Alsatians love France as a child loves its mother," Boppe told me.

Arbogast Zorn had encountered difficulty in learning anything about the Glautsch chemical works in Ottmarsheim.

"The plant is sealed off and employs exclusively German immigrants," he said. "Materials arrive by barge from across the Rhine. The fields and Harth forest to the west are patrolled by German soldiers. All most unusual." He gazed at me soberly.

"And we may draw our own conclusions on the reasons for this security," I replied. My conclusions were already clearly drawn.

Their meeting lasted very late. I could not understand all they discussed, for occasionally they lapsed into their own dialect—something between an aspirated, rolling German and a harsh, guttural French, but pleasing and soothing all the same. A number of staunch young partisans came in, were briefed, and departed. I tried to contribute as much as I could but was lulled into dreamy detachment by the voices, the thick air, and the dull light.

"Clayton?" Boppe's shadow swaddled me as he stood before the lantern. "You are asleep?"

"Oh. No, just thinking," I apologized.

He smiled kindly. "You need not excuse your exhaustion. You have given a great deal today, and heard still more. It is time for you to retire."

"No, please. Not until you're finished. I'm fine," I argued, stretching.

"Young men must rest," said Arbo Zorn. "There is so much to be done. Old men have no need for sleep."

"I believe," Boppe said, "that soon someone must cross into the lost provinces to warn the people and to do the work that must be done. We are all too old, but we shall find the right person for this task. Someone who will not be suspect."

I remained silent, waiting. It was not my place to interfere, to offer myself to them, and I was not yet certain this was what I was meant for. I still nurtured some hope that I could make an impression at the Quai d'Orsay, or that Daunt would return to give me other counsel.

It had become clear over the course of the evening that Boppe was their acknowledged, though undesignated, leader. Before I departed he assured me he would contact a friend at the Quai d'Orsay, if only to warn them. We all agreed that independent action was preferable and that we could not wait for assistance from officials mired in their own stupidity and blindness.

Arbogast Zorn suggested that in future I contact him at his family's home in Bercy. The circus was too public and vulnerable a location for our meetings. We exchanged pledges and expressions of gratitude, and I left those three old Alsatian clowns brooding over their decades of struggle and despairing at the prospect of a sudden, distant denouement in which they could not play an active role.

Though I had dozed during the long evening in the railroad car behind the Cirque Mediano, as soon as I stepped into the balmy Paris morning I felt wide awake and I began a restless, furtive walking, as though my tired feet could delude my mind into believing it too might rest.

I walked swiftly, stalking the empty streets until I came to the Seine, then stood watching the water run past, silver and lambent with moonlight. Although I rarely smoke, for some reason I wanted a cigarette at that moment when I knew I could not have one.

I crossed the river by the Pont d'Austerlitz, passed the *gare* and gardens, and continued drifting, unwilling to turn toward my bed.

Before even the first sliver of lavender creased the eastern sky I found signs of life in the city. I must have traipsed far into the outskirts of Paris, and now I had come to an unfamiliar *carrefour,* at the center of which workmen were assembling a platform and scaffolding with ropes on suspended pulleys. I stopped to watch.

When a van arrived and the men began unloading its contents I realized what they were building. The two upright posts and crosspiece were in place when they unloaded the triangular blade sheathed in leather.

The *lunette* was hammered together—a slab of wood with a hole at its center rather like one half of a stocks. In front of this a long board was erected in an upright position and a metal counterweight hoisted.

A crowd began to assemble slowly in the predawn as the workmen hammered and adjusted, examining and testing each part of the device. Finally the keen-edged blade was unsheathed and glinted in the light of lanterns which hung on the scaffolding. A stuffed dummy was brought from the van, strapped to the upright board, and a practice run conducted on it. The mechanism was in perfect working order.

By now I was fascinated by the spectacle unfolding before me that dawn. The crowd was not large but eagerly questioned a cordon of *flics* about the condemned man: an apache named Latouche who had committed crimes of all descriptions. A despicable man, they murmured, and awaited his appearance.

A prison van rattled into the wide *carrefour*. A memory pierced me as I glimpsed the rows of compartments and the man stepped out between two guards, his hands bound. As he passed close before me with his spiky black hair and small eyes I felt a shock of recognition and pushed forward to get a closer view. But it could not be the same man. This was the apache Latouche. I craned over the straw hats and workmen's caps of the crowd, but my eyes fastened on his neck as he walked away from me and on the beads of perspiration soaking into the collar of his prison shirt. I stared at the back of his neck as he mounted the platform.

Along the curb outside the crowd several women had set up umbrellas and were selling fruit. An old blind man squatted against the stone wall clutching a violin case, a cup before him. His hands trembled as he struggled with the clasp on his case.

Above me on the scaffolding Latouche stood steady and silent before the hooded executioner. In the pearl light of dawn I tried to dismiss the face, but my mind kept insisting that this was another of the guests at Madame Orgueil's, the man who called himself Aristo.

I heard a click, a swish as the guillotine fell, a thud and a muffled cry, and the man, Latouche or Aristo or whoever he may have been, was no more. The crowd began to disperse.

I watched them load the body into the morgue van, and the workmen, already back on the scaffolding, began to undo their predawn labor.

My eyes followed the receding van out of the *place* and I saw the long, coarse, blackened conglomerate walls of the Santée Prison on my right. I had no idea where I was until I saw those dreadful walls. As I started up the Boulevard Arago the old blind violinist began to play, with an unsteady bow and weak hands. It was a melancholy folk ballad, an eerie gypsy wail, mountainous and eastern in its drift, and he played very badly. The notes scattered into the dawn like shards of shattered glass, shredding the gathering light, jagged and broken and only token fragments of what they might have been in the hands of a more skilled violinist, but the blind man played with increasing vigor as I hobbled off on tired, tired feet into my own scumbled dissonance.

IX

The following days were maddeningly uneventful.

Each morning began beneath circling flies buzzing into my face as I lay under a single sheet at the Rue du Sommerard. After checking the morning post for messages which never came and discovering my blue telegram still nestled unclaimed in Daunt's box at the Paris post office, I repaired to my daily confrontation with Underwood.

Appointments were set and broken; meetings at the embassy, the Quai d'Orsay, and neutral locations planned and, at the last moment, shifted, delayed, or canceled. But the constant prospect of a meeting prevented my taking matters into my own hands. Underwood derived obvious enjoyment from this game, which he saw as a test of our respective ingenuity, perseverance, and manipulative skills. For me the game provided no pleasure.

The weather grew more oppressive. Besides daily reports of cabinet meetings, stock market collapse, and German threats was news of sunstroke and apoplexy in Paris as the temperature approached forty degrees. At midweek the windstorms began, tearing chimneys and roofs from buildings. On these days one had to beware of bricks and tiles falling from the sky as one walked the streets.

At length this stagnation convinced me to approach Théophile Delcassé, the Navy Minister who had impressed me at the embassy function before my trip to London. But Monsieur Delcassé did not open his doors to any American who wandered over to the Rue St.

Dominique. On my third visit to his office I was informed by an assistant that he was busily engaged in meetings regarding the current crisis and asked not to bother them again.

I felt constantly observed, though I could never actually detect anyone following me: I watched for the old man from Berkeley Square, the man in the frock coat off the Dover ferry, even Moors in green knit caps, while I vainly trekked the city, semidelirious with boredom, waiting for the sun to set and my room to cool sufficiently to permit sleep. I even paid a return call on Apolline, but she spouted the same anapestic gobbledygook and on second hearing its inspirational value had diminished.

Finally I received a brief note informing me that Guillaume had returned to Paris and inviting me to supper at his mother's. He was obliquely disconsolate; matters had obviously not improved in London following my departure. I noted that the dinner invitation was for a Thursday, the Inspector's day, and found this odd but encouraging. I located Marie at the Rôtonde—she had already made appropriate arrangements with the Countess—and at six o'clock we set out together for Auteuil.

The little greengrocer at the corner of the Rue Molitor and the Rue Erlanger was closing for the evening. A fat woman in a thick green apron retrieved crates of produce from the sidewalk. After a day in the heat the market smelled of rot.

Marie insisted upon bringing sweets from the *patisserie* next door. The baker in his white skirts and cap stood beckoning her in the doorway with a long loaf of braided bread.

"Here we go," I said to Marie a moment later as we

mounted the steps to the little house. She seemed far less apprehensive about this reunion than I.

Inspector Pernicieux, wearing his pince-nez and a *boutonnière,* opened the door while Guillaume and the Countess sagged in their seats behind him.

"What a great pleasure this is," he declared, and we stood beaming at each other. "And Marie. This *is* a surprise." But he seemed oblivious of the implications in her presence there. Though past sixty, he appeared to have grown younger over four years. His mustache was more thickly rimed with gray, but the hair on his head was still black and his eyes as eager as ever.

"Yes, what a surprise," said Guillaume, rising and glancing icily at his mother. "I suppose this is your doing, Mama?"

The Countess flushed and fanned herself but said nothing. Marie slipped past the Inspector and smiled at Guillaume.

"It was my idea," I said.

"It is quite unlike you, Clayton," said Guillaume. He sank back into his seat. "I did not know you were so clever at managing other people's affairs."

"No, Guillaume," Marie began to protest but I interrupted.

"It was meant to be a reunion," I said, tugging at the corner of my mustache. "I'm sorry if it displeases you. I hoped we were all old, dear friends. Nothing more."

"It does not displease me," Guillaume replied with conspicuous irony, but his dark eyes shone shyly as he beheld Marie. I sensed that although he felt compelled to display his annoyance at heart he *was* pleased to see her.

"So here we are, together again. Can it really be four years? But how wonderful," said the Inspector, pouring drinks and zealously playing host. "Such dreadful times we live in." He acknowledged the state of the world in a way which sought to dismiss it and carried on abruptly to his own life, over which he regaled us for some time with childlike delight.

"So at present I am engaged in the 'Affair of the Statuettes,' as it is called. The theft from the Louvre, surely you've heard of it?" He eyed me suspiciously in case I had not.

"That is hardly a homicide case," I noted.

"Indeed. But with my artistic notoriety, which I owe in large part to my mentor here"—he nodded at Guillaume, who gulped his *porto*—"I enjoy a broader range of assignments. Who better to seek the culprits who despoil our great artistic heritage than the Painting Inspector, eh?" Marie laughed gaily while he exchanged a charming look of shy, almost adolescent affection with the Countess, and embarked upon the story of his newest canvas, an homage to the poet.

"Within a sunken galleon, illuminated by a mysterious light and filled with chests of unknown cargo, stand the poet and his little dancer. Through holes in the ship's hull, creatures of the deep observe the couple in their iridescent chamber. I am calling it *The Muse Inspiring the Poet*."

At this first direct reference to Claudie, Guillaume wriggled uncomfortably in his seat and lighted a cigarette. The pleasant wine smell of a poaching sauce drifting from the kitchen could not surmount the stale odor of the poorly ventilated sitting room. The air felt starched so that all movements were crimped and flat. For several beats of silence I wondered who would speak first, or if the subject would be changed. The Inspector was at a loss, and Marie stepped bravely into the breach.

"How has your work been going, Guillaume?" she asked. "I saw a wonderful poem last month in *La Mercure*."

"Oh, that was something old I reshaped. A calligramme." He sulked a moment, the cigarette clasped wetly between his lips. "I have done no work worth speaking of in a long time."

"Your muse does not inspire you?" she said, and I expected the playful, jesting tone of this remark—precisely the tone she had criticized in Patrick at the Rôtonde earlier in the week—to arouse in Guillaume either self-pity or a burst of anger. But she knew him far better than I.

"We fought," he replied.

"You and Claudie?" I pressed him, emboldened by Marie's example and sucking an untrimmed end of my mustache.

"We fought," he repeated. "After a cowboy picture. One of your American films with the men on horses riding about the desert shooting handguns at one another. It was wonderful but she did not care for it. She said it was stupid and that I was stupid to like it. She was tired and said things whose impact on me she could never imagine."

"Which proves you are human and she is a child," said his mother.

"It proves nothing of the sort."

"But *we* always fought so fiercely. Do you remember, Guillaume? That night at the Gingerbread Fair du Trône when you became incensed over a magic show which you said possessed no magic." Marie's cheerfulness still seemed contrived to me, but Guillaume brightened briefly at this memory.

"But this is not the same. With you I always knew—" He stopped, afraid to pursue the thought, and changed course. "So this is what you've planned for our 'reunion,' Clayton Peavey. You have come to help me sort out my life. How kind of you all, my dear friends."

Outside a rising wind snapped the trees along the

Rue Molitor. The Countess observed that a new storm was approaching, and Inspector Pernicieux busied himself securing the shutters.

"No one pities you except yourself, Guillaume." Marie stood slim and bright-eyed before him, full of that sweet candor I had always found her most appealing characteristic. "We all respect you too much to believe we can arrange your life for you."

"Then why is everyone staring at me in this ridiculous way, as though I were some piteous specimen of another life form?"

I stifled my inclination to laugh by sucking on my mustache again. Marie answered him.

"Because we all love you too much to be content seeing you so bored and unhappy."

"Yes, that's it," chimed in the Inspector, though his involvement in this conversation had been intermittent and frivolous. "An artist must be at work to be happy. You told me that yourself."

"He's right, Guillaume."

"Of course he's right. I told him that myself." His seriousness lapsed and he had to make a concerted effort to conceal a smile beneath his cranky scowl. "But one must find joy and inspiration in one's work. One cannot search for these things. They must simply be there."

"Nonsense," said Marie. "You cannot permit yourself to think only of her and her affairs, no matter how great your love. You *must* remember yourself."

He gazed at her sadly. The shy pleasure he had evinced on first seeing her blossomed in his eyes.

"Yes, yes. London was a terrible mistake. There was nothing for me there. I was so thrilled by her success in Paris. I wanted to bask in that reflected glory again and again. But I was not part of their world in London. It was a mistake to have gone. Now I am home." He looked at me, and I understood the drift of his thoughts. "So what is to become of me now, Clayton Peavey?"

"I have a question for you, Inspector." I pretended to change the subject, though in fact I was indirectly broaching the subject of deepest concern to me. "I saw a man executed the other morning. I had never seen the guillotine in use before."

"A truly French instrument, don't you think?" he said proudly. "Efficient yet eloquent."

"I have my doubts about that, but I thought I recognized the condemned man. He was an apache called Latouche, though that is not the name I knew him by."

The Inspector ran his fingers along his nose and pursed his lips. "Yes, of course, Latouche, I know the case. Raiding post offices in the faubourgs by automobile. Running down innocent bystanders with his vehicle. An odious character."

"Was this man ever called Aristo?" I asked, and Guillaume eyed me curiously, his memory jarred but as yet unfocused.

"Aristo? Yes, I believe one of his ruses was to attire himself elegantly and gain admission to salons of the sort where seances and other foolishness occur. These attract a certain stratum of the well-to-do. Among his many skills Latouche was an accomplished pickpocket, and with the other guests in states of trance and general distraction he had little trouble looting these salons of jewelry and other valuables. And yes, I do recall that on his forays into higher society he had the audacity to call himself Aristo."

The Inspector sniffed, ruffling the little black nose hairs. Guillaume, his memory now quite refreshed, stared at me. Marie sat quietly gazing at the Inspector with her small, gentle eyes while the Countess fanned her flaccid face.

"The remarkable thing," I continued, "is that this man, this Aristo, was at the seance we attended the night Charles was murdered four years ago."

"Well, now he is dead," said the Countess, assuming that the subject of this unpleasant fellow's execution could be dropped.

The Inspector's appetite had been whetted.

"And you witnessed the execution?" he said. "You're quite certain it was the same man?"

"I recognized him, and now you have confirmed the name." I flicked the droop of lank hair from my eyes and smiled. "Does one still hear in Paris of that Madame O-? Madame Orgueil, I believe her name was."

"Oh, I hardly follow such matters," said the Inspector with a shrug, but the Countess had certainly heard of Madame Orgueil.

"She is very exclusive and highly regarded, though my friend Madame Dubord claims she is merely an elaborate fakir. Probably in league with your Aristo, I shouldn't be surprised."

"I shouldn't be surprised," I mimicked her and turned back to the Inspector. "But I would be amused to learn more about Madame Orgueil, since I have inadvertently crossed her path again. Do you think, Inspector, you might inquire at the Préfecture or among your private sources where she is located, her activities and reputation, or if she is even in Paris at all?"

"It would be a pleasure to serve you," he said. "I recall the name now, but no serious complaints have ever been lodged against her."

Though I had no notion of how I might induce information regarding Fritz or the pale man from her, I was encouraged to have an ally in my search for Madame Orgueil.

"Madame O-'s involvement in all of this has many

tentacles, does it not?" Guillaume whispered to me as we moved from the drawing room to the dining table. "Though it was a true coincidence that you witnessed that man's execution, eh, Clayton?"

"Yes, Guillaume." I smiled. "A true coincidence."

The meal was bountiful and delicious but we languished over our plates, talking in circles or not at all, and only the Inspector ate with his accustomed relish. As he drank wine, Guillaume grew more gregarious.

"I feel a great change coming over me," he exclaimed. "London was the prelude, no, the silence before the next movement in my life's symphony, and so I felt lost there. It is a change coming over all of us. I feel I must *act* now, for once. Not merely contemplate and abstract, but look outside myself, to my country. I am ready to march forth, only I do not know in what direction to march."

"Ooh la la." The Countess had begun tittering as he spoke. "Now he is a patriot."

"I feel the same thing," I reinforced him. "Something must be done." He understood; our resolve was like a door that had been hinged and began, at that moment of hinging, to sense the direction in which it would open.

"But Americans are always rushing off in some new direction," Guy Pernicieux informed me. "Is that not how they became Americans, by rushing off in a new direction? If they had stayed where they were they would still be something else."

"While the French," I retorted, "are creatures of habit who determined centuries ago how best to do everything and refuse to alter that prescription one iota."

"I think you are wrong there, Clayton," he argued. "France has always been a changing, dynamic culture."

"Perhaps so," I said, "but it has been my observation that you French have a deeply conservative nature.

Everything must be done a certain way, even at a certain time of day, for that is the correct, the French, way of doing it. It is as though life were some very precise recipe and unless the exact combination of ingredients were employed in the same manner each time, the result would be aberrant and unsatisfactory." I surveyed their amused faces and concluded: "We wouldn't want the sauce to curdle, would we, Inspector?"

"But this profound conservatism sustains a culture capable of encouraging an avant-garde which is neither crushed nor assimilated." Guillaume insisted upon having the last word. "It is this contradiction which produces the greatness of French art and literature, the aesthetic life which all the world knows as France."

"Bravo, Guillaume," Marie rejoiced at this flash of the old bombast, and I believe I saw Guillaume blush.

"An excellent point." The Inspector conferred his blessing on the argument.

"Yet from my experience," I countered, "the avant-garde of France are also creatures of habit. Only theirs are outrageous habits rather than mundane ones. But habits nonetheless."

While Guillaume rubbed his red ant scar and considered what I had said, a windstorm swept in from the Bois de Boulogne, crackling and dry with thunder.

"I still believe it is in France, and in Paris, that the most innovative, creative impulses arise." As Guillaume spoke, the windows began kicking at the jambs and a gust down the chimney blew soot onto the rug. One of the Countess' lace antimacassars took flight across the room. "And that is why France must be saved," he was shouting now, transported by his percussive accompaniment. "And *we* must save her." He rose, eyes wide with excitement, yet oblivious of the elemental chaos raging around him.

The Inspector and I managed to latch the windows

and close the flue while Marie calmed the Countess with a glass of cognac and a comforting pat.

When we had shut out the storm I noticed the Inspector observing me with a puzzled expression, but I thought little of it. The wind rattled the world around us, occasionally toppling some object and sending it skittering noisily down the street. We sat over our digestifs, the Countess fanning herself and chatting quietly with Inspector Pernicieux while we three young people reminisced over four years past, bringing tears to Guillaume's eyes several times. He never again achieved the rapture of that moment when he spoke of saving France.

Soon his mother's head was drooping slightly, jerking upward as she awoke, then once more slowly dropping forward onto her full bosom. As she dozed she made a faint gurgling sound in her throat.

"You will not forget about Madame Orgueil?" I reminded the Inspector as we took our leave.

"I shall look into it tomorrow morning, Clayton, since it is of such great importance." I was content that he remain uninformed and dotingly amused by my interest in Madame O-, but again I detected a quizzical expression. When he accompanied us to the front door his darting eyes surveyed up and down the street very quickly.

We three rode together back into town to a small left-bank café. We sat at a corner table over cognacs and espressos until it was quite late, nearly two in the morning, when Guillaume spoke once more of Claudie.

"Despite London, despite all my doubts, I cannot stop believing in her for an instant, or believing in the possibility of all I have imagined when I am with her." He coughed and his bleary eyes watered, either from emotion or the smoky atmosphere in the café. "It is best we be apart now, for a little while. . . . She is so young and she must be given room . . . room to grow. . . ." He was forcing himself to say these things, then halted abruptly. "Oh yes, it is all quite rational. Yet I think of her constantly."

"But do you draw inspiration from that?" I asked. "In that case there is nothing wrong with your obsession."

"Yes, I must constantly forgive and forget the evil, open my eyes only to the light. Let her light draw the words from my soul."

With promises to meet for lunch the next day and kisses all around, I returned to another night with the flies beneath my single sheet at the Rue du Sommerard.

X

This hateful hiatus in my adventures ended on the Monday following our dinner in Auteuil, when Inspector Pernicieux summoned me to the Préfecture.

It was altogether a banner morning: my telegram had disappeared from Daunt's postal box, evidence of his return to Paris; and Underwood informed me, rather dourly, that Monsieur Théophile Delcassé had requested my presence at a meeting two days hence at the Rue St. Dominique.

Thus fortified, I set out for the Paris Préfecture and news of the mysterious Madame O-. A sentry at the porte cochere directed me through a cobbled courtyard and up a circular stairwell to the Inspector's private office. This was generously appointed with comfortable chairs, a large writing desk, and even a small hassock on which the aging detective could rest his feet. Two of his smaller canvases adorned the walls.

Madame Orgueil, he told me, no longer maintained a salon proper but lived clandestinely, holding private sessions for a selected clientele. His informants believed she was at present engaged in a lengthy soothsaying for a certain eccentric man of letters, a very reclusive and erudite gentleman. She could be found late evenings at his apartment on the Boulevard Haussmann. He gave me the address.

"I feel you are not being entirely forthright with me about your interest in this woman," said the Inspector. "I have provided the information you desired, but your secretive manner distresses me."

"I noticed that the other night," I said. "But why do you believe I am deceiving you?"

"It is not a matter of deception, Clayton, so do not treat me as a fool. You are merely omitting things. I know of your interest in the current crisis in Morocco. I cannot doubt you believe there is a connection between those events and this occultist. You need not reveal your specific conjectures. I quite understand that, but I should be pleased if at least you admitted their existence."

"Very well, I admit I have suspicions. Does that make you feel better?"

"On the contrary, now I realize I did see what I thought I saw. I am more concerned for you than before."

I eyed him skeptically and asked what he had seen.

"Were you aware that you were followed to Auteuil last week?"

I shook my head.

"You were. I saw a man in the street when I opened the door for you and thought nothing of it. He passed by. But when I went to latch the windows during the windstorm I saw him again, standing at a doorway down the block as though about to knock. That is an old police tail's trick, and I was startled to see him outside in the storm."

"Can you describe this man for me?"

"I did not see him clearly the second time, and on the first occasion I thought too little of it to remark closely on his appearance. He was a well built, brawny sort of fellow with a narrow, intense face. I did notice very sharp, high cheekbones. Perhaps in his late twenties, and blond." He paused as though trying to embellish the description or weighing his next statement. "Decidedly Germanic, if I may indulge my prejudices, and perhaps my imagination, just a whit. A decidedly German-looking fellow."

The placid facade I tried to maintain could not conceal from the old detective the consternation this news brought me. He nodded to indicate he read my thoughts.

"I do not doubt that you are correct," I said.

"You are involved in matters with very high stakes," he speculated. "I fully appreciate that you cannot confide in me, but let me say that if there is any way in which I can assist you, or if you need my support or influence regarding some indiscretion you find yourself forced to commit, do not hesitate to ask, Clayton. I shall help you however I can and demand no explanations."

I smiled gratefully at this man whom I had seen only as a meddlesome adversary when I met him four years before, and later as a silly old fool. Suddenly I recognized that he could be a useful accessory in my work. "But why should you wish to help me?" I asked.

Inspector Pernicieux shook his head, and the normally prim, affable countenance was transfigured by a shadow of fear and angry determination.

"As a youth I witnessed the Germans marching through the streets of my beloved Paris," he enunciated slowly in a voice I had never heard him use before. "I do not wish to see that sight again as an old man. Once is quite enough."

"Thank you, Inspector. Our hearts are in the same place."

But he shook his head firmly and rose from his seat, circling the desk to me with his hands clasped behind his back.

"When you have spent a lifetime in this city, as I have, then you may say that, Clayton. Until then, you can only guess at my emotions"—though these were so clearly etched across his face I did not need to guess at anything. I embraced him and assured him I would keep him informed of my activities.

"I would not instruct you in your work," he said as I turned to leave. "But do not take anyone at face value in such a business. Not anyone," he repeated, and I began shuffling through all the innocent faces among my acquaintances—from Paul to Underwood to Daunt himself —wondering whom to suspect.

I left word at Guillaume's apartment, knowing that he must accompany me on my visit to the Boulevard Haussmann, and returned to the Rue du Sommerard in high anticipation of a message from Daunt. Again I was disappointed. Throughout the afternoon I heard thunder outside Paris and watched swaths of black clouds forming like bloody stanches on a wounded sky.

The first electrical storm passed over us as we discussed our strategy and expectations in the Café Henner. Guillaume was greatly excited by the prospect of a confrontation with Madame O-. As we set out shortly before ten the rain had ceased and the air was still, almost unbreathably dense. My clothes clung to me and my skin felt lacquered to my face and body.

I waded through the thick evening and rested before the church in the Place de la Trinité, constantly vigilant for brawny young blonds with high cheekbones or anyone else who might be loitering on the periphery of my life, examining kiosks or stepping into doorways or opening newspapers. I saw no one, and when the intrepid Guillaume had regained his wind we proceeded down the Avenue Mogàdor to the Boulevard Haussmann.

The building at No. 102 was of flat, chamois colored stone. We entered between fluted columns engaged either side of a brass handled door. The boulevard we left behind was lined with plane trees.

Our heavy breathing echoed in the open foyer. We

ascended to our left up a sweep of carpeted stairs with a black and gilt-leafed balustrade, and found the apartment of the eccentric member of the literati.

An elderly serving woman, pink and puffy with the heat, opened the door. When we told her we had come to see her master she replied, "Monsieur is not receiving visitors," and blinked her pale, moist eyes. I leaned against the door and we forced our way past her into a cramped vestibule. The serving woman gasped and flapped her wrist at us as we opened the next door.

The inner room was entirely lined with cork. Shuttered windows closed off the only means of escape for the eddies of yellow fumigations issuing from a pair of silver censers suspended above the bed.

Monsieur lay upon his bed, an oily olive face peering up at us, swaddled in a long nightshirt and woolen pullover, with scarves and mufflers and gloves, all of them dotted with tiny burn holes from the censer sparks bursting out sporadically above him. It was apparently as unbearable for this frothy, oleaginous rodent to find us in his cork lined burrow as for us to behold him.

"Get out, get out," he shrieked. "Close the door, Françoise," he instructed the frightened maidservant, who had come into the room after us. The reeking fumigations floating over the bed were drawn toward the open door behind us like a cloudbank rushing across a windy sky.

I ducked the approaching clouds, and around the corner of the bed I saw gray skirts purled in pale mauve. The black-booted feet were short and broad. She sat on a stiff little tabouret stool and bent over a lap tray on which was spread a deck of tarot cards.

"What is the meaning of this intrusion? You must get out," wheezed our host, and he ducked his head beneath the covers. A bed table toppled from his knees, disordering the books and papers, bound black notebooks, manuscripts and correspondence and scraps of watercolors surrounding him on the bed.

When Madame Orgueil raised her eyes toward us their radiance was almost serene. The maid shut the door and the storm clouds receded. "What do you want here?" She displayed no sign of recognition and shuffled the tarot cards in her plump, white hands.

"You know who we are," I stated. "I want to know the whereabouts of Fritz Amgott. Where did he go when he left Berkeley Square?"

"Who? What are you saying?" Did her eyes or mine flicker when I mentioned Berkeley Square?

"Herr Sturm, perhaps you know him as Herr Sturm. And who is the pale man, the man who was at your seance four years ago, the one the wraith pointed at?" I stood above her, barraging her with questions, and she stared at me. Although her eyes remained calm I felt her hunch over the table and draw into her ancient shell, a cream colored cape with *bois de rose* collar. She was a weak old woman, defended only by a bedridden asthmatic and a serving woman more aged than herself. A compulsion came over me which I had never felt before —a sense of acute danger coupled with a sensation of power, and with it the willingness to employ physical force to achieve my ends. This ugly mood, which has taken hold of me several times in my life, frightens me as much as it is frightening to those around me. The gentleman in the bed peeked with one terrified eye from beneath his notebooks and papers as I grasped the soft shoulders of Madame Orgueil and forced my weight down until she gulped and her eyes dropped.

"Françoise, please call the concierge. Call the police. Françoise, do not simply stand there," he huffed.

"Oh, please," said Françoise. "Oh, please."

"Who was your host in Berkeley Square last month?" I repeated, shaking the old medium by the shoulders.

Suddenly the balance shifted, she regained her dignity, conquered her fear, and as she did so I heard noises in the vestibule, the click of the front door and a soft footstep. I glanced at Guillaume.

"I do not know what you mean, young man," said Madame O-. "And your physical abuse shall not improve my memory, I assure you."

I removed my hands from her shoulders, and her pale green, translucent eyes rose once more to my face. I stepped back, wondering whether she was about to call some vengeful spirit down upon me.

"It is not a futurist conclave we are speaking of here," I screamed at her. "This is the future of Europe. Of France," I added, thinking that even so unlikely a prospect for patriotism as Madame Orgueil might be stirred by this appeal. "These men are our enemies." I lowered my voice and spoke more distinctly. "Now, what can you tell me about Fritz Amgott, or Herr Sturm? And who is the pale man in Berkeley Square?"

"I do not know a Fritz Amgott or Herr Sturm," she said quietly, and I heard the door fly open behind me. "As for my host in London, his name is—"

A single shot rang out, its echo quickly damped in the cork lined room.

"Oh dear God protect us," cried the muffled voice from the bed, and I believe at this point the eminent author fainted.

A solidly built blond man dressed in tight black pants and pullover and black gloves faced me from the doorway. I thought, I can't feel anything, I must have been shot; and Madame Orgueil choked and slumped to the floor. Blood seeped through her cream cape.

As the long smoking muzzle and intense blue eyes of

the blond man turned on me, a deafening blast of thunder caused him to hesitate an instant.

Guillaume and Françoise stood behind the open door. The assassin was unaware of them until Guillaume brought his hands down together on the man's wrist. The gun dropped to the floor.

He cursed in German and reached down for it. Another clap of thunder seemed to enter the very stones of the building and reverberate there for several seconds. The simultaneous flash of lightning directly outside in the street illuminated Guillaume, in a magnificent display of agility, kneeing the German in the face.

A tree collapsed against the building, and I heard glass shatter before the next thunder sounded, this time a few blocks distant.

The blond man staggered backwards, blood gushing from his nose. I lunged toward the gun just as poor Françoise followed her master into insensibility, her plump starched person coming to rest upon the discarded weapon.

The intruder, suddenly disarmed and outmanned, cried out something unintelligible and fell across the maid, trying to slide her off the gun and pawing at the floor. While Guillaume stood stunned by his accomplishment I stomped with my bootheel on the man's right hand and heard the tiny bones crunch like a chewed carrot. He howled terribly.

I took Guillaume's arm and we hopped over the pair of prone figures at the door and through the vestibule onto the landing. Grasping the gilt balustrade, we swooped down the carpeted stairway and out the door past fallen branches into a drenching rain slashed by bolts of lightning so near they made the wet air tingle with electricity.

I ran blindly for two blocks and ducked into the

bowered pathways of a small, overgrown park while the rain soaked Paris.

Guillaume followed me into the little park. We did not speak but looked at one another and then away, scanning the street, panting. Then our eyes met again, and still the rain did not let up. As though on cue we ran beneath the flailing plane trees along the Boulevard Haussmann, Guillaume slogging along after me in the long climb home.

Somewhere I lost him in the storm. I ran at a steady, modest pace which I felt I had the strength to maintain all night if necessary, and I kept asking myself why the man had shot Madame Orgueil and not me.

I sat on the single stone bench in the little garth at Guillaume's building, awaiting his arrival. That question "Why?" utterly confounded me, though I knew Timothy Daunt, had he been present, would have reminded me to count my blessings and not always to complicate matters with that most inscrutable of questions.

After fifteen minutes Guillaume walked through the arched passageway off the Rue Henner. Dripping and gasping for breath, but smiling triumphantly, he led me upstairs to cognac and a long consultation over what to do next.

Madame Orgueil was dead, one adversary crippled, and one Parisian author terrified; but we had learned nothing.

XI

It was decided during our night of consultation—and I employ the passive voice intentionally, for the decision was not made but evolved as a function of time, tension, the storm, and the cognac—that we must go into hiding or disappear from Paris entirely, before the next German assassin found us. Guillaume agreed to go directly to the Zorns in Bercy, a presumably safe hideaway. I would urge Inspector Pernicieux to erect a smokescreen over our activities on the Boulevard Haussmann, attend my meeting with Delcassé and the diplomats, and join him in Bercy no later than evening of the second day, a Wednesday. This resolved, we pledged our allegiance and parted company.

I set out early the next morning for the Préfecture. The storm had passed, washing the heat and accumulated filth from the air. Faces and windows shone fresh and clear, women sold produce from street stands with a smile, sparrows and pigeons snuffled in the dirt. It was such a pleasant morning I felt confidence for the success of all my endeavors.

"'If you can tear yourself away from your *statuettes,* I have a homicide case for you," I told the Inspector. "Madame Orgueil has been shot."

"So I understand," he said. "I had hoped for a quiet morning." He rubbed his forehead and rolled his eyes. "I slept rather poorly through the storms last night. But I see I shall have no peace today."

"You expected me?"

"Complaints were lodged against two mysterious young men by the distressed author. I had little difficulty deducing the identity of these two 'ruffians,' but Clayton, you've gone a bit too far this time, don't you think?" He chastised me with a look of weary resignation.

"Surely you don't think that I . . . it was our blond German friend who killed her."

"Indeed, but my duty requires that I hold you for questioning." I rose quickly, and the Inspector smiled for the first time since I had entered his office. "I shall not follow my duty in this case, Clayton. I shall trust you and let you go, though I don't know why I should. Moreover, I shall try to see that neither you nor Guillaume are apprehended over this business."

"I knew I could count on you. I cannot thank you enough."

"What *you* must do is leave Paris as quickly as possible. With my colleagues and the cohorts of that German looking for you there is no safe place for you in the city."

"That is precisely what I intend to do," I agreed.

"I can obscure your trail and suppress the reports of our literary plaintiff for perhaps two days. Even that is more than I *should* do. But my retirement is near . . . and I very much look forward to it. Now I must ask you to leave, so as not to further jeopardize my position or your own safety."

He said this with strict formality, but I knew it distressed him to throw me out as much as it offended his sense of duty not to arrest me on the spot.

"I shall be out of Paris within two days," I assured him as I moved to the door. "And I do appreciate the irregularity of what you're doing. It is in a great cause."

"Yes, yes. God be with you, Clayton. Let us hope you prove more resourceful than our enemies."

* * *

Underwood greeted me at the embassy with his normal condescension when I insisted that the meeting be moved up a day.

"And why should three governments alter their plans because of the death of some elderly clairvoyant?" He ignored my efforts to explain the connection between Madame O- and the Teutonic Accord.

"Because it is of critical importance to all of us, not to mention the danger to myself. By tomorrow I might not be available for a meeting."

"Tut-tut." Underwood frowned. "Tell me, Peavey, are you still an employee of the U.S. State Department?"

More games, I thought. "Yes, of course I am."

"Well, to remind you of that the Ambassador suggested I assign you a piece of work which needs doing today, if you can spare the time." I looked doubtful. "It's just the thing for you. It will occupy your mind and keep you out of harm's way until tomorrow."

"Why is there always someone looking after me in this world?" I moaned as he described my new assignment.

"Apparently you require looking after."

"I suppose you'll be coming to the meeting at the Rue St. Dominique tomorrow?"

"To be sure." He cracked his square jaws with that mocking smile and I turned on my heel and stalked out of the embassy.

The Bibliothèque Nationale, where the thoughtful Ambassador had assigned me to do research in several diplomatic journals, was the ideal place for me to spend my last day of waiting in Paris. I felt safely sequestered from the hectic world outside in the still, high-ceilinged Salle de Travail with its long, hardwood tables. The slightly musty library air had a comforting familiarity, and with only the rattling of turned pages, a few stifled coughs, and the faint murmur of subdued voices to disturb me my stomach settled and I became pleasantly drowsy as I leaned over the thick bound journals and scribbled notes.

In this soothing atmosphere my mind wandered freely and I began to regain a sense of continuity in my life. I needed this repose, the security I have always felt in a great library, to measure my thoughts and clear my head. As I sat there a profound, almost desperate, sense of loss came over me. Guillaume spoke ardently of shattering the old rules and values, creating new parameters for life and art, and of the great coalescing which would follow, but I had slowly come to recognize that within these vast possibilities lurked an entirely new suffering which man had not yet faced. I admired, but could not share, Guillaume's unbounded optimism for the future. All the world was changing—by the time I was ready for retirement like Inspector Pernicieux, in forty or fifty years, I knew that everything around me would be inalterably, unrecognizably changed. But as we mastered the world around us, unraveling the ancient riddles, we had increasingly to confront the mystery within man. Our responsibility for our actions would grow as the handy explanations of God and Nature lost their relevance.

A lump came to my throat as I felt this profound sense of loss and with it a surge of comfort and peace, because I knew this library would be the same fifty years hence, these books and the truth in them would not have changed for all the frantic innovation swirling around them in the world. Or so it seemed to me as I sat drowsily over those fat volumes in the Bibliothèque Nationale and awaited my inevitable disappointments on the morrow.

* * *

I first noticed the old man the next morning, standing in the Rue du Sommerard in his ragged coat and enveloping hat. He was such a pathetic old cur I could not seriously believe he had been sent to spy upon me, and there was surely no threat inherent in his presence; still, he made me extremely uncomfortable.

I collected Underwood at the embassy and proceeded to the Ministre de la Guerre, crossing the Seine by the Pont Alexandre III. This was the newest and most ornate bridge in Paris (completed for the Exposition of 1900) and spanned the river between the Esplanade des Invalides on the left bank and the Grand and Petit Palais on the right. From the bridge we could see the tall, gilded dome and spire of the Hôtel des Invalides between rows of lampposts and elms lining the broad esplanade, and to our left the stately Quai d'Orsay. Standing by a massive pylon, in the shadow of a winged horse and rider charging to the defense of the motherland, I saw that same old man in the ragged coat at the far end of the bridge. I pointed him out to Underwood, who laughed at me.

Across the esplanade we turned into the Rue St. Dominique, a narrow street of serried ministry buildings bearing tricolors and RF insignia. This was no place to display for visiting dignitaries like the Quai d'Orsay but a dark, working street for plotting *revanche* and mobilizations.

We assembled promptly at ten o'clock in Delcassé's office, a cold, uninviting room with a big clock ticking off the seconds while we met. There were seven of us: myself, Underwood, and the American Ambassador Henry White; an Englishman named Lord Keith who was the antithesis of Daunt in every way—pink where Daunt was tan, lumps and bulges beneath his suit where Daunt was hard and taut; and three Frenchmen: Théophile Delcassé, short and swarthy with large ears and tired, discreet eyes beyond oval pince-nez; General Cran, an ordnance expert familiar with Glautsch who was all mustaches and brandenburg buttons and wore knee-high boots with spurs; and the nameless representative of the Troisième Bureau, who was all buckteeth and eyebrows, great flaring white bushes that had received a lifetime of devoted grooming.

We commenced by discussing the weather.

"I understand the post office at Rennes caught fire in the electrical storms the other night," said General Cran. "And the worst is yet to come."

I coughed loudly and singlemindedly.

"Yes, Monsieur Peavey," Delcassé acknowledged my impatience. "So you are the young American who has been harassing my assistant this past week?"

"Yes, it is I. I apologize for my rude insistence, but I felt that you, of all Frenchmen, would appreciate my concern and understand the threat hanging over us all."

"And what exactly is that?" he asked, apparently pleased by my assessment of him but outwardly reproving.

I described Daunt and the Teutonic Accord, its connection to Morocco, to Fritz Amgot and the Glautsch chemical works, and my surveillance of the house in Berkeley Square.

"Extraordinary," said Delcassé when I had finished.

"Rubbish," grumbled Lord Keith, while Underwood smiled insipidly.

"And you believe this attack will come through Belgium?" The man from the Troisième Bureau jiggled his eyebrows scornfully.

"Only because German strategy requires a quick, decisive victory over France and this cannot be accomplished from the east." I glanced at Delcassé as I made this tacit reference to Alsace-Lorraine, but he hid his well-known convictions behind a mask of studied deliberation.

"Baron von Schoen paints a somewhat different picture," he noted, in reference to the German Ambassador in Paris. "You understand, of course, that the violation of Belgian neutrality would be political suicide for the Germans, even in the unlikely event they achieved a swift victory over France?"

"It is political suicide only under the existing political order. The Wilhelmstrasse is intent upon a war which will destroy that order and replace it with a new one." This argument gave them pause, and I plunged to the heart of the matter. "The Teutonic Accord will allow them to do this. For that reason it is a matter of grave consequence to France, and a matter of life and death to the lost provinces," I concluded and awaited the inevitable rebuttals.

"Lord Keith?" Delcassé acted as our moderator.

"While I respect Mr. Peavey's sincerity in this matter, we must remember that his analysis is based entirely upon information supplied him by Timothy Daunt. From what I understand, Daunt has a rather lively imagination and a strong partiality to playing a lone hand. This has created considerable misgivings about his usefulness to the service. He is, in fact, an expert on Moroccan affairs and has operated quite successfully within that limited sphere for many years. But his boldness may have overstepped itself now. I was not personally aware that he had returned to the continent."

"But the men who met with Fritz Amgott at Berkeley Square went on to Downing Street," I protested.

"Many people visit Downing Street," Lord Keith replied calmly. "And not all of them obtain what they are seeking there." He paused to let me mull over that. "As for Fritz Amgott, I defer to my French colleagues. I know the name, of course, but that is all."

"General Cran?" said Delcassé, and the little general fluffed his mustaches. He spoke in a high-pitched voice.

"The Amgott Munitions Fabriken rivals Krupp. In some areas, possibly naval weaponry, it may have surpassed the Krupps. Hans Amgott is a powerful figure in the Zollverein. I am well aware that the Glautsch chemical works is manufacturing gunpowder, though I think Monsieur Peavey has overestimated its capacity. Nonetheless . . ." He rambled on for several minutes, fingering his brandenburgs while comparing ordnance capabilities and supplies and citing figures to assure us of French parity in this area.

"If you are so certain the British are not tempted by the Glautsch offer, why have they said nothing in support of France in the present crisis? They have quietly allowed the Germans to establish a foothold at Agadir. Might this not suggest a new Anglo-German rapprochement? And if so, what is the price for each country?"

Ambassador White was obviously embarrassed by my bluntness, for in diplomatic circles everyone is constantly assuring everyone else of his probity and good intentions, no matter the facts. Only Delcassé sympathized with my emotion.

"It is a legitimate argument, Monsieur Peavey," he said. "Though I must discount the possibility of a permanent German base at Agadir."

"I should think not," snapped Lord Keith.

"Perhaps legitimate but invalid," Delcassé explained. "I think I have something which may adduce the contrary and set your mind at rest." He tapped a locked leather case and glanced at General Cran, who tilted his head to one side. The eyebrows flared, Lord Keith shrugged, and Delcassé removed from the case a thick volume. Its pages were edged in gold and it was bound in blue silk ribbons (for the French employed the traditional formalities in the preparation of dispatches and reports while at the American embassy we were already using typewriters). He slid the thick volume across the table to me.

"This is a report, to be issued next week, prepared jointly by General Henry Wilson of the British Staff College and General Dubail of the Ministre de la Guerre. It is the result of more than five years of military and diplomatic conversations between our governments, carried out in secret since the signing of the Entente Cordiale." I glanced at the opening pages while he continued, weighing his words, careful not to say too much or permit me to look too long. "The report details the transport, housing, and victualing of British forces on the continent, and the apportionment of squadrons and commands in a French-English mobilization in case of German attack." He took the secret report from me as General Cran squeaked out the inescapable conclusion.

"There is no Teutonic Accord, monsieur."

"Certainly not," huffed Lord Keith, and Delcassé nodded.

Deflated, I sat silently a moment and tried to reassess my position, seeking some way to prove the veracity of Daunt's contentions. But the five-hundred-page report on a French-English mobilization lay before me.

"I still believe the munitions supply has to be tempting." I sucked on the corner of my mustache and scanned their faces. "Why else do the British waver in support of their allies in North Africa?" I repeated.

"My dear fellow, we are not wavering," Lord Keith

reproached me. "We merely obey our government's policies," he added, clearly implying that I did not.

"Of course you do," the Ambassador comforted him with a stern glare at me. I was hardly listening, for I had begun to see that just one thing could erase this British temptation and vanquish all chance of a Teutonic Accord: if there were no Glautsch chemical works there would be no temptation.

"Are you satisfied now, Peavey?" It was Underwood, of course. But I was engrossed and shook my head stubbornly.

"Good heavens," cried Lord Keith in exasperation. "The fellow is mad."

With images of Glautsch in ruins running through my head I gazed around the table and saw only cartoon caricatures: General Cran and the eyebrows as proud Frenchmen who indeed, as Daunt once told me, exaggerated all affairs connected with themselves into something grandiose, full of smug self-containment and myopia; Lord Keith with his modest civility and stodgy industriousness, yet underlying this a fear of rational discourse on the French scale; and three foolish Americans, utterly out of their depth, one thick-headed and square-jawed, one friendly and ingratiating but dull, and the third simply mad. It was a hopeless conference.

"We have the situation in Morocco well in hand," Delcassé told me. "And if there is an attack from the east, or the north, we are prepared." He tapped the Wilson-Dubail report. "I for one appreciate your concern, and I shall personally see that a full re-evaluation is made of the Glautsch plant. As for your friend Daunt, I fear he may be engaged in a personal crusade against this man Amgott, perhaps having to do with a long-standing grudge formed in Morocco. You may have unwittingly been drawn into assisting him. Had that occurred to you?"

"And the pale man?" I ignored his insinuations regarding Daunt, which had already occurred to me. Underwood forced a laugh.

"The pale man," replied Lord Keith haughtily, "need not bother you. He may well be a futurist, an occultist, even a cabalist, but, whoever he is, he does not have the ear of the British government. Of that I can assure you."

And that was all. We left Delcassé sitting beneath his tall clock. The mountainous report lay open before him, and General Cran perched at his shoulder.

With no intention of doing so, I promised to continue my work at the Bibliothèque Nationale and to report to the embassy the next morning. The long sought meeting had confirmed the futility of following formal procedures any longer.

Had Apolline been inside my mind at that moment she would have told me it was all a case of parallax: that the substantive situation did not alter, had not altered from the outset, but my ever-changing point of view as I circled the issue caused it to appear constantly in a different light. I could hear her voice drumming against my skull: "Parallax. Parallax."

But I could not relax. Or forget. Or ignore Delcassé's reminder that I might have been drawn into a personal feud between Daunt and Fritz.

I walked along the Boulevard St. Germain and was tempted to turn toward St. Sulpice, but it was growing hot and humid and the smell of fish heads and vegetable clippings in the gutter sickened me.

Near St. Germain-des-Prés I stopped to watch a street performer: a flabby woman standing on a board balanced at a fulcrum with dogs at either end. Her act was grotesque, pathetic; the faces in the crowd swarmed around me like frozen masks of horror. It was then I noticed the same old man with his hat pulled down on his head. He tottered toward me, his hands plunged deep in the pockets of his ragged coat.

I backed away from him and found a rear table in a café. He took a table near me. I regarded him cautiously and sat over a *café crème* for half an hour. At one point I noticed his thin, knuckly hands clutching a pencil and writing something on a napkin.

I was tempted to go over to his table and confront him. He inspired no dread in me, but neither was he making any effort to conceal his surveillance.

While I contemplated approaching him he rose and made a halting, unsteady progress through the tables toward me. As a waiter shuffled past, the old man lurched in my direction, knocking against my table and sending my coffee cup onto the floor. He fell to his knees and began mumbling apologies.

Two café waiters hustled him into the street while I followed, trying to make out what the old man was saying. His voice was a feeble rasp from the depths of his coat.

"It's all right, it's all right," I assured the waiters, but they pushed the old man away from me and then escorted me back to my seat.

When my table had been set right and a fresh coffee served I noticed the stained café napkin wedged under the ashtray.

A message was scrawled across the napkin in the original cipher (beginning with C, proceeding by threes). It did not take me long to decode the message, which was but a single word:

I looked for the old man in the street, but he had gone.

Now at least I knew where I must go from Paris, not that there had ever been any doubt. Daunt's message was at once confirming, avenging, and sundering. It was also quite clear. It puzzled me that he had not delivered it in a more conventional fashion. Once again I felt he was teasing me, though whether for his own amusement or out of a sense of danger and urgency I could not determine.

Without bothering to return to the Rue du Sommerard I walked to the Seine and turned upriver toward that "lesser arrondissement" where the Zorns lived.

It is less than a mile from the Quai d'Orsay to the Quai de Bercy, but it is difficult to believe they lie upon the same river in the same city.

The Bercy district is a narrow rectangle of stone wine caves and brick warehouses dropped between a switchery of railroad tracks leading into the Gare aux Marchandises on one side and the docks of the Seine on the other. It is an island cut off from the rest of Paris. The *entrepôts* of Bercy receive wine from all over France, and the names of the cobbled alleyways which slice through the district reflect this: Macon, Médoc, Cognac, St. Estephe, Margaux, Laffite, St. Emilion, Vouvray.

I crossed the river where the railroad tracks ran down to the quai among piles of rock and gravel. Workmen were unloading barges onto a revolving chute. On the bridge several old men were fishing. They had newspapers stuffed beneath their caps as sun shields. I could read the dire warnings of war on the backs of their necks as I passed.

I left the quai and descended into the tree-lined *cours* of Bercy, rich with the smell of wine and oak casks, bustling with drays and railroad cars which drove down the middle of the little alleys.

The building on the Rue St. Estephe where the

Zorns were living was a small two-story structure backing onto a weeded vacant lot. Unpainted shutters tilted off broken hinges. Few people lived in this district, and the frayed, graying laundry flapping in the heavy air bespoke the sorry mixture of the destitute, the dissolute, and the desperate who must certainly inhabit such a place.

At the door the dog Cuntz, who once leaped through gilded hoops in the Place St. Sulpice, lay dreamily by a plate of uneaten scraps swarming with flies. I pushed open the corrugated metal door and found the Zorns in their dingy rooms on the second floor.

Guillaume appeared comfortably at home there. Seated on the floor, he was working on a new poem. Claudie had returned from London, drained by her two months with the Ballet Russe. She was dressed in crumpled old clothing, content to be back with her family and merely an Alsatian *saltimbanque* once again.

I described my meeting at the Ministre de la Guerre and Daunt's message confirming the inevitable next step.

"Just 'Mulhouse'—that's all it said?" Guillaume asked, and I showed him the stained café napkin.

"What more need he say? After my conference with Delcassé and the others, this can mean only one thing." I paused and surveyed the room, my eyes coming to rest on Arbogast Zorn. His thoughts lay hidden behind lusterless eyes. "I am going," I said. "Tonight or tomorrow morning, as you advise."

The old clown nodded—I would always think of him as an old clown—and Guillaume paced about the room.

"And I shall go with you," he said.

A weak "No, Guillaume" escaped Claudie, and she went to his side in a swift, supple movement. This seemed to harden his resolve, while at the same time gratifying him. He took her lovely hands and raised them to his lips.

"It is best so," he said. "I can no longer tolerate myself as I am, and neither can you." She bit her lip and shook her head. "You know the truth in what I say." He glanced at me and straightened his back as he spoke. "This is our moment of destiny, Clayton and I, the end towards which everything, from the day we first met, has been leading. We cannot turn away now, no matter how dangerous our course. Surely *you* understand this, Claudie."

She nodded, and her face flashed a brave smile while her eyes searched that squalid apartment until they fastened on Arbogast Zorn. "Oh, *mon oncle,*" they seemed to cry, "I do not want to understand so much. I wish to know nothing. Then I could be happy." But he had no comfort for her.

"We must rouse Bruno," he said. "Perhaps he will lead our young friends across the border."

Bruno Spahn was a young Alsatian partisan who had come out of the lost provinces earlier in the week, the man the sodality of clowns had been awaiting. He was safely ensconced at the Zorns' for the duration of his stay in Paris and was preparing to cross back into Alsace.

Bruno was a strapping youth with rosy cheeks and a wide gap between his front teeth. His coarse, gravelly voice lent a comical quality to his boyishness and robust good health. I would come to appreciate his pluck and experience with the Germans in the days that followed.

We decided to start the next morning, which would bring us to the border on Bastille Day. Bruno believed "the oppressors," as he called the Germans, would be occupied controlling patriotic demonstrations within Alsace that day and their vigilance at the border might be slightly lessened.

As we planned our departure I saw each of the Zorns growing restless. At last the silent one, Arbo's brother, Gaspard, nodded his head as though he had reached a difficult decision.

"I will come with you," he said.

"And me too," exclaimed young Thiébaut immediately. He could not be deterred from this by his mother's and sister's entreaties nor by my own observation that a party of five was rather cumbersome and more easily detected than three or even four.

"But you may split up. You may need five to create diversions in the crossing," Arbo Zorn suggested. "You do not know what you shall encounter. I believe there cannot be too many comrades." Bruno agreed, so it was decided that young Thiébaut would accompany us.

At sunset we sat outside on a row of upturned oak barrels, the smell of wine washing over us in a soft breeze blowing off the Seine. The warehouses of Bercy were deserted, and I felt at peace, safely hidden there, husbanding my strength for what lay ahead. I began to whistle, knowing that I had discharged all my duties and was now free to do what I had long known I must do. Old Zorn shook his head and held a finger to his lips, and I fell silent.

Bruno Spahn described the current situation in Alsace, the hardening of resistance since the passage of the sham constitution, and the worsening repression.

"We must rouse the people and prepare them for a German attack," he told us. "The oppressors shall not pass as easily across the Vosges as they expect. We shall give the motherland time to mobilize, and all men will see what we Alsatians are made of."

"You know," observed Arbogast Zorn, "it is a great irony that the Germans have always told us, 'I shall not give you freedom until you give me love,' but have never understood that we could not give them love until they set us free. Had they understood that, they might have won over Alsace, and *revanche* might have died in old hearts like mine."

"But it has not died," said Bruno Spahn.

We sat in silence for several moments until Arbogast Zorn sighed deeply and asked me what I would do when I reached the lost provinces. I answered him almost without thinking, listening to the words pour from my lips as though someone else were speaking.

"I will go to Mulhouse and find Fritz. I expect Daunt will be there. And then . . ." I hesitated as the end hung above me, menacing and smoky and smelling of chemicals and the river, my endless uncertainty at last solidifying into a tangible, and terrifying, shape. "And then I shall destroy Fritz Amgott and all he has created."

Arbo smiled. "I have a gift for you," he said and left us sitting on our barrels. He returned with a short-nosed pistol, tarnished with age, which he handed to me. "This was mine in the Legion thirty years ago," he explained. "I had always intended that it find its way back to Alsace, but now I see that I shall not be able to carry it there myself. May it serve you well."

We slept little that night in the crowded apartment. Guillaume was up late working on his new poem, "Phantom of the Clouds." When it was nearly complete he read me the opening lines: "It was the eve of July 14 and I went out in the street to watch the *saltimbanques*." It continued in that vein, describing the scene in St. Sulpice with the hindsight of four years while evoking our enterprise of the next day.

One line caught in his throat and struck me particularly: it spoke of the rosy color in the cheeks of "certain young girls who are near death," and I glanced at

Claudie, who lay sleeping in a corner of the room. I had observed a change in their relations since the troubles in London and the apparent reconciliation here. No longer did Guillaume mysticize her, no longer did she regard him as a benefactor; they had begun to see each other more clearly, with all the faults and blemishes, and in this I sensed that they might achieve their potential, individually and together.

I no longer fretted over Guillaume's lack of fitness, his incessant smoking and romanticizing of our adventures. I felt certain that he would be no hindrance once we crossed into the lost provinces, and that his devotion to the cause of France and to the Zorns would elicit great things from him.

I dozed fitfully through the night. Before dawn I awoke and found Kasia Zorn preparing provisions for our journey. For the first time we began to converse, softly in the predawn light.

Kasia told me she had awakened in the violent thunderstorms of two nights past, the night on which Madame Orgueil was murdered, and felt her dead son's presence in the room. There were odd knockings. A window opened and a vase fell from a table and shattered. She was convinced it was not the wind and thunder which caused this but a visitation from Sébastien. She related this so vividly and with such intensity that I could not doubt that on the night of Madame O-'s death the wraith had returned to watch over his family.

The others awoke one by one. At dawn we collected the foodstuffs which Kasia had prepared and took our leave with a great clasping of hands and kissing of cheeks all around the room.

Claudie stood on her toes to kiss Guillaume. She broke down in childish sobs as he drew himself from her slender embrace and bid farewell to Arbogast Zorn.

Upriver the cruel sun sat upon the waters, lilac and coral beneath belts of thin cloud dispersing in the morning sky. We rode the train into the rising sun.

Before us lay what the Emperor Franz Joseph called an "open sore upon the body of the German Empire." Paris lay abandoned at our backs.

XII

Our train traced the course of the Seine east through dripping forests and across fawn glistening downs. Low, gray mists blanketed the fields, and funnels of vapor spiraled off the river like tiny hurricanes. There would be no storms this day, just the sun-dulled sky and our smoky compartment with Guillaume beside me working over his poem.

"I cannot end it," he said.

"Perhaps it will end itself," I suggested peevishly.

"That is precisely what I am afraid of." He read me the closing section describing a young *saltimbanque* balanced on a ball, not unlike Sébastien on his barrel. Suddenly the boy disappeared. Here he was at a loss: he added a pair of lines, scratched them out, added another pair. After a long gaze out the window he added a final couplet. "Yes, that's it," and he read: "But each spectator searched inside himself for the wondrous child / Century upon century of clouds." He leaned back and shut his eyes, content with the enchantment.

Bruno Spahn looked more perplexed than troubled by Guillaume's behavior, while Gaspard Zorn was too deeply moved by his imminent return to the land he had left as an infant even to notice. But young Thiébaut listened and heard and did not like what he heard. Unlike his dead brother, young Thiébaut knew at seventeen how history functioned and the thin thread upon which events hung. He sensed what awaited us: drenched by tepid rains and unable to air itself, the open sore still festered after four decades, beckoning to us from across the Vosges as we arrived that afternoon in Belfort.

Outside the city, crowned with fortifications dating from Gallic times, was a long, flat-topped outcropping of rock against which sat Bartholdi's Lion, symbol of the heroic defense which had saved Belfort in 1871. The lion caught the setting sun full in its face as our train pulled slowly into the station. It was sculpted of rust colored stone, nearly one hundred feet long and half as high, its head lifted and forepaws braced, with rippling rust stone muscles in the forearms and tensed hind legs. The eyebrows were furled angrily, the nostrils flaring and the mouth open as though the lion were about to roar. On top of the mammoth rock in matching red brick stood a garrison flying the tricolor flag.

I squinted through the bright sunlight glancing off our compartment window, expecting to see the wondrous child appear above the lion, pierced with arrows and pointing east. Somewhere out across the mountains it thundered.

The city was alive with Bastille Day celebrations. In the central square, brass bands played the "Marche Lorraine" and the "Sambre et Meuse," and the promenading crowds responded eagerly to the music.

"We must rest here tonight," Bruno Spahn told us. He sat listening to the music, sipping a Kanterbräu. His voice assumed the emotionless monotone I had come to expect of Alsatian partisans. "On the other side, you will hear no music. We hide behind our shutters on the fête days, embarrassed to behold the drunken merrymaking of the oppressors. Schoolchildren are imprisoned for tearing down pictures of the Kaiser and old men are murdered because they have stolen four eggs. And for this they call us *Wackes*."

The next day saw no dawn: a dark nimbus sky encased Belfort and I was sticky with perspiration before I had walked a block.

We took the high road toward Mulhouse. Bruno said we could not enter Alsace along this road without proper papers. He had arranged to meet a farmer with a horse-drawn cart who would take us to a mountain pass which cut north from the main road and was guarded by a small, isolated border station.

When we reached the appointed meeting place the farmer had not arrived. After enduring the curious stares of a few passersby we began walking up the side road. We had gone less than a mile when the cart came into view, and soon we were jouncing along to the pleasant clip-clop of horse hooves.

We drove for several miles through gradually ascending farmland and orchards, past grazing cattle and old stone farmhouses with peculiar, hipped, three-sided roofs, the entire front wall of the building resembling a truncated gable. Colorful flowerbeds surrounded the houses, and farm women waved and called out to us as we passed through Rougemont and Masevaux.

Beyond Masevaux the woods thickened with pines and fir trees. The two-horse cart slowed as we climbed into darkening pine forests. It was cooler at midday in the mountains than it had been at dawn in Belfort—the sweet smell of evergreen all around us and the wet, soggy ground, thick with pine needles, cushioning the jolt of the wagon. By comparison to the rugged peaks of the Atlas, the Vosges were no more than gently rolling hills, rather like the so-called mountains of New England.

We turned off on a logging road near Bourbach-le-Haut. Dark clouds drifted over the mountains to the east, while behind us, through the rose gray evening sky, I could see sunlight on the green fields outside Belfort. We skirted an open meadow and emerged from the pine forests at a ridge. A quarter mile below us I saw daubs of white smoke and the iron cross flag with a black eagle holding a wreath of oak leaves which flew over the small booth at the border station. Here the farmer turned back and we proceeded on foot to the pass.

Across the pass the logging road ended and we dropped steeply through pines and roundleaf oaks along a rough trail marked by rock cairns. A light mist brushed our faces while the sound of water filled my ears; water dripping from the trees, coursing down countless muddy runnels like little creeks in the rutted trail, gushing from a hidden underground spring. I felt thankful for this cover of sound, for I imagined that every cracked twig, every displaced pebble or the splash of a boot in a puddle echoed across the mountainside to the German guard station less than a mile away. I expected at any moment to hear shouts, dogs barking, and pursuing footsteps. Several times Bruno raised a hand for us to halt and stood listening through the rush of water, then touched his lips and proceeded. In this manner we crossed the Col du Hundsrück and entered the lost provinces.

"We are safe now," our guide told us when we had dropped well below the pass. "The weather has been our friend, I think," and he grinned his gap-toothed grin and filled his broad chest with the air of Alsace.

We rejoined the road two miles below the border station with the clouds breaking up overhead and a brief half hour of sunset stretched across the mountaintops behind us.

Bruno insisted it was too dangerous to follow the main road down into Thann and enter the city by night. He guided us to a small woodsman's cottage a few hundred yards off the road. There we were lodged for the night by the woodsman and his wife, who accepted us without question after Bruno explained our mission and the Zorns' history. Given the proximity of the guard station, they were a bit apprehensive over our presence and quite eager to see us on our way early the next morning.

The storms had passed, and we descended a mile of switchbacks until abruptly the pine woods ended and we stood looking out across the vale of Thann, brightly glimmering in the cool dawn beneath a cerulescent sky. Patches of mist were caught in hollows in the mountains. The valley was dotted with village steeples standing along the Thur river until it ascended and narrowed far to the east and was reclaimed by the mountains.

I stood enchanted by this lovely, peaceful scene, so far removed from the storms of nature and politics which swept across Paris and seemed to be sweeping across Europe. The local farmers were assembling from the surrounding countryside for the Saturday market in Thann: carts passed us with milk cans clanking and chickens clucking, wine in plain green bottles, waxed rounds of cheese and sausages dangling over the sides, fresh produce, and textiles. The smell of fresh-baked loaves wafted through the cool morning air.

In the smiling faces of the local farmers was no sense of danger or oppression nor even that weary sadness I had detected in Alsatians outside their homeland. I wondered if, contrary to the view from afar and the reports of Bruno Spahn, life went on as usual for these people. Their easygoing, natural outlook shaped a subtle change in my attitude toward Alsace and my mission there. This began a bucolic interlude of two days which I still find difficult to place within the continuum of events which preceded and followed it.

I slipped off the road to relieve myself and stood in the dewy silence, my back to the sun, wishing I could become rooted to that spot like one of the nearby oaks and never continue to Mulhouse or return to Paris.

Grasshoppers and spiders perched on pale green ferns no bigger than a stalk of grass. Big black bumblebees probed dandelions and other blossoming wild flowers. The dew coated tiny spiderwebs like patches of barely translucent fine pearl lace, embroidered by the purple and yellow flowers and tossed about on a thick brocade of green. The little webs dipped with the weight of the dew and sparkled in the sunlight.

Bruno called me and I rejoined my companions on the road. We followed the river Thur through Moosch and Bitschwiller, gathering a company of horses and carts and families with whom we entered Thann.

Thann was not as small a village as I had imagined, but it was more ancient and built around a large Gothic cathedral. On this market day the village was jammed with merchants and artisans and their customers from a dozen surrounding villages, and we passed inconspicuously into the town center, as Bruno had assured us we would.

Pink-cheeked girls in braids, gingham, and wooden clogs served local wine and braised brochettes in the square near the church. Some of them had enormous black bows wobbling on their heads. All along the narrow cobbled streets, merchants displayed their wares. I sensed no brutalization or oppression among these people. Their lives seemed perfectly natural and uncomplicated by political considerations. I observed just two or three small clusters of black-booted German soldiers with sabers at their hips, standing in the square behind the Collégiale. I tried but could not bring myself to fear them, and they paid us no heed, as the marketing farmers of the countryside paid them none. The only evidence I saw of Bastille Day was a discreet tricolor display of charcuterie cleverly arranged like a French flag in a shop window.

Roadways led in a half-dozen directions from the church and market with medieval buildings, their walls chipped and cracked, leaning over them. We followed one of these avenues, bridged the river Thur, and walked down a narrow lane by a stone wall. At an opening in the wall we turned in and crossed a small orchard of flowering plum trees, vines, and crab apples to the stone house where we would stay in Thann.

Although Bruno secured false identification papers for us, he advised us that in the absence of the bustling Saturday market Guillaume and I would attract attention in the village—if not from the German immigrants themselves then from informers who abounded among the local citizens—and he recommended that we remain under cover until we set out for Mulhouse.

"I don't see why we've come here if we can't even walk the streets," groused Guillaume. "What will become of us in Mulhouse?"

"Mulhouse is a large city. Thann is a village," Bruno answered.

"Are there really informers among the people here?" I asked, again struck by the dichotomy between my impressions and Bruno's analysis of the Thannois.

"It is an easy way to buy favors," he said. Sensing my skepticism, he continued, "We are not slaves here. The oppression is subtle and you must look closely to perceive it. You must stay long in Alsace before you understand our sadness."

Bruno took Gaspard Zorn into town, leaving us in the care of our hosts, a family named Metzger living with the husband's mother, who had known Gaspard and Arbo Zorn's mother a half century before. I contented myself to postponing my mission for a few days and allowed the fresh air and bucolic simplicity of life in Thann to caress me.

The old lady's name was Griselda. She had a single

front tooth angling out of her gums and made a funny, wet sound when she spoke. She told us rambling stories of her past and legends of Alsace and was particularly taken with Thiébaut, whom she treated as a child. Guillaume and I found her tales endearing, but I think Thiébaut would rather have been out fighting Germans.

"Tell me, little one, do you know how Thann was founded?" she asked him, and he shook his head. It was late afternoon and we sat on stone benches beneath a bower of bougainvillea and honeysuckle, lulled by old Griselda's gurgling voice. "It was after the death of St. Thiébaut. His faithful servant came to this spot in the summer of 1161. He leaned his pilgrim's staff against a fir tree and went to sleep, but when he awoke the staff had taken root in the soil. He could not remove it. Sparkling lights burst from the top of the fir tree and were seen by the master of this region. He hastened to the place, recognized that he was in the presence of a miracle, and vowed to build a chapel on the spot. The chapel is the Collégiale, and around it has grown the town of Thann."

She smiled and sucked her single tooth. The doughty Thiébaut was won over and encouraged her as she launched into another legend, involving Louis Quatorze and a yellow dwarf named Chamillo who helped the great king take Strasbourg in 1683. Her tale made no mention of the Peace of Westphalia but I neglected to point this out.

It was past nine o'clock, still light and mild in the garden, when Bruno and Gaspard Zorn returned from the village with Griselda's son Balthasar Metzger. He was a short, sober man who printed calico tissues. He showed us the round wood roller carved with intricate raised designs which he employed in his craft. While Griselda and his wife prepared dinner in a warm little kitchen with dimity curtains, we men discussed politics.

"I am confused by what I see here in Thann," I told

them. "I feel none of the urgency and commitment to change which were so strong back in Paris. Can you explain this?"

"You are right," Balthasar Metzger admitted. "We live as we have always lived. What else is there to do? But something is missing within. We work but have no desire to perfect our work. The energy to create and excel has been lost. We merely pass through life."

"But you don't think that Arbo Zorn and Boppe and the others"—I directed my question to Bruno Spahn—"You don't think they have exaggerated the situation, that in their long absence from Alsace they have lost touch with the reality of life here?"

Bruno shook his head, but Gaspard Zorn answered me.

"I am beginning to wonder that myself," he said. "I am disheartened by the weakness I have encountered in Thann. These peasants have been asleep for so long it may be impossible to rouse them."

"Not difficult at all, you will see," replied Bruno. He looked sternly at Gaspard, resenting the reference to "peasants." Perhaps, I thought, the Zorns *are* of a different world from their forefathers and no longer can understand.

"It is all well and good for you to speak of rousing the peasants," said Guillaume, "but what I want to know is when are we going to Mulhouse." He glanced at me, and this reminder of our mission caused my own nearly forgotten sense of urgency to flare briefly within me.

Bruno had found a guide who would put us in contact with friends in the city, but said that we must wait another day in Thann and depart Monday morning. Though I had strong misgivings about further delay and questioned the usefulness of Bruno's comrades in Mulhouse for the job we must do with Daunt, it was agreed that we remain with the Metzgers until Monday. The Zorns, of course, would not leave the mountains.

We ate a filling dinner of a local dish called *choucroute*: a mound of sauerkraut topped with all forms of boiled pork—ham, bacon, a chop, and a sausage—and served with hot mustard and a thick slice of dark bread. We drank several bottles of fruity white wine with our *choucroute*. Putting politics aside for the evening, we drifted off to sleep in the stone farmhouse.

The following morning we were permitted our single venture into the village, to attend early mass at the Collégiale. As I sat in the Gothic cathedral, gazing up at three tall, narrow stained-glass windows within the alcove formed behind the altar by the vaulted arch, a sensation of timelessness and of the antiquity of Thann swept over me. The village was 750 years old (reckoning by the date in Griselda's legend of St. Thiébaut) and had known many masters. How much, I wondered, could our concerns, or those of Fritz Amgott, change life as it was lived by the Thannois and their neighbors? No German oppressors would bother us in the church; the vault seemed to me to extend across the entire vale of Thann —nothing could harm us here. The same soothing somnolence and sense of continuity which I had felt in the national library at Paris comforted me in the old church. Dreamily I gazed at Griselda muttering the litany with her jowls jiggling and her eyes watering, clinging to the pew in front of her with knobby, purple hands.

After church we returned to the Metzgers'. Bruno read to us from the local newspaper, but the words passed over my head. We picked cherries and, through the buzz of late afternoon, listened to Griselda telling Thiébaut about his grandmother. In the evening we prepared reluctantly to leave Thann the next day with Bruno's friend.

But our plans for a Monday morning departure were disrupted.

I awoke before dawn. The wind out of the mountains and a heaviness in the air signaled the approach of another storm. As I lay awake, restlessly imagining the day before me, I heard a pummeling at the door and a deep growling.

Quickly the entire household was awakened. Our bearded visitor, with his growling dog, wore a military-style jacket with epaulettes.

"They know you are in Thann," he told us. "Or they know someone is hiding here, and they have begun a search of the houses. They are coming this way. You have perhaps half an hour."

Within minutes we had crossed the orchard behind the Metzgers' house, scaled the pocked wall into the cobbled lane, and followed the lane until it turned into a dirt road at the edge of town. Bruno led us across a small meadow to a road running north from Thann through the mountains to Cernay. Slivers of sunlight pierced the slate-gray eastern sky like stationary bolts of lightning, and I heard the thunder of a distant storm.

Suddenly I heard a closer rumbling, a mechanical thunder and the clamor of wheels on the road behind us. An armor-plated, motorized vehicle was pursuing us at a rate no greater than our running speed. Mounted atop the armored vehicle was a Maxim gun. Two German casque helmets, black with gold eagles and spike tops, flanked the mechanism of the menacing gun.

We clambered up a terraced vineyard, but the motorized monster turned from the road and followed us overland at the same steady pace. Already Guillaume was limping, his gait resembling the awkward canter of an overweight show horse.

"We cannot outrun them," Bruno said. "But I think we may be able to go where they cannot."

We scrambled up a steep escarpment covered in brambles and heather. At the ridge in a stand of fir and oak were two enormous stone wheels, twice as tall as a man and set at an oblique angle, a fortification from medieval times. We could not stop to admire them, for the rumble and clank of our pursuers drew closer.

Between the ridge upon which we stood and the next rise in the mountains lay a long swale a half mile wide. The open swale appeared a particularly vulnerable position to me, and when Bruno motioned us to cross it I asked whether the Germans would not easily follow. He shook his head vigorously and grinned.

"They cannot," he said and hurried down into the little valley.

When I was a hundred feet out I began to understand his thinking. The low-lying meadow was soft from the constant rains. Even near its edge our feet stuck in the earth and our trouser legs were matted by the wet rushes growing there. As we ventured further the flooded swale turned to swamp. We sank to our ankles in the muck and plodded forward awkwardly while the first heavy drops of rain fell. Glancing back, I saw the Germans and their grumbling black monstrosity hovering at the edge of the swale. Then they plunged forward after us.

Bruno had planned well, because soon the vehicle began to sink into the mire. We saw the Germans, a half-dozen of them in their spiked helmets, hopping around by their disabled machine, arguing and gesticulating, while we waded through the heart of the swale. We sank nearly to our knees with each step but were almost out of range of the Maxim.

As I began to despair whether I could lift my throbbing legs again and proceed, a powerful bolt of lightning illuminated the entire valley. Every tree and the face of the mountains opposite froze in its light, and in the ensuing thunder the Maxim gun burst forth with its first volley of shots.

Gaspard Zorn was grazed on the shoulder and cried out as a spot of blood appeared on his coat. Bruno Spahn fell to his stomach and motioned for us to fall as well. Hidden by the tall rushes all around us, we crawled toward the far side of the valley while the Maxim strafed the air above our heads and bullets embedded themselves in the mud with a splash and a sucking sound.

The mud soaked my chest and caught in my hair and nose as I inched forward on elbows and knees, trying to hold my face clear of the muck which oozed between my fingers.

Suddenly the tops of several junipers across the swale seemed to ignite. Tall green flames tipped in red and blue flared from the thin trees. I halted, and when Guillaume came grunting up to my side we lay gazing at this apparition in awe and terror.

"It is St. Elmo's Fire," shouted Bruno from a few yards ahead of us. "A good sign." He glanced back at us immobilized in the mud behind him and added, "It is real," as though we needed this assurance to continue, and I believe we did. Gathering our remaining strength, we gradually outdistanced the Maxim's range. Slowly the soil beneath us solidified as we crept out of the swale toward the row of junipers which had displayed St. Elmo's Fire.

At last we dared stand and look back. The German monster was mired on the other side. Two German soldiers had crossed partway with rifles but had turned back at the point where they sank to their knees, apparently less desperate to chase us than we were to escape. They could not circle the valley and would be a long time extricating their vehicle. Though my arms and legs ached from the exertion and I was coated with mud, for the moment at least we had escaped.

Bruno attended Gaspard Zorn's injured shoulder and suggested we make for the "Gallus house," hidden in the woods above that valley, where we would find a change of clothes and the Zorns could rest.

"I regret that my plans did not work out and you must make your way to Mulhouse alone. Our work lies in these mountains and the time has come for us to part," he said softly.

"You have already helped us more than we could ask," I assured him. We changed into old denim workclothes and peasant caps at the Gallus house. Gaspard seemed strengthened, at least in resolve, by his wound, and Thiébaut was obviously emboldened by his first encounter with the Germans. An impish smile played upon his taut features, and his eyes glowed with excitement. Our brief reprieve had ended. All the burden of my task and the obstacles which stood in the way of its accomplishment lay upon me once more.

"It is but twenty kilometers to Mulhouse," Bruno told us. "If you follow the next river valley eastward into the plains you should reach the city by nightfall. And once you arrive there . . ." He broke off and gazed at us as if to say that some power greater than his would determine our success or failure.

I tried to find a comfortable place in my belt for the pistol Arbogast Zorn had given me in Bercy while Guillaume folded his poem "Phantom of the Clouds" and slipped it inside his shirt.

"Just keep that gun and your hands hidden. Keep your eyes lowered and your mouths shut, and you can probably pass for *Wackes* in the eyes of the oppressors,"

Bruno warned us. He embraced us and we clasped hands with the Zorns.

Supplied with our identity papers and peasant clothing, and armed with our vast unwarranted audacity, we took leave of the Zorns and Bruno Spahn. We climbed out of the valley of the muddy swale and so began our descent into Mulhouse.

XIII

The Glautsch chemical works was located in Ottmarsheim, an industrial district several miles east of the city of Mulhouse, across the Harth Forest in a tangle of canals, railroad tracks, and roadways on the banks of the Rhine. Standing at the edge of the Harth we could smell the plant before we could make it out through the haze. We had reached the heart of the open sore, and above us the purulent sky rained dark chemical mists over the factory's multiple smokestacks, ringed in red and black.

The wary vigilance of our journey from the mountains had proved unwarranted: we encountered several doses of the abuse levied upon all *Wackes* by the German oppressors but, following Bruno's advice, kept our mouths shut, our caps pulled down, and our eyes lowered, thus apparently displaying sufficient humility to placate our harassers. We entered Mulhouse undeterred at sunset, found a small hotel near the station, and slept soundly.

The next day we shuffled along the busy, gray streets of the city like a pair of wayward peasants, crossed the Grand Canal du Rhône au Rhin, and left the dull, horizonless sprawl of a very ugly metropolis in early afternoon.

The Harth is a strip of forest five miles wide, laced with canals and a few narrow roads. We cut through its damp, shaded depths, occasionally sighting a deer or hearing a bird call, walking softly over tufts of grass and matted leaves beneath birch and blackthorn and hazel.

I had resolved to destroy the Glautsch chemical

works. Though my knowledge of explosives was limited, I felt certain there was sufficient firepower at Glautsch to accomplish this. But first, Guillaume reminded me, we must find and destroy the master himself.

We emerged from the forest and crossed a cornfield. The stalks were head high, but a farmer's dog detected us and chased us from the field. Now the tall gates of the plant came into view, flying the iron cross flag with a black eagle at its center and guarded by several armed soldiers. We skirted along a side canal, crossed a pair of railroad lines which terminated at the plant, and approached from the south. A stench of chemical discharge filled the moist air.

Out of view of the gates we reached the wire-mesh fence which surrounded the plant and I followed Guillaume up and over, urging him on. The fence backed up against the wall of the huge main structure, large enough to serve as hangar for a zeppelin. Slanting chutes and conveyer belts led from the factory building to barges drawn up at docks on the canal. From the top of the fence we stepped onto the roof of this structure, and clinging to exhaust tubes and pipes for support we clattered across fifty feet of roof to an opening. We ducked inside and dropped onto an elevated catwalk. The vaulted chambers of the Glautsch plant spread out below us.

The arched ceiling above our heads was crisscrossed by exposed ductwork and supporting joists. Concrete columns supported the roof, with galleries and catwalks at intermediate levels along the walls, strung together by an intricate system of steel supports. A series of wheels, cranks with pulleys, and the chutes we had seen from outside were suspended over four enormous tanks, twenty feet across and twice as deep, which occupied the center of the floor. Ladders were attached to the tanks and scaffolding rigged above them on inverted funnels which drew off the thick mephitic mist bubbling up from these chemical caldrons. When I wiped the sweat from my lips the skin on the back of my hand tasted of chemical vapor. I could well imagine what a week's work in the plant did to one's eyes and lungs.

We could see a few workmen in beige suits and caps prowling the concrete floor around the big vats. It was not long before the distinction between hunter and hunted disappeared. Two uniformed and armed men crossed the floor and peered around the vats and into the network of pipes and cranks behind them. They appeared to be searching for something other than us, for they did not scan the scaffolding or even look up. We shrank back against the ceiling and waited.

Suddenly a valve at head level belched steam. Guillaume jumped, cried out, and drew back. We had been spotted, and one of the men called out for us to come down. When we did not respond they came to a ladder which led upward to the section of gallery where we hid. Before they began their ascent, a third man strode between the bubbling vats, his high-topped black boots clacking on a steel walkway. Even from above at this distance I recognized the pinched waist and bushy mustaches of Fritz Amgott.

The armed men pointed in our direction, and Fritz, sensing that we were not, as we appeared, a pair of Alsatian farmers lost in his plant, led them up the ladder. When they were about thirty feet below us I drew the pistol from my belt, cocked it, and for the first time in my life fired at another human being.

My aim was not true, but our enemies, after hanging precariously on the ladder a moment, hastily retreated to the safety of the main floor as a second arrant shot winged over their heads. I pushed Guillaume before me and we ran in a half-crouch along the top gallery toward the shelter of the tall metal housing which funneled off the fumes from the big vats.

We glanced at each other as we crouched in the shadows and surveyed the floor below us. I could see into the bubbling vats, which were filled with a bilious green chemical mixture.

I heard the armed men shouting to the beige clad workers to clear the floor, and one of them returned my fire. His shot careened off the metal cowling behind which we cowered. I heard footsteps on the concrete floor beneath us, and Fritz and his two guards appeared at a mechanical lift which buzzed and began to climb toward us.

Before they reached our level, Guillaume and I slunk along a narrow catwalk and descended a ladder to the next lower gallery, so that when the men stepped from the mechanical lift we were directly beneath them.

My third shot hit one of the guards. In their distraction, searching for us below, we fled down the gallery. I heard Fritz's boots in pursuit, and the mechanism of the plant ground around us like steel teeth gnashing on a troublesome piece of gristle, trying to pry it loose and spit us out on the floor.

Our walkway ended in a blocked-off storage area of long wooden crates. A single set of rungs ran up the wall to an opening onto another level of the plant. Below us was a twelve-foot drop to the next gallery, and below that the last of the great bubbling vats. I heard a single pair of boots coming slowly along the gallery above us.

"This is it," I said to Guillaume. Wiping the foul taste from my mouth and firing a single blind warning shot upward into the gallery, I began to climb the rungs toward the safety of the next level.

As we climbed the sound of the boot clomps ceased. It seemed unlikely I had hit Fritz with my blind shot.

Perhaps he was watching us. I tucked my head between my shoulders, and we reached the next level unscathed.

I shuddered to see how neatly we had caged ourselves. In a small enclosure, beneath a corrugated metal roof, was a control room filled with gauges and valves and dials, walled on all sides—and inescapable. Now I heard the steady footsteps approaching along the gallery and beneath them the sound of voices and boots on the plant floor.

"Come down from there, you imbeciles," Fritz's brittle voice called out in baneful victory. "Come down or I shall cook you in your roost."

I drew my dangling legs into the control room, quickly reloaded my pistol, and tried to assess our situation. I believed Fritz would enjoy cooking us in our roost.

"There is no exit," the voice informed us. "Throw down your weapons and descend."

I glanced helplessly at Guillaume, who was frantically peering into the recesses of our little cage, and dropped my gun onto the walkway below. Before climbing down, I twisted wheels and turned switches and levers on as many of the gauges in the control room as I could, hoping at least to muck up the operation and perhaps create a diversion which might allow us to escape. There seemed little chance of this now.

Slowly I descended the rungs, Guillaume following me. His nervous hands slipped and one of his feet kicked my jaw as he struggled to catch himself. The painful throbbing in my face dulled my senses, and I was numb when we reached the bottom of the ladder and faced Fritz. He stood alone, waiting for us.

He was a smaller man than I remembered, and his icy stare was vivid sky blue; on another face, with another disposition, those could have been beautiful eyes. The color was startling in its luminosity. But there was nothing beautiful in their expression, and his voice was crisp with pleasure at our misfortune.

"And now, my meddlesome friends," he said, raising a heavy pistol and aiming its long, dark snout at us, "to complete a task which ought to have been done long ago."

"Indeed it should, Herr Sturm," came a disembodied voice from the catwalk beneath him. "Some time ago. . . ."

Fritz gaped into the shadows beneath and behind him as though he had forgotten something. A shot rang out, and he spun backward and dropped his gun into the vat. He reached for his side and staggered one step toward us. Another shot sounded and blood appeared on his forehead. He collapsed across the guardrail. A trickle of blood from his head dripped down into the vat and sizzled across the surface of green bile.

For a moment he swung suspended and I thought he would topple after his gun into the great caldron of chemicals, but he achieved his equilibrium and hung crumpled over the railing, his thin arms dangling as the droplets of blood sizzled across the surface of the vat.

"No time to lose now, lads," said Daunt, emerging from the shadows on the catwalk beneath us. "This is not Telouet and I have no accomplices here. But I do know a way out."

As he spoke I heard voices shouting below us. The first malfunctionings to result from my dial-twiddling in the control room released clouds of foul-smelling vapors across the plant.

Guillaume and I, so close to death and rescued once more by our eternal benefactor, simply stared at him in disbelief as he stepped into full view.

"Come on then," he shouted, and he raised a movable metal chute so that we could slither down to his level. He lit out down the gallery, and we barreled along after him toward the far end of the building.

He turned abruptly through a small doorway which emerged into an insulated corridor off of which several small offices opened. He slammed the door and we proceeded down the corridor. It ended at a sliding steel door.

"We've an hour to get away from this doomed building," he said. "Before Glautsch commits suicide."

"What do you mean? What are you talking about?"

"I have arranged for a small fire to break out in a vulnerable spot on the main floor, behind one of those tanks. When the tank blows there will be a chain reaction of explosions such as none of these Germans has even conceived."

"But how can we get away in time?" I beseeched him. Guillaume was probably already imagining our heroic deaths in the cause of France.

Grinning with self-confidence, Daunt turned to me and dangled a set of keys before my face.

"I have taken the liberty of borrowing Fritz's automobile, which is parked just beyond this doorway. It is swift and, thanks to our friend's precautions, virtually invulnerable to gunshots. If we can cross the yard to the car we should be able to elude any pursuit the Germans send after us."

He slid back the door and waved us through, but as I stepped forward I was greeted by a volley of gunfire and shrank back.

"Damn," he snapped. "Bloody damn awful. They're waiting for us. Very well," he added with a touch of disappointment but not a shred of dismay. "Stand away from the door, lads."

He peeked out, drew fire, and when he stepped back into the corridor he pulled my discarded gun from his pocket, having alertly recovered it on the walkway in the moment after Fritz was killed.

"You'll have to be more careful with your toys, Clayton," he said, indicating the gun. "Especially ones as useful as this."

"What shall we do?" I asked, sucking furiously on my mustache.

"It appears there are two of them, but soon we'll have them at our heels and a whole battalion outside. I will go first, stop and fire on them, then you run behind me to the Daimler. I'll continue firing and follow you." Guillaume drooped and shook his head forlornly. "Chin up," Daunt told him. "It's our only hope, and we'd best take it now."

I nodded and nudged Guillaume toward the big steel door. Slowly Daunt wheeled it back. The Germans began firing, and Daunt stepped past us and returned their fire two-handed.

"Now, run for your bloody lives, you imbeciles," he cried out. Even in the direst straits he possessed sufficient composure to take pleasure in using Fritz's epithet for us.

We took flight across fifty feet of tarmac with Daunt behind us, a hail of bullets spewing from his guns. It was a two- or three-second scamper, but it lasted a dreadfully long time.

Fritz's car was a Daimler Pullman Limousine, fully enclosed, with side lamps and running boards. Armor plating had been mounted over the honeycomb grate and across the car's long hood and four doors.

I knelt on the running board and found Guillaume at my side, panting and hugging his chest but very much alive. Daunt was already in the driver's seat starting the car's engine.

"Crank," he screamed at me, and I cranked. When

the engine started he threw open the doors for us, handed both guns to me, and told me to keep shooting until we had cleared the corner of the building. I could neither see nor hear anything in the roar of the answering fusillade, so I shut my eyes and fired away with both fists, my elbows knocking against my ribs with the fury of the recoil.

Daunt swerved the big car past our adversaries and screeched down the length of the plant toward the main gate.

"Duck down in the seat," he told us, "and hand me that helmet." I set a spike-topped German helmet on his head and crouched behind the seat with Guillaume.

From a distance the approaching Daimler appeared to have just its German driver in the front seat, whisking the master safely away from his plant. Daunt slowed and the tall gates swung open.

At that point when it was just too late to close us in, he accelerated to full throttle and we roared past the startled guards, who drew their guns and tried vainly to slam the gates shut.

Soon we sat up in our seats while Daunt flew through cornfields, over cobbled gassens and rain-slickened bridges, across two canals, and finally into the sheltering trees of the Harth, where he found a main road leading south.

"Where are we going?" I asked him when I had recovered my powers of articulation.

"Basel," he said. "It's less than thirty miles and we can cross the Rhine there and be safely in Switzerland by the time Glautsch blows up."

XIV

"Your timing remains extraordinary, Mr. Daunt," I complimented him.

We sped south through a forest of birch, hazel, and oak, crossed several small waterways, and emerged into flat farmland near the river. We were on our way to the safety of Basel, and I felt strangely secure, swaddled in the padded leather seat of the big black Daimler with Daunt at the wheel—three German industrialists on an evening outing in the Harth.

"So does yours," he replied. "If you had not provided the necessary diversion at the right moment I might have been caught planting my fuse at Glautsch. So the gratitude runs in both directions," and he extended his right hand to me.

Guillaume sat mutely in the back seat, content merely to be breathing. At last he spoke.

"What will happen now?"

"To us?" Daunt said. "We'll escape into Switzerland, with any luck."

"No, no, I mean to the world," Guillaume said.

"Ah, that is a big order. You want my opinion, do you?"

"I'm willing to hear it," Guillaume admitted.

"Indeed? The Teutonic Accord has been foiled and the German attempt to woo the British is ended. Fritz's death helps to assure that. We shall resist all temptations and stand by our allies. Besides, once my little device goes off there will be no temptation left. The Glautsch plant is a giant bullet aimed at the heart of the Reichsland." His laugh was bitter. "Mind you," he continued, "the French would like to decline the German challenge at Agadir, but I fear they will not be allowed that privilege. The Germans are committed to act now, for better or worse, with or without the Teutonic Accord. There is no turning back."

Nor was there any turning back for us when we sighted the first roadblock outside Kembs. Two carriages were turned sideways across the road, and several German soldiers stood waiting for us, their horses grazing nearby.

Daunt accelerated and returned my apprehensive glance with a shrug. A few warning shots ricocheted harmlessly off the Daimler's armor plating. "Oh, jolly good fun," he said and drove straight into the barricade, splintering the wooden carriages and scattering the soldiers and their terrified horses out across the fields. In like manner we broke through a second roadblock a few miles south near Rosenau.

Past Kembs, Daunt swerved violently onto a bumpy, narrow side road, blinded on both sides by tall cornstalks. We were bouncing about inside the car when suddenly he came upon an old farmer plodding down the road on a cart. Without slowing, the Daimler veered into the cornfield, sweeping out a wide swath of stalks around the immobilized farmer, and we somehow regained the road and continued our flight toward the bridge from St. Louis to Basel. There was no sign of pursuit.

"Quite a nifty bit of driving," I said, and Daunt accepted my flattery with a wry smile.

"So you see no way of averting war?" I asked, and he shook his head.

"But this war, if it comes," said Guillaume, "is but a

moment's detour from the course of this century. The old world will die quietly."

"Would that were so," Daunt replied. "But this is only the beginning of the horror." He turned to me. "Don't you agree, Clayton, that your friend sees the world reborn but does not conceive of the terrible process of rebirth? What has become possible remains far out of reach."

"Perhaps," I admitted, then thought better of this. "No, of course, you are right. It *will* be terrible. But it is possible. At least the possibility exists."

"Our boy Fritz thought that it was possible—nay, easy. 'War is the cleansing synthesis,' and then the *Kultur* troops will penetrate the last bastions of stupidity and inefficiency, and we shall rush forward into paradise. The futurist doctrine, eh? But it did not turn out to be so simple for Fritz, nor shall it be for the rest of us."

"Then you believe the futurists held a strong sway over Fritz?" Guillaume asked from the back seat. He leaned forward with his broad, fleshy chin resting on the seat between us, his plump hands each side of his chin.

"Yes, mad egotists always like to have psychic phenomena to bolster their arrogance. It comforts them that there is a spirit on their side, something irrational and outside themselves which sustains their convictions. Fritz felt he could single-handedly rend the Entente Cordiale. The futurists confirmed his belief in the inevitability of that."

"And the pale man?" I asked, but Daunt carefully ignored my question and pursued his own line of thought.

"Poor Fritz. His father was a powerful figure in German industry during the last century. He was also a fanatic about his only son. He tried to forge Fritz as he cast his steel, as though he could create a tougher human alloy by manipulating the development of his son. He forbade Fritz to attend the university, for that was unworthy of a master of industry. Fritz grew up in the shadow of the great Amgott Munitions Fabriken in Bremen, constantly surrounded by the noise and soot of the factory. His only escape was the family mansion. He was a weak boy in continual ill health and suffered beneath his father's palling heritage of power and his social isolation. He could not become the bright new alloy of Hans Amgott's dreams. Finally he rebelled. He married against his father's will and came to Mulhouse to oversee the conversion of the chemical plant. He fled in disgrace following his wife's suicide. That was how he came to Morocco, but his hatred of the forces which had conspired against him, and particularly of his father, tortured him. It fostered the self-destructive notion that he could shape the future of Europe to his own ends. A death instinct. Fritz's curse from his father."

"But who is the pale man?" I asked again when he had finished recounting Fritz's life.

He shook his head. "The threat is past. There will be no Teutonic Accord, but I cannot reveal the identity of the man you call 'the pale man.' The British government will deal with him. Quietly, without the public scandal of an investigation. Can you not accept that?"

I tilted my head in accord, but realized I could never accept it and wondered why he persisted in this mystification. "It makes me feel that all of this was a personal vendetta between you and Fritz. That we have been used in it," I said firmly, more to test his reaction than out of genuine ongoing belief in this possibility.

Daunt snorted. "You are a deucedly suspicious fellow, Peavey, though I suppose that will serve you well in the future. As for your scenario of duplicity, you don't really believe that anyway. And if it were true, what then? Have I misused you, or merely used you?"

"I suppose we've been rather a useless lot, anyway," I agreed.

"Not at all, old sport, not at all."

"There is one thing I would like to know," Guillaume interjected from his position leaning over the seat between us. "When you sent Clayton to London, how did you know he would recognize the man in Berkeley Square? How could you possibly have known he was the pale man from Madame Orgueil's?"

Daunt glanced at me and smiled. "Instinct," he said, and he winked at Guillaume.

We had entered the Alsatian border town of St. Louis. The Rhine in this area is not wide and is broken by jetties, small islands, and roadways. It was unclear at any given moment which side of the border we were on or which direction we were headed. Daunt slowed as the bridge to Basel came into view a mile away.

A major roadblock had been erected at the border station leading onto the bridge: a dozen soldiers with automatic weapons and rifles knelt before a pair of carriages, wooden horses, and upended barrels.

The road ran south of the bridge, crossed a narrow canal, and doubled back along a bight in the river. Past the border station the road climbed a slope to the point where it crossed over the embankment and the bridge began. Across the Rhine the lights of Basel filtered faintly and invitingly through the mist. The river flowed placidly beneath the embankment and an overcast, starless sky.

Daunt stopped the car.

"I think it best for you to get out here," he said.

"Excuse me?"

"Oh, I'm not deserting you now that I'm done using

you in my evil schemes, Clayton, but it's too risky for all of us to charge that barricade in the Daimler. If something should go wrong . . . if I am stopped, or shot . . ."

"And what are we to do?"

"Follow the embankment toward the bridge. It is but a fraction of a mile from here. After I break through I will retrieve you from the approach to the bridge." He pointed to the spot where the road crossed the embankment.

"And if not?"

"Can you swim?" he asked, flicking his head toward the Rhine flowing past.

I nodded and Guillaume gulped but said that yes, he could swim.

"Well, thank God for that," said Daunt, "because you may have to."

Suddenly there was a deep roar of thunder far upriver. Another storm approaching, I thought, but when the ground trembled I scanned the northern horizon and heard another great roar and saw giant flames searing the dark sky and black smoke spewing out into the night.

"And so goes Glautsch," Daunt said contentedly. The German cordon at the border was momentarily distracted by the repeated explosions and tall flames visible from so far away. Within the Daimler were only smiles and a deep sense of satisfaction.

"All right, get out then," Daunt ordered us. "Now is the moment, while the bastards are confused. I'll meet you at the bridge."

We hopped from the car and slithered down the embankment out of sight of the border station. Enormous orange and blue chemical flames illuminated the night. The German cordon stood clearly before us and the bridge beyond.

Daunt honked the bulb horn twice and sped up the

last quarter mile to the border. We ran along the riverbank toward our anticipated meeting place beneath the bridge.

When they saw him accelerating down upon them, the Germans turned from the conflagration at their backs and crouched in readiness. Then they opened fire, a spray of bullets rattling off the armored Daimler and cracking the V windscreen, but still Daunt pressed on, faster and faster.

Thirty feet from the barricade something happened. It must have been the intense barrage of bullets—perhaps one of them puncturing the car's fuel tank while another sparked against the armor plate or the road—because suddenly the big Daimler exploded and hurtled forward, enveloped in flames and black smoke, into the stunned soldiers, scattering men and carriages and barrels in all directions off the bridge approach. A second explosion shook the ground, and the car came to rest in a cloak of flames barely across the border.

I stared for an instant at the horror, then grabbed Guillaume's arm and pulled him after me into the cool river. Green rushes, slippery with industrial waste, floated in the shallows, but as we moved away from the western shore the water cleared and we swam more freely.

The Germans at the border were momentarily too astounded by what had happened to notice us. When they did, we were well out into the river and drifting away from them, downstream into Switzerland. They fired a few futile shots into the dark water around us.

Looking back from midriver I saw the local police arriving to see what extraordinary things had transpired at the border. I could not tell if the salty taste on my lips was from some discharge in the river or was just my choking tears. I put my head back into the water and swam as hard as I could toward Switzerland, until the ache in my arms and chest overcame my grief.

We were pulled far south of the bridge and reached the eastern shore within the city of Basel.

Guillaume was not a strong swimmer and lagged behind. I had to wade back into the water to drag him out. Then we both collapsed exhausted on the Swiss banks of the Rhine, and we cried: cried for relief at our own escape, of course, and cried for Daunt.

Gazing back across the river, I saw explosions continuing in the distant glow from the Glautsch plant, black smoke and tall flames, and heard sirens rushing to the scene at the border.

On the bridge approach, in a miniature version of the inferno raging thirty miles upriver, Daunt sat in his pyre: the blackened hulk of the Daimler with the flames subsiding around it and a thin drift of black smoke rising from it like the phantom of the clouds dispersing into a sultry evening over the Rhine.

We lay on our backs, winded and drenched, gazing in awe and wonder at those twin smoking beacons of victory and defeat. Our mission was complete. The Great War had begun.

EPILOGUE

Of course, the Great War did not begin in the summer of 1911 nor, when it did, did Great Britain enter it upon the side of Germany.

I have always believed that the destruction of the Glautsch chemical works at Mulhouse so far set back German preparedness that it was in large part responsible for giving the British and French an extra three years to make their own preparations for war, and I remain to this day very proud of my small part in assuring their eventual victory in the Great War.

The memories of those days rush through my head like the trains through the little valley outside the window of the room in which I have written this account: filled with never known or else forgotten people, headed someplace else. . . .

Guillaume and I reached Geneva and from there took the train to Paris. My report was received at the American embassy with a mixture of admiration, rebuke, and bemused skepticism.

I often imagined the Zorns in the mountains above Thann, awaiting the German attack which did not come. Gaspard Zorn never returned to Paris: he was arrested and held in a German prison as a saboteur and apparently tortured and died there. Thiébaut eluded "the oppressors" and reached Paris. I understand that he was a valiant soldier in the war and afterwards returned to Alsace and became a leading political figure in the reintegration into French life.

Arbogast Zorn did not live to see Alsace restored to

France. He died in 1916 at the depth of despair following the battle of Verdun. I think, or I would like to believe, that he died knowing that with British and American assistance the lost provinces eventually would be recovered. I do not know what became of the sodality of clowns, of Darius Boppe and Clovis Vogel.

Guillaume and Claudie were married in 1913, by which time she was a much-admired performer in the classical dance and on the popular stage. They were happy together the first year of marriage, though Claudie was away from Paris with increasing frequency. When the war broke out in 1914, Guillaume, recently naturalized and in a fit of patriotic fervor, enlisted in the infantry and was sent into battle.

By that time I had returned to Washington. I spent most of the war years there and in London. Though I have lived my life quite differently from his, I always recalled Timothy Daunt and considered him my model for what an agent should be.

I did not see Guillaume again during those years, though once I saw Claudie, on tour in New York with Diaghilev. I went backstage after the performance to congratulate her and ask after Guillaume. She was cordial but changed, no longer a girlish *saltimbanque* but a dynamic, aloof presence. She spoke with me briefly and departed with a beautiful male dancer on one arm and a bouquet of roses in the other. We had no real opportunity to converse.

The rest of the old Rue Ravignan gang met varying degrees of success. Max, oddly enough, lived many years as an eccentric character in Montmartre, prophesying on the steps of Sacre Coeur and writing his gloomy poems. He later converted to Christianity and found new avenues for his mysticism.

Apolline never emerged from her hallucinations.

Paul, with whom I continued a sporadic correspondence, referred obliquely to her in his letters, but the lack of substantive news was clear indication of her continuing deterioration: Max had been right when he told me she was gone.

Paul was perhaps the most successful of the gang, aside from the little Spaniard, of course. He finally designed his own ballet at the war's end, a futuristic vision called *Revolutions Per Minute*. Marie also created ballet decors, painted, and remained an integral part of the artistic life of the left bank for many years.

As for that other futurist Tommaso, he prospered in his native country, where his militaristic designs were popular. Later, I understand, he became a close personal friend of *Il Duce*.

And Inspector Guy Pernicieux, the Painting Inspector of the Paris Préfecture? Following his retirement he did not shrivel up but blossomed, dying in 1939 at the age of eighty-nine after three decades of prolific artistic output during which he became a legend of sorts. I visited him occasionally on my returns to the continent and we spoke of the past, of Guillaume and of the Countess. I was gratified that Inspector Pernicieux did not live to see the hated Germans marching through his beloved Paris again.

Guillaume served admirably at the front until 1916, when he sustained a severe head wound. He was transported to a sanitarium near the Swiss border and trepanned. He remained there for several months of painful convalescence.

Back in Paris he never fully recovered his strength and was subject to fits of deep depression, seizures, and hallucinations. He was forced to abstain entirely from alcohol, which induced the seizures. Claudie was rarely in Paris, and he was too weak to follow her tours. In the presence of her youth and boundless vitality he must have felt an enfeebled invalid at the age of thirty-eight. She attracted many swains and became a minor celebrity, and I think he imagined, and was probably not mistaken in this, a multitude of liaisons and infidelities across the continent. During these last war years Guillaume wrote powerful, brooding, violently patriotic but apocalyptic poetry, filled with images of war and a future far less bright than he had once imagined. I believe it was his greatest work.

In 1918 a severe epidemic of Spanish influenza struck Paris. In his weakened state he contracted the disease. As his condition worsened, and with Claudie far from Paris, he slipped into delirium.

Paul reported to me that Guillaume hallucinated long conversations with Claudie, who learned too late of his final illness. He raved to her over art and dance and poetry and the meaning of life, and then responded in her own voice full of the love and admiration and gratitude which no longer existed. I could almost hear the conversations in Paul's vivid letters and see Guillaume propped on his pillows, his plump hands weaving calligrammes in the air as he spoke, punctuating and emphasizing the salient points for Claudie with his perennial battlecry: "And that is all."

He died on Armistice Day in 1918, lying delirious in his bed while the crowds in the street beneath his window celebrated the defeat of the German Kaiser with cries of "*À bas Guillaume . . . À bas Guillaume . . . À bas Guillaume . . .*"